PRAISE FOR

HAZEL CREEK

"Walt Larimore isn't just a great storyteller. He paints word pictures that linger like country wood smoke—so strong you can't get it out of your mind. Once you experience *Hazel Creek,* you'll never want to leave."

—Chris Fabry, author of ECPA Fiction winner
Almost Heaven

"This captivating story took me to a simpler time when humans were closer to creation and to the creator. I found in it echoes of Christian classics—Catherine Marshall's *Christy,* for one—and that puts Larimore's book in the best of company. Being in the Great Smoky Mountains wilderness when it was still wild nourished my soul!"

—Julie L. Cannon, author of *I'll Be Home for Christmas*

"A powerful, heartwarming story of courage, love, and faith, *Hazel Creek* is sure to leave the reader ready for a sentimental journey into an era and region that has charmed the hearts of millions."

—Eric Wiggin, author of *Skinny Dipping at Megunticook Lake* and *Emily's Garden*

"A compelling story of courage and faith."

—Augusta Trobaugh, author of *Sophie and the Rising Sun* and *River Jordan*

"Walt Larimore's *Hazel Creek* stands right along with Catherine Marshall's *Christy* or Francine Rivers's *The Last Sin Eater*. This book will stir your emotions at a deep level, entertain, and open your eyes to a different time and world far back in the Great Smoky Mountains. I hated to see it end, and I'm thrilled to give *Hazel Creek* my highest recommendation."

—Miralee Ferrell, author of *Love Finds You in Sundance, Wyoming*

WALT LARIMORE

HAZEL CREEK

A NOVEL

HOWARD BOOKS
A DIVISION OF SIMON & SCHUSTER, INC.

New York   Nashville   London   Toronto   Sydney   New Delhi

Howard Books
A Division of Simon & Schuster, Inc.
1230 Avenue of the Americas
New York, NY 10020

First Howard Books trade paperback edition March 2012

HOWARD and colophon are trademarks of Simon & Schuster, Inc.

For information about special discounts for bulk purchases, please contact Simon & Schuster Special Sales at 1-866-506-1949 or business@simonandschuster.com.

The Simon & Schuster Speakers Bureau can bring authors to your live event. For more information or to book an event contact the Simon & Schuster Speakers Bureau at 1-866-248-3049 or visit our website at www.simonspeakers.com.

Designed by Jaime Putorti

Manufactured in the United States of America

10 9 8 7 6 5 4 3 2 1

Library of Congress Cataloging-in-Publication Data

Larimore, Walter L.
    Hazel Creek : a novel / Walt Larimore.—1st Howard Books trade paperback ed.
        p.   cm.
    I. Title.
    PS3612.A64835H39 2012
    813'.6—dc22
            2011020333

ISBN 978-1-4391-4182-3
ISBN 978-1-4391-9681-6 (ebook)

To Kate
Love You More

May 24, 2009

A Century

She didn't look one hundred years old.

"This must be the best view from any nursing home in the country," I said, sitting in a rocking chair next to her wheelchair. I placed a brown bag at my feet and gazed at the lush, rounded mountains, which undulated in wave after wave, stretching to the horizon over twenty miles away—where the highest mountains separated North Carolina and Tennessee.

A wry smile slightly lifted the corners of her wrinkled lips. "To gaze across the great ridges, which like giant billows blend their sapphire outlines with the sky."

"Nice," I said. "Poetic."

"Not mine. They're from a writer named Christian Reid."

"Haven't heard of him."

"Her," she said. "Frances Christine Fisher Tiernan. But she wrote under a pen name. It allowed her to compete with her male counterparts—kinda like one of my sisters before . . ."

"Before what?"

"That's all I'm gonna say 'bout that." She turned back toward the ancient mountains, clothed in their spring coat of fresh leaves.

I chuckled. "I guess I need to add Reid to my reading list."

"If you'd been taught fine readin', like my sisters and I were, by the likes of Horace Kephart, you'd have read much more just like it."

"Don't know that name, either."

"Sad," she said. "One of the best-known authors at the start of the last century. He wrote famous books like *Our Southern Highlanders* and *Camping and Woodcraft*, and scads of articles for *Field and Stream* magazine."

"You read him a lot?"

"Read him? I *knew* him—loved him like a second pa. He lived near where I was raised. And that's all I want to say about that."

She turned back to face the peaks and valleys from which, I would soon learn, she had come—a wilderness that had shaped her past and personality as much as its view inspired us.

"I brought you something," I said. "It's not wrapped very pretty, but . . ."

"Magnolia blossoms," she said, smiling and reaching for the bag. "Smelled 'em comin' down the hall." She opened the bag and placed her nose in it, taking a slow, deep breath. "Ah, just like the ones on my family's homestead. That old tree could perfume acres at a time." She took another sniff. "Just like I remember—a bit like heaven and summer all rolled into one."

She removed one and held it at arm's length, slowly twirling it and admiring it as if it were the Hope diamond. "Just look at that, Doc. Must be nine—no, ten inches across. Looks like freshly starched linen and smells even better!"

"They say the magnolia tree is rare in the Smokies. But your family had one?"

"Sure did. *Magnolia grandiflora*, the queen of the South. Gives new meanin' to the term *white-on-white*. Just look at all the shades of pure, silky white against the deep green leaves. It's an astonishin' and marvelous flower." Her smile went from ear to ear as she gazed at the bloom. "What a wonderful birthday gift."

"Did you have a good party today? Heard people came from all over to celebrate you making it to the century mark."

"Said who?"

"One of the ER nurses who had come up here."

"You must be talkin' about old Louise Thomas—who claims I look as old as Seth himself."

"Seth?"

"You know, Adam's son."

"Adam?"

"Adam and Eve, sonny." She shook her head. "Louise was tryin' to get my goat, saying I looked as old as Seth when he died."

She was quiet for a moment—waiting for me to ask. Finally, I took the bait. "Which was how old?"

"The Good Book says he lived nine hundred and twelve years. Course, any fool knows Jared and Methuselah lived longer; Jared, nine hundred and sixty-two years, and old Methuselah, nine hundred and sixty-nine years. But I don't want to live that long. Gettin' to one hundred is hard enough. It's 'bout wore me out!"

"Sorry I couldn't make it up for the party. I've been running since sunup."

She turned to look at me and patted my arm. "You doctors are always as busy as one-armed paper hangers."

"Well, Miss Abbie," I said, "I'm here for a bit."

"You know much about me?" she asked, still gazing over the mountains as the lights of the small hamlet of Bryson City began to illuminate the valley below us.

"Just what I've read on the chart. Other than all the medical stuff, I know you're a widow. Active over at First Baptist Church. Have kids that have moved elsewhere—"

"More important, I don't smoke, or dip, or chew," she interrupted, smiling, "or dance with boys who do."

"Well, that's a good thing," I said with a chuckle. "Might shorten your life.

"Where'd you grow up?"

"Out on Hazel Creek. Not twenty miles from here as the crow flies. But it used to take all day to drive out there."

"What road is it on?"

She looked at me like I had two heads. With a laugh, she explained, "The town of Proctor was out on Hazel Creek—it's now part of the Great Smoky Mountains National Park. But we was all forced to move out when they built Fontana Dam and the government stole our land for the park."

"When was that?"

"Nineteen hundred and forty-four. I was thirty-five years old when we left our old home place. My grandpappy had homesteaded the land."

"Proctor musta been a hole in the wall."

She shook her head and looked at me once again as if I was dimwitted. "Heckfire, son, because of Calhoun Lumber Company, Proctor had well over a thousand citizens in the 1920s. It was bigger *then* than Bryson City is now. But our farm was a long way from town—about six miles up valley. And walkin' those miles seemed to take an eternity back then."

"Well, Miss Abbie—"

"You've made that mistake twice now."

"What?"

"Callin' me *Miss* Abbie. It's *Mrs.* Abbie," she corrected. "Was married nearly seventy years to a wonderful man." She showed me her wedding band. "One of my most prized possessions. Was my mama's . . . once upon a time."

"Well, Mrs. Abbie, I bet it was a unique time to live back in the Roaring Twenties."

She laughed. "No one accused Proctor of bein' a roarin' anythin'. But Hazel Creek *was* unique. Some called it the 'Wild East.' Others, like Reid, called it the 'Land of the Sky.' Hazel Creek had wild animals like panthers and bears, Cherokee Indians, desperados, lumbermen, moonshiners, revenuers, visitors from all over, mysterious wanderers, more than one world-famous writer, Civil War heroes, murderers, rustlers . . . even a flesh-and-blood Haint.

Tarnation, without him—and the Good Lord—we would have for sure lost our farm."

"A *Haint*? What's a Haint?

Abbie laughed again. "It's a term we used on Hazel Creek to describe a ghost—or a person whose soul was haunted. You know, hainted—a Haint."

"Sounds like an interesting person—and a mysterious place."

She nodded, looking back over the mountains. "It was—and so is he."

"The Haint?" I inquired.

"No, the Lord. He's mysterious and works in wonderful ways. And Hazel Creek certainly had more than her share of massacres, secrets, adventures, and whodunits." She turned to look at me. "Got time to hear about a few?"

"Sure!"

She turned back toward the mountains and, with a faraway look, began . . .

Part One

SUNDAY, MAY 4

through

SATURDAY, JULY 12, 1924

1

Smoking

*G*ood! she thought. *No one's seen me.*

Abbie's movements were quick, her dark brown eyes alert, almost anxious. She wore a dress made out of secondhand cloth, the original bright floral patterns faded to a pale tan, and a straw hat, equally pale and limp. She glanced in all directions once again to be sure she was alone.

Hurrying around the corner of the barn, she stopped to catch her breath. She brushed her long auburn hair away from her eyes and peeked back around the corner, embarrassed by both her nervousness and rapid panting.

She tried to relax by taking a long, slow, deep breath, then letting the air escape slowly through her lips as she rested the back of her head against the rough planks of the old barn. She smiled as she recognized the pungent, earthy aromas that always wafted around their barn—scents that brought back warm memories of playing in the barn with her younger sisters.

A rustling sound caused her to look up. A flight of swallows divided in midair. As she stepped out from below the eve of the barn, four ebony crows cawed as they arose from the field, flapping their heavy wings and making dark silhouettes against the bright sky.

The young girl again cast furtive looks in all directions and then slowly moved back into the shadow of the barn. She reached behind and pulled out a roll of papers that were tucked under her belt and tore a page from the two-year-old Sears, Roebuck catalog. She had found the remains of the catalog where she had stashed it—in the corncrib. Many of the pages had been removed so that only a thin sheaf was left. She read one of the ads:

Doctor Warner's health corset. Adapted to ladies deficient in bust fullness and those desiring bust support for both slim and stout figures. The special features of this corset give light and flexible support to any lady with an elegant figure and assure her a well-fitting dress.

Abbie studied the ad and then looked down over her own lean body. "Shoot! I ain't *never* gonna have no figure," she muttered as she looked at the busty model wearing the doctor's corset. "If'n I had a chest like her, Bobby Lee would be comin' to court in a hurry." She rolled up the remaining catalog and placed it securely behind her belt.

She sighed and, taking the page, carefully tore out a small rectangle. "I don't reckon any boy's gonna take a hankerin' to a flat-chested mountain girl. Won't never happen!" Reaching into her pocket, she pulled out a small cloth sack and shook into her palm a handful of dried brown corn silks.

Carefully she held the catalog page in the palm of her left hand, cupping it so that it caught the corn silk as she gently ground it between the fingertips of her right hand. She dropped the remaining corn silk on the ground and dusted off her right hand. She concentrated on rolling as perfect a tube as possible but, having never done it before, was a bit awkward. Then she licked it thoroughly and squeezed the ends together. Sticking it in her mouth, she retrieved a kitchen match from her pocket, struck it on the side of the barn, and applied it to the tip of her home-made cigarette.

The paper ignited, and a thin, curling tendril of smoke rose as

Abbie held the cigarette between two fingers, as accomplished cigarette smokers did in the silent moving pictures she had seen. She sucked on the end, got a mouthful, and inhaled—and in an instant began to cough violently. She tried to stifle her coughs by clamping her free hand over her mouth.

Recovering, she began to strut back and forth holding the cigarette at a jaunty angle between her lips. She ignored her watering eyes and began to act out another of her many imaginary dramas—ones in which she was always the star.

"So you suppose you can put *that* over on me, do you?" she said in what she considered a threatening tone, her eyes narrowed as she looked through the rising smoke. "I'm here to tell you that I don't let *nobody* pull that kinda stuff on *me*! If you try it, you'll be plum sorry!"

She stopped and smiled as she thought about the dramatic streak that ran through her soul—a trait that found little outlet on her family's isolated farm. She had read a few smuggled romance novels, had seen a few movies, and had created from them a world in which she played out her dreams.

"You'd better stop or I'll let you have it!" she hissed.

At yesterday's crime movie at the Calhoun Lumber Company Cinema down in the company town of Proctor, she had been impressed by the showdown between the hard-eyed detective and the ferret-like criminal. Pulling her hat down farther over her eyes, she said in a voice that she imagined was frightening and tough to any fan of crime movies, "I'll plug you if you take another step!"

As her pretend opponent exited, stage right, she carefully watched him, her hand perched on the butt of the imaginary mother-of-pearl-handled derringer wedged between her dress and its belt.

Back and forth she walked, punctuating her speech with left-handed gestures, occasionally puffing the cigarette while being careful not to inhale the smoke.

Stopping, she quickly looked toward stage left. "Well, if it ain't Bobby Lee Taylor," she said gutturally, as she turned to saunter over to the imaginary character, sexily swaying her hips from side to side. "What brings you back to Hazel Creek, big boy? I thought you'd stay away once you became a famous pitcher for the St. Louis Cardinals."

She took another puff, tilting her head back, as she pretended to listen to his response.

"I don't care what you say, Mr. Baseball, I know you've come back for my little sister. You always liked Corrie better than me. Ain't that right?" She pointed her cigarette at him. "She's four years younger than you. You should be ashamed!" She turned to show him her profile and softly ran her free hand down her hip. "And besides, I'm much more voluptuous and womanly than she—"

She heard a loud snap behind her and spun around.

"Whatcha doin', Abbie?"

Abbie was shocked to see two of her sisters, thirteen-year-old Darla Whitney and almost-eleven-year-old Corrie Hannah, who had stepped around the corner of the barn, staring wide-eyed at her. She quickly put the cigarette behind her back.

Whit with her brown eyes and wealth of glossy brown hair was pretty, almost fragile looking, while Corrie with her bright red hair and green eyes was the feisty beauty of the family.

"I know what you're doin'. You're smokin' a cigarette!" Corrie shouted. She came closer and reached out her hand. "Lemme try it, Abbie."

"Get away, Corrie! You ain't smokin' no cigarette."

"If you don't let me, I'll tell Pa on you."

Corrie was by far the most impulsive and daring of the four Randolph sisters. She was already somewhat of a tomboy and cared little for the things that young girls were supposed to, such as dolls. She drew closer and insisted, "Lemme try to smoke it!"

"You stop that, Corrie!" Whit said. Then she shook her head as she gazed at her older sister. "You shouldn't oughta be doin' that, Abbie. If Pa found out, he'd whup you!"

"He ain't gonna find out unless you'uns tell him. Now you two get on back to the house and leave me alone."

"I ain't goin' 'less you lemme try smokin' that cigarette," Corrie said stubbornly, her bright green eyes flashing. "Come on, Abbie. Lemme try it!"

Abbie held the cigarette high to keep it out of Corrie's grasp, but even as she did, a strong tenor voice sounded from behind them.

"All right, Lauren Abigail! Get rid of that cigarette."

All three sisters spun around at once. Abbie felt her throat constrict and suddenly found it hard to breathe.

Her father had come around the opposite end of the barn and now stood before them in his faded overalls. His thick auburn hair stuck out from under his battered straw hat, and his bright blue eyes, which Abbie had always admired, were fixed on her and filled with a growing anger. Just under six feet, strong and lean, Nathan Randolph moved forward and in disgust reached out and plucked the remains of the homemade cigarette from Abbie's fingers. He threw it to the ground, stomped on it, and shook his head in disgust.

"Pa, whatcha doin' here?" Abbie asked, her voice cracking.

"Was workin' on that old truck of mine and heard you girls talkin'. Kinda disturbed 'bout what I'm seein'. I swan, Abbie! I wouldn't of thought this of you!"

"I . . . I didn't mean no harm, Pa."

"Didn't mean no harm? You're the oldest, Abbie. You know better."

Corrie piped up. "I don't see what's so bad about smokin', Pa. You do it your own self."

"You hush up, Corrie Hannah! This ain't none of your put-in. You're too young to understand things like this."

"I ain't but four years younger than Abbie!" Corrie countered.

Nate Randolph's blue eyes hardened and he barked, "Now Corrie, you and Whit get on to the house!"

Abbie heard the steel in their father's voice and had learned, as had her sisters, that it was best to be instantly obedient at times like this. The two younger girls both turned and ran.

Whit rounded the corner first, but Corrie paused to stick her tongue out at Abbie before disappearing. "You're gonna get whupped!" she cried, and then vanished.

2

Magnolia

"What in the blue-eyed world were you thinkin', Abbie?"
"I don't know, Pa. I was just . . . I was just playin'."
Abbie looked up, and her lips trembled. "I was just pretendin' I
was in one of them movie shows."

"And you have to smoke a cigarette to do that? Abbie, I'm
downright ashamed of you."

Her head dropped as she whispered, "I'm real sorry, Pa."

"Well, that's good, but you're durn lucky it's the Lord's Day or
you'd get a switchin' from a sprig off the magnolia in the back-
yard." He turned his back on her for a moment, as if in thought.

Abbie was relieved, as she had made two trips to the magnolia tree in her life, both times after she had disobeyed her pa.
The memory of the punishments lingered sharply in her mind.
The first time he'd let her pick her own switch. The old magnolia, planted by her pa's pa, was now a giant and exuded the most
beautiful of perfumes from its blooms. She had pulled the small-
est twig she could find off a lower branch, which had been a mistake, for her father had said, "All right. I gave you a chance to get
a good switch. Now *I'll* pick one."

He had picked what seemed to be the most enormous switch
she had ever seen and switched the back of her legs. She could
still feel the stings. After the second offense, she had chosen more
wisely and her father had not protested.

Nate turned back to her and put his hands on her shoulders. She saw something in his tanned face—an expression that at first she could not identify. Then remembering how her father always stressed that she, as the oldest, needed to be a role model for her sisters, she suspected he was not nearly as disappointed with her smoking as he was with her poor example. In a tremulous voice, she said, "I'm awful sorry, Pa. I didn't expect Whit and Corrie to find me."

He put his arms around her and held her tightly. She could smell the sweat and earth on him. As he released her, he kissed her forehead and said, "You're a good girl, Abbie." He held her out at arm's length. "Reckon I forget you're fourteen—be fifteen just next week. But you seem lots older these days."

Abbie studied his face and full beard. Even though he was only thirty-four years old, decades of exposure to the elements had toughened his face, leaving creases and crinkles that stood out around his eyes when he smiled or laughed, which he was prone to do. She loved him—not just for the toughness that always made her feel defended and protected, but also for the softness that communicated that he loved her and deemed her special.

He looked away and said, "Well, do your playactin' all you want—just don't smoke no more cigarettes, ya hear?"

"I won't do it no more, Pa."

He drew her close and hugged her again. "I love ya, Punkin. I just don't love whatcha done. It purely hurts me. But it don't make me love ya no less, ya hear?"

Abbie smiled and nodded. She loved when he called her *Punkin*—it always gave her a warm glow.

"Got a question for ya."

She knew what he was going to ask and smiled.

"What's one thing you can do to make me love you less?" he asked.

Even though she knew the answer, she demurely lowered her head and whispered, "I don't know."

"Nothin'!" he said, beaming. "And what's one thing you can do to make me love ya more?"

"Nothin'?" she asked softly.

"Nothin'!" he said. "Nothin' ya could ever do to make your pa love ya more." He pulled her into another hug and then straightened up.

They started back toward the house, and when her father took her hand and squeezed it she forgot about his rebuke. He had a large hand, almost as hard as oak, and his grip made her feel even more safe and secure. Now as he held her hand in his and looked down at her, his forehead was ridged with lines, and his eyes were troubled.

"Are you worried about somethin', Pa?"

"Well, I reckon I am a mite."

"You still worried about the lumber company gettin' our land?"

"Seems like the Calhoun Lumber Company wants to own the whole of Hazel Creek—to cut down all of the trees put here by the good Lord. Since they moved into our valley, back in '07, they've been buyin' up every piece of land or timber right they can get their hands on."

"But they won't get our place, will they, Pa?"

"Not as long as I can fight 'em off, Punkin!"

Abbie looked into his soft eyes. "There's somethin' else, ain't there?"

Her pa didn't answer.

"You worried about Mama?"

His mouth drew taut.

"About the baby that's comin'?"

Nate nodded. "But I'm prayin' that your ma will be all right. We'll just have to trust the good Lord." He smiled down at her. "You get on to the cabin. Your ma needs ya. I'll be in shortly. I need to run off those desperados that you left in that saloon back there. If they draw on me, I may just have to gun down one or two of 'em."

"Just don't shoot Bobby Lee," Abbie said, as she turned to run toward the cabin. "I think I like him."

"Then I may just have to shoot him for sure!" her pa shouted after her.

Abbie walked up to their cabin and was greeted by Lilly, the family's stocky Mountain Cur pup; Julius, their huge long-haired orange cat; and Jack, a gray tabby, who bounded lightly up the porch, meowing loudly.

"Get away, Jack! I ain't got time for you!" Abbie said.

As soon as she entered the cabin, Corrie blurted, "Did he switch you, Abbie? Did it hurt?"

"You hush, Corrie Hannah," Callie Randolph instructed. She was sitting in a rocking chair holding her youngest, six-year-old Anna Katherine, in her lap. "It ain't none of your put-in."

Suddenly Abbie laughed. She was a good-humored girl and she shrugged her thin shoulders, saying, "No, Pa didn't switch me. But he was plum disappointed in me."

She walked over to her mama, knelt beside the rocker, and gently poked her sister in the stomach. Anna giggled.

"I was smokin' a cigarette all right, Anna, just like blabbermouth there told you."

"Now, don't call your sister names, Abbie," Callie warned.

"Yeah, don't call me no names!" Corrie called out loudly.

Callie smiled a smile that warmed the room. Abbie always thought her mama a pretty woman, and she still was, even though the pregnancy had caused her to swell. At thirty-two, Callie still had bright red hair and glimmering green eyes, both of which she had passed along to Corrie. She smiled as she lovingly tousled Abbie's hair.

"I'm sorry you got fussed at," Whit added as she came over and put her arms around Abbie's waist. She was the most tenderhearted of the Randolph girls. "I was right saddened over it."

"Why, it don't make no never mind, Whit. I was just playin', but I shouldn't have smoked that ol' cigarette. Anyways, I ain't never gonna smoke no more. It bit my tongue like fire and made me cough like nobody's business."

Her mother smiled at her and then laughed.

"I ain't *never* gonna smoke no more, Mama. I don't see no fun in it."

Suddenly Nate Randolph's laughter echoed through the door of the cabin as he walked in with an armload of chopped wood. "So Abbie, you ain't gonna sin if it ain't fun? Is that the way it is? I reckon if you find somethin' that's fun, you'll do it even if it's a sin. Is that the way of it?"

"Don't be foolish, Nate," Callie said with a smile. "She's a good girl."

"You'd say Jezebel was a good girl, Callie, if'n she was your own." Nate grinned at her as he walked over and gently placed the back of his fingers on her cheek. She took his hand and softly kissed it.

Whenever he showed affection to their mama, the girls quickly took notice of it. Abbie had never seen another mountain man do this, and she loved her pa all the more for it.

"Abbie, since next Saturday is your birthday, how about you take the afternoon off?" Callie said, having forgiven Abbie for the smoking incident. "Whit, you and Corrie have your afternoon chores. When Abbie gets back, then all of you girls will need to start the milkin' and fixin' supper, I reckon."

Nate turned to step outside. "I'll finish up my chores and then wash up. I'll look forward to bein' with this group of good-lookin' daughters of yours for dinner."

"Hey! They're yours, too!" Callie said as she chuckled.

3

Rustling

Abbie was walking briskly toward the forest above their cabin as the warm spring breeze blew across her brow. Her pa had given her permission to hike up to the top of their property, to a steep ridge rising over a thousand vertical feet above their cabin. From there she could view northeast to the 5,600-foot-high summit of Silers Bald—the side of which birthed the headwater of Hazel Creek.

As Abbie walked, she recognized the familiar scent of wood smoke lacing the air—likely from the Rau farm, the next home place just up the Sugar Fork, which tumbled down their valley to where it merged into Hazel Creek in a joyous confluence of icy cold waters. Abbie savored the feeling of sunlight warming her hair just before she plunged into the woods.

Entering the forest, she scanned the path ahead and listened for any unusual sounds. She instinctively focused on the birds chattering in the tree canopy, as they could give her clues of any danger that lay ahead, since they could see and hear far better from their lofty perches than she could from the forest floor. For some reason she could not explain, she felt safer in the woods than she did in the meadows. The great trees cast a pleasantly cool shadow over her as the leafy canopy rustled in the breeze.

After walking nearly halfway up to the ridge, Abbie came across a large clearing containing an ancient mountain bog. She breathed deeply the mustiness rising from the bog as she admired the massive virgin hardwood trees surrounding it. Some of the chestnut trees were so gigantic that eight grown men could circle the trunk with their arms fully extended and barely touch each other's fingertips. Many of the oldest trees were nearly two hundred feet tall and up to twelve feet in diameter.

Poplars, she thought as she looked toward a group of trees on the other side of the swamp. She gazed up to the lowest branches of many of the older trees, which were fifty or sixty feet off the ground.

On their property alone, Abbie had counted over a hundred different types of trees, from the oak, hickory, black gum, and red maple of the lower altitudes to the high-altitude black spruce and balsam. She loved the oldest cherry trees, which reached a height of sixty feet and a diameter of over four feet. And throughout the forest stood remarkable yellow locust and chestnut trees, which furnished not only prodigious amounts of wood when felled, but also, while alive, a phenomenal amount of mast to feed man and beast.

From her earliest memories, she had enjoyed walking alone in the mountains. While her sisters seemed to enjoy community and family events, Abbie took the greatest pleasure in being in the woodland. She had studied the sounds of the birds and could mimic the sounds of the whip-poor-will, the great horned owl, the vireo, and the chickadee. Two Cherokee Indians who had befriended her family, James Walkingstick and his father, Jonathan, along with the old midwife herbalist of the valley, Madeleine Satterfield, whom everyone called *Maddie*, had taught her how to recognize virtually every plant in the woods. She knew which were poisonous and which part of each safe plant could be used for eating, seasoning, healing, dyeing clothes, and making baskets.

She felt a wisp of wind begin to blow, threw her head back, and smiled up at the sunbeams coursing through the clearing, thankful for their warmth. She took in another deep breath of the moist air and then slowly let it out as she sat down leisurely on a log overlooking the marsh. The flutelike whistles of a male wood thrush—ending with a high, liquid trill of *tut, tut, oh-lay-oh-leeeee*—bounced across the treetops as a large whitetail doe cautiously emerged from the woods to take a long, cool drink of water.

She spent a few minutes watching the doe drink as a riotous migration party of warblers celebrated a stop on their journey north. Whenever she had the opportunity to see a warbler party in progress, she stood in amazement as they fluttered through the branches in flocks, feasting on insects trying to hide in the budding leaves. Their gaiety was contagious.

A harsh crackling sound abruptly interrupted the tranquil scene. The deer instantly bounded into the forest. As quick as a cat, Abbie jumped up and spun to face the direction of the sound. She heard the slow, then accelerating noise of snapping, popping wood—a tree was falling! *Is it one or two ridges away?* she wondered. For a moment, she wasn't sure. The cracking sound grew louder and louder and ended in a final, massive thud. Then the forest was completely silent—even the birds.

Abbie was familiar with the turbulence a dead tree caused when it fell. To clear land, her pa, like his pa before him, didn't usually cut trees down. It was backbreaking work, so the men *girdled* the trees instead. They would chop and peel the bark completely around the base of the tree; the tree would begin to die and then, in time, fall over or be felled. The now-downed tree would be completely dried out without the rot that might have occurred had the tree been left on the ground to dry. As a result, by the time she was a small girl, Abbie had heard many, many dead trees fall over; however, the sound Abbie had just heard was *not* that of a dead tree falling. She was almost sure she had heard a live tree fall—and a massive tree at that. She felt confused. Only the Calhoun Lumber Company was cutting down the majestic giants up and down the Hazel Creek valley, and the company was under *no* circumstances allowed anywhere near the Randolphs' land or that of their neighbors, the Raus.

Abbie remembered her pa threatening Mr. L. G. Sanders, the manager of the company's Hazel Creek operations, to stay off their family property. Sanders had been caught trespassing on their property more than once. Her pa was sure the man was illegally scouting their forest.

Sanders had tried everything he could to convince her pa to sell their property, and being unsuccessful, he had turned his efforts to trying to buy some of their more valuable trees individually. The Raus had sold two trees to Calhoun. After all, a large walnut or cherry tree could bring a family a significant amount of money. But her pa would never consent to this, seeing it as treason to his own pa's memory.

She darted around the swamp and through the woods in the direction from which the sound had come. Her Cherokee friends, the Walkingsticks, had taught her how to move quickly through the forest without making a sound.

As she picked up speed, she remembered stories of tree rustlers in the valley before she was born. Since the Calhoun Lumber Company had purchased so much land in the lower Hazel Creek watershed, rustling had disappeared in that part of the valley. But whenever the men gathered together and talked, they discussed the fact that all of the remaining larger and more valuable trees were located in the upper reaches of Hazel Creek and her tributaries, as well as on the few remaining family farms and forests, including her pa's.

Maybe I'm plum wrong. Maybe it was just a big ol' rotten tree that fell! Abbie told herself, hoping against hope that her intuition was incorrect as she moved quickly through the virgin forest in the direction of the sound. After crossing a second ridge, she stopped. She heard voices coming from over the ridge just in front of her. Now she *knew* something suspicious was going on! She crouched low to the ground and began to creep up to the ridge. As she went higher, the sounds of men's voices became clearer.

Abbie crept toward a massive buckeye tree just at the top of the ridge with a small laurel bush hugging its base. She felt her breathing becoming shallower and faster—and could almost hear old Jonathan Walkingstick whispering, "Little Abbie, slow your breathin' and it will slow your heart. Keep in control." She knew something was wrong, maybe even dangerous. Was it her instinct or her imagination? She knew she had a vivid imagination, although it was much more realistic than her sisters thought.

Once under the laurel bush, she took a deep breath and slowly raised her head to look over the ridge into the hollow below. She gasped. A tiny stream of water flowed out of the base of a boulder at the top of the hollow. She knew *this* valley. *This is on our property. It's where we gather spring onions.* The pungent plant was always one of the first to emerge in the spring. Also called *wild leeks*, *wild garlic*, or more commonly *ramps*, they were the first greens of the season her family traditionally consumed. Maddie, the midwife and herbalist of the valley, called them a *tonic* because she said they provided necessary vitamins and minerals following the long winter months without any fresh vegetables. She and her sisters had harvested them here just a month ago. They named the little valley *Ramp Hollow*.

What she then saw shocked her. *My tree!* There, on its side, was *her* majestic walnut tree! Abbie and her sisters had played under this tree more times than she could count. The tree was a much-loved and ancient giant, reputedly the largest remaining walnut tree in Hazel Creek. It was almost nine feet in diameter—and now it had been tragically sawed down. And she knew why.

A crew of men was working rapidly to cut the massive trunk into six- to eight-foot lengths. She recognized some of the crew, as they lived down valley in the lumber town of Proctor and worked for Calhoun Lumber Company. Abbie was close enough to see their sweat-dampened shirts as they worked, talking to one another in hushed tones and only when necessary.

A black man was driving a pair of oxen up the hollow toward

the fallen tree. Abbie knew the oxen would be used to haul the logs down to Hazel Creek. There the logs would likely be loaded onto the narrow-gauge train to be hauled to the Calhoun Mill, located where Hazel Creek flowed into the Little Tennessee River. She knew that the logs could also be floated down the creek, which was the way they were most commonly sent downstream, but it was slower. *With stolen logs, best to get 'em off the mountain quickly*, she thought.

Then she saw two men standing halfway up the opposite ridge just above the crew. Her eyes were instantly drawn to the shorter man. He was holding his Winchester rifle, and a pearl-handled .22 pistol was holstered at his side. Abbie hissed, "That's Sanders!"

Standing next to him was a tall stranger—wearing a long, dark duster designed to cover the upper and lower body of a horseman as he rode. He had a Stetson pulled down on his forehead as he chewed on a twig. What was more remarkable to Abbie was his bright red goatee. She had seen goatees on store catalogs' models, but had never seen one on a person.

L. G. Sanders was standing guard over the whole illegal operation. He glanced around himself constantly, seeming to search the woods for unwanted visitors. Abbie knew he'd use his rifle if he needed to.

I need to get Pa. Now! Abbie slowly lowered her head, crept back down the ridge, and then sprinted home through her primordial forest as fast as she could.

Decision

Abbie came running out of the forest toward their cabin with her hair streaming behind her. She didn't break stride as she spotted her pa working outside the barn and sprinted toward him.

He looked up and she ran into his muscular arms, grasping him tightly and gasping for air. "Pa, I saw him! I saw *him*!"

He smiled. "Old Gray Back? That big old black bear?"

Abbie was trying to catch her breath. "No, Pa! I saw *him*!"

"Abbie, what are you talkin' about?"

"Sanders!" Abbie was still panting. "Pa, he and some stranger with a bright red goatee and his men are rustlin' my big old walnut tree up in Ramp Holler! *My* tree!"

Nate was clearly taken aback. His blue eyes hardened. "Abbie, are you tellin' me the truth?"

"I am, Pa! I heard a tree fall, and I snuck up onto the ridge above them. Sanders and his crew have cut my tree down! They have oxen up there and they're sawin' my tree into logs."

He lifted her chin to look into her eyes. "I'm proud of ya, Punkin. But now I need to get my gun. I don't want you sayin' a thing to worry your sisters or ma, you hear?"

She nodded, and Nate turned and walked quickly to the cabin. Abbie followed, trying to keep up. Nate's boots thudded on the porch as he rapidly entered the cabin, reaching for his .44-40 Winchester rifle. Abbie could see him touch his thumb to the magazine gate. She knew he'd be feeling the spring tension to see it was full of cartridges—any one of which could, with a proper aim, easily kill a man at a hundred paces.

Abbie, still panting from her panicked run, stood with her back against the wall catching her breath. Whit and Corrie stared at her, wide-eyed, while Anna Kate played on the floor. Corrie had stopped stirring the cook pot.

"Nate?" inquired a soft voice. Callie looked up at her husband, concern showing on her face.

He said nothing but grabbed a box of shells and began putting them in his shirt pocket.

"Nate, what's the matter?" Callie stood, straightening her calico dress over her pregnant abdomen. She looked at her oldest. "Abbie, what is it?"

Abbie couldn't stay quiet. "Mama, a crew from Calhoun is rustlin' my big old walnut tree up in Ramp Holler."

"Abbie says she saw Sanders and his men cuttin' up one of our trees," Nate said. "My guess is that they're gonna haul it off as fast as they can." He continued to put shells in his pocket. "They're rustlin' our tree!"

Callie began to tremble. "Nate, you *cannot* go up there! That man's evil! Plum evil. They say he's killed other men and gotten off scot-free. You know that!"

"Gotta go, Cal."

"No! You ride to town and get help! Sheriff Taylor and some of the boys would come runnin' if ya asked 'em. We can't lose ya, Nate!"

Abbie could see tears forming in her mother's eyes.

Nate turned, his face taut. "Callie Jean, you know as well as I do that no one in Proctor wants to pick a fight with the lumber company. Calhoun has bought most of 'em out. And by the time I get to town and back, they'll likely have the logs on company property, and then we'll have no claim at all."

Anna began to cry. Whit picked her up and looked at her

father as he continued loading the rifle. "Please don't go, Pa," she pleaded.

Nate leaned the rifle against the wall, walked over, and hugged Callie—softly kissing her on the cheek. "I'll be careful, Cal. Don't worry." Then he walked back to his gun and picked it up.

Callie sat back down on the rocker, rubbing her stomach as she cried out, "I'm beggin' ya, Nate. Go next door and get Tom Rau to help you. Please don't go alone! If they shoot you, what are the girls and me gonna do? Calhoun'll get the farm, Nate, and that's exactly what they want. Since you won't sell to them, they're gonna shoot you!"

"Cal, I'm *not* gonna get shot. But they're cuttin' up Abbie's tree and I aim to stop 'em. I can't save the tree, but I can sure enough stop them from stealin' it. I can make Calhoun pay a top price— and maybe get Sheriff Taylor to give L.G. a bit of time in the town jail. And if'n they don't buy it, another company will."

Callie looked down and began to weep.

Nate's face visibly softened, as did his voice. "Cal, I'll be back here for dinner before you know it, and, I might add, some of your strawberry rhubarb cobbler. I love ya, Cal. I'll be back. You have the girls have my dinner ready, you hear?"

Callie smiled as she wiped her tears. Nate walked back to her and kissed her on the forehead.

Abbie ran up to hug her pa as he picked up his rifle and turned toward the door. "Don't go, Pa! Let's go get help!"

He hugged her closely. "I'll be back, Abbie. You don't think I'd miss your cookin', do ya?" He smiled at her as she let him loose, then turned and dashed out the door.

After Nate left, Callie slowly rocked as she called her girls around her. "We best pray for Pa, girls."

5

Confrontation

A s Nate approached the ridge above Ramp Hollow, he knelt down and then crawled the last few feet to the ridgetop. He was as quiet as he could be, knowing that he'd be about as welcome as a scorpion in a boot. He positioned himself at the bottom of a large rock. Well protected by the dense brush, he was able to survey the scene.

Abbie was right! Nate thought. L. G. Sanders was just above the stump of their enormous walnut tree, sitting on a flat rock with his rifle across his leg. He was short and chubby. The hair showing under his off-center hat was black and, as always, greased back. He held a scrimshaw pipe between his teeth and looked uncommonly relaxed for a man committing such a serious crime. Next to him was the stranger with the red goatee that Abbie had described. He looked as out of place and as up to no good as a wet rat in a crowded café.

Nate recognized most of the crew. He had seen them working up and down the valley. They were mostly lumbermen from other states, especially Maine and Minnesota, who sold their services to the top bidder, usually for a dollar a day. They worked for lumber companies that slowly bought up and then clear-cut the virgin hardwood forests up and down the spine of the Appalachian Mountains, stripping the ancient forests and leaving behind a pockmarked and hideous terrain of stumps, branches, and brush that was subject to massive fires—not to mention the destructive erosion and devastating landslides that could occur for years after they left. They were slowly demolishing and annihilating his beloved valley!

Hidden in brush, Nate had the advantage. *This is gonna be fun!* he thought as he carefully pulled his rifle up to his shoulder. He knew he could shoot Sanders through the heart and not be convicted for it. A man defending his property from a rustler was as righteous as a man defending his home, his wife, his children, his church, or his own life. Judge Hughes in Bryson City would release him within a day or two, and the world would be better off without this snake!

Small puffs of smoke rose from Sanders's pipe as he talked in muffled tones to his mysterious friend. Nate took careful aim, inhaled, and then slowly exhaled. He refined his aim and then slowly pulled the trigger.

Before Sanders even heard the crack of the rifle, his pipe burst into minuscule shards, splintering in every direction. The stranger next to Sanders immediately flipped backward and disappeared. For a moment, Sanders sat there stunned. Then he leaped to his feet as Nate sent a second shot whizzing close by his ear—just as his guest's Stetson hat began to rise from behind the rock the men had been sitting on. Nate aimed at the hat, shot it, and watched it catapult up into the air and flip several times before falling behind the rock.

The work crew froze. Nate shouted, "Drop your tools and put your hands up! Any man who doesn't put his hands up will be shot through the heart!"

The men confusedly looked around for the source of the command. Nate shot again, just above their heads, and they all instantly dropped their tools and shot their hands into the air. Sanders, though, held his rifle in a ready position.

Nate stood. Positioned where he was, none of the men could see him except Sanders, but Nate kept his eyes and ears tuned for any sound or motion from the stranger who had disappeared. He carefully aimed the gun at Sanders's chest and calmly ordered, "Sanders, drop your rifle and pistol, or I'll drop you."

Sanders glared at Nate.

"Now!"

Sanders squatted down, placed his rifle on the ground, and then stood up.

"Drop the pistol!"

Sanders pulled the pearl-handled pistol from his belt and laid it on the ground. Nate could see that Sanders was trying to control his rage as he stood and spit out the mouthpiece—all that remained of his favorite pipe. Nate kept his rifle pointed at Sanders.

"Tell your friend to come up from behind the rock."

Sanders looked behind him and said something. Then the tall man stood up with his hands above his head.

"Pull your duster back!" Nate commanded. "Lemme see your belt."

The man followed the instructions, revealing pistols in holsters on both hips.

"Drop them to the ground, mister."

The man picked up his Stetson, put it on, and nodded, before carefully placing each gun on the ground and standing upright.

Sanders nodded. "I got no beef with you, Randolph. Why'd you shoot at my friend and me? Ought to have you arrested."

"Me?" Nate said. "It's you'uns who are rustlin' my tree."

Sanders stared angrily at Nate as his face reddened, and the veins in his neck stood out in fury. Then he took a deep breath and flashed an obviously strained smile. "Randolph, we ain't rustling your tree. This here's a tree we done bought from your neighbor, Tom Rau."

Nate knew Sanders was trying to buy some time. "He can't sell you a tree if'n he don't own it. This is my property, and ya know it."

"Ain't true!" Sanders sounded friendly now. "We bought this tree, and we have a claim purchase down at the mill."

"You're lyin', Sanders! My property goes to the ridge behind you, and you know that to be true. So, either you buy this tree from me at full value, or I'll commence to shoot you and your crew one kneecap at a time. And ya need to know, I've got more bullets than you and your crew has knees."

Sanders's face began to glow crimson again. "Randolph," he growled, "you'll pay for this!"

"Sanders, either you're gonna agree, in front of these witnesses, to buy my tree at full market value, or you're gonna face the judgment seat of our Lord for rustlin' a tree on a man's property." Nate cocked his rifle and aimed it at the middle of Sanders's chest. "Your call."

Sanders began to shake in fury. Nate suspected he was beside himself at being threatened by what he considered a mountain bumpkin. But his reason seemed to overcome his emotion as he visibly calmed down again.

"Okay," he growled, through gritted teeth. "We'll pay you market value."

Nate nodded and lowered his rifle. "Our family attorney is over in Bryson. You know Frye?"

Sanders nodded.

"When the attorney lets me know the money's in the bank, I'll let you come back, haul off the tree, and claim your weapons and your crew's tools. So until then, leave your guns, and you and your men get off my property! You can take the oxen with you."

Sanders and the crew turned to walk down the hollow while Nate followed from a safe distance, watching carefully for men who might try to curl around behind him. He could hear no telltale signs of anyone following him; nevertheless, he kept his senses sharpened until the men were down the valley and walking on the road toward town, well off the Randolph property.

As his crew rounded a bend in front of him, Sanders and his friend stopped a few paces from Nate. Sanders turned and snarled, "If it's the last thing I do, I'll make you pay! It will only take one bullet to stop your clock!"

Nate did not doubt the truth of his threat.

Suddenly, Sanders's attention was drawn over Nate's shoulder as he and his friend's eyes began to widen. The lips of each separated, as if they were trying to say something. Sanders involuntarily stepped back and stumbled a bit before catching himself. Then the two men spun around and quickly walked away, frequently checking back over their shoulders.

When they were safely down the road, Nate turned and looked over his shoulder to see the apparition he had guessed had flustered the men. Sure enough, thirty paces up a hill off the side of the road, standing between two large, thick rhododendron bushes, stood a short, skinny old man, with his unkempt and long curly gray hair streaming out in every direction, making his head look as large as a bear's. In the middle of the ball of hair was a long, thin face smeared with what looked like white pancake makeup, with two eyes opened as wide as saucers.

Nate smiled and walked toward him. "I swan. Jeremiah Welch, seein' you like that would scare the ticks off a bear. And that clay on your face makes you 'bout the scariest-looking Haint in these here mountains, that's for sure! I see you've been up in our kaolin pit."

The slight old man closed his eyes, nodded, and smiled—showing a toothless grin that spread from ear to ear; then he raised his long, spindly arm and pointed back up the trail.

"Guess you saw what those men were doin'. You been followin' us very long?"

Welch nodded and then in a surprisingly deep bass voice said, "For a bit. Heard the tree fall from where I was up on the Little Fork. Scurried down the valley and then heard two shots. Then I ran more quickly. I was worried, my friend. But by the time I got down to y'all, you was herdin' this crew like sheep to slaughter."

"You see that tall man in the dark outfit? Had a goatee."

Welch nodded. "Yep."

"Know who he is?"

Welch shook his head.

"Well, if I'm in need of a witness of that gang cuttin' down my tree, can I come a-callin'?"

The old man's eyes opened wide. He quickly shook his head, spun around, and disappeared into the bushes without a sound.

No wonder folk think he's a ghost, Nate thought as he sat down on a log by the road and listened to the comforting gurgling and babbling of Hazel Creek. He was surprised to feel himself begin to tremble a bit. He realized the confrontation with Sanders had been more unnerving than he had let on. Nate sat his rifle on the log. He knew Sanders's threat was as real as any could be, as he was a known killer who had gotten off—with the help of the company lawyers and money under the table—after murdering in other valleys.

Nate could fight when he needed to. He had proven that many times as a younger man—one time even winning a boxing championship in a lumber camp full of brawlers. But he wasn't a naturally violent man, and a large part of him hated the conflicts that reverberated up and down Hazel Creek. Nate was sick at heart at what the lumber company was doing to the watershed of his beloved Hazel Creek, a valley that had been as unspoiled and untouched as the day the good Lord created it.

Nate shook his head, for he had no doubt Sanders would try someday, some way, to carry out his threat. The only protection he had was the reassurance that the mountain people, including the Haint, would always look out for his and his family's backs—as he did theirs.

Picking up his rifle, Nate stood and turned toward home. The afternoon shadows were beginning to lengthen, and it was good to see the trees all covered with new leaves. The wildflowers by the path were welcoming and gave him hope that at least he could keep his part of this glorious wilderness safe.

As he thought of his girls, he began to pick up his pace. *Reckon they'll be glad to see me. I hate to trouble my girls and Cal, but I had to do it.*

Indeed, when they saw him striding up the path toward the cabin, the girls, who had been waiting and fretting since they had heard the two shots echo down the valley, began to cheer. Corrie, Whit, and Anna leaped from the porch and raced toward their pa, while Abbie stayed in a rocker by her ma.

The young girls were crying in relief when they hugged him and clung to him as he walked up the steps to Abbie and Callie.

"It's all right. Sanders agreed to pay full price for the tree. There was no violence and no harm done—other than the loss of Abbie's magnificent tree."

But he could see suspicion and fear in Callie's eyes. Likely she knew, as he did, that this problem was far from over.

"All right, girls," Nate directed. "Let's get us some dinner!"

The sisters cheered as they scurried inside.

6

Dinner

"Sing us a song, Abbie," Anna said as the girls prepared supper. "Sing us a good one."

Abbie laughed and thought for a moment as she stirred the red-eye gravy. She had many fond memories of the family sitting together and singing old songs. They loved singing hymns, gospel songs, ballads, and ancient music from the mountains and the old country. In fact, there was hardly a day went by that the Randolphs couldn't be found singing or playing music together.

All of the Randolphs had musical ability. Whit played the mountain dulcimer, Abbie a gourd piano or a real one, Corrie a fiddle, which her pa had made from cornstalks, and Anna the *cat paws*—two wooden spoons with a single handle that were fashioned from a solid piece of hardwood, and were the first instrument each of the sisters learned to play. Also, all of the older girls could skillfully pick or strum the old flattop guitar that had belonged to their grandpa.

However, the instrument they used the most was called the *sacred harp*, which referred to the human voice. Their mama often told them that this was the holy instrument given to each human at birth. "Make a joyful noise unto the Lord, all the earth: make a loud noise, and rejoice, and sing praise. Sing unto the Lord with the harp; with the harp, and the voice of a psalm," she would often say, quoting the 98th Psalm. She believed that any human could sing—and that all should.

More times than not, the family just sang a capella, in four-part harmony. They'd sing while working, sewing, spinning, walking, or even while just sitting on the porch.

Because Mama revered the sacred harp, and felt that all of the Lord's gifts needed to be developed, stewarded, and tended well, when they could afford it, each of the girls would take singing lessons from Reba Johnson—who had the best singing voice in the entire valley.

Abbie began to sing:

Red, red, red is the color of my true love's hair,
Her lips are like a rose so fair,
And the prettiest face and the neatest hands.
I love the grass whereon she stands,
She with the wondrous hair.

The younger girls smiled with delight, and when she started the next verse, they all joined in:

Red, red, red is the color of my true love's hair,
Her face is somethin' truly rare.
Oh I do love my love and so well she knows,
I love the ground whereon she goes.
She with the wondrous hair.

Callie smiled as she listened to her girls' lovely voices. Nate was smoking his pipe while he rocked. Then the sisters all faced each other and sang the last verse:

Red, red, red is the color of my true love's hair,
Alone, my life would be so bare.
I would sigh, I would weep,

I would never fall asleep.
My love is way beyond compare
She with the wondrous hair.

"Reckon that song's on Bobby Lee's lips?" Nate said, his mischievous eyes glancing at Callie.

Callie smiled back at him. "He'd have to change it from red to auburn hair if'n he wanted to sing about our Abbie."

"Maybe he'd sing it to Corrie," Whit said. "She's the one with red hair."

"I've got no more interest in Bobby Lee than I have with a wormy apple," Corrie shot back. "'Sides, if'n he tried holdin' my hand, I'd punch him one."

"Girls, girls," Nate chided. "As beautiful as each of you is, I reckon there'll be men a plenty tryin' to court you."

"Shouldn't we have some rules," Callie asked, "for when the boys start comin'?"

"Reckon so," Nate said, nodding and puffing his pipe. "The first is that he is to call me *Sir*, and you, my dear, *Ma'am*—as in *Yes, Sir; No, Ma'am;* and *I wouldn't think of it, Sir,* and *I will remember that good advice, Ma'am*—just the same way my daughters do."

The girls moaned as they continued their cooking.

"I like it," Callie laughed. "Any others?"

"Yes. I'll tell him he is not to touch my daughter in any sort of unseemly way—for if I see it or hear about it I will likely be incited into an uncontrollable and overly violent action on my part, such as reachin' for my shotgun."

"Pa!" Abbie exclaimed.

"Yeah, Pa," Corrie added, "you wouldn't want to be arrested for shootin' at the sheriff's son, would you?"

"After all," Abbie commented, "so far, Bobby Lee Taylor's just guilty of lookin' at me when we're at church or in town."

"Lookin'?" Nate said. "More like gawkin' or oglin'."

"Nate," Callie cautioned, "watch your language around my girls."

"Well, it's true." Taking a puff of his pipe, he added, "I think to each young man that comes to court one of my daughters I should say somethin' like this." He cleared his throat. "Young man, there is really only one rule when it comes to seein' my dear daughter and it is this—simply that you care for her as much as I do."

"Aww," the girls sighed together.

"But right now, the boys are really only shoppin' with their eyes," Callie said.

"Which reminds me that I need to add another rule. I'll tell the young men that they may only glance at my daughters from the neck up. No peekin' from the neck down."

"I like your rules, Nate. My girls are blessed to have a pa like you!" Callie said, turning to her girls. "But I don't feel right not helpin' you girls with dinner."

Abbie knew her mama felt bad that she had not been able to do most of her normal chores because of her difficult pregnancy. "You'll be back at it before Hallowed Eve. And when you're back in the kitchen, it will be with a beautiful new baby in your arms."

"The only kind we make," Nate said, laughing.

Whit laughed and looked at Abbie as she began to sing:

Is Abbie fit to be a wife, my boy Bobby?
Is she fit to be a wife? Bobby won't you tell me now.

Corrie answered, singing:

She's as fit to be a wife, as a fork fits to a knife,
But she is too young to be taken from her mother.

As Abbie blushed, the family laughed. Whit continued:

Does she often go to church, my ma Callie?
Does she often go to church? Callie won't you tell me now?

Callie picked up the verse:

Yes, she often goes to church in a bonnet white as birch,
But she is too young to be taken from her mother.

"I think that's quite enough," Abbie scolded.
Whit, giggling, couldn't stop herself:

Did she tell how old she is, my boy Bobby?
Did she tell how old she is, Bobby won't you tell me now?

The younger girls threw their arms around each other and joined their mama and pa in answering the question—quite to Abbie's consternation:

She's three times six, and seven times seven, twenty-eight and
   eleven.
But she is too young to be taken from her mother.

"Sometimes," Abbie said, unable to keep a smile off her face, "I feel that old havin' to live with you girls! Now, back to work, everyone."

One rendition of the song was not enough and as the supper cooking went on, the girls sang it several times—adding additional verses that were as old as the hills.

"Mama," Whit called out from the kitchen, "the first of the spring onions, turnips, potatoes, and cabbage are ready to bring in from the garden. And we picked some beautiful greens."

Callie looked at Nate before responding. "I told your pa that I thought March too early to plant this year. But he declared the whip-poor-will had called and the oak leaves were as big as a squirrel's ear—signs from the good Lord that it was time to plant. So, I guess we have to declare him righteous about that, eh?"

"Mama," Abbie added, "he had us only put in the cold-tolerant plants since the frost comes sometimes until the end of May. But the greens look plum dreamy."

"Speakin' of dreams," Whit said, "I had a real bad dream about the Haint last night. I dreamed it came to our loft window and scratched to get in. Oh, it scared me, I tell you!"

Corrie scoffed, "That's foolishness, Whit! First of all, there ain't no such thing as a Haint. Second of all, if'n there was one, it wouldn't be tall enough to scratch on our loft window. It's too high up in the air."

"There is too a Haint! And maybe it just used a long stick and that's what I heard," Whit insisted.

"Or maybe it can fly," Anna Kate added.

Whit put her hands on her hips and glared at Corrie. "June Cable saw the Haint her own self. She says it's shorter and smaller than any grown man in the valley. And it can float across the ground without makin' a sound. She thinks it's an elf or a fairy or a Little Person of some sort."

"See," Anna said. "Told you it could fly."

"June Cable couldn't tell the truth if they paid her for it!" Corrie sniffed. "The Haint's just an old superstition—just like them Little People that the Cherokee people believe in and the Leprechaun the Irish lumbermen talk about."

Abbie thought about her sisters' words. Virtually every mountain person in the Hazel Creek valley had a fervent belief about the strange figure that had come to be called *the Haint*. Some claimed that it was a ghost that haunted Hazel Creek, but others insisted that no such creature existed.

Abbie knew the facts about Jeremiah Welch, but she doubted she would change Whit's or Corrie's mind. Her pa had introduced her to the Haint one night the previous autumn when he had taken her hunting up in Bone Valley for a few days. But it was to be a secret that she and her pa would share. "I'll introduce each of your sisters to him when they're fourteen—just like I did you," he had said.

Finally the meal was ready. Under Abbie's direction, the table had been set, and the family stood around it. They joined hands, and when they bowed their heads, Nate prayed, "Father in Heaven, thanks for providin' me safety today amongst those rustlers. Bless this food, bless this house, and especially be with my girls' ma as she carries our baby. In Jesus' name. Amen."

They all sat down in the sturdy white oak chairs that Nate and his pa had crafted. Nate was a good woodworker, and many times Abbie heard her mama say these chairs would outlast any store-bought ones.

As she sipped her sassafras tea, Corrie shook her head. "I wish we had us some store-bought coffee. Ain't nothin' better than coffee, is there, Pa?"

"Well, coffee is mighty good, but it sure costs a heap." Nate shook his head. "'Bout like buyin' gold, it seems."

"When I get grown up, I'm gonna marry me a rich man so I can drink coffee three times a day," Corrie said.

"Where you gonna meet a rich man?" Anna asked.

"At the guest house in town?" Whit wondered out loud.

"Naw," Corrie answered. "Everyone knows Bobby Lee's one of the best baseball pitchers in western North Carolina. And the coaches of the St. Louis Cardinals' farm team in Asheville have been comin' out here to scout him for over a year."

"So," Abbie inquired, "are you planning to use him to find a rich baseball player?"

"Yep, and one who can buy me store-bought candy, too, and have it in every room in our mansion."

"Then your teeth will rot out," Anna commented, "and you won't be able to keep no husband with rotten teeth."

"Candy will not make your teeth rot out," Corrie said, glaring at Anna. "Rafe Semmes eats candy all the time. He's rich. I bet he eats candy with every meal. And he's got *all* his teeth."

"I doubt he eats candy all day long, Corrie," Callie said. "His ma wouldn't let him do that. Besides, his pa's the pastor and they ain't rich."

Anna was digging into her cobbler industriously. It was smeared all over her lips and cheeks when Whit said, "Anna Katherine, you stop eatin' like a pig! You ain't got no manners a'tall!"

Anna, however, merely grinned at her sister and continued to stuff the delectable dessert into her mouth.

"Let her alone, Whit," Callie said, laughing. "Does me good to watch her enjoy her treat. She can pick up manners later on when she gets a bit older."

Finally, when the supper was done, Callie stood to begin clearing the table.

Nate said, "No, Callie, you just go set yourself down in that rockin' chair. That's what I made it for."

"That's right, Mama. We'll clean up," Abbie quickly added.

After the dishes were cleaned, the family joined Callie on the front porch to watch the dusk settle. Abbie took a seat beside her father. He was whittling a piece of aromatic red cedar. She watched as the sunlight seemed to dissolve and the darkness slowly descended on the distant crests of mountain ridges.

Though much of the lower Hazel Creek valley had been stripped clean of its ancient forest, the upper and side valleys were as pristine as when they had first been created. Abbie often imagined that the Garden of Eden didn't have anything over the Smoky Mountains wilderness.

Living in the mountains pleased her. The Smokies were rounded and smooth and for much of the year wore petticoats of morning mist that gave them a mystic quality. But unless it was rainy season, the evenings were usually crisp and clear, allowing the family to see from their porch to the distant peaks that marked the darkening ridge of the eastern continental divide. Abbie could not imagine living anywhere else—nor did she want to.

As Julius lay in Abbie's lap, Whit sat between Nate's legs, stroking a purring Jack, as her pa scratched Lilly's head and drew on his pipe.

Abbie let out a long, contented sigh as night descended upon Hazel Creek.

7

Dawning

First light had broken when Callie heard their rooster, Hezekiah, begin to crow. Callie was thankful for him and his
brood. The food and the eggs the hens provided were a lifesaver,
particularly during their long winters—and all the more when
Nate could keep the coons and foxes out of the henhouse. The
worst offender of all was Pretty Boy—a raccoon so named by
Corrie when Nate had brought him home as an abandoned kit
after a hunting trip a year ago.

At that time, he was a mere handful of fur, ring-tailed and
black-eyed. Anna had hand-raised him on a bottle, but as of last
fall, far from being able to sit in the palm of her hand, Pretty Boy
weighed thirty pounds and was strong enough and equipped with
enough sharp teeth to keep Lilly or any full-grown dog wary of
and away from him.

The girls had tearfully put him out of the cabin in November,
before the first snow, and he had survived the winter well, but he
still visited the homestead often—at least once a day. Hezekiah
crowed again.

I'll bet that old rooster thinks he makes the sun come up! she
thought as she lay on her side, softly stroking her protuberant
belly. *You'll be here in just a couple of months more, my sweet baby, and
then I'll be able to sleep on my tummy again.*

Nate was already gone, probably in the barn milking the cow.

She smiled, thinking of the day when Abbie as a little girl named their milking cow *Star* because of the white spot on her black face. She found herself wishing they had another milk cow, so they could add to their meager income by selling even more milk, along with the cheese she made, in town—at least until she began having trouble with the pregnancy.

She rolled over to face Nate's side of the bed and pulled his pillow to her face. Breathing in his scent, she felt a deep gratitude for him. *He's such a good man to me,* she thought, *and a wonderful pa for my girls.* Nate not only worked from before dawn to dusk to keep the farm and homestead going but he also worked from time to time at the livery stable in town. He had a knack for working on engines and had even earned enough to buy an old broken-down pickup truck from the lumber company, which he had expertly repaired, although they didn't often use it given the outrageously high cost of gasoline: twenty cents a gallon!

Maybe he's workin' on that truck, she mused. *Sometimes I wonder if he loves it more than me.* She chuckled.

As the dawn's light filtered into the cabin, Callie began to make out the features of their common room, where she and Nate slept each winter. A ladder on the wall went up to the children's sleeping loft.

Once the baby is born, we'll be able to move back to our bedroom, she thought. She looked forward to the privacy. This year they did not move back during the first week of April, as they usually did when the days warmed, because the pregnancy was so difficult. Nate wanted her in the main cabin with the girls in case any problem should develop. *He worries too much. But I do like being with my girls.*

Looking up at the rafters and roof, she smiled at a warm reminiscence of the day when their neighbors had gathered from all around the Sugar Fork and Hazel creeks for raising their new bedroom. The addition of it and the dogtrot, the eight-foot breezeway between the new bedroom and the original cabin, were luxurious to her. Also, she had been so pleased when Nate had replaced their old leaky roof with newly split white oak shakes he had riven from a virgin log.

She looked up at the mantel, where a wedding picture of the two of them taken by Harve Fouts hung next to her mother's pendulum clock, which slowly ticked away the time. His full name was Nathan Hale Randolph—named after the Revolutionary war hero who, before he was hanged by the British, said, "I only regret that I have but one life to give to my country."

As more early morning light crept into the cabin, Callie could see the huge logs making up the walls of the cabin—nearly eighteen inches across and each carefully split and then hand-hewn by Nate's pa, Caleb. He had chosen the rock for the fireplace from the newly created fields of the farm. He and Nate had chinked the spaces between the cabin's logs, which were notched at the corners, with the unusually white clay they had discovered near a spring high on the family's property.

Years after the cabin had been chinked, they had learned that this white clay was called *kaolin* and was highly valued for making medicine and porcelain. Callie chuckled again, thinking, *We have the most expensive chinking in western North Carolina.*

Callie was sad that Abbie could not remember her grandpa Caleb, but she loved telling her daughter the story of how proud he looked when he held his first grandchild. "She's like a piece of heaven distilled into a precious little body," he had said as he stared down at Abbie, his eyes misting as he held her little hand. "One of God's angels for sure!" he had insisted.

Callie and the girls would visit his grave each season of the year. His plot lay next to Nate's ma's in the small family cemetery on a high ridge at the top of their property. To Callie's dismay, Nate would seldom go with her or the girls to the family plot. The visits were therapeutic to Callie—especially Decoration Day in the summer, when she and the girls went to clean the family graveyard and repaint the small picket fence surrounding it. Callie felt her heart healed a bit more each time she visited the cemetery. It gave her time to sit beside the small graves and ponder the memories of her three boys, Nathan Jr., Samuel, and George; her second, fourth, and sixth born.

Well, it's time to get stirrin'. As Callie pushed herself to a sitting position on the side of the bed, she threw a shawl over her shoulders. *Brr, it's sure colder than usual,* she thought. Fortunately, Nate had stacked fresh hardwood logs in the fireplace over the coals that were left from the evening meal, and the new fire radiated a welcoming warmth that felt more inviting with each step she took toward it.

After warming in front of its glow for a few moments, she glanced at the cooking oven and smiled. She knew before she even looked that Nate had built a small pile of the faster-burning, resin-soaked pinewood called *fatwood* in the cook box.

Callie was more than pleased with her cookstove. The Randolphs were one of the few mountain families to own one, even though almost every home in Proctor had one. But no one had a porcelain stove from Germany like the one Nancy Cunningham had at her Clubhouse in Proctor, where dignitaries and tourists often stayed.

She took a sliver of the rich pine and lit it in the fireplace. The sap in the wood ignited quickly, and she slowly carried it, shielded by her other hand, to the cooking stove, where she guided it under the pile of fatwood to light the fire. She shut the door to the stove and reached for her large iron skillet. Placing it on the stove, she added a dollop of lard from a small jug near the stove.

Turning toward the loft, she called out, "Girls! Time to rise!" She heard no movement or response. She called more sharply, "Lauren Abigail, Darla Whitney! Time to stir, girls! Corrie Hannah, you and Anna Katherine get up. Now!"

Corrie's voice floated down, "Mama, even if it's a school day, can't we rest a bit longer?"

"Not today. Mr. Faulkner's comin' early to pick you'uns up. If'n you miss him, it will be a long walk down to the schoolhouse."

At that moment, Callie heard the gate open in the yard and knew she'd hear Nate's boots on the porch in a moment. "Girls, Pa's comin'! Best get up."

Instantly the girls were up, out of their beds, and scurrying down the ladder.

8

Breakfast

Abbie was at the cookstove when her pa entered the cabin and quickly shut the door behind him. "It's mighty cold out there for a late May morn, girls! Reckon it must be the Blackberry Winter."

"What's Blackberry Winter, Pa?" Anna asked as she carefully climbed down the ladder.

"It's what the Cherokee Indians call the last cold snap of the spring. At least that's what Jonathan Walkingstick says. Anyway, you girls get washed. I brought a chunk of bacon from the smokehouse and some milk from the springhouse." Placing them on the cooking table, he kissed Callie on the cheek and then turned to hang his coat on a peg by the door. Abbie spread the melted lard in the pan. Then she expertly thick-sliced the bacon and placed it in the skillet. She loved the smell of Pa's smoked bacon. *Best in the whole valley*, she thought.

As Corrie washed her face, she called over her shoulder, "Pa, can't you wait a week so I can help you with the corn plantin'? School's out at the end of the week—just five days."

"Sorry, Precious." Nate smiled and tousled her hair. "You need your learnin'. Mr. Faulkner says the *Almanac* and the moon are tellin' us to plant this week. Besides, I've got a bunch of boys comin' up from Proctor to help out."

"Corrie," called Abbie over her shoulder, "no time to sit and chitchat. Come help me put out the settin'. Whit, get the milk poured and then come help me with the biscuits."

"You can at least say please," Whit complained.

"Please," Abbie said, sarcastically.

"And you can at least say it like you mean it!" Whit said, sticking her tongue out at her sister.

"Girls, girls!" Callie fussed as she sat at the table next to Nate. "Remember your manners."

After Abbie took the bacon out of the skillet, she poured in some flour and milk, mixing it into the grease to create the milk gravy her family enjoyed with biscuits.

Abbie began to hum as the gravy was cooking. Meanwhile, Whit took some hard biscuits out of the biscuit tin, placed them in a pan, and put them in their small Dutch oven.

"Don't leave the biscuits to burn, Whit," Abbie instructed as she stirred the gravy.

Whit again sounded irritated. "I reckon I know how to heat biscuits, Abbie!" she said.

Abbie smiled at her. "I know you do. Sorry."

Abbie realized the younger girls sometimes resented her role as their substitute ma—a role the problem pregnancy thrust upon them all. In a way, if she were honest, there were times she resented having to take over her mama's role also. "Corrie, be sure to put the preserves and honey jar on the table," she said as she leaned over to kiss Anna on the cheek.

When the breakfast was on the table, the family prayed together and then pulled out their chairs to sit. The bacon, biscuits, gravy, preserves, and honey were shared all around. Steam rose from the serving plates as they were passed. They all ate hungrily, and the food rapidly disappeared.

"Anna," laughed Whit, as she observed the creamy-white mustache on her youngest sister's upper lip, "you look just like Mr. Barnes," referring to the general-store owner in Proctor who sported a thick white mustache.

Corrie looked at her dad. "Pa, can I *please* stay home from school and help you with the plantin'?"

He scratched his auburn-brown beard. "Tell you what, Corrie. If you have a good week in school, maybe you can stay home from school and help me on Friday. That is, if your mama says it's all right."

"What about me?" Abbie and Whit cried out together.

Abbie saw her mama frown. She looked back to her pa, who seemed to quickly pick up on her irritation. "Tell ya what, girls. If you have a good week in school, I'll let you all work the corn with me Saturday."

"What about me, Pa? Why can't I go to school?" whined Anna.

"'Cause I need you to be here to help your mama and Emily Rau in the house. And you'll be startin' school the next school year."

Anna smiled.

At that instant, Julius jumped up on the table. Nate broke off a small piece of biscuit, dipped it in the gravy, and fed it to him as he purred.

"Pa, you shouldn't let that ol' cat eat on the table," Abbie protested. "It's not good manners."

"Why, I reckon Julius's manners is better than lots of folks I seen," Nate said, grinning. "And cats are cleaner than most humans. They wash all the time." He stroked the long-haired orange cat and then added, "But I reckon you're right, Abbie. Your mama tends not to like havin' a cat eat at the table with us. Right, Callie?"

Abbie could see her mama's stern look as her pa gently put Julius on the floor. Then hearing a noise outside, Nate said, "I reckon that's the men that'll be helpin' me in the fields."

"Who?" Callie asked.

A voice shouted from the outside. "Mr. Randolph? Me and the boys is here to help!"

"Sounds like Mr. Gabriel," Abbie said. Gabriel Johnson was

one of the company's lumbermen and would occasionally help Nate on the farm.

"Yep, it is," Nate said. "And I still don't feel quite right about it."

"What?" Callie said.

"Well, on the one hand havin' Gabe and some of the other black men help out here on the farm is a mighty fine thing. Gives me the help I need, gives the men some extra income to help their families when the lumberin' is slow."

"And they are good Christian folk," Callie added.

"Agreed," Nate responded. "But at the same time these men are part of the company that's destroyin' Hazel Creek and may end up destroyin' the life we love. Makes me feel like a hypocrite sometimes."

"I think it's a good thing you're doin', Nathan," Callie said, reaching over to squeeze his muscular forearm. "I think the Lord is pleased."

Nate smiled, nodding, then rose and peered out the window.

"Be right out, Gabe!"

He plucked his hat and coat off the peg beside the door, then turned and gave each of the girls a kiss. He knelt by Callie's chair to give her a hug and a kiss. The girls all watched closely as he whispered, "I love ya, Cal." Abbie knew it was his favorite name for the love of his life.

"Y'all do good work today at school, ya hear?" he said over his shoulder as he left the cabin, closing the door behind him.

"Okay, girls," Callie commanded as she pushed back from the table, "get dressed. Mr. Faulkner will be here soon." All of a sudden her face twisted in pain and she quickly sat down.

Abbie rushed around the table. Her mama complained of having pains with this baby earlier than she had with any of the others. Abbie sensed something was different about this pregnancy, but she wasn't sure what.

"I need just a moment, Abbie," her mama reassured her. Abbie directed the cleaning of the kitchen. When they were almost finished, Emily Rau arrived. She came in smiling, a small, plain young woman of seventeen. She was what the mountain folk called *a simple child*, who was not able to finish school and still lived at home with her parents. She took care of Anna and helped Callie with chores while the girls were at school.

"You shoulda left the dishes for me, Abbie," Emily scolded. "I don't mind doin' 'em."

"You've got enough to do takin' care of Mama and Anna, not to mention the chores," Abbie said. "If it weren't for you, I wouldn't be able to go to school. I wish we could do somethin' more for ya, Emily."

"I appreciate the work, Abbie, and I like takin' care of Anna. We're good friends, ain't we, Anna?" Emily smiled at Anna, who nodded and returned the smile.

As the girls hurried to get ready for school, Abbie felt a warm glow of gratitude to Emily and whispered to her mama, "We have to do somethin' nice for Em. Maybe we can buy her a present when the crops come in."

"Or from the profit from your walnut tree," Callie whispered.

Even as her mama spoke, Abbie heard Lafe Faulkner's call from outside, and all the girls hurriedly put on their coats and ran to where his wagon was pulling up.

9

Dream

Abbie knew that Lafe Faulkner enjoyed carrying them to school as much as they enjoyed riding with him—and it sure saved the girls a long six-mile walk that even in good weather could take a couple of hours.

Abbie also knew that it gave him an excuse to sell his and their milk and cheese to Barnes General Store as well as dropping by the town café to have a small bite of breakfast and large heaping of local gossip.

Then he would entertain himself playing checkers the rest of the morning. He was able to relax in his retirement due to the money he collected in a Confederate soldier pension and earned from leasing his fields out to another family to farm.

Abbie marveled at the old man's healthy appearance. He was lean as a rake handle and at the age of seventy-nine was still, unlike most of the older folks in the valley, as straight as a pine. His long silver hair was tied in the back with a thong, and his light green eyes twinkled whenever he spoke to the girls.

Nate had told the girls that Lafe had served under General Stonewall Jackson in the famous Stonewall Brigade during the Civil War. He had been in the house when the general died of pneumonia, with Mrs. Jackson at his side, after the Battle of Chancellorsville. Lafe had even been part of the contingent that had marched with the body back to the Virginia Military

Institute for the general's burial. And, most important, Lafe had soldiered with Nate's father, which greatly strengthened their families' already strong friendship.

"Come on, Mr. Lafe, tell us a story," Corrie pleaded.

"What story do you girls want?" Lafe said.

"How 'bout a story from your Civil War days?" Corrie grinned, "Like the one 'bout Jeb Stuart."

Lafe frowned and looked at the three girls sitting beside him on the wagon seat. "You girls won't lemme forget that confounded war, will ya? Heckfire, it ended a long, long time ago. Fact is, next April ninth will be sixty years!"

As he fussed at the girls, Abbie saw Lafe's eyes soften. She knew General J. E. B. Stuart was deeply admired by Mr. Lafe, not only because *Jeb*, as his men had called him, distinguished himself as the temporary commander of the wounded Stonewall Jackson's infantry corps, but also for his mastery of reconnaissance and use of his cavalry contingent in support of offensive operations. Often Mr. Lafe would talk about General Stuart's dandy clothing, including his red-lined gray cape, yellow sash, hat cocked to the side with an ostrich plume, red flower in his lapel, and copious use of cologne.

"Well," Lafe began, "one story I particularly like is when Jeb set out with twelve hundred troopers. Findin' a weakness in the enemy's flank, he took his men completely around the baffled Union army, returnin' after a hundred fifty miles with one hundred and sixty-five captured Union soldiers, over two hundred and fifty horses and mules, and wagonloads of various ordnance supplies. His men met no serious opposition from the weaker Union cavalry. His darin' and pluck were a Southern sensation, and Stuart was greeted with flower petals thrown in his path when he returned to Richmond. Why, he had become as famous as Stonewall Jackson in the eyes of the Confederacy. Still is to this day."

As he finished his story, Lafe suddenly pulled the wagon to a stop, staring at the scene on his side. "I wish you gals would look at how Calhoun has ruined our land!" He nodded to the three girls who sat beside him and added, "Why, just two decades back there wasn't a finer view of the virgin forests of Hazel Creek than right here! You could see as far south as the Snowbird Mountains in Graham County. Now the haze from the lumber mills on the river stops your eyesight before it even gets started."

Abbie was sitting between Corrie and Whit. She ran her eyes over the valley and felt a deep sadness. The hills in the lower valley were all clear-cut except for some scrub saplings. The branches that had been lopped off by the cutters were scattered across the hills, brown and dead; combined with a shroud of burn smoke mixing with the early morning mist, the scene of destruction left a pall of death over the mountains.

"It's ugly, ain't it, Mr. Lafe?" Abbie said. "Looks like a giant just raked all the trees down."

"I don't like it, either," Corrie added. "I hate that old lumber company! I hope Pa doesn't let them do this to our place."

"This is what happens when Calhoun buys land, girls," Lafe said. "The hills are stripped, the fish in the streams die, and most of the birds and animals that aren't killed clear out. And after Calhoun wrecks one valley, he just moves on and destroys another. Word is they're lookin' to clear-cut every inch of Hazel Creek."

"Why doesn't somebody stop them, Mr. Lafe?" Corrie said.

"'Cause Calhoun gets a lot of money from our trees—and he pays the folks that work for him very, very well," Lafe said sourly. "His men take the logs down Hazel Creek to the Proctor mill, saw 'em up, and dry 'em out in them enormous brick ovens. Then they load the lumber on the train, and it goes not only to the big cities all over these United States, but even across the Atlantic Ocean to Europe. Reckon if the Calhoun Company had its way, every tree in North Carolina would be cut down."

"Will they be comin' to get our trees?" Corrie asked.

"I fear so, child. The only reason they ain't moved higher up Hazel Creek is because the land's so steep, and men like your pa haven't sold to them. But now that the easy-to-get trees are gone, I fear they'll be a-comin' up to the higher parts of the valley later this summer and fall."

"It's like the dream I had last night," Whit said, almost in a whisper.

Lafe looked down at her as she continued. "I dreamed I woke up and walked to the window in the loft. There, in front of our house, lit up by the full moon, was the Haint. He was lookin' up at me. Then he turned away from the house toward the Hazel Creek valley. He raised his arms and swept them from right to left. As he did, all the trees fell down flat on the ground. Then he turned back to the cabin and looked straight up at me. I'm sure it was the Haint."

"I've often heard of him," Lafe said.

"Whit," Corrie complained, "you said before that you dreamed about the Haint last week. I think you're lyin'!"

Whit looked down at Corrie. "I *don't* lie, Corrie. Never have. Never will! 'Cause 'lyin' lips are abomination to the Lord: but they that deal truly are his delight.' Proverbs chapter twelve and the twenty-second verse."

Corrie rolled her eyes and whispered to Abbie, "I hate when she does that."

Abbie laughed. "Wouldn't hurt you to pick up your Scripture memorization, Corrie. Like it says, 'Thy word have I hid in mine heart.'"

"I know. I know! It's Psalm One-Hundred-Nineteen and the eleventh verse."

Whit looked back at Lafe. "But I couldn't stop lookin', Mr. Lafe. Then the Haint turned back toward the forest and squatted down. He didn't move for a few moments. Then he put his arms straight in front and slowly stood up, liftin' his arms over his head. When he did, the forest just came back. It reappeared. And then, in an instant, the Haint just disappeared. I couldn't stop shakin'. It scared me a mite."

Abbie felt the gooseflesh on her arms. "I think it *was* the Haint you saw," she said. "I don't think it was a dream."

"Ain't no such thing as no Haint!" Corrie scolded. "Just an old wives' tale 'round here."

Abbie and Lafe exchanged knowing looks as he called out to the mules and slapped the reins on their backs.

10

Cat's Eye

The girls jumped off Mr. Faulkner's wagon just as the school bell began to ring. As they ran to the schoolhouse, Lafe hollered after them, "Remember now, I won't be able to fetch you'uns this afternoon! Y'all be able to walk home or catch the train?"

"Course we can, Mr. Lafe!" Corrie called back.

"Thanks, Mr. Lafe!" Abbie yelled, smiling over her shoulder. "Hurry up, Whit!"

"You ain't my boss!" Whit complained.

Lafe smiled and waved. Abbie waved back, and the girls ran through the front door of the one-room schoolhouse. She knew that if they arrived after the last ring, their teacher would punish them, but they skidded into their seats just ahead of the last peal of the bell.

Abbie saw Mr. Simmons scowling from his desk. She was convinced that he was upset that they were *not* late. She believed he actually enjoyed punishing children.

Josiah Simmons was a widower the Calhoun Lumber Company had brought to Proctor from Pennsylvania. He had set up the company-financed school, which most of the locals welcomed. Prior to this, parents had to pay tuition of a dollar a month for each child who was in the one-room school, which the School Board used for paying the teacher's salary and for buying school supplies.

Sheriff Zach Taylor had accompanied Simmons in traveling

up and down Hazel Creek to inform each of the families of the new state law requiring them to send their school-age children to school, and warned each set of parents of the state-mandated consequences if they didn't. Although Zach was officially a deputy sheriff, serving the sheriff of Swain County, whose office was in Bryson City, everyone just called him *Sheriff*. And most of the mountain folk were happy for the school and the new teacher, although none of them knew much about him.

Abbie heard her father disapprove of the threats from the new schoolmaster and the fact that the school was a lumber company operation, but he had told her a number of times, "I'm pleased for my children to get more schoolin' than I had."

The only problem for the Randolph girls was how far they lived from school—a four-hour walk round trip. However, once Lafe volunteered to take them to and from school in his wagon, the decision was secure.

At ten o'clock, the students were playing outdoors during recess. Some of the girls were playing hopscotch, but most of them were crowded around Zina Farley, who brought a Montgomery Ward catalog to school to show her friends. It was called *The Wish Book*, because the four-pound catalog listed just about anything a person would need or could ever want or wish for.

The girls were crowded together on their stomachs flipping through the pages. "Looky here!" said Abbie, pointing to a picture of an electric stove. "Don't reckon there's one of these west of Sylva. There sure enough ain't one in Bryson City! At least that's what Pastor Semmes says."

"Bet there ain't one west of Asheville!" said Zina Farley.

"Pa says we won't never have 'lectricity up at our place. But it don't make no never mind," commented Abbie. "I can cook better in our fireplace, on top of our cookstove, or in our Dutch oven than anyone could on any old 'lectric stove."

"My pa told me about when 'lectricity come to Proctor," commented Angie Oliver. "It was after the lumber company come here and begun to build up the town. Calhoun brought the power system *and* the phone system with him."

Abbie said, "My pa says he wishes that we didn't have no 'lectricity or phones in Proctor because then there wouldn't be no stinkin' lumber company!"

All the girls nodded as Zina turned the page and then they gasped, for there was a page full of radios in just about every size and shape imaginable. "Says here, 'These are the first production radio sets incorporating a loudspeaker. All previously produced sets required the use of headphones. These radios allow the entire family to listen.' I'd sure love to hear one."

Angie whispered, "One Sunday afternoon after church I sneaked up to the Clubhouse. I wanted to listen to the Victor-Victrola through the window. But they were playing one of *these* newfangled radios. They was all listening to a show that come from a radio station in Asheville, and I heard one of 'em say that some of the programs come all the way from New York City!"

"Wait till you girls see what's in the back of this Monkey Ward Wish Book!" Zina said as she flipped through the pages to one showing plump women in bras and corsets.

"Zina Farley! How can you look at those pictures? Why, they're downright sinful!" said June Cable.

"You don't have to look if you don't want," scoffed Zina. "Besides, you ever seen fatter women? Tell you what: these here women don't have to do no work, I guess. Give 'em a week on our farm and I bet you they wouldn't need a corset to hold in all that fat! It'd plum fall off of them right quick."

All the girls giggled.

The only girl not playing hopscotch or looking at the catalog was Corrie. She preferred playing marbles with the boys. A crack shot, Corrie loved the challenge of beating the boys. She took the marbles she won to the Barnes General Store and traded them for candy, some of which she shared with her sisters, so as to buy their silence.

"Corrie, that was a great shot!" shouted Bobby Lee, the son of the deputy sheriff, and named after the famous general, Robert E. Lee. He was a tall, slender boy who had his father's good looks and the same black hair and dark eyes. "You knocked him clear out of the circle, Corrie!" Turning to another boy he scoffed, "Semmes, she's plum kickin' your pants."

Corrie saw Rafe Semmes, the pastor's son, sneer at the comment. At the age of thirteen, he seemed a replica of his father. His fair skin was covered with freckles and his eyes were a light blue. He was stockily built like his father, and pugnacious. She knew he disliked girls in general, and her and her sisters in particular. Rafe was a bully, and she did not trust him for a second.

Corrie heard the other boys laughing as she lined up her next shot. She was on all fours, with her marble balanced and ready to shoot. She shut her left eye tight and squinted through her right eye as she aimed. When she released the marble, it shot across the dirt like a bullet and smacked into Rafe's last remaining marble, knocking it completely out of the ring.

"Hooray!" shouted the small group of boys. Though she was a girl, she knew they admired her skill.

"Corrie whupped Rafe!" one of the boys shouted.

Corrie grinned at Rafe and then reached out to pick up the marble she had just won. Quick as a snake, his hand shot out and grabbed her wrist. With the boys taunting in the background, he growled, "You ain't takin' my best marble!"

The suddenness of his grasp shocked Corrie and the pain that shot up her arm made her wince. He began to twist her wrist. He was bigger and stronger than she was, but she stubbornly refused to cry out.

"That's my best cat's eye, Corrie Randolph!" Rafe snarled. "You cain't have it. You try and take it, and I'll break your arm!"

Corrie glowered back at him and said, "Lemme go, ya ol' snake! Or I'll bust ya!"

He twisted her wrist even harder and whispered, "You and what army, you little rat?"

Just then, a fist flew out of nowhere to slug Rafe's arm. He yelled in pain as he released Corrie's wrist.

"How 'bout me?"

Corrie looked up to see Bobby Lee glaring at Rafe. His fists were doubled up.

"Bobby Lee, why'd ya do that?" asked Rafe as he sat up, rubbing his arm. "Why you helpin' some old girl who ain't nothin'?"

"You just pick on somebody your own size, Rafe."

Rafe stood up, kneading his aching arm, and announced, "Bobby Lee, you're just sweet on her sister." Looking down at Corrie he scowled, "I'll whup you next time! I'll show you." Looking at the boys crowded around, he cried out, "I'll show you all!" He wheeled around and took off running across the schoolyard.

"You all right?" Bobby Lee asked Corrie, who was massaging her wrist.

"Why'd ya do that, Bobby Lee?" Corrie said. "I reckon I can take care of myself."

"That's what I was worried about, Corrie," laughed Bobby Lee. "I was worried you were about to stomp Rafe. And we can't have our pastor's son whupped in the schoolyard. It wouldn't look right, would it?"

"Well, you hit him your own self!"

"Reckon so, but we can't have a girl beatin' up on him, can we?"

Corrie nodded and then looked up at him. "Is it true?"

"What?"

"That you've got eyes for my sister."

"Naw," Bobby Lee said, blushing and looking down, scuffing his shoe on the dirt. "Whit's too young for me," he said, laughing.

Just at that moment, the school bell rang, signaling the end of recess.

"That's not who I meant," Corrie said as she spun around and began to run toward the schoolhouse. "And you know it!"

Bobby Lee laughed as he reached down to gather up Corrie's marbles. "Hey, come back! You forgot your marbles!"

11

Tyrant

A in't but an hour of school left, thought Corrie, staring out the window at the tree line on the edge of the school property.

Corrie loved the outdoors, and the tempting sight of the woods around the schoolyard made being indoors almost unbearable. *That old Mr. Simmons! I wish he would drown in the creek!* Corrie couldn't remember another person she disliked more than this particular teacher. Simmons was not just overly stern and downright unfriendly, he was unfair!

What she hated the most wasn't when he would give her a whack across her bottom with his punishing rod, but when he would put a clothespin on her ear. The pain would not only build and build the longer the clothespin stayed on her ear, but her bruised earlobe would be a surefire giveaway to her mama and pa that she had acted up in school that day.

"Corrie Hannah Randolph!" A voice spoke from just over her shoulder. Corrie turned to see Mr. Simmons staring at her. "If you don't recommence your lesson this moment, Miss Randolph, you'll be punished. Do you understand?"

Corrie nodded and tried to concentrate on the open book on her desk. Simmons bent over and repeated his question: "I said, do you understand me, young lady?"

"Yes, sir," Corrie whispered, feeling her face getting hot. She knew Rafe was smiling from ear to ear. She'd get him for that!

Corrie looked around at the students and noted that they were all staring.

"All of you get back to work!" Simmons commanded. "And I want silence. Understood?"

All was quiet as the students returned to their assignments, until the sound of a book falling to the floor caused the children's heads to whip around. Corrie watched Whit reach down to pick up the book, saying, "I'm sorry."

Mr. Simmons at once marched down the aisle toward Whit. Corrie's heart beat faster, for she knew that Whit was likely in for a paddling. Whit's face turned white, and she clasped her hand over her mouth, fear in her eyes. "I'm so sorry," she repeated.

Whit was the most tender of all the Randolph girls, and Corrie had been disgusted that Whit was the one who almost never got a switching from Pa. He could just scold her and reduce her to tears. As Corrie watched her sister begin to tremble, she thought, *Mr. Simmons better not hurt her like he does some of the kids!*

He approached Whit's desk. "Darla Whitney Randolph," he snarled, "did you *not* understand my order for silence?"

Whit slowly nodded. "I . . . I didn't mean anything, Mr. Simmons. It was an accident!" she stammered.

"Get out of your seat!" Everyone in the class knew what was coming next. Whit began to whimper as she stood. Simmons shoved her forward, and she stumbled to the front of the room.

"I will not tolerate such obvious and willful disobedience. I will have to punish you."

Huge tears began to tumble down Whit's cheeks as Mr. Simmons went to his desk to get one of his rods. She was trembling, and suddenly Corrie could not stand it. She quickly stood and ran to the front of the class, positioning herself directly between her sister and Mr. Simmons.

"You ain't gonna paddle her! All she did was accidentally drop her book."

The class gasped. Although they had seen Simmons paddle

children unmercifully, they never saw a student challenge him to his face.

Simmons seemed to compose himself. "Very well." He took a deep breath and seemed to be thinking. Then a wicked smile crossed his face. "Darla Whitney, you go back to your desk. And you, Corrie Randolph, you hold your arms up."

As Whit ran back to her desk sobbing, Corrie, staring straight into Mr. Simmons's eyes, defiantly lifted her hands, palms up.

He walked to her side, facing the class, and then like lightning raised the rod above his head and brutally smacked it across both her palms. Corrie's cheeks flushed as she turned her gaze out the windows toward the forest, but she didn't move or speak, which only seemed to increase the teacher's fury. He whacked her hands again and again, all the time searching the girl's face. Although Corrie flinched and flushed with each whack, she made no sound.

Finally, Mr. Simmons seemed to come to his senses. He looked around to see the shocked students. Most of the boys were wide-eyed and the girls all had hands clasped to their mouths in horror, and several were crying. He seemed to suddenly realize that this time he had gone too far. Corrie felt her entire body trembling, and her face drained of all color, but she did not utter a sound.

"Go back to your chair!" he growled stiffly.

Corrie walked slowly to her seat, her hands still held out in front, her eyes seemingly transfixed on the back of the room. Her palms were on fire and when she looked at them she saw that they were a bright reddish blue and starting to swell.

Mr. Simmons stood. "Class, attention!" Everyone except Corrie jumped to attention and faced their tormentor. "I don't think any of you need to discuss this incident with your parents. That is, unless *you* want to be paddled. I can *not* abide a child who tattles. Do you understand me?"

"Yes, sir," chimed a few students, weakly.

"Then we will continue with our lesson."

As soon as Mr. Simmons dismissed the class, Abbie ran over to Corrie's desk. "Are you all right?" Abbie whispered.

Corrie's face was still as pale as paper, but she whispered, "That old buzzard didn't hurt me none! Let's get outta here."

Whit was on one side and Abbie on the other as they walked away from the school with Corrie. Whit began to cry.

"Hush up!" scolded Corrie. "Don't let him see you cryin'. That's just what he wants!"

"But why'd you take my punishment, Corrie? I was the one who dropped my book, not you!"

"Everybody knows that, Whit. But I knew you couldn't take that man's vengeance. And I knew I could."

"But Corrie, I thought he was gonna kill you!"

"He 'bout tried."

They turned when they heard footsteps running behind them. Bobby Lee and Rafe were running up to them.

"That's about the bravest thing I ever seen, Corrie!" said Rafe.

"Why you're tougher than leather," Bobby Lee commented as he quickly looked over his shoulder and then back. He lowered his voice. "My pa's gonna hear 'bout this! He's on the School Board. That old man Simmons is the meanest person in the valley—except maybe for Mr. Sanders. My pa's gonna either string him up or run him out of town!"

"Don't you go meddlin', Bobby Lee!" warned Corrie. "Next thing you know, he'll be comin' after you. He's kin to Sanders and ain't no one gonna get rid of no company man—at least not without payin' a high price!"

"Don't make no never mind, Corrie. My mind's made up." With that, Rafe and Bobby Lee turned and ran toward town.

Corrie stared after the pair as a train whistle echoed up the valley. She turned to her sisters. "If we hurry, we can jump on the afternoon train goin' up valley."

❧ ❧ ❧ ❧

Riding on a flatcar of the narrow-gauge Smoky Mountain Railway Company train, Corrie placed her palms on the cool metal. "Makes my hands feel better," she said.

During the ride, the girls hatched a plan to keep their pa from finding out about the paddling. Whit would help Abbie with the cooking and Corrie would help watch Anna. That way, Corrie could hide her hands.

The plan worked well until they sat down for supper and it came time for the blessing. When Callie took Corrie's hand, Corrie flinched in pain. When Callie saw the severely bruised and swollen hand, her eyes widened in surprise. "Oh my goodness, Corrie, what happened?"

"I . . . I just fell, Mama."

Abbie could see that her mama knew Corrie wasn't telling the truth. She also knew that when Corrie stiffened her neck, there would be no getting the truth out of her.

Nate stood up and walked around the table to his daughter. "Lemme see," he commanded.

With her head bowed, she lifted her hand.

Nate's eyebrows raised. "Lemme see the other one."

Corrie hesitated and then raised the other hand.

Nate held her wrists tenderly as he carefully looked them over, saying nothing for a long moment. "Corrie, this didn't happen from no fall. Could only happen with several hard blows." He looked across the table to Abbie and softly asked, "What do you know about this?"

Abbie knew she couldn't lie to her pa. She looked at Corrie, whose eyes widened as she shook her head as if to say no. She suddenly gained her courage and looked at her pa. "Mr. Simmons beat Corrie, Pa. He beat her hands real bad with a rod."

Callie gasped as her pa's eyes narrowed in concern.

"It's my fault, Pa!" cried Whit. "He beat her 'cause I dropped my book in class!"

Abbie added quickly, "Pa, Corrie stood up to Mr. Simmons. She stood between him and Whit. Simmons was gonna beat Whit—just like he beats all the kids at school." She could see that her pa was deeply shaken as Whit began to cry.

Whit sniffled and then looked at her pa. "She took my punishment, Pa."

Callie reached out to grasp Nate's hand. "Best to see the sheriff," she encouraged.

Abbie knew that would not be likely.

Nate looked into Callie's eyes. Abbie could see the rage welling up in his soul.

"Don't reckon I'll be goin' to visit no sheriff." He took a deep breath, and then released it before saying in a voice that was strangely calm, "I ain't been to school for a spell . . . but reckon I'll be goin' to make a visit there tomorrow!"

12

Defender

When Nate came in from the barn to join the girls for breakfast the next morning, he knew he wouldn't be able to participate in their usual morning conversation.

However, during breakfast, Abbie, Whit, and Corrie didn't say much. Nate suspected they were nervous about what he would do that day. He and Callie knew the girls stayed up late talking about what might happen at school. He had been relieved when Abbie finally said, "We've got to get to sleep, girls. There's no point in talkin', 'cause Pa's gonna do what Pa's gonna do."

Emily came early, and when Lafe arrived to pick them up for school, Nate said quietly, "All right, girls, let's go."

As the girls walked to the wagon, Nate and Callie talked in hushed whispers on the porch. Then after he kissed Callie, he walked quickly toward the wagon, just as Lafe was going to swat the reins on the back of the mules. "Hold up, Lafe! I'll be joinin' you."

"Oh, headin' into town with me, Nate?"

"Nope. I'll just be ridin' to school with the girls."

Lafe looked quizzically at Nate as he climbed into the wagon.

"Don't look at me like I'm crazy, Lafe. A man's got a right to see about his children's education, don't he?"

"Reckon," Lafe answered, but he gave Nate a wondering look as he snapped the reins across the mules' backs.

During the ride to school, Lafe and Nate were uncharacteristically silent. Only when they pulled up to the schoolhouse did Lafe speak. "Nate, you all right?"

"I'm tolerable."

"You seem a right bit . . . well, quiet-like."

Nate smiled at his friend. "I'm fine. Just want to have a talk with my girls' teacher." Nate turned to Abbie. "Abbie, what do you do first?"

"Do first?"

"Yep. In the classroom, after the bell rings, what do you do?"

"Well, first thing is, we each go to our seats. Then we have the Pledge of Allegiance and sing the national anthem. After that, we say the Lord's Prayer, and then we start our lessons."

"All right. You go on in and get your day started."

"Pa," whispered Whit nervously, "what you aimin' to do?"

"Don't you fret, Whit," Nate replied, as he bent over to give her a hug. "You just go about your day."

"Yes, Pa."

"All right. Y'all go on in. No matter what happens, I'll either be here at the end of the schoolday to take you'uns home or have someone come bring you home."

Just that moment, the school bell began to ring and the children all sprinted toward their class.

Throughout the preliminaries, everything seemed normal. Abbie kept looking out the window, but her pa was not to be seen. After about half an hour, when all the children were working on their spelling, and Mr. Simmons was walking up and down the aisles, the door suddenly opened.

Abbie spun around in her chair to see her pa entering the door. As he strode quickly down the aisle, Abbie felt a combination of pride and trepidation. Her father was an imposing man. She turned to stare at Mr. Simmons, who looked up with surprise, then said, "Why . . . uh . . . Mr. Randolph. Good to see you."

Nate walked slowly up to the teacher, who retreated backward a few steps toward his desk. "Mr. Simmons," said Nate in a cool voice, "why'd ya beat my girl?"

Simmons began to change color, and his voice was pitched higher than usual as he spoke. "Why, Mr. Randolph, perhaps we should . . . ah . . . step outside to talk a bit. The children are busy studying just now."

Her pa looked around and noted that every child was staring at him. Abbie knew not a single pupil was studying. "Mr. Simmons," Nate answered with a firm voice, "I ain't lookin' for no privacy. I come to make something clear to you." He looked around the room and said, "Corrie Hannah, come up here."

Abbie watched Corrie slowly walk up to him. "Show this man your hands, Corrie."

Corrie slowly lifted her arms and held her hands out, palms upward. Mr. Simmons's face showed little expression, but his eyes widened a bit as he stared at the ugly, deep purple bruises and the terrible swelling that made her fingers look like sausages. Abbie thought he might have even winced. Pa's face was set and his mouth was drawn into a straight line. Abbie had never seen him so resolute!

Nate stepped closer to Simmons, who tried to back up but was stopped by his desk. "What kind of man are you to beat a child like this?"

Simmons sputtered for a moment and then attempted an explanation. "Discipline is crucial to molding a child, Mr. Randolph. As the Bible says, 'Spare the rod, spoil the child.'"

Nate glared at him. "So, you believe in the Bible, Simmons?"

"Of course I do."

"That so? Frankly, I think it's a shame you don't know it better! I may not be the best Christian in Hazel Creek, but since I was a child we was required to memorize the Good Book. And it's obvious to me you ain't done the same!" Nate glowered at Simmons.

"Mr. Randolph, what makes you think I don't know Holy Scripture? In point of fact, I too have studied it since I was a child."

"Then you should know the Bible does not say 'Spare the rod, spoil the child.' It says, in the book of Proverbs, thirteenth chapter and twenty-fourth verse, 'He that spareth his rod hateth his son: but he that loveth him chasteneth him.'"

Simmons's eyes widened.

"Jesus loved children," Nate continued. As he looked over to Corrie, he said, "'Whoever receives one little child like this in my name receives me.'" Looking back at Simmons, he said, "Jesus also said, 'Whoever causes one of these little ones who believe in me to sin, it would be better for him if a millstone were hung around his neck, and he were drowned in the depth of the sea.'"

Abbie felt pride in her pa. Their mama always encouraged the family to study and memorize Scripture. She knew her pa had hidden more Scripture in his heart than he let on.

Nate let the silence run on for what seemed like a long time, then said, "I don't have a millstone to put around your neck, Simmons. But, where's the rod that you used on my girl?"

Simmons, now visibly trembling, attempted to counter his opponent. "Mr. Randolph, I . . . I *have* to discipline my students. You said it yourself. The Good Book says, 'he that loveth him chasteneth him.'"

"No question about that, Simmons. But this time you've gone too far. And your mistake was to beat *my* child."

Simmons tried to bluster, but his brow was damp with sweat. "I teach here at the request of Mr. William Rosecrans Calhoun himself—whose general manager is a relative of mine—and I discipline with *his* authority. If you have a problem with my methods, I suggest you take it up with Mr. L. G. Sanders."

Abbie saw the color rising in her father's cheeks and that his fists were clenched. She took a deep breath as her father took a half step toward Simmons, who leaned back over his desk.

Simmons's voice was almost a squeal as he cried, "Randolph, you better leave my classroom right now!"

Abbie gasped as she saw Simmons reach behind him and grab the rod sitting on his desk.

"Simmons, you either take your treatment like a man here in front of the students or I'll drag you outside and whip you like a dog!"

"Pa! Look out!" Abbie screamed as in one swift movement Simmons raised the rod in his hand high above his head. But before he could bring it down, Nate's hand shot out, seizing Simmons by the wrist. Simmons shrieked as Nate twisted his arm, then plucked the rod out of it with his free hand. He tightened his grip on Simmons's wrist and watched him wilt in pain. Abbie knew her father's strength and understood why the teacher's face was twisted and pale. Nate bent Simmons's arm unmercifully behind his back, then pulled him around his desk and pushed him to the front of the room and against the blackboard.

Nate growled, "Simmons, hold out your hands, palms up. You do this, and I'll show you more mercy than you showed my Corrie. If you don't, I'll take you outside and mark your face!"

Nate released Simmons's wrist, turned him around, and took a step back. Simmons slowly lifted his hands.

"Palms up!" Nate commanded.

Simmons began to turn even whiter as he lifted his trembling hands. Before Abbie could blink, her dad whacked both of Mr. Simmons's palms with the rod. Simmons cried out and pulled his hands to his chest.

"Your hands or your face," Nate said coldly. "Makes no difference to me."

Simmons looked around wildly but saw no help, so again he held out his hands. Nate repeated the punishment for a total of seven times. When he was done, he broke the rod across his knee and dropped the pieces on the floor.

Nate turned toward the class. "Children, I believe that in most instances vengeance belongs to the Lord. And Jesus himself said, 'Whosoever shall smite thee on thy right cheek, turn to him the other also.' But the Bible also teaches a man to provide for and protect his own, and 'specially for those of his own house. In fact, if a man don't, God's Word says he hath denied the faith, and is worse than an infidel—why, he ain't no man at all."

Nate turned to look at Simmons, who was still trembling against the blackboard. He turned back to the classroom and pointed at Simmons. "If this man ever touches another one of you, then you come lemme know."

Abbie saw her father turn back to Simmons. For a moment she thought he might slug the trembling teacher. She could barely hear him whisper, "You ever even touch one of these children again, and I'll be back. And next time you won't be standing when I'm done."

Nathan turned and began to walk out. Abbie was surprised to see him stop at Corrie's desk, then slowly bend over, and kiss her on the head. "I love you, Precious."

Abbie never felt more proud of her pa! As Nate turned to leave, Simmons cried out in a tremulous voice, "I'll have the law on you, Randolph!"

Nathan turned to face Simmons. "School's supposed to end in two days—on Friday. Simmons, as far as I'm concerned, that's when your job ends. You'd best be out of this valley and findin' a new job for next school year." Nathan turned and left the schoolhouse without a backward look.

As the door slammed behind Nathan Randolph, the children all turned back to face Mr. Simmons. He was still pale and tremulous as he slowly walked up to his desk and sat in his chair. In almost a whisper, he commanded, "Get . . . you get back to your spelling!"

13

Summoned

For the remainder of the morning, class was calm. Mr. Simmons seemed to speak in a softer voice. What surprised Abbie even more—even though it should not have—was that student mistakes or misbehavior that might normally result in a reprimand or a smack across the hand with the rod just did not happen. In fact, Mr. Simmons didn't even pick up the pieces of his broken rod—but from time to time Abbie would notice him uncomfortably looking down at his bruised and swollen palms.

Just before the lunch break, the children were working on math problems at their desks. Mr. Simmons was sitting at his desk. Abbie saw that he was staring out the window at the forest. He nodded to himself, as if having reached a conclusion, and then turned to the class. Abbie quickly looked down at her paper.

"Bobby Lee Taylor," called Mr. Simmons.

Abbie looked at Bobby Lee, who was sitting behind her on another row. Bobby Lee's face turned pale.

"Yes, sir," Bobby Lee nervously answered.

"Come up here."

Bobby Lee got out of his chair and slowly walked forward. *What did he do?* Abbie thought to herself. *He ain't done nothin'!*

When Bobby Lee was at the side of the teacher's desk, Mr. Simmons gestured for the boy to lean over. Then Mr. Simmons whispered in his ear.

Bobby Lee stood up and said, "Now?"

"Yes, now! Run as quickly as you can."

"Yes, sir," replied Bobby Lee as he turned. His eyes met Abbie's, but she couldn't tell what he was thinking. He quickly walked out the door and she turned to see him running toward town.

"Time for lunch!" Mr. Simmons ordered.

As she left the schoolroom to go outside for lunch, Abbie went to Corrie and Whit and joined them as they walked together to sit on the grass under a large chestnut tree. The other girls quickly joined them. No sooner had they sat down than the gossip began.

Zina began, "Wow, Abbie. Your pa beat the stuffing out of old Simmons!"

June chimed in, "He's gotta be the toughest man in the valley."

Abbie looked down. "Wasn't anything, really."

"Why it was, too! Wish my pa would take up for me like that," commented Angie, the oldest of the girls.

"I reckon most girls' pas would take up for 'em."

Whit, who was munching on an apple, swallowed and commented, "Ain't every girl loves and protects her sister like my Corrie did."

Corrie looked up at Abbie and then at Whit. "What's the matter, Whit?" Abbie said softly.

"I feel so bad 'bout gettin' Corrie in trouble."

Corrie reached over and gave Whit's hair a playful tug. "Just forget about it. That's what I aim to do."

Angie said, "Whit, Corrie Hannah's just built stronger than most of us. What she did was right." She turned to Corrie and added, "Corrie Randolph, I've never seen such mettle in a girl. Why, I believe you'd spit in old Satan's face if you'd half a chance!"

For the first time the girls laughed—even Whit giggled. The girls ate in silence for a moment, and then Corrie said, "If Pa hadn't done that, I would've hit old Simmons right between the eyes with a rock myself."

Whit looked at her sister in shock. "Why, Corrie, you don't mean that!"

Corrie looked up at her next older sister and Abbie could see the venom in her eyes.

"Tell me I wouldn't, Whit? I'm tellin' you, if someone attacks my family or me, the justice is mine. You just remember that!"

"But Corrie, you can't take the law in your own hands!" Whit said.

"Why not? That's what Pa done!" Corrie cried.

"That's what's got me a-feared." Abbie looked away.

"What's got your mind, Abbie?" said Whit.

"I'm a-feared 'bout what Bobby Lee's been sent to do."

"What's that?" said Whit.

"He's done been sent to get his daddy. Simmons is gonna have Pa thrown in the jail. That's for sure!"

The afternoon classes began uneventfully. The only peculiar thing Abbie noted was that Mr. Simmons kept looking out the window at the road down to town. Abbie knew what he was looking for. She tried to concentrate on her work. Then she heard it. At first it was a low rumble. Abbie was sure that none of the other students heard it, but she saw that Mr. Simmons did.

At first he looked up, then as the sound grew, he walked to the window. In a moment other students could hear it, and they all turned toward the window to see a car turning the bend and driving quickly toward the schoolhouse. Mr. Simmons began to walk toward the back of the room. "You students continue your work. I don't want anyone talking. And when I get back, you'd better be at your desks. You hear me?"

The class responded, "Yes, sir!"

By now the car was outside the schoolhouse and the motor was turned off. Mr. Simmons walked out the door, closing it behind him.

No sooner had the door shut than all the children jumped out of their chairs and ran to the back of the room. Abbie could hear Simmons's voice through the door but couldn't quite make out what he was saying. They all startled when the door opened and in walked Bobby Lee, closing the door behind him. The children surrounded him as he whispered, "Simmons sent me to get Pa." He looked at Abbie. "Simmons wants your pa arrested and thrown under the jail in Bryson City."

"That ain't funny, Bobby Lee," Abbie said. "They've actually got a dungeon under the jail over there."

"That's right," June added. "It's a room dug below the Swain County jail. I never seen it, but my pappy has. He says it's a log room within a log room—with stones filling the space in between. The only entrance to the dungeon cell is in its ceiling, and it's a locked trapdoor from the floor above it."

"Bobby Lee," Corrie whispered, "he ain't gonna arrest my pa and throw him in the dungeon, is he?"

Bobby Lee smiled at Corrie. Abbie thought she saw a softness and a warmth to his eyes that weren't usually there. "Aw, Corrie, I done told Pa the whole story. I told him about your beatin' and how you stood up to Mr. Simmons, and I told him how this man's been beatin' us the whole year. Pa got his gun and drove here real quick."

"That doesn't mean he won't arrest Pa," Abbie said. "Simmons is a company man, a relative of Mr. Sanders. Bobby Lee, you know the company *always* gets its way. The company *always* wins!"

"Corrie, my pa will do what's right! He was born here in Hazel Creek, just like your pa. He knows how to care for the mountain people. You can trust him."

Just then, loud voices could be heard outside. The students all turned to the door as Bobby Lee slowly cracked the door open. Simmons was furious and shouting, "And then that maniac began to hit me with the rod! I thought he was going to kill me on the spot. You need to arrest him and arrest him now—for assault and battery! And if you don't, I'll be sure to see that your boss, the sheriff in Bryson City, does! Even though everyone calls you *sheriff*, I know you're just a deputy. You gotta knuckle under what the sheriff says."

"Mr. Simmons," Taylor said calmly, "I'll take care of this."

"You may not know this," Simmons hissed, "but Mr. L. G. Sanders's sister was my dear, departed wife. You best treat me like family, Taylor. Sanders sure will."

"I don't need to remind you, Simmons, since you are an educated man, that I'm the law here, not Sanders."

"Then where were you when I needed you, Zach Taylor?" Simmons snapped. "That man would have killed me if I hadn't stood up to him and commanded him to leave."

"You're a braver man than I imagined, Mr. Simmons—standin' up to Nathan Randolph like that. He's one determined man."

"Well," Mr. Simmons responded, straightening the front of his coat, "a man must do what he has to do to protect himself and his students."

Some of the boys giggled, and Bobby Lee turned and placed a finger over his lips. "Shh!"

"Well then, Mr. Simmons, I bet you wouldn't mind me talkin' to some of the students, would you?"

Simmons was silent for a moment. Abbie *knew* Simmons didn't want Zach Taylor to come in that room. "I'm afraid the School Board won't allow me to let anyone in the class. It's to protect the students, Taylor. My job's in the school. Yours is to go arrest that vicious criminal!"

"Mr. Simmons, maybe you've forgotten that I'm on the School Board. And any member of the School Board can enter any class in any school on Hazel Creek whenever he takes a notion."

Simmons was silent. Abbie could see the color drain from his face.

"And I'll tell you somethin' else, Mr. Simmons. I'm the law here on Hazel Creek. Don't you tell me where I can and can't go!"

Simmons still stood between the sheriff and the schoolhouse.

"Now, you'll either kindly step aside, or I will move you aside! Your choice."

Bobby Lee quietly and quickly shut the door, and the children scurried back to their desks. The last child had just sat down when the door creaked open.

Zach Taylor stood at the door with his hands on his hips. "Children, most of you know me. You just keep at your work. I need to talk to one or two of you."

He walked to the front of the class, then glanced at the broken pieces of rod lying on Mr. Simmons's desk. Zach sat behind the desk and looked across the classroom as Mr. Simmons entered the back of the room. The children's eyes darted between Simmons and Taylor.

"Back to your lessons!" commanded Mr. Simmons.

After a moment of silence, the sheriff's voice came from the front of the room. "Corrie Randolph."

14

Investigation

Abbie saw Corrie's head shoot up as she looked up at the deputy sheriff. "Yes, sir."

"Can you please come up here?"

Corrie stood and walked to the front of the room to stand before him.

"You're Nathan's third girl—that right?"

"Yes, sir."

"My boy's been tellin' me a bit about you."

Corrie spun around to glare at Bobby Lee, who was smiling ear to ear. Corrie turned back. "I don't need no boy a-talkin' none 'bout me!"

"I understand," Taylor reassured her, smiling. Then he turned serious. "Corrie, can you show me your hands?"

Corrie looked back at Abbie, who nodded, and held her hands out. Sheriff Zach Taylor was a man who had been hardened by his work, but Abbie thought she saw his eyes widen a bit as he gazed upon the bruises and swelling. Several of the students in the front of the class gasped.

Abbie saw anger forming in the sheriff's eyes. "All right, you can go back to your seat, Corrie."

As Corrie returned to her seat, the deputy swiveled the chair so that his back was to the class. He didn't move for several moments. There wasn't a sound in the classroom, only the songs of the birds outside. Taylor turned around, stood, and leveled his eyes on the teacher. In a hard-edged voice, he said, "Simmons, I'm gonna go up to the Randolph place. But I won't be arrestin' Nate. I'm gonna see if he wants to press charges against you. If he does, you'll be in the Bryson City jail by this evening, and no Mr. Calhoun or Mr. Sanders is gonna stand up for you when they see what you done to this little girl!"

Abbie could see Sheriff Taylor's fists clench. "You're a lucky man, Simmons. If you'd done this to my boy, I'd have done you worse than Nate did. And I'll tell ya this, if Nathan Randolph doesn't file charges, then I'm bringin' you up before the School Board myself!"

Zach Taylor looked at the children sitting at their desks. His jaw was firm, but his voice softened. He drew in a deep breath and then slowly let it out. "I want to apologize to you children. You're good young'uns, and your folks are good people. But I'm sorry for what you've had to put up with this year. I want each of you to let your folks know what has happened here. You let them know I'll be by to give my regrets, in person, to each one of them."

He took another deep breath and continued. "This school is dismissed—for the summer. Y'all go home now. Tell your parents we'll let them know when the School Board's gonna meet to fire this man."

He looked back at Simmons, who was stone-faced. "You might as well get packed up. You've made enough of our board mad that it won't be no trouble to get a vote to put the skids on you. When they hear about this, they might just order me to lynch you on the spot! You best make the afternoon train to Bryson City."

Simmons's face began to flush and his lip quivered in anger. "You and I are not done, Deputy. I'll be getting a friend or two and we'll be meeting you in your office in a bit. Don't make me have to look for you."

Zach laughed. "Don't worry, Simmons. Last thing I would want to do is make you try to hunt me down."

Simmons spun around and quickly walked toward the back of the building and slammed the door shut behind him.

Zach Taylor paused a moment. "After he's had a chance to steam down the road a bit, I want you children to leave and go home. Nobody walk home alone, ya hear?"

The children all silently nodded and stood to leave. The sheriff motioned Abbie and her sisters over to where he stood with Bobby Lee.

"Bobby Lee, can you walk with the girls to the store?"

"Yes, sir."

"Get Mr. Barnes to draw up a soda for each of you. You girls want a soda?"

The girls all smiled.

Zach nodded. "After I meet with your former teacher, I'll take you girls home."

"But Pa's comin' to get us," Abbie said.

"Your pa came down to my office earlier, and then he caught one of the trains up to the farm. He said he'd be waitin' for us there."

As the sheriff drove off, Abbie looked around. Simmons was nowhere to be seen and she hoped to never see him again. But she suspected he'd have revenge in his heart. She imagined that he was like a trapped cobra she'd read about in a book—just coiled in a basket, seething with anger, until the opportunity came to either strike or spit his fatal venom.

Nate had taken a late afternoon break from his fieldwork and was sitting on the porch drinking a glass of sassafras tea with Callie while Anna played at their feet. Lilly jumped to her feet and began to bark as Sheriff Taylor pulled his car to the front of the cabin. After he turned it off, the children filed out. Callie looked worried.

Taylor slowly walked around the car and stopped to lean against the fender. He reached into his coat pocket and pulled out his pipe.

"Lilly, hush up!" commanded Nate, and the hound fell silent and slunk under the porch.

Zach packed his pipe with tobacco from a pouch and placed it in his mouth. Abbie wondered why he was taking so long to talk. Then Zach reached into his shirt pocket, took out a kitchen match, and bent over to strike it off the bottom of his boot. As the flame subsided, he lit his pipe and took a long draw on it. Only then did he approach the porch.

Nate looked at Zach. "Simmons file charges against me?"

"Nope," replied Zach, looking away as he took a puff on his pipe. "After I took a look at your girl, his days around here were done." He took another draw from his pipe. "I saw what he did, Nate. And my boy told me what he's been doin' all year. I told him that as far as I was concerned his time in this valley was over—it was time for him to leave."

"Did he?"

"I didn't think he was gonna. Came by my office with Sanders and a stranger. Made me think he or Sanders had hired a body-guard or gunslinger to try to scare me. Anyway, when they realized I wasn't changin' my opinion or my mind no matter what the threat, they backed off and left, but not before the stranger told me that he and I weren't finished."

Nate had a bad feeling in his stomach. "Man have a bright red goatee?"

"Sure did. You know him? I haven't seen him around here before."

Nate nodded his head as Abbie stifled a gasp by putting her hand over her mouth.

"I seen him the day Sanders was rustlin' our walnut tree. You seen him, Abbie, didn't ya?"

Abbie's face paled as she nodded.

"Anyway, got a message from the train depot sayin' Simmons was on the afternoon train to Bryson with all of his belongin's."

"The stranger go with him?"

"Not that I know of. But no need to worry about him or Sanders, Nate. I could handle them both without breakin' a sweat. Especially with what I've just learned."

He reached back into his shirt pocket and pulled out a telegram, unfolded it, and handed it to Nate. "Thought you might be interested in this."

Nate read the telegram aloud:

TO: SHERIFF ZACHARY TAYLOR
    JOSIAH SIMMONS FLED FROM HERE LAST YEAR
AFTER BEING CHARGED WITH FELONY ASSAULT AND
BATTERY OF CHILDREN IN HIS CLASSROOM STOP
SENDING OUTSTANDING WARRANT FOR HIS ARREST BY
POST STOP HOPEFUL YOU CAN HELP US APPREHEND
HIM STOP

Nate folded the telegram and handed it back to Zach. "Who is this from?"

"A sheriff up in Pennsylvania—from the county where Simmons worked before. Wish I had done a bit more checkin' before we hired that man." Zach paused to take another puff of his pipe. "After gettin' this telegram, I phoned up the sheriff of Buncombe County over in Asheville. I've asked him to have the varmint apprehended this evening when the train gets there and hold him on charges of felony assault upon a child and battery, and anythin' else I can think of in the meantime."

"Why not call Bryson City and have the sheriff there pick him up?"

"I'd prefer to have a federal agent in Buncombe pick him up. The closest federal agents are up there, and they are much more difficult to bribe, if you get my meaning."

Nate smiled. "I've always thought you were an easy bribe."

Zach's face hardened. "Not funny, Nate."

"No offense intended, Zach. I was just a-pullin' your leg."

"Well, you may have to testify against him, or at the very least, give a statement."

"I'd be right happy to, Zach."

Zach nodded and then looked at Corrie. He smiled at her. "You got a mighty brave girl, Nathan Randolph. I'll have to give you your due."

"How about you join us for a sit, Zach?"

Zach smiled. "Reckon I've a moment to visit, if you've the time. After all, we may be related someday."

"Related?" Callie said.

Zach winked at Abbie, and then took a seat on the edge of the porch. "Nate and Callie, I understand your daughter and my son have eyes for each other." He turned to Nate. "Reckon they should court?"

Nate could see his daughter blush. "I'm not so sure, Zach. At least not until he comes and asks me. Wouldn't that be proper?"

Zach laughed. "Reckon it would, Nate."

Callie leaned forward. "Zach, Nate and I believe the physical, spiritual, and emotional union of a man and a woman is a wonderful gift of God."

"Me, too, Callie," Zach said. "I know it was with my Hannah."

"And," Callie continued, "I believe the weavin' of a young man's and young woman's hearts in a romantic relationship prior to a marriage is also a wonderful thing—provided it's done within God's boundaries of a betrothal commitment to marriage and stayin' within the protections he has given."

"Reckon it wouldn't hurt them to see each other from time to time, would it?"

"Could," Callie answered. "I believe that the buildin' of affections of a boy and girl without a betrothal is outside the lovin' principles that God has given us in his Word. Both physical and emotional purity are important to the Lord."

"Well, I guess I best talk to Bobby Lee about this. That be okay with you, Abbie?"

Abbie looked out across the mountains and then at her pa. Nate nodded to Zach and his heart warmed as his oldest smiled at him and then nodded to Zach.

"My Hannah always said that parents should be very involved with their sons and daughters in preparation for marriage. And hopefully, my son and your daughter will joyfully trust the Lord to use us to provide oversight, protection, and wise counsel to them."

"Amen," Abbie whispered as her sisters jumped and cheered with glee.

Dinner that night was abuzz with more conversation. The topic of discussion was, of course, the possibility that Bobby Lee would come and ask Nate for permission to court Abbie. Speculations abounded around the kitchen as to when that might be. Most supposed it would be Abbie's fifteenth birthday, which was less than a week away.

The discussion then turned to Simmons, as the girls recounted the day's story to Callie and each one told her how proud they were of their pa. It was no surprise to Abbie that her pa fended off the praise. "Any man would do the same."

Abbie could see the gratification in her ma's face as she reached across the table to touch Nate's arm. He placed his hand on hers.

"Nate, it makes me plum pleased when you stand up for our girls."

The girls giggled, but Abbie could imagine how delighted her mama was for the way he cared for her and his girls.

He smiled and added, "Best that will come of this may be a son-in-law."

"And," Whit added, "a new teacher."

"Whoever we get," Abbie said with conviction, "he'll be better than Mr. Simmons!"

❧ ❧ ❧ ❧

At bedtime, Abbie was still writing and sketching in her journal. She loved writing in the journal and did so most every day. She secretly hoped to become a writer or an artist one day, but couldn't see a way a girl could make a living doing either. Her pa had already turned in and the girls sat around to talk a bit. Finally Callie scurried the younger ones up the ladder to the loft and off to bed.

As Abbie hugged her mama good night, Callie pulled her close.

"Abbie, I need to talk to you for a moment."

Abbie sat back down as Callie took her hands and gave them a squeeze.

Callie looked down at the floor and back up at her daughter. "Abbie, I think you know how special you are to me."

Abbie nodded.

"I think the Lord is buildin' you into a lovely woman. I love the Christ-like characteristics I see in you. And I see in you the skills, knowledge, and heart necessary to be a hospitable, gracious, industrious, and lovin' wife."

Abbie blushed. "Thank you, Mama."

"And you know I expect a lot from you, correct?"

Abbie nodded again.

"I have a very difficult question for you. Do you think you shoulda been the one to stand up for Whit, not Corrie?"

Abbie felt the color rise in her face. "I'm sorry, Mama. But before I could even think, Corrie ran to the front of the room to stand that man down. It just plum shocked me, Mama. I couldn't move. I was frozen."

Callie smiled. "I know she's feisty quick to act, Abbie, but you're the oldest and the most responsible. No matter what, you're the one who always needs to take care of your younger sisters. I need to know I can depend on you no matter what. You hear?"

Abbie nodded.

"Abbie, I'll always love you so much. And I *always* want you to do what's right. If I'm not around, I want to know that you'll care for your sisters, that you'll bring them up right."

Abbie nodded as she saw tears welling up in her mama's eyes as her mama drew her close, hugged her long, and then said, "Now up to bed with you."

As Abbie climbed the ladder to the loft and then into bed, a cacophony of thoughts swirled through her mind. The lamp went out downstairs and she heard her mama climb into bed next to her pa.

Abbie couldn't sleep. Her spirit was troubled. Something in her mama's eyes and voice bothered her deeply.

15

Fifteenth

Abbie laughed out loud as she and Whit walked out of the woods. She was pretending to be the world-famous singer and theater and film actress Fanny Brice. Whit giggled as Abbie shook out her long auburn hair and belted out a tune.

The family was planning a small party in honor of Abbie's fifteenth birthday and she and Whit had been sent up to Ramp Hollow to gather some greens for the evening meal.

Unlike most onions, ramps had not only pungent bulbs, but also shoots that were eaten as greens. After being cleaned, the roots and greens would be chopped and fried in rendered bacon fat, with some cracklings added, and then the whole mess cooked down.

"You think Bobby Lee's comin' tonight?" Whit asked.

"I hope so." *But,* she wondered to herself, *will he?*

"I'll pick some mint from the garden for you," Whit said.

"Why, sweet sister?"

"'Cause if he comes, you don't want to have ramp breath, do ya?"

Abbie laughed. "Thanks for takin' care of your sister."

As they turned to walk toward the cabin, Abbie became concerned. Usually before dinner on a warm evening, her mama would be rocking on the porch with the windows wide open.

Walking up to the porch, she stopped. The shutters were closed on all the windows. She found herself backing up a step. Abbie felt a chill across her back. *Somethin's wrong!*

The door of the cabin cracked open and Corrie stuck her head out. "Abbie, Whit! Pa says come in here now!" Then she slammed the door.

Now I know somethin's wrong, Abbie thought. *This ain't right!* Dropping the basket with the greens, she ran up the porch. She quickly lifted the latch and started to push the door open. *Why's it so dark inside?*

Suddenly the door was pulled open and a chorus of voices inside the cabin yelled, "Surprise!"

The shutters flew open, and as the warm afternoon light flooded the cabin, Abbie could see the room was packed with people.

Her friends from school rushed up along with her sisters to hug her. Maddie Satterfield was behind her mama, laughing and clapping. The Walkingsticks were standing by Maddie, smiling and nodding. The entire Rau clan was there, as were the Faulkners, Barneses, Taylors, Semmeses, and many others—friends from up and down Hazel Creek.

"Where are all of your mounts and carriages?" Abbie asked incredulously.

"Hidden in and behind the barn," Nate said, laughing. "We were worried sick you'd see 'em anyway."

"I can't believe it!" Abbie said, blinking back tears. She was even more astonished when she saw Maybelle Semmes walking toward her, holding a beautiful frosted birthday cake. Everyone was cheering.

"Reba Johnson baked this just for you," Maybelle told her. "Her friend Linda Pyeritz helped her prepare and frost it, and then they wrote 'Happy 15th Birthday, Abbie.'"

From around the room came a chorus, "Happy Birthday, Abbie." Rafe and Bobby Lee were obnoxiously whistling via fingers stuck between their lips.

She saw her pa sitting by her mama, smiling and looking so proud. She ran over to him, hugged him, and then stood, beaming.

"Thank you both. Thank you so much!"

"I have a small surprise for you," Callie said.

Nate turned around and picked up a brown-paper-wrapped box held together with a piece of twine.

"For me?" Abbie said.

"It is!" Nate nodded. "Unwrap it. Don't keep everyone waitin'."

Abbie pulled off the twine and wrapping, leaving a plain box. The label on the box said *Barnes Emporium*.

"Go ahead," Whit encouraged.

Abbie noticed the room was completely silent and that everyone leaned forward. She reached down and pulled off the lid. As she recognized the contents, she stifled a gasp.

"They're the most beautiful shoes I have ever seen!" she exclaimed. "Store-bought, churchgoin' shoes. Fit for a queen," Abbie whispered as she lifted the pair out of the box.

"Fit for a princess," Nate whispered as the room murmured in approval.

"I can't believe it," was all Abbie could whisper.

"I wanted you to have them," her mama said. "They're to match the dress I'm hoping your pa will help me buy you next year. That right, Nate?"

Nate smiled and nodded.

Callie looked back at Abbie and said, "But don't even think of wearin' them for every day. These are for special events only. Ya hear?"

Abbie nodded.

"And thank your pa. He made them possible."

"Thank you, Pa! This is the best day in my life!" She gave him a long hug.

"I love you, Punkin."

"I love you, Pa."

"You get on and enjoy your party. Ya hear?"

"I will, Pa."

"Come on over to the table, Abbie," Maybelle instructed. "You need to blow out the candles on your cake, make a wish, and open up some more presents!"

The guests moved to the front lawn for the dinner and some after-dinner dancing and singing. The party quickly moved into full swing. The lemonade was a perfect balance of sweet and sour. The cake had been delicious, especially with scoops of the home-made ice cream the Barneses brought from their store.

Lafe supervised the games, while Sandy Rau and Maddie ran the kitchen. People from town, as well as up and down Hazel Creek, dropped by throughout the afternoon to eat, visit, play games, catch up on gossip, and dance to the music played by a group of black musicians, including Gabe and Reba Johnson, who were hired by Mr. Barnes to play all the mountain songs that Abbie and her family loved. Proctor's only photographer, Harve Fouts, who now worked for Calhoun, was there to take pictures of the event and the families.

Abbie was sitting on the front porch watching the festivities when Bobby Lee ran up to her.

"Mind if I sit a bit?"

Abbie smiled. "I don't. Not a bit."

"Nice party, eh?"

"It is. Very nice."

"How's it feel to be fifteen?"

"Not bad. In fact, I rather enjoy it."

"I bet I know why, Abbie."

"You do?" Abbie said, laughing. "Since when did you learn to read a girl's mind?"

Bobby Lee smiled. "I betcha it's because fifteen is the courtin' age in Hazel Creek. So now, if your pa will let you, you can find a guy to court. And I'm gonna be keepin' a lookout for eligible bachelors for you, I'll tell ya that."

"You will?" Abbie said coyly.

"Well, maybe not. After all, I reckon you'll have plenty of boys sniffin' up the Sugar Fork a-lookin' for ya. Why, that's for sure. Won't hardly be able to keep them away."

Abbie smiled.

"That is . . ."

She turned to face him. "That is what?"

"That is unless I came up here from time to time." Bobby Lee blushed and looked down. He was quiet for a moment. "Um . . . er . . . Abbie . . ."

"What?"

"Would you mind too terribly if I come up to call on you from time to time?"

Abbie smiled. "To visit . . . or to court?"

Bobby Lee took in a deep breath and then slowly let it out. "Um . . . I think I'd prefer the second?"

"To court?"

He nodded.

"You gotta ask Pa first."

"Um . . ." Bobby Lee looked away. "Guess I already did."

"You did? What did Pa say?"

Bobby Lee smiled again. "He said it would be right fine by him."

"And Mama?"

He nodded again. "And your ma agreed."

It was Abbie's turn to blush. Her mind was reeling. *I've got to get control. I've got to remember the ritual.* She thought for a moment as she scanned her memory for the custom she had practiced in her head since she was a little girl and waited for what seemed a lifetime to repeat. When she was sure she had it, she nodded once and began: "Can I trust you to court me?"

"You may, my lovely," he said, quoting the words of the mountain tradition that was generations old. "After all, don't I have honest eyes?"

"So has a sheep," Abbie responded. "But have you discretion?"

"Do I have keen eyes?"

Abbie continued the ritual: "So has a fox, but it is tricky."

Bobby Lee smiled at her and she felt her heart beating like fire. "Do I have kind eyes?" he said.

"So has a puppy." Abbie laughed, putting her hand to her mouth. "But it is so foolish."

"Do I have lovely eyes?"

Abbie looked down for a moment. This was the moment she had awaited for so long, but never thought would arrive. She looked up at him, smiled, and said, "You have all four."

He smiled as he took her hands in his and knelt on one knee. "Then, Miss Lauren Abigail Randolph, shall we court forevermore?"

She looked back at Bobby Lee, reached out, and completed the ancient rhyme and ritual: "Yes! And to you, I open my heart's door."

"Really?"

"Really!"

Bobby Lee gently and softly kissed the top of each of her hands and then they both stood and laughed as he pulled her close, hugged her, and twirled her around. The family and friends who were watching the ceremony erupted in wild cheers.

He whispered in her ear. "When you blew out your birthday cake candles, what did you wish for?"

"Love," she whispered back. "That is what I want!"

"I believe I can grant your wish, Abbie. And I think we're in for some excitin' times."

It was hard for the girls to go to sleep that night. They could not quit chattering about the courtship ritual they had witnessed.

"'Bout the most romantic thing I've ever seen," Whit said.

"Better than any weddin' I've ever been to," Corrie added.

"But that don't mean nothin' 'cause you *hate* weddin's," Whit said, laughing.

"A lot of girls marry at fifteen here in Hazel Creek," Abbie commented. "Sixteen at the latest. So, it may be just in the nick of time."

"Then maybe we oughta get you courtin', Whit," Corrie said. "You're thirteen. How about I talk to Pastor Semmes about sendin' Rafe up here to court you?"

"Wouldn't court Rafe if he was the last boy in the valley," Whit said, scowling. "He's too dadburn uncivilized."

"Corrie's almost eleven. Maybe Rafe should court her," Anna suggested as the other girls laughed.

"I'd rather whup him than court him," Corrie said. "'Sides, he don't never talk to me. He's still mad that I won his best marble." Corrie smiled at Abbie. "I'm happy you and Bobby Lee will be courtin'. But I'll tell you this much, I ain't courtin' no poor boys. Nope. I'm only gonna court someone who's rich."

"I know, I know," Abbie said as she laughed. "When Bobby Lee's playing for the St. Louis Cardinals, he's to find you a prosperous and wealthy baseball-playing bachelor who can whisk you away to the life of your dreams."

Corrie applauded. "Yes!" she exclaimed. "That's exactly what I want!"

The girls all took their pillows and began beating Corrie on the head as they laughed.

16

Carnival

For most of the mountain people on Hazel Creek, day-to-day life was a struggle. Throughout the spring and early summer, locals were working their fields. Then in the fall, harvest, canning, and butchering began—as well as the fall hunts and trapping for meat.

During the winter months, the labor became even more diffi-cult and the rewards scarcer. To the outside reviewer, life may have seemed devoid of excitement or color—but that was a dramati-cally inaccurate perception, especially during the Independence Day celebration, when Nate allowed Abbie to drive his truck down from the farm.

Because gasoline was in short supply and very expensive, the family usually used their horses or their feet for most of their transportation needs. But today was July Fourth, a very special day on Hazel Creek!

"When did the carnival start comin' here? How many years ago?" Anna asked as she sat on her pa's lap in the passenger seat.

"Been over a decade," Nate said. "Since before you were born, that's for sure. Calhoun brings the carnival in by train. They've been settin' up a couple of days accordin' to Bobby Lee. This year they even have wild animals."

"Like what?" Anna said, her eyes widening.

"Lions and tigers. Plus camels and bears."

"Yippee!" Anna shrieked.

"I've been lookin' forward to this for quite a while," Nate said. "It's one of my favorite days."

"Why?" Anna asked. "'Cause you wanna see the animals?"

Nate laughed. "That's part of it. But most just because it's a day of fun and frolic. Everyone up and down Hazel Creek gets together. Folks take a day to leave their fieldwork and housework to visit one another and celebrate Uncle Sam's birthday. Other than the Christmas tree celebration, it's about the only time everyone gathers."

"Is that why so many politicians come, Pa?" Abbie asked.

"Yep. They furnish the tables of food in return for us mountain people havin' to swallow their speeches."

"Seems like a fair enough bargain," Whit observed.

Nate laughed again. "Depends on the food, honey."

It was ten in the morning when Abbie pulled into the parking lot, and the festivities had already begun. The girls were bubbling with anticipation as they disembarked from the truck. The air was filled with the sounds of the calliope and of the screams of those who happily endured the flight of the Ferris wheel and other seemingly death-defying rides.

"Looks like it's bigger than ever," Nate said as he put Anna on the ground and stretched out, looking over the row of carnival attractions that lined a crowd-filled alley with booths on both sides as far as the eye could see.

"Girls," he said, "before we begin our caper, y'all remember to stick together. You could get lost in this crowd. Ya hear?"

"Oh, Pa, we know where the truck is. If we got separated, we'd just come back here," Corrie said impatiently.

"Let's go!" Anna shouted. "I want to ride the Ferris wheel."

"I'm *not* gonna ride that thing!" Whit said quickly. "It could fall over and kill everybody on it."

"Well, I *am*!" Anna announced defiantly. "I was too little last year, but now I'm big enough, ain't I, Pa?"

Nate reached over and touched Anna's hair fondly. "I reckon

you're grown enough to handle it. What about you, Corrie? You think you'll do it?"

"I rode it last year, Pa," Corrie said quickly. "I didn't think it was scary a'tall."

"Remember, we all stay together. Let's go."

Abbie said, "I'm sorry Mama ain't here with us."

"You know she shooed us out of the house. Said she'd be rightly upset if we didn't come. And she'll be with us at next year's carnival with that little baby of ours in her hands."

"And," Corrie said, "maybe next year Bobby Lee will be here with his new wife."

"Corrie Hannah!" Abbie scolded.

Nate laughed. "Reckon you two are plannin' to meet up here, that right?"

Abbie blushed.

"Come on, girls," he said. "Let's go have us a frolic!"

Nate left the girls at the flagpole in the center of the carnival ground, after instructing them to stay within a stone's throw of the pole until he returned from purchasing some tickets for the rides and drinks.

The people who passed by fascinated the girls. "I've never seen so many strangers," Whit observed.

"They musta come from all over," Abbie said.

"Look at that odd wagon!" Anna said.

Indeed, there was a very peculiar-looking and large coach with a colorful striped awning stretching from its side. A gypsy woman sat at a little table, and Corrie, the most impulsive of the girls, walked excitedly forward.

The wagon was strikingly different from all the farm wagons Abbie had ever seen in the valley. It had a curved top, and there were shuttered windows in the side of it—real glass windows! It was painted with intricate patterns of red, yellow, green, and other bright colors, making a splash of color against the carnival behind it. The wheels were painted bright yellow, and Abbie was filled with admiration at the beauty of it.

As the girls walked up, the gypsy looked up from her chair, placed her hands on the table in front of her, and looked from one girl to the other. Then she slowly stood. She was much taller than average and was a most exceptional-looking woman—having a dark olive complexion and the blackest eyes that Abbie had ever seen. Black eyebrows arched over them, and her skin looked as smooth as silk. She had a wide mouth, large and well formed, and as she stared at them for a moment, Abbie wondered if something dangerous or mysterious might be lurking in this woman—or her past.

"Why are you staring at me?" she asked, looking down at the girls. "Have you never seen a gypsy before?"

"No, I ain't," Corrie said defiantly.

"Well, you look all you please, missy." The woman smiled.

She was wearing a multicolored skirt that came almost down to the tops of her black boots. It was separated from her blouse with a belt that had some sort of embedded gems. Her blouse was a brilliant red, and she wore a bright yellow kerchief that could not contain the wealth of jet-black hair that dropped beneath it and escaped to cover her forehead.

"What's your name?" Corrie asked.

"My friends call me Maria. But some call me Gypsy Mary."

As their pa walked up behind them, the woman smiled. "I'll tell your girls' futures, if you wish, sir."

"Thanks, but I think we'll decline," Nate said.

"We just wanted to come and see you," Corrie said.

"Don't be rude," Abbie cautioned.

"Are you tellin' lots of futures?" Corrie said.

"I tell a few, but people around here don't seem to believe much in it. At least they say they don't. Pity, I say."

At that moment Sheriff Zach Taylor strolled by. Zach looked

very handsome—tall and broad-shouldered as he was. His eyes lit up as he saw the Randolphs, and he came over at once.

"Well, if it ain't the prettiest girls in the county," he said.

"Where's Bobby Lee?" Abbie asked, hardly able to suppress her excitement.

"Well, before I answer that, I want to tell you somethin'."

"Which is?" Abbie said.

"I'm really glad Bobby Lee chose to court you."

Abbie smiled and nodded.

Zach put a hand on each of her shoulders. "Tell ya this, Abbie: I'll be mighty proud to have you as my daughter. My Hannah would agree. Just sorry she's not here to tell you herself."

"Me, too," Abbie said softly.

"Well, about Bobby Lee: he's finishing up some chores with his pals Rafe Semmes and David Rau. Should be here before lunch. Told me he'd find you as soon as he got here. That be okay?"

"How's he gonna find me in all these people?" Abbie said.

"How does a mountain lion find his prey? My bet's he'll find you lickety split!" Zach said, laughing.

Abbie smiled.

"You gettin' your future told?"

"She don't need her future told," a voice growled. "She needs to be arrested."

L. G. Sanders strode up to Zach, looking angry as the Randolph girls stared up at him. He shook his head with disgust.

"That girl's done broke the law, Sheriff," he said, his voice rising with anger. "It's your duty to arrest her."

"What girl? Who in tarnation are you talkin' about, Sanders?"

L.G. walked toward Abbie and pointed at her. "That Randolph girl."

Nate stepped between Abbie and L.G., but was silent.

"What law did she break, L.G.?" Zach said.

"She's not old enough to have a driver's license."

"Maybe not. But why would she need one?"

"Saw her driving her pa's truck down here and parking it out in the lot." Sanders turned to glare at Nate, and then turned back to Sheriff Taylor and said accusingly, "You gonna enforce the law?"

Sheriff Taylor smiled lazily, his eyes half-hooded as he studied the shorter man. "You got any witnesses?"

"Why would I need witnesses?"

"Well, I reckon it would be your word against the girls, and their pa's. By my count, that would be five to one."

"I reckon Judge Hughes over in Bryson City would be willing to consider my testimony, me being who I am here at the company. I'd be willing to take that risk. So, I recommend you go ahead and give her a citation. I think a fine would be in order, also."

"Reckon it would be a shame to do that, L.G." Zach rubbed his chin as if in thought. "Because maybe the judge would be interested in hearin' the girls testify about you rustlin' their walnut tree."

L. G. Sanders's face reddened. "I paid for that tree, fair and square. In fact, I got robbed on the price of that old tree."

"Maybe so, maybe not. But I imagine the judge might be sympathetic to the testimony of these cute little girls whose mother is heavy with child."

"You know he'd have no interest in that tree, Taylor. It's old business."

"Maybe so. Maybe not. But Corrie bein' beaten by a relative of yours is still unfinished business to me—as is the murder of old Mr. Cable. He was gunned down not long ago and not too far from his cabin. Some say it was done by a lumberman intent on stealin' his land out from under his family."

"Heard tell it was an accident. I had nothing to do with it. And even if I did, there ain't no evidence to the contrary," L.G. said. "Besides, that family's been planning to sell their land to me for some time."

Zach leaned forward until he was nose to nose with Sanders.

"I've been investigatin' that so-called accident, Sanders. There was no fight, so he musta known the scoundrel that murdered him. And he was shot right between the eyes with a .22, probably a pistol. Maybe it was the .22 pistol you're wearin'."

"Ain't no way to prove that," Sanders said.

"Been workin' with the State Bureau of Investigation, Sanders. You might be surprised what the SBI can prove these days."

Sanders opened his mouth to speak but then saw something in the sheriff's eyes that made him change his mind. He clamped his mouth shut, wheeled around, and stalked off.

"You don't need to be a prophet to know that man's no good," Maria commented.

"You're right about that," Zach said. "Now, can I pay you to read my little friends' futures?"

"I don't charge money for this, Sheriff," Maria said. "I will tell their futures for free. And how about you, Sheriff?"

"Depends," Zach said. "You a fortune-teller or a prophet?"

"Does it matter?" Maria asked.

"Yep. The former is frowned on in the Bible, the latter approved."

Maria narrowed her eyes and stared at the sheriff for a moment. "Can I trust you?"

"I'm the law."

She smiled. "Yes, but can I trust you?"

"As long as the day is, you can trust him," Abbie attested.

"Then let's call me a prophetess."

Zach Taylor had a good sense of humor. He at once came forward and said, "Then in that case, why, sure, lady. By the way, I don't know your name."

"Some call me Gypsy Mary. But you can call me Maria."

"I like that name," Zach said as he stuck his hand out. "Go ahead. Tell me what's gonna happen."

Abbie saw Maria's eyes sparkle as she looked into his eyes. She rested her hands on his head. When she looked up, there was a slight smile on her face. "I see a wonderful, dark, mystifying woman in your future. She will make you very happy."

Sheriff Taylor laughed aloud. "Why, I'm hopin' a Miss Agnes Morgan's in my future. We're seein' each other when I get over to Bryson City, but she's a blond woman."

"Then she is *not* for you." Maria shook her head firmly, continuing to gaze into his eyes. "Not enough fire in a blond woman. No, I see a mysterious woman with an olive complexion. Don't let these blond women turn you aside from your true future."

Sheriff Taylor was still smiling. "I'll have to think on that, Maria. Am I gonna be rich or take a long journey?"

"For that we will have to have a full conference. It takes more time for such things—assuming the Lord wants me to tell you these things . . . or . . . perhaps other things."

"All right then. I want the full works." He turned to Nate. "Y'all go on."

Nate laughed. "I reckon we'll wait. That way you can't be kidnapped without a fight."

Zach smiled and nodded.

17

Gypsy

Nate and the girls watched as Zach and Maria sat down next to the wagon.

After a few minutes Corrie wrinkled her brow, saying, "How could it take so long to tell one man's future?"

Whit said, "I think Sheriff Taylor might be takin' a likin' to Maria."

"Why, he wouldn't marry no gypsy. Half the women in Swain County are after him," Nate observed. "She'll have to find her a gypsy man to marry."

"Ain't nothin' wrong with a gypsy marryin' a white man, is there, Pa?" Corrie asked. "Plenty of white men are marryin' Cherokee women around here."

"You got a point, Precious," Nate said. "But I'd bet many folks would still look down on it."

Finally Sheriff Taylor stood up, smiled at Gypsy Mary, and walked toward the Randolphs with a thoughtful look in his eyes. "Well, I don't have to worry about what I'll be doin', girls. Miss Maria here has told me all about it." He turned and winked. "I'll see you later, gypsy lady."

Maria's smile beamed.

Zach turned to Nate. "Let's leave these girls to have a good time. I need to show you something." He turned to Maria. "Mind keepin' an eye on these girls for a little bit?"

"I'd be pleased to," Maria said.

After giving the girls some last-minute instructions and sitting them under Maria's awning, Nate left with Zach.

As the men walked away, Maria sat down. "Gypsy Mary says that there go two fine men. And I can tell you from experience that not all lawmen, or men for that matter, are so kind."

At that moment, Mr. and Mrs. Barnes came strolling by. Millard was a short man, but trim and fit. His round, mild face contained an almost continual jovial luster and was framed by thick brown hair, graying sideburns, and crystalline light blue eyes. Abbie thought his thick white mustache to be one of the handsomest in town.

Etta Mae Barnes was, compared to her husband, a large woman. *Not fat*, Abbie thought, *just big. Actually, she has a fine figure. And she's not homely, just plain.*

"Well, hello, young ladies." Millard smiled broadly. "I suppose you had your future told."

"Not yet. But I think *you* ought to," Corrie said pertly. "Both of you. Gypsy Mary here says she can tell futures better than anybody."

"Oh, I don't believe in that poppycock!" Etta Mae said quickly.

Millard turned to her. "Well, you know, I think maybe it might be a good idea. I mean, after all, you keep saying I'm going to outlive you because you're always so ill. Maybe this lady here can give me some advice on my next wife."

"Millard!"

"Well, you're the one that started it, Etta Mae. Now I think we're gonna have to do all we can to get me set up and ready for when you depart this vale of tears. Maybe we ought to just give this woman a chance. She might point me to just the right one for after you're gone."

Etta Mae's face turned scarlet. She grabbed Millard by the arm and said, "I don't want to hear any more of this foolishness! Come along!"

As the two left, Gypsy Mary said, "That is a funny woman. I don't think she knows how to treat a husband. Maybe I should give her lessons."

"Have you been married, Maria?" Abbie inquired.

"No, but I have common sense. Everyone knows you don't make a husband love you by pretending to be sick all the time like that woman does."

Abbie felt her jaw drop open. "How'd you know *that*?"

Maria smiled and leaned forward. "It's my gift."

"Gift?" Abbie asked.

"Yes," Maria whispered. "It's the gift I've been given by God."

Corrie grabbed Abbie's arm. "Look, here comes Belle Rogers."

Abbie turned quickly to see a couple coming along the midway. Belle Rogers was a woman with a less-than-stellar reputation. She lived in a house on the outskirts of the north end of Proctor along with two other single and suspicious women. Since they lived just outside the official city limits, Calhoun's "morals" sheriff, L. G. Sanders, could do little, and the county officials practically winked at the whole affair. "After all," they said, "it *is* a lumber camp."

Belle Rogers was an attractive woman in her late twenties. She had red hair and green eyes, and her face was very becoming in spite of too much makeup. Rings glittered from her fingers, and her dress was cut daringly low in the front—the plunging neckline accentuating her extremely thin waist.

Abbie remembered shopping in Barnes General Store one day when Belle entered to purchase some supplies. Abbie had never forgotten how Mrs. Barnes gave her husband a tongue-lashing once Belle left, viciously accusing him of flirting with Belle.

Beside Belle walked a tall man, just over six feet, slender but muscular with dark auburn hair and dark eyes. He had a chiseled face with a very distinguished-looking bright red goatee.

Corrie whispered, "Look at that man. Ain't he handsome?"

"I don't think he's a good man, Corrie. I seen him up with Sanders when they was rustlin' our tree," Abbie whispered as

Corrie gasped. But the sight of the unusual couple also fascinated her.

"And Belle for sure is not a churchgoin' woman," Whit said.

"Yep," Abbie said. "Everyone knows that Belle did time in the penitentiary for cuttin' a man up into pieces with a bowie knife in a bar fight over in Sylva."

"To me," Corrie said, "she looks wild and dangerous. If rumor has it correct, she's never done an honest day's work in her entire life."

"Tell your future, lovely lady?" Gypsy Mary called out, and at once Belle, who held the strange man by the arm, said, "Let's find out what lies ahead of us, darling."

"Good times lie ahead of us, baby. I can tell you that!" But his eyes went to Gypsy Mary, and he said, "But you'd better hang on to me, Belle. That's one good-looking future-teller there."

Belle's eyes danced. "You keep your hands off her, or I'll put rat poison in your whiskey."

"I will tell your futures at once."

Belle stuck her hand out and said, "Tell me that I'm going to be rich and famous."

After concentrating on Belle's eyes for a few moments, a strange look came across Gypsy Mary's face. She grew very sober, and Belle suddenly looked at her, also becoming very serious. The two women locked eyes, and finally Belle said, "What did you see?"

"In your eyes, nothing, but I see something in you. You are unhappy, and you need a great change in your life."

Belle's face flushed beneath the rouge. "I don't need any preaching from you, gypsy . . . you . . . you lowlife! Come on, darling."

"Wait a minute," the stranger said. He put his hand out and said, "What about me?"

Maria's face flushed and she tersely said, "You sure you want a lowlife telling your future?"

"You bet, lady. If you're up to it."

Maria stood closer to him and looked intently into his eyes. As she gazed, her eyes widened. She looked down at his left hand and noticed he had a gold band on his ring finger.

Suddenly he turned away and said, "I know what's ahead for me, lady. No gypsy woman is going to change it, either. My motto comes from the Bible: 'a man hath no better thing under the sun than to eat, and to drink, and to be merry.' Don't need your type, gypsy. I'll make my own future," he growled. "Come on, Belle. Let's get out of here. It's getting gloomy."

The man put on his Stetson as he looked down at Abbie.

"I can tell you your future, little lady. You want to hear it?"

Abbie felt her cheeks blush and was too shocked to respond.

He bent down and she could smell the whiskey on his breath. "If your pa does not sell his farm to the company, then it is quite likely that you will not make your sixteenth birthday. It would be a shame for a pretty girl like you to have never been kissed."

The man leaned toward her and before she could think, Abbie slapped him across the cheek as hard as she could, knocking him back a half step.

Anger shot across his face as his hand flew up to slap her. But before his open hand could move forward, Maria grabbed it and stepped between them.

With his free hand he threw back his coat and reached for a bowie knife that was sheathed on his belt.

Belle pulled on his arm. "Come on, darling. No need to waste time with this gypsy or these little hillbilly girls. They're just white trash."

The man continued to glare at Abbie and then his face softened as he looked at Belle. "Reckon you're right, Belle. Let's move on." He looked down at Abbie. "But you will be sorry you did that, young lady. You be careful where you walk, you hear?"

The couple turned and quickly walked away.

"I feel bad for the way they treated you girls," Maria said.

"I'm sorry for what they said to you, Miss Maria," Whit said.

"Me, too," Anna added.

Maria stooped down and smiled at Anna. "Not to worry, little one. Gypsy Mary has to get used to such things. Insults come with those who have my gift and with being a gypsy. I just consider the source." The large woman walked over to Abbie and took her hands.

"I see you are still in shock."

Abbie nodded.

Maria looked at the couple as they disappeared into the crowd. "Belle, she's sad, but I think down deep she's nice. Not the man. He's dangerous. I think he would have tried to kiss you. But your slap stopped him in a New York second. We need to tell your pa."

"No!" Abbie said.

"Why not?" Maria asked.

"He's got too much on his mind as it is. No need to bother him."

Maria looked uncertain. "I hope you're right."

Corrie spoke up, "Did you really see bad things for them in their eyes?"

"Not just in the eyes, Corrie. I can see people's spirits—deep into their souls. But even without my gift, anyone could just look at them and know bad things are coming."

Abbie looked at the two and said, "They're real bad people, aren't they, Miss Maria?"

"Like I said, Belle has some good in her, but she will not let it come out. As for him, I think he's as evil as old Scratch himself. There's only one end to a man like that—and it is not any good. The only question is how many will go down with him."

"Who's old Scratch?" Anna asked.

"It's just a nickname for ol' Satan himself. And that man's a devil if I ever saw one." Her face grew tense, but she quickly shook it off. Looking up, she smiled. "Well, the sheriff and your pa are heading back this way."

The girls looked around. "I don't see 'em," Whit said. "Do you, Maria?"

Maria smiled. "Not with my eyes, but by the time you get to the flagpole, they'll be there. So you girls scoot along. Go have a good time. But don't forget. I owe you a telling of your futures."

As they walked away from the wagon, Whit took Abbie's hand. "I thought he was gonna hurt you, Abbie."

"Me, too," Abbie said. "'Bout scared me to death." She felt a chill go down her spine as she remembered seeing him standing with Sanders above the trunk of her beloved walnut tree. "I knew he was bad stock the first time I saw him."

"You think he's gonna come after you?" Whit asked.

"Not if Pa has anythin' to do with it," Corrie said defiantly. "Pa will protect us. You can mark that down."

Abbie's intuition told her otherwise. *That man is truly evil,* she thought. *There's no tellin' what his type would do.*

Abbie shivered as yet another chill ran down her spine.

18

Ferris Wheel

Abbie's mind continued to ruminate on the threat from the man with the red goatee as Pa treated the girls to saltwater taffy, caramel-covered apples, and lemonade. Abbie continued to wrestle with whether she should tell her pa of the interaction or not. Finally, fearing what he might do to the man, Abbie decided to keep the whole affair to herself.

Looking down at Anna Kate, who was devouring her spun-sugar "fairy floss"—the local name for cotton candy—Abbie smiled and decided to put the earlier events behind her and enjoy the rest of the day.

Abbie and her sisters had great fun on the carnival rides and playing games at several booths, but were bored almost to tears by the politicians' speeches. However, they all enjoyed listening to the band Calhoun had hired to play both popular and patriotic music. It was the same group of black musicians, including Gabe and Reba Johnson, and Rick and Linda Pyeritz, who had played at her birthday.

Abbie kept looking around, hoping to see Bobby Lee. *What's keepin' him?* she wondered. She went to get another glass of lemonade for Nate, who found a place to sit down and rest on the grass under a large shade tree. The girls stayed with him, and after Abbie brought the lemonade back, he gave her a ticket and said, "Let's see you ride that Ferris wheel."

Actually, Abbie was afraid of the Ferris wheel. She disliked heights. Corrie knew this and grinned at her. "Come on. You ain't gonna be a scaredy-cat, are you?"

"No, I ain't!" Abbie said and turned and marched away. When she got to the Ferris wheel, it was full, so she was waiting at the end of the line for a seat when a voice behind her said, "I'd better ride that Ferris wheel with you, my fair lady." She turned to see Bobby Lee. Her heart began to beat wildly.

"I wouldn't want you to get scared and fall outta that thing or somethin'," he said.

"I don't believe I'm scared of any old Ferris wheel!"

He smiled. "Well, I think you might be, and I'm here to protect you not only from fallin' out of that wheel, but from any boys who might be lookin' to take your hand from mine."

As the two stood there talking, Rafe came walking up and, ignoring Bobby Lee, said, "Hi, Abbie. You gonna ride the Ferris wheel?"

"I guess so."

"Well, I'd sure like to ride with you."

"You don't have to do that, Rafe. I'm ridin' with her," Bobby Lee said.

"I guess you can take the next car, Bobby Lee," Rafe said.

"I'm takin' this one, and I'm ridin' with Abbie."

"Abbie," Rafe said, "looks like you're either gonna have to choose between us or ride with the both of us."

"Rafe!" Abbie exclaimed. "You *know* Bobby Lee and I are courtin'."

"I know," Rafe said. "But I thought I'd give you one last chance to make a change. You know, court a preacher's kid."

"I appreciate the offer, Rafe, but my mind's made up. This here's my man!"

Bobby Lee smiled at Abbie as he put his arm around her shoulder.

"Well, I'll be a monkey's uncle!" Rafe said as a smile beamed across his face. He stuck out his hand and shook Bobby Lee's like it was a pump handle. "Well, you two'll make a mighty fine couple, I'll tell you that."

"I think so," Bobby Lee said as Abbie felt her cheeks warm.

"Well," Rafe said, looking around, "if'n you two don't mind, I'll be takin' a walk to find me another pretty girl that's available."

The Ferris wheel attendant hollered, "I don't have time to wait. Are you getting in?"

Abbie reluctantly got in and Bobby Lee quickly jumped in after her. After the safety bar was placed across their laps and clamped, Bobby Lee said, "I reckon I'd better hold your hand." He reached out and took Abbie's hand, but she surprised herself by jerking it back.

"You don't want to hold my hand?" Bobby Lee said.

"I've . . . I've just never held hands with a boy in public . . . that is, if'n you don't count Pa."

"It won't hurt none," he said as he gently placed his hand in hers.

Abbie felt a chill go up her spine as their fingers intertwined. She looked up at him and smiled. "I think I like it."

"Me, too."

Abbie took a deep breath as she summoned her courage to tell Bobby Lee about the man with the red goatee. She thought that if Bobby Lee would tell his pa, it might provide her and her family a bit of protection. But, all of a sudden, the chair was airborne.

Abbie's scream was muffled by the calliope music as the Ferris wheel began to move higher and higher. Despite her initial fear, she found herself delighted with the view up and down the valley. She could see the mountains far off and even could see where their truck was parked. Then the problems of the morning and the difficulties of day-to-day life in Hazel Creek flew away in an instant.

"I like bein' next to ya," she said as she leaned into his muscular body, trying to forget the goateed man's threat.

Bobby Lee let loose of her hand and put his arm around her

shoulder, pulling her closer. "I kinda like it, too," he said, laughing nervously.

Down and around they went, saying nothing, Abbie just enjoying her first experience of being close to a boy. She laid her head on his shoulder and felt as if she were flying across Hazel Creek as the air blew her hair. At times she was hardly able to breathe from the thrill of it all. When the ride was over, which occurred far too quickly for Abbie, they got out and walked over to Abbie's family.

As they came near, Whit's eyes were dancing. "I saw you two holdin' hands. That all right, Pa? I mean, I know they're courtin', but is hand holdin' all right? Who knows what it could lead to? Or are you gonna have to take a shotgun after him and get 'em married?"

"What's this? My girl's holdin' hands with a young man?" Nate said. His eyes were sparkling. "Well, I'll have to speak to him and ask him if he's intendin' to marry her."

"Well," Anna said, "he's right there, Pa. Why don't you just talk to him right now?"

"Reckon I can?" Nate asked Anna.

"Of course!" Anna said laughing. "You're the pa!"

"Okay," Nate said, looking up at Bobby Lee. "My girls want to know your intentions, young man."

"Don't you dare, Bobby Lee! They're just bein' silly," Abbie said as she and Bobby Lee sat down together.

"Why, I don't think we're bein' silly." Nate reached over and pulled Abbie close. "What's silly about a pa askin' the intention of a boy that's courtin' his girl?"

"Pa, we're *just* courtin'!" Abbie said.

Anna looked up at Pa. "If'n they can hold hands, can they kiss?"

"Anna!" Abbie cried out. "You're embarrassin' me."

"It's all right, Abbie," Bobby Lee said. He then turned to the girls. "For you'uns' information, I'm courtin' your sister and hopin' the Lord will make it clear to me and Abbie, as well as your parents and my pa, that me and Abbie are meant for each other in marriage. And when he makes that clear to us all, then I'm here to tell you all that I'm lookin' forward to spendin' my life with this beautiful young woman and helpin' your pa with all the bad that's comin' his way."

"Bad? Comin' my way?" Nate said.

"Yep. The way I figure it, as these lovely young ladies grow up, each one of them is gonna have at least three or four, maybe even five, boys chasin' after them. So, if five fellers apiece come fightin' amongst themselves, let's see, we'll have three girls, with five courters per girl. Why, that's fifteen young bucks I'll have to help you watch out for."

"But if the St. Louis Cardinals draft you to play for them, Bobby Lee," Corrie said, "then you won't be here to protect me from no boys!"

"Ah, in the very, very unlikely event such a thing were to happen . . . then what would we do?" Bobby Lee asked as he scratched his chin, appearing to be deep in thought. Suddenly his eyes brightened and he held a finger up in the air. "But I do know the deputy sheriff of these here parts pretty well. I reckon he'll help me!"

The girls all found this hilarious, and Abbie was happy that the attention had been turned from her.

Finally Whit leaned over to Abbie and whispered, "I like him a lot."

"Me, too," Abbie whispered.

"Found out the name of that man," Whit said. "He's Reginald Knight."

"Who told you?"

"The sheriff. He came by and Corrie blabbed her mouth about the whole thing to him."

"Did Pa hear?" Abbie asked.

"Nope. But the sheriff said he'd been watchin' Mr. Knight very carefully. Feels he's up to no good. Said he'll keep his eyes even more peeled now."

Abbie nodded, but she wasn't sure it would be enough. "Pa's gonna have to know," she whispered.

Whit nodded. "I think so."

19

Jean

One of the tents had a stage on the front side that featured three young boxers who would take on any challengers. The boxers stood there allowing those passing by to feel their large arm muscles and their leather gloves. The largest and oldest of the three was called Okay Donovan.

The manager of the boxing attraction shouted out, "Come on now! We need another man here! I need *any* man who will stand up to Okay Donovan! Twenty dollars to anyone that can stand up to my man for three three-minute rounds!" Even raising the stakes to thirty dollars attracted no takers, though several of the lumbermen were obviously considering it.

Finally, Millard Barnes spoke up. "I'll tell you what. If any good man here will take him up, I'll add the finest first calf heifer in the county. I just won her at the raffle, and I have no place to keep a cow. There she is right over there, boys; a blue-ribbon winner. As fine an animal as lives in Hazel Creek."

The cow was brought forward, and Abbie said, "She's beautiful, Pa."

"You like her, Abbie?"

"Oh, I'd give anythin' for a nice young cow like her!" Abbie said. She dearly loved animals, and Star, their milk cow, was getting old. "Look at her udder—it's well attached. She's got a lot of good depth to her—has good capacity for feed. She'll make a fine milk cow."

Nate smiled at her. "There was a day I'd have been mighty happy to fight a man for a fine animal like this. But your ma don't like me fightin'."

"Pa," Abbie interjected, "Mama's been wantin' another cow so we'd have extra milk and cheese to sell in town."

"But I'm a churchgoin' fella now. I need to leave my scrappin' days behind, don'tcha think?"

"That ain't the reason you don't fight," snarled a voice behind them.

Nate turned to see Sanders walking up.

"You're just too blamed chicken to face up to a real man, ain'tcha, Randolph?"

Nate stood to face the man. "Well, if'n it ain't L. G. Sanders. What rock did you crawl out from under?"

Sanders's cold eyes narrowed and an evil stare projected from them. Abbie had seen his wicked gaze directed at others he hated—it was an icy look meant to freeze an opponent, almost like the look of a rattlesnake in a just-shaken jar.

"You remind me of a bad cold, Sanders, always showin' up at just the wrong time and makin' folks feel puny."

Sanders frostily, purposefully, and unhurriedly pulled back his coat, revealing the pearl-handled .22 pistol that was holstered at his side. "Just doing my job, Randolph. As the manager of the lumber company, this here's my event, and I call 'em like I see 'em."

"Sanders," Nate said, "you're too rotten to see straight even if'n ya tried."

The crowd gathering around them chuckled, which perturbed Sanders.

"I've never been scared to fight a man," Sanders said, fingering the handle of his pistol as he looked down at Abbie and Bobby Lee. "Guess your little girl is having to learn the hard way that her pa is a coward. And I reckon her sniveling little boyfriend is finding out his future father-in-law is nothing but a lily-livered, yellow-bellied weakling." He looked back at Nate. "Tough thing for the kids to learn, I suspect."

Nate felt his face flush. He had half a mind to put out Sanders's lights right then and there. But he took a deep breath and slowly let it out as he thought how he might respond. Before he could collect his thoughts, Bobby Lee stepped by and thrust both of his hands into Sanders's chest, knocking him back a step.

"You be careful what you say, mister!"

"You think 'cause your pa's the sheriff that that will protect you from me, you little snot nose?"

Nate reached out and firmly grasped Bobby Lee by the shoulders. "Not worth wastin' your time, son."

Sanders glared at Bobby Lee, sneered, then looked over Nate's shoulder at the massive fighter before spitting out a stream of tobacco juice. Wiping his sleeve, he glared back at Nate. "Guess a little fellow like you'd have no chance with a real man like that, eh, Randolph?"

Nate smiled and looked down at Abbie. "You like that cow, Punkin?" Nate said. "Then I'll get her for you and your mama."

"Why, you can't fight that big fella, Pa! He's a professional. And he's huge."

"When I was a younger man, Abbie, I never lost a fight." He looked up at Sanders. "And I ain't plannin' to lose to Donovan today—or in the future to you, Sanders."

"But he's awfully *big*," Bobby Lee warned.

Nate smiled at him. "Your pa will tell you, Bobby Lee, the biggest men are often the easiest to whip. You know, the bigger they are, the harder they fall." He looked back at Sanders. "Them, and the ones what are stiff-necked and prideful."

Abbie watched as her pa turned and began to move through the crowd. When he got to the platform, he hopped up on it and looked across the crowd. "I'm here to show this flatlander how mountain men fight—and to win that milkin' cow for my girl."

Donovan was a massive man, over six and a half feet tall

and weighing well over two hundred fifty pounds. His face was scarred and battered, and Nate heard he'd been a professional fighter whose career washed out and now he was touring the country with the fair. Nate also suspected Donovan found no difficulty in getting rid of the crude talent that came at him. Most of them were likely untested farm boys and young lumbermen who came in swinging blindly, which would allow him to flatten them with one well-placed blow to their noses or chins. Nate suspected that very rarely did any of them go more than one round before ending up on their backs watching stars circle their heads.

"What do you think, Donovan?" the manager asked.

The boxer shrugged his shoulders and smirked down at Nate. "Shouldn't take too long. It's your life, little man." Then he looked down at his manager and grinned. "Bring him in."

"All right, fellow," the manager said to Nate. "You come along. We'll get you dressed out."

As they entered the tent, Nate could see the crowd surging forward to buy tickets.

Abbie and Bobby Lee watched as the crowd paid their entry fees and poured into the tent.

"Can't we go watch?" Corrie said.

"Nope," Whit said. "Children are *not* allowed. See the sign by the entrance?"

"Hogwash!" Bobby Lee said. "We can watch."

"How we gonna get in?" Abbie inquired. "They ain't gonna let us in there without a ticket."

"Follow me, girls," Bobby Lee said. "I've got me an idea." He led the girls through the crowd and around the side, where he lifted up the edge of the tent. He and the girls scurried under. Inside the tent, there were bleachers set up on four sides of the boxing ring. Bright light illuminated the canvas, surrounded by the darkness that enveloped the seats. No one noticed them.

Donovan got into the ring. His boxing gloves were gargantuan. The boxing ring's canvas floor bounced and gave way under his hulking body as he began to dance around the ring, punching at the air.

Nate made his way through the crowd wearing a pair of over-sized boxing shorts, and he had a small boxing glove on each hand. As he entered the ring, the locals began to cheer and shout for him. Compared to Donovan, he looked like a midget.

"He doesn't have a chance!" Abbie gasped.

"If I could bet," Bobby Lee said, "I'd bet on your pa."

"Me, too," Corrie added.

The manager slid under the ropes and walked to the center of the ring. "I'll be the referee." Looking at Nate, he announced, "Gentlemen, I need to announce a substitution. Mr. Donovan will be replaced, at the request of Calhoun Lumber Company, our hosts today, by Mr. Reginald Knight."

"What?" Nate and the large boxer bellowed in unison.

"That ain't fair!" Nate cried.

"Bait and switch!" Millard Barnes shouted.

The referee looked at the booing crowd. "It ain't my choice!"

Nate nodded, but Donovan didn't move. "Take a break, Tiny," the referee said as the crowd separated to let a tall man make his way into the ring. Abbie gasped as she saw his bright red goatee. Knight and Donovan touched gloves as the larger man left the ring.

The referee called the two men to the center of the ring and lifted his hands to hush the crowd. "You know the rules?" he asked Nate.

"No, sir," Nate said.

"That ain't true!" Abbie whispered to Bobby Lee. "He's boxed before."

"Bet he's just bluffin' the man," Bobby Lee responded. "Playin' dumb to Knight to make him overconfident."

"Well, no head butting," the referee began, "and you can't hit below the belt. No wrestling, kicking, or unfair tactics will be tolerated. Each round will last three minutes separated by a one-minute rest period. When I come between you, you must separate without throwing a punch. At a knockdown, the one scoring the knockdown will go to his corner while I count. If you're down, you've got ten seconds to get up. Break a rule, you get disqualified. You got that?"

Nate nodded.

"You remember me, Randolph?" Knight said as he punched his gloves together.

Nate's eyes narrowed.

"You're going to be sorry for putting a hole in my Stetson, son," he said as he stepped toward Nate. "I have boxed in lumber camps from Michigan to Maine and have not lost a single bout. Several of my opponents were dragged from the ring unconscious. I just want you and your people to be properly warned."

Nate leaned into Knight until they were nose to nose, each staring the other down without blinking.

The referee stepped between them. "All right. You men go to your corners."

Knight walked over to the corner, grabbing the ropes as he stretched and waited. He seemed unconcerned, and Abbie grew worried. "I'm a-feared that man could hurt Pa bad," she whispered to Bobby Lee.

"If what he says is true, I suspect he could. But I'm in your pa's corner," Bobby Lee said.

"Oh dear," Abbie said. "I wish I hadn't got Pa into this."

"I'm tellin' ya," Bobby Lee reassured the girls, "my pa says yours can whup any man in Hazel Creek. My money's on your pa."

The bell rang, and Nate came out, his hands down at his sides. He almost looked like he was walking leisurely down a forest path. Knight came out with his left hand high, guarding his head, and his right cocked as his feet danced across the canvas like a professional. "Get your hands up, you fool!" he growled.

Nate smiled and put his hands on his hips. Knight began circling, and Nate simply stood there turning around looking like a rank amateur. Suddenly Knight leaped forward and unleashed a left, but Nate simply raised his glove and deflected the blow as he quickly dodged it.

Knight then tried a right with the same effect. He circled for a few seconds and then unfurled a series of blows with one hand after the other. But Nate skillfully protected his body with his arms and gloves and dodged each powerful blow.

Apparently Knight was not accustomed to boxing anyone as quick as Nate. Try as he may, he could not land a punch. He continued to swing, seemingly becoming more frustrated. Finally, after trying to land a massive roundhouse with his right hand, which Nate had to block with both hands, Knight landed a left upper cut into Nate's abdomen, lifting him off the mat and knocking the air out of him.

The blow obviously hurt Nate as he sank to one knee in agony, unable to breathe for a moment. Abbie felt herself gasp, as the referee didn't rush in to protect her pa when Knight drew back to throw a final blow. At just the last second, the bell clanged and the referee jumped between them, ending the round.

Nate struggled to his corner, where someone placed a stool under him as he collapsed. Abbie saw Millard Barnes jump into the ring with a bucket of water, a large sponge, and a towel. She wanted to run forward as Mr. Barnes tended to her pa, but found herself frozen in place.

"He'll shake it off, Abbie," she heard Bobby Lee say. "Don't worry."

The second round went better with the crowd wildly cheering for Nate. It was as if the cheers energized him. Nate was able to land several blows to Knight's chest, but it looked to Abbie like he was hitting an oak tree. They went around and around each other, prodding and jabbing for the entire three minutes. Knight, try as he might, was never able to get to Nate's head.

As the bell clanged and Nate turned to his corner, Knight stepped toward him and launched a haymaker.

"Look out, Nate!" Millard screamed. Nate instantly squatted and turned as Knight's massive fist skimmed across his head and knocked Nate backward and into the ropes—almost causing him to plummet out of the ring. The referee was between them at once. Abbie could see her pa's eyes were glazed as he crawled back into the ring and backed toward his corner, not taking his eyes off Knight. The crowd loudly and lustily booed.

As Millard whispered instructions to Nate, Knight walked to his corner shaking his head. The referee marched up to him and said, loudly enough for most to hear, "What's the matter with you?"

"You want me to win, don't you?" Knight snarled. "And I plan to."

"Fairly!" the manager exclaimed. "They say you're the best boxer in any lumber camp. Why can't you hit him? Why can't you take him out?"

"Can't you see? He's too blamed fast—quick as a weasel! I can hardly land a blow. And I'm about winded. I don't usually need more than a round."

"Well, you'd better get him quick or I'm going to lose a ton of money! And your boss is going to owe me big!" the referee barked.

Finally the bell clanged to signal round three. Nate seemed to still be groggy as he stumbled toward the middle of the ring, apparently still affected by Knight's unblocked blow. Just then the large man let out a bellow, launched himself off his stool, and charged Nate like a half-crazed bull.

Abbie's hand flew to her mouth as the crowd gasped.

As Knight charged, Nate instantly came to life and took a half step back as he threw a roundhouse punch to the right side of Knight's head and quickly stepped out of the way. The large man's ear split open and began to spurt blood as he sprawled out on the mat, while the crowd laughed and cheered for Nate.

Knight jumped to his feet, his face a brilliant, raging red as he threw himself toward Nate with his arms flailing.

Nate nimbly dodged the huge man's thrashing arms and managed to smash Knight right in the mouth. Blood poured from the man's upper lip and dripped down his goatee, but the blow only seemed to make him more insane. He again rushed toward Nate like a wild man, screaming at the top of his lungs. As he did, Nate spun around like a top, which seemed to confuse the fighter and slowed him down just enough that when Nate threw a powerful uppercut, it caught Knight squarely in the chin and popped the big man's head backward. His whole body crumpled as he fell flat on his back, lying absolutely still.

The referee stared in disbelief as he made Nate retreat to his corner and then proceeded with the count as slowly as possible. He paused before the last count, but saw there was no hope. His man was out like a light.

"All right," he said as he stood and took Nate's arm. "You win, fair and square." As he took Nate's elbow, and pushed his arm up in the air he announced, "Gentlemen, the winner. And the first man in history to knock out boxing champion Reginald Knight! He'll win thirty dollars and the milk cow."

Abbie and her sisters jumped up and down, screaming in glee and hugging one another as hard as they could. Abbie turned to Bobby Lee, who was beaming.

"I knew he'd do it, Abbie. I *knew* it."

As Abbie reached up to hug him, he leaned forward and gave her a kiss on her cheek. It was the most wonderful thing she had ever felt as she heard her sisters cheering in the background.

Once washed up and fully dressed, Nate came out and found everybody waiting to congratulate him. As he walked out of the tent, a cheer went up. The men all gathered around him, patting him on the back.

Nate smiled, but looked for his girls. After he hugged each one and shook Bobby Lee's hand, the crowd separated to reveal Millard Barnes leading the beautiful milking cow toward them.

As Millard held out the halter, Nate took it and placed it in Abbie's hand. "She's yours now, Punkin. You like her?"

Abbie nodded.

"You asked for her, so she's yours now. And you're gonna have to care for and milk her every day. You know your mama can't in her condition. You and the girls up to it?"

Abbie smiled, nodded, then reached down and stroked the silky hide. Stooping down and putting her arms around the cow's neck, she gave her a hug. Then she straightened up and reached her arms around her pa.

Nate winced and moaned quietly.

Abbie pulled back. "I'm sorry, Pa. You hurt?"

Nate smiled. "My ribs are too bruised for a proper hug, even by my Punkin. So, how about a hug around my neck?"

Abbie hugged his neck and said, "Thanks, Pa. I'll always think of you every time I see her. And I'm gonna name her Jean."

"Jean? You mean your ma's middle name?"

Abbie nodded and smiled.

"I never saw anything like that!" Millard said to Nate, slapping him on the back. "I don't believe there's a man alive that can stand up to you, Nate Randolph."

"I don't like fightin', Millard. I hope that will be my last one. This dog's gettin' too old for that type of game. But Abbie wanted the calf—and she's got it."

"Well, you sure showed up Mr. L. G. Sanders, Nate. Reckon he won't be a-callin' you a coward anymore."

As the crowd began to move away, Nate said, "Don't be too sure, Millard. A snake like that might back down for a moment, but before you can shake a stick at him, he'll likely be back. And I'm sure a man like Knight won't cotton well to bein' embarrassed like he was today. I suspect he'll come for me sometime."

20

Berries

Abbie had just finished filling her bucket with black-berries when Whit hollered, "How much more we gotta pick, Abbie?"

"I reckon we got enough to have earned a swim!" Abbie called back.

They had come to the cleared land where Hazel Creek drained into the Little Tennessee River to harvest wild berries. Abbie looked at the river and felt the heat of the afternoon sun beating down on her. Suddenly the thought of the cool water was irresistible, and she yelled at her sisters, "How about we go down to the river and take a little swim? Could cool us off a mite."

Corrie, who loved to swim, yelped, "Last one down to the river's a rotten egg!" She took off in a burst with Whit on her tail.

The girls raced across the meadow toward the river. The waist-high grass had not been cut and was sprinkled with Queen Anne's lace. At the edge of the field they bounded through a grove of large trees on the river's edge. *I reckon they'll be gone soon if Calhoun has anythin' to do with it!* Abbie thought as she ran through the trees.

As Abbie ran down the bank, Corrie and Whit were already down at the river's edge, giggling and peeling off their clothes—except their underwear—and putting them on rocks at the edge of the river. Abbie looked up and down and then across the river to be sure they would not be seen.

"You're the rotten egg, Abbie," teased Corrie.

Abbie smiled and took off her clothes and stared at her underwear. "Someday I'm gonna have me some store-bought underwear with ribbons and lace, just like in the Sears and Roebuck catalog."

As she waded into the river, she closed her eyes as the cool water wrapped around her legs, her stomach, and then her chest and shoulders. She took a deep breath and went under the water.

This is mighty fine! she thought to herself. She was thankful that her pa had made sure each of the girls knew how to swim when they were very young. Her pa told her she was the best swimmer in Hazel Creek. Abbie felt comfortable in the weightlessness of the cool river. She loved the water, which was noticeably warmer than the icy water of Hazel Creek.

After holding her breath as long as she could, Abbie surfaced and took in another deep breath of the warm air. She began to walk toward the bank, feeling the cool mud oozing between her toes. Now standing in knee-deep water, she looked down at her sisters, who were sitting in the water with only their heads showing above the surface.

The girls laughed and splashed in the cool water until Whit cried out, "Someone's a-comin'!"

Abbie immediately whirled around to look upstream. Sure enough, a raft was coming around the bend of the river. Three boys were using poles to guide it through the rapids and around a large boulder.

"Oh, my gosh! What can we do?" whispered Whit.

"Ain't no time to get out now!" Corrie said quickly. "Let's stay here and stay quiet. Maybe they won't see us."

"Let's move closer to the shore and under some of those overhangin' willow limbs," suggested Abbie.

Corrie and Whit nodded, and the girls, with only their heads showing, slowly moved under the branches. "It won't give us much cover, but let's pray it hides us enough."

"Well, I'll be dipped!" exclaimed Corrie. "You see who that is?"

Abbie squinted, and then her eyes widened. "It's Rafe, David, and Bobby Lee! If they see us, we won't never ever live this down!"

Suddenly the boys stopped poling as Rafe began to point at them and howl like a coyote. Then the girls heard the sound of laughter as the boys saw them and began poling as fast as they could—right toward the girls.

"We caught 'em, boys! We done found us some girls!" shouted Rafe. He may have been the pastor's son, but he was mischievous and always looking for another source for gossip.

"Who's that skinny-dippin'?" hollered David Rau. "I can see clothes there on the bank!"

Why ain't he workin' up at his pa's farm? thought Abbie. *This is terrible! They're gonna know who we are in a minute!*

She was right, for Rafe shouted, "I'll be a monkey's uncle! It's them Randolph girls. Abbie, Whit, Corrie, you got any clothes on? Or you naked like jaybirds?"

"Let's let 'em be, boys," Bobby Lee cautioned.

"Not me, Bobby Lee. I mean we done found us a bunch of bare-tailed girls! Reckon we ought to chase them out of the water, Rafe?" laughed David.

"I've been wantin' to go swimmin' myself!" Rafe said. "How 'bout we stop this raft, hop out, and have us a swim?"

"They best not!" Corrie growled. "Why, I'll drown the whole bunch myself! It'll only take one funeral to get rid of that whole bunch of rats!"

"You girls want us to come a-swimmin'?" shouted Bobby Lee. "Or just float on downstream?" The raft was drawing nearer.

"I vote we go swimmin'!" Rafe shouted.

Whit began to whimper. "They're gonna see us naked!"

"Don't worry, Whit," Abbie reassured her. "Water's too murky for them to see. Just stay down and we'll be all right."

The boys were poling as hard as they could. But the current suddenly took hold of the raft.

"Come on over here, ya 'fraidy cat!" yelled Corrie. "I'll beat you like a rug if'n you even get close. Rafe, your pa will be preachin' your burial service before you know it. That is if the snappin' turtles here in the river don't chew up what's left of your fat ugly body!"

As the raft began to sweep by the girls, the boys realized they were no match for the river's powerful current. But it didn't prevent them from trying to save their pride.

"I'll get you back, Corrie!" shouted Rafe. "You'll get yours!"

"Just let 'em go!" Bobby Lee said. "'Sides, don't want no boys seein' my girl in her birthday suit. Ain't that right, Abbie?"

Abbie smiled and blushed.

"Yeah, they ain't worth the trouble!" chided David.

"Anyway," yelled Rafe, "we done seen lots prettier girls than you'uns!"

"Not me!" shouted Bobby Lee. "I think you Randolph girls are the prettiest in the valley!" he yelled as the raft glided by.

As it disappeared around the bend, the girls giggled and teased each other.

"My lands!" exclaimed Whit. "That was a close call!"

"For them, not for us!" replied Corrie.

"Oh, I think they're just bein' silly," sighed Abbie. "They didn't mean no harm."

"You're just sayin' that 'cause you're smitten with Bobby Lee," Whit complained.

"Ain't nothin' wrong with that, I'd say," Abbie replied.

The girls continued their good-natured banter as they got out of the river and allowed the sun to quickly dry their skin. After they were dressed, they picked up their containers and walked back to the edge of the meadow. The girls had berried there for many summers and knew all the best spots. The blackberry bushes were thick and tall and chock-full of large, juicy berries.

"Keep an eye out for rattlesnakes," Abbie warned.

Whit giggled. "Do snakes eat blackberries?"

"No!" laughed Abbie. "But sometimes they just come out of the trees to warm themselves on the rocks. So, be sure to shuffle your feet as you walk through the grass. If they hear you comin', they'll light out."

The girls picked in silence for a few moments.

Whit broke the silence. "Abbie, you think Mama's gonna have a boy or a girl?"

"I don't rightly know, Whit, but I know Pa sure wants him a boy. And a boy sure would be able to help Pa on the farm."

"I think we help about as good as any old boy!" complained Corrie.

Abbie laughed. "I think you're probably right, Corrie."

"Even so, Maddie says Mama's gonna have a girl."

"How you know that?"

"Overheard Maddie tell Mama at one of her visits."

"How does she know?"

"It's just somethin' she knows. It's her job to know things like that."

"Well, I just hope she's wrong!" Corrie commented.

"Not me!" exclaimed Abbie.

"Me, neither!" added Whit.

Abbie smiled. She was delighted for her mama and pa. She knew how they had been praying for another child. This one, boy or girl, would be an answer to their prayers.

When the girls filled their pails to overflowing with the dark purple berries, they sat under the shade of a big tree to rest and wiped their brows. As they sat, Abbie noted that Whit seemed to be deep in thought. "Penny for your thoughts."

Whit furrowed her brow and looked at her older sister. "You worried about Mama?"

Abbie thought for a moment. She wondered, *Do I hide my concerns from my sister? Or do I be honest?* She chose the latter.

"Yep. I'm a mite distressed. Mama's more swollen up than she was with Anna at this same point in the pregnancy. She seems to be in more pain. Maddie's been makin' more visits than she usually does, and she's a-givin' Mama more potions than normal. So, I reckon I am worried."

Abbie thought a moment and then decided she needed to reassure her sisters. "But Mama's is a mite older than she was before. And Maddie says that havin' a young'un when you're older can be easier. And ol' Maddie's done delivered a mess of babies in her six and a half decades of life."

Once again the girls nodded. It was Whit who spoke next. "Still, I just got a bad feelin' in my stomach, Abbie."

"It's gonna be all right," reassured Corrie. "We just need to keep Mama in our prayers."

But in her heart of hearts, Abbie felt the same way Whit did.

Suddenly a clap of thunder caused the girls to startle. They looked up to see an ominous bank of dark clouds moving down the river toward them. As they jumped to their feet, a powerful downrush of wind blew across them.

"It's a bad storm what's blowin' in, girls. Grab your buckets. We best try to outrun it!"

And try they did—although outrunning storms in Hazel Creek was never an easy task.

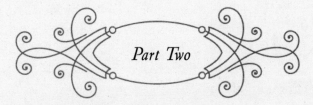

Part Two

TUESDAY, SEPTEMBER 9

through

FRIDAY, OCTOBER 10, 1924

21

Grace

During the summer of 1924, the people in Hazel Creek followed three major news stories: first, they received daily reports from the Summer Olympics in Paris, France; second, they debated the merits of President Calvin Coolidge signing the Indian Citizenship Act of 1924 into law, granting citizenship to all Native Americans born within the territorial limits of the United States; and third, and most important, the School Board was choosing a new teacher.

Small towns are extremely serious about three offices: the pastor, the mayor, and the schoolteacher—in that order. In selecting these, for better or worse, the entire community gets involved.

After Josiah Simmons caught the train out of town, he somehow escaped apprehension and disappeared from western North Carolina. Rumor held that L. G. Sanders had someone pull him off the train in Enka, the last stop before Asheville, where the sheriff of Buncombe County and a federal marshal were waiting. Simmons's whereabouts were still unknown, although a poster with his mug was hanging in every post office up and down the Appalachian Mountains of western North Carolina and eastern Tennessee.

In the wake of his departure, the School Board's selection process for a replacement became quite heated. Part of the community insisted that the schoolteacher should be a man, in order to maintain appropriate discipline. Others felt that a woman would be a welcome relief from the likes of Simmons with his harsh ways.

Horace Kephart, an author known internationally for his writings about the Smoky Mountains wilderness and the craft of camping, and one of the more respected individuals in the area, presented his candidate, one Miss Grace Lumpkin, at a School Board meeting: "Miss Lumpkin trained to be a teacher at Brenau College in Gainesville, Georgia, graduating in 1911. After volunteering in France for a year, she worked for the Young Men's Christian Association and taught an adult night school for poor farmers and their families."

The crowd seemed to murmur positively about her education and civic-mindedness.

Kephart continued, "For the last five years, Miss Lumpkin has spent her summers living in the various watersheds in the mountains of western North Carolina. Some winters she stays in the mountains to teach, and others she teaches in the flatlands. Her recommendations from each school board for which she has worked are stellar. I give her my highest recommendation."

Before sitting down, he passed out a folder for the board to review.

Some who testified that evening labeled her a "flatlander" and "gypsy"—the last label used to designate the fact that she did not seem to be able to establish roots anywhere in the mountains. Nevertheless, given her training and experience, and the fact she had chosen to live in Hazel Creek that very summer, the School Board met with her, examined her credentials, and grilled her in the manner of the Spanish Inquisition questioning the beliefs of a suspected heretic.

Millard Barnes was concerned that some of her beliefs bordered on communistic, while Nancy Cunningham thought her convictions on feminism bespoke a warm heart of compassion. She reminded the School Board, "Don't forget, we in Swain

County have long been leaders in granting qualified women the right and opportunity to excel. Just look at the opportunities you have each given me to operate the Clubhouse. And don't forget February 26, 1917."

Several in the audience looked confused. Nancy smiled and explained: "That was the day the North Carolina Senate passed a bill allowing the women of Swain County to vote. It was the first suffrage victory in the North Carolina General Assembly—and none other than my dear friend and our own state senator, pharmacist Kelly Bennett of Bryson City, submitted the bill. There'd be no better place for a woman of Miss Lumpkin's beliefs and qualifications to teach progressive ideals."

Although "progressive ideals" were not considered an ideal qualification by most parents, her strict religious upbringing and encyclopedic knowledge of the Bible, world events, and the various subjects she would teach eventually won them over.

The School Board sessions were private, of course, but the board members told their families the details, and the families managed to get the word out to everyone else in the Hazel Creek watershed.

"She's too blamed pretty to be a schoolteacher. She won't last a term out," Millard Barnes insisted. "She's just *too* good-looking."

Zach Taylor grinned at Barnes and countered by saying, "It's better to be good-lookin' than it is to be ugly, I always say. Besides, some of the women around here are ugly as a pan of worms! I like to rest my eyes on a good-lookin' young woman now and then."

In the end, the adherents of Miss Lumpkin won, and she stepped into the vacancy left by Mr. Simmons with an elegance and resolve that startled both students and the rest of the community.

Within an hour of commencing the first day of class, Rafe Semmes, to no one's surprise, challenged Miss Lumpkin's authority. When he refused to be quiet, she marched to the back of the room, reached out, and grabbed his ear, jerking him to his feet. She was not a large woman, and Rafe, at the age of thirteen, was strongly built, like his father. She led him to the front of the room and picked up a stick that Mr. Simmons had left before turning to him. "Rafael Semmes, you're stronger than I am, but you are not stronger than your father, are you?"

"No, ma'am," Rafe said, turning pale.

"I'm not going to struggle with you. Take this stick to your father right now. Tell him I said to give you ten hard licks right across your bottom. Go now!"

Rafe turned pale and began to whimper, "Please, ma'am, don't make me do that. My pa will bring the welts!"

"Very well. I'm going to give you one more chance. We're going to leave this stick right here. I don't propose to use it myself. I think it's disgraceful to spank a child publicly, but if chastisement or punishment is necessary, I'm sure your father will assist me in caring for that chore."

From that day forward all Miss Lumpkin had to do was to pick up the stick and put her eyes on a potential troublemaker, and all was well.

When Bobby Lee reported the incident to his father, Sheriff Taylor stared at his son and then broke out into an infectious grin. "Well, if that don't beat a hen's peckin'! I swan, she's not only prettier than a pair of green shoes with yellow laces, she's spunkier than a robin redbreast pullin' worms in the spring! I reckon we done got us a teacher!"

22

Giant

"A in't that a gypsy wagon, Miss Lumpkin?" Anna asked. She pulled at Grace's sleeve and pointed over toward a dark grove of eastern hemlock trees.

Miss Lumpkin had volunteered to bring the Randolph children home after school, as she was traveling to visit a family up in Bone Valley who had decided not to send their children to school that year. She reined the horse to a stop. "It is unique, Anna. I don't think I've ever seen one like it."

"Well, we have!" Corrie said. "It was at the July Fourth festival. It's the gypsy wagon, that's what it is!"

"After the festival, Rafe told me that *all* gypsies are bad," Anna said tentatively. "Real bad."

"I wouldn't think so, dear," Miss Lumpkin said.

"Rafe says they steal things. He says they cook babies and then eat 'em. That's what he said!" Anna said.

"That's a horrible thing to say!" Grace exclaimed.

"I know this much, Anna," Corrie added. "Rafe don't know nothin' 'bout nothin'. Come on. Let's go!"

"We'd better not," Anna said nervously. "They might kidnap us."

"I wouldn't think so," Grace replied, laughing. The girls all liked her sweet smile and soft laughter.

"Anna, how are they gonna kidnap *all* of us?" Corrie demanded, her green eyes flashing. I bet it's Gypsy Mary's wagon and I wanna see her again. The rest of you do what you please."

Corrie hopped out of the carriage and began to run, and Abbie watched as Grace giddyupped her horse toward the gypsy wagon. Two large workhorses were unhitched and grazing beside the camp.

Corrie ran up to the wagon, coming to stand before the woman who was sitting on a stool and cooking something over a fire. As Grace stopped the carriage, the girls all hopped out and ran up to Corrie's side.

The woman merely watched as the girls approached.

"Hi, Miss Maria," Corrie said. "My name's Corrie Randolph and these here are my sisters Abbie, Whit, and Anna. We met you at the fair in July."

"I remember you girls," the woman said. "It's good to see you again."

Corrie pointed to Grace, who was walking up to them. "This here's our teacher, Miss Lumpkin." Looking back at the gypsy, Corrie said, "At the carnival, you offered to tell us our futures sometime."

Maria smiled. She was wearing a dark green skirt with a brilliant yellow blouse that looked as if it was made of silk. Her black hair hung down her back, tied together with a fine golden chain. Golden earrings flashed in her ears, and she looked very mysterious in a place like Hazel Creek.

The gypsy stood up. "My name's Maria," she said to Grace, sticking her hand out.

"I'm Grace."

"It's very nice to meet you."

"What's your last name?" Corrie asked as the women shook hands.

"I am Maria Petrova."

"What kind of a name is that? I ain't never heard nobody named anythin' like it," Corrie said.

Maria laughed. She had a husky voice, deep for a woman, and her eyes flashed as she studied Corrie. "You ask many questions for such a small girl. My name is Russian."

"You're from Russia?" Abbie said, her curiosity overcoming caution. "I've seen that on a map. It's a long way from here."

"Yes, a *very* long way. Anyway, I remember promising to tell you your futures, if you and the Lord are both willing."

"That's right!" Corrie said at once.

"No, you don't!" Abbie quickly responded. "We don't believe in—"

A loud voice broke in: "What are you doing on lumber company property?"

She turned to see Mr. Knight striding toward them. Under the rim of his Stetson, she could see displeasure crawling across his face like a black cloud crossing the sun. When he came to stand before them, he ignored the girls and glared at Gypsy Mary.

"I am not harming anything," Maria said. She stood fearlessly facing the man, and her attitude seemed to enrage him.

"I don't want a gypsy on lumber company property, or even in this valley—especially one that embarrassed me and my Belle."

"What about your wife, Mr. Lumberman? Does she know about *your* Belle?"

"My personal life is none of your business. But this land is my responsibility. So you need to get off now! You hear me?"

"As soon as I have finished cooking, I will leave."

Knight stepped forward and snarled, "I said you will leave now!" Before anyone could react, he reached out, grabbed Maria by the arm, and began shaking her. She did not wince, but neither could she pull away. "You get your trash out of here! I won't be telling you again!" Knight shouted.

What happened next came as such a shock to Abbie and the girls that they could never agree on the exact order of what happened.

Abbie kept her eyes fixed on Mr. Knight, wanting to say something but being too afraid, when suddenly a colossal man—the largest man any of the girls had ever seen, much bigger than even Okay Donovan—stepped from the rear of the wagon. He was behind Knight, and while Knight was still shaking Maria, he reached out with his huge left hand and grabbed Knight by the collar of his suit. He lifted Knight as if he were a pillow, and Knight's words were cut off as he yelped, "What the—"

He said no more as he kicked, his dangling feet at least a foot off the ground. The enormous man towered over Knight, who was no small man himself, and seemed to be holding him up with effortless strength. He had thick, wavy, coal-black hair, a fierce curly beard, and dark blue eyes. He was so gigantic that Knight looked like a child in his grasp. Whit let out a small cry of alarm, but none of the other girls moved—the sight mesmerized Abbie.

As Knight kicked and struggled, to no avail, the mammoth man reached around with his equally massive right hand and grabbed Knight by the front of his jacket, letting go with his left. He spun him around and stared at him intently. Knight was speechless—obviously shocked, as was Abbie, by the giant.

Maria said something in what Abbie thought had to be Russian, and the giant slowly lowered Knight to the ground, but he held on to the front of his coat. He lifted his hefty left hand, now clenched in a fist, and menacingly shook it in front of Knight's face.

"You turn me loose, you brute!" Knight growled as he rubbed his sleeve over his bright red goatee and pulled back his coat, showing the handle of his bowie knife.

Again the woman spoke, and the huge man released his grip. As Knight backed away, the gypsy man pulled back his coat, revealing the carved handle of an even larger and more magnificent hunting knife sheathed on his belt.

"I'll have the law on you! You get off the lumber company's property!" Knight was sputtering as he quickly backed away.

"You'd better be gone by the time I get back or I'll fill your no-good gypsy hides with buckshot."

As Knight turned and lumbered away, Abbie said, "He's not a nice man. But this *is* company property. Maybe we'd all better leave."

"No, he is *not* nice," Grace said.

"I told the girls the same this summer," Maria said, "and he's only confirmed my prophecy." She went over to the big man and reached up to pat him on the arm. She smiled up at him, said something in their language, and then turned to the girls. "This is my brother, Daniel Petrov."

"Petrov or Petrova?" Whit asked.

Maria smiled. "I'm Maria Petrova, he's Daniel Petrov, but everyone calls him Danya."

"But," Whit protested, "you said you were brother and sister."

Laughing, Grace said, "Can I try to explain?"

Maria nodded, smiling.

"In Russia, women have an *a* on their last name. The men do not. Is that correct, Maria?"

Maria nodded and looked at Corrie. "Maybe your family needs some metal work done. Danya is good at that. Or you may want some wood chopped or a field plowed. Or," she said, pointing at his knife, "he can forge a prized Russian hunting knife for your father. This is one of the ways we earn our living. Show them, Danya."

As he pulled the hefty knife out, Corrie stepped forward and reached out. "May I hold it?"

Danya smiled, knelt down, and handed it to her.

The girls gathered around, admiring the beautiful artistry of the massive blade and handle.

"It's called a boar knife," he said, his tenor voice surprisingly soft and gentle.

"More beautiful than any I've ever seen." Corrie handed it back to him, using both hands.

Danya smiled from ear to ear. "Thank you, little lady. It took me many weeks to make it. And with this blade's razor edge and my aim, I can stop a charging boar in his tracks from fifty paces if he threatens us."

"I don't know about that, but why don't you come along with us?" Corrie said. "Maybe you can camp on our land for a night or two. We can ask Pa."

"Good." Maria turned to Danya and said a few words in Russian, and at once he began moving their large workhorses into position.

"I've never seen horses that beautiful—or big," Whit commented.

"Percherons," Maria explained as she gathered up her cooking supplies. "They stand seventeen hands tall and weigh over two thousand pounds each."

"My father raises them in Georgia. The breed comes from France," Grace explained as she looked at the horses with obvious admiration, "and they were originally bred to be used as warhorses, then for pulling coaches, then for use in agriculture and the hauling of heavy goods."

"They also have Arabian blood," Maria added, "which adds mystery to their strength. These are the best workhorses the good Lord ever created."

"We'll be happy to help ya," Corrie said, beginning to pick up items.

The tall woman looked at Corrie, and her face grew serious. "I am not used to much kindness. Maybe if the Lord gives me a word, then I will give you or your family a prophecy."

23

Gypsy Dinner

Nate watched Grace's carriage pull up, followed by the gypsy wagon. His curiosity was drawn to the two gypsies that were walking up to him—a woman with enormous dark eyes and a colossal, fierce-looking figure of a man beside her.

"Pa, that's Maria, who we met this summer, and her brother, Danya," Abbie said as her pa met them at the fence.

"Mr. Knight wouldn't let them stay on company land," Corrie said. "Threatened to shoot 'em till Danya here handled him like a bad puppy." Her eyes were sparkling. "They could stay on our place, can't they, Pa? We've got plenty of room."

"Perhaps. But I should get to know 'em a bit first."

After introductions were made and handshakes exchanged, Maria smiled and said, "We would be glad to do anything that needs doing." She had exceptionally white teeth that shone against her complexion, and her eyes showed caution as she examined Nate. "My brother is a blacksmith and works with all kinds of metal, but he has also managed a farm in the old country and can do anything on your farm you might need."

"Can they stay, Pa?" Corrie asked. "Please."

"Corrie, hush up!" He looked at Maria. "We'll be glad to have you stay—but just for supper." Nate had the typical mountain man's suspicion of flatlanders, outlanders, and strangers, and the two who stood before him were about as outlandish and strange as any flatlanders he had ever seen.

"Can they camp on our property tonight?" Corrie begged.

Nate looked at the strangers for a moment. "For now, why don't you put your wagon down there by the creek? Your horses are free to graze."

"Thank you, sir. You are very kind. Come, Danya," Maria said.

"Can I go with them, Pa?" Corrie said.

"No, you've got to help fix supper," Abbie said.

"Oh, shoot! I want to talk to Maria and Danya."

"You mind your sister, Corrie," Nate said at once. "Go on in now and get supper ready. There'll be plenty of time to talk . . . later."

He turned to the teacher. "Miss Lumpkin, how are you today?"

"Mr. Randolph," she said, with a slight nod. "I just offered the girls a ride home. I hope that is all right."

"I'm obliged—and appreciative," Nate said. "Can you stay for dinner?"

She smiled. "I'd love to, but it seems you already have company and—"

"Another guest is no problem. There's always room for new friends."

"Thank you," she said, "but I need to visit a family up valley and then Miss Cunningham is expecting me at the Clubhouse this evening. Perhaps another time."

Nate nodded and Grace reined the horse and left. As her carriage disappeared down the road, Nate kept his eyes fixed on the gypsies. *Biggest feller I ever saw in my life. I hope it ain't so . . . what I always heard about gypsies. I'd better keep a sharp eye on 'em!*

Much of the cooking in the Randolph home was done in the fireplace that took up most of one end of the main room. A large iron pot hung from a crane in the middle of it, and about the hearth were trivets, griddles, pothooks, and spiders—which were cast-iron frying pans, made with legs for cooking on the coals of the hearth.

The fire crackled cheerfully and sent a warm glow out over the cabin as the girls moved around. They had learned how to stay out of each other's way and obeyed Abbie as she supervised the making of the meal.

Sweet potatoes were roasting in the ashes as Abbie worked on the main dish, which was called *potlikker*. It was made up of collard greens, flavored with a ham shoulder, carrots, onion, and pods of red pepper. Abbie was also preparing corn pone, baking it in a large skillet with a heavy top. "Mountain folk never eat potlikker without pone," her mama always said.

Another pot held a huge mess of beans flavored with a large chunk of fatback. After adding onions, Abbie stirred the beans until finally, when the meal was ready, she said, "Corrie, can you run down and tell Maria and Danya that we're ready to eat?"

Corrie shot out the door and, as soon as it closed, Nate shook his head. "I don't know about these gypsies. I've heard you have to watch them carefully."

Callie laughed. "You are judgin' them before you know them, Nate. Don't forget what the Bible says about judgment."

"What? 'Judge not, that ye be not judged'?"

"Jesus does say that in . . ." She thought a second. "In Matthew chapter seven and verse one. That's true. But in John chapter seven and verse twenty-four, Jesus also says, 'Judge not according to the appearance, but judge with righteous judgment.'"

"Guess you're right, Cal," Nate admitted. "I'll give 'em some time to get to know 'em."

Callie smiled at him and nodded her agreement.

Corrie soon returned with the gypsies, and the huge form of Danya seemed to fill the door of the cabin as he ducked to enter. Nate got up and said, "Glad to have you both at our table."

After Callie met and greeted the two strangers, Maria said,

"Thank you for inviting us. Most people are afraid of gypsies. They think we are thieves."

"Do you steal babies and eat 'em?" Anna asked.

Callie looked shocked. "Anna!"

Her question also caught Maria off guard. Then she threw back her head and let out a peal of laughter that shook the cabin. A smile also spread across Danya's face, revealing teeth as large and white as the ivories on a piano.

Maria leaned down to Anna. "Of course not, little one. My brother and I love children. One day I pray to have many of my own."

She paused to look up at Nate. "People often believe gypsies steal, lie, and cheat. And maybe the bad ones do. But we have never taken a single thing that is not ours. We will not steal from you. I promise." Then she smiled. "And we do *not* lie."

Danya looked around the cabin and his eyes widened when he saw a large ball hanging from a rafter with insects flying around. He cocked his head as he stared at the sphere that looked like it had pieces of paper glued to it. At the bottom of the orb was a hole through which the creatures flew in and out.

"Bees?" he said, pointing up.

"No, a hornets' nest," Abbie replied.

"You let hornets in your house?" Maria said incredulously.

"Many mountain homes have them. You've never seen 'em in a home?" Whit asked.

Maria and Danya shook their heads as they continued to look up in disbelief.

Whit explained, "They don't sting anybody, and they catch all the house flies. They'll be goin' to sleep for the winter soon, but they'll come out again in the spring."

"I like to watch 'em catch flies. They just zing down on 'em," Anna said, laughing.

"Well, everybody have a seat," Nate commanded. "I'm as hungry as a bear comin' out of hibernation."

"But fortunately," Callie said, "not nearly as mean."

They all laughed as they sat. Nate looked at the two guests. "We always thank the Lord for the food."

"We do also. My brother and I were Russian Orthodox in the old country. Over here we just worship in the closest church to where we are camping."

"Well, we'd be pleased to have you visit our church some Sunday. But tonight we're pleased to have you both here at our table," Nate said.

The girls all extended their hands. For a moment Maria and Danya didn't know what to do. But then they held out their hands. The girls' hands looked minuscule in Danya's, causing everyone around the table to smile.

Then they all bowed their heads as Nate prayed, "Lord, thank you for this food, and bless it to the nourishin' and strengthenin' of our bodies. Bless these guests, our new friends. In Jesus' name. Amen."

Both Maria and Danya made the sign of the cross before beginning their meal.

24

Music

The plates and bowls were filled with steaming potlikker and sides and the cups topped up with sassafras tea. As they ate, Nate asked curiously, "Why'd ya leave the carnival? At least I assume ya left 'em."

"The carnival heads down south for the winter months. Danya and I, we fell in love with the mountains and decided to stay and work around here for the winter. We'd both like to settle down—maybe find our true loves, isn't that right, Danya?"

"Yes," he said, between bites.

"How'd you get to the United States all the way from Russia?" Callie said. "If you don't mind my askin'."

"Not at all, Mrs. Randolph—"

"'Callie' is fine with me."

"And 'Maria' with me. Anyway, I came to the United States eight years ago," Maria began. "When I got off the boat, in Philadelphia, I knew some English—words I learned during the long ocean crossing. But then I lived with my great-uncle, my grandfather's brother, and his wife. They taught me more. Both of them were born in this country. I worked in a factory and saved money and then last year sent for Danya."

Abbie was curious. "What about your uncle and his wife?"

"They are very old now and their house is very small. So, Danya and me, we purchased a gypsy wagon, and we travel from place to place looking for work and hoping to save enough to buy a small piece of land to start a farm. This spring we came across the carnival and decided to work a season with them."

"What was it like in Russia?" Corrie said.

"Very cold. They have much trouble. We knew a revolution was coming, and my people were scared. People are very poor there—at least most of them."

Danya said practically nothing, but when the meal was finished, he bowed toward Callie and said, "I thank you for the dinner. It was delicious."

As the girls cleaned up, Nate invited the gypsies to join him on the porch. When the girls came out, Maria and Callie were sitting in rockers while Nate and Danya were smoking their pipes on the edge of the porch.

"Your father has been questioning us about everything under the sun," Maria said. "But now, we pay for our supper." Her eyes gleamed.

"No!" Callie said at once. "We don't take money from people who are our guests."

"Not with money. I will show you." She got up and picked up a bag she had left on the porch.

Anna walked over to Danya and picked up his hand. It was enormous. She put her tiny hand inside it, stretching out her fingers. "You're so big!" she said, looking up into his face.

"Yes. Danya is big. And you are *very* little." Danya smiled, and Anna began to ask him questions.

Maria reached into the bag and pulled out what looked like a guitar.

"Never seen nothin' like that," Nate said. "Whatcha call it?"

"It's a balalaika," she answered as she held it up. It was a triangular instrument with a neck and three strings and painted red; a scene of horses pulling people in a carriage over a field of snow was painted on the base.

Abbie thought it was the most beautiful instrument she had ever seen.

"I will sing for you, and then Danya will join me."

Maria stood as she began to play the instrument. Her fingers moved more quickly than Abbie could follow them, and her voice was husky and deep. The words were in Russian, and when she finished the girls applauded.

"What was the song?" Anna said.

"It's a sad story about a young man who loved a woman," Maria explained. "She went off and left him, and he died in sorrow."

Nate grinned. "Do you know any happy songs?"

"Yes." She spoke to Danya, then said, "Danya is a much better singer than me. It is funny. I, a woman, have a deep voice. He has a high voice, but he can sing well."

Indeed, Danya did sing well. He had a pure tenor voice, and Abbie sensed that if he really let go, he would rattle the windows of the cabin. It was a very simple song and evidently a happy one. When Danya finished, he said, "Someday I want to learn some English songs."

"Why, Danya, we can teach you a mess of songs," Abbie said. "Girls, let's get our instruments."

The girls played and Nate and Callie joined them in singing several mountain ballads. A lantern was lit and dusk fell across Hazel Creek. The gypsies applauded, their eyes gleaming at the finish of each song, and they picked the choruses up very quickly.

Finally Maria stood and said, "Now, maybe I tell you all your futures."

Callie looked hesitant. "I don't rightly know about that."

"You are afraid to know what will happen?"

"I don't think anybody, other than the good Lord, knows the future. And besides, the Bible warns against divination," Callie cautioned.

"I don't want no stinkin' divination, Mama. I just want my

future told!" Corrie said. She moved closer to Maria and looked carefully into her eyes.

"Perhaps *not* tonight," Callie cautioned. Each of the girls knew the tone in their mother's voice. "Maria, I don't know about your Russian Orthodox religion, but we believe the Bible teaches that divination and fortune-tellin' are the same thing. And we cannot in good conscience take part. I hope you can understand."

"Completely," Maria said, sitting back in her rocker.

"Maria is *not* a fortune-teller, Mrs. Randolph," Danya said. "She's a prophetess."

"A prophetess?" Callie asked.

Danya nodded. "In the old country, when we were children, a monk visited our parish. He claimed to be the great-grandson of a famous hermit monk named Feodor Kuzmich."

"Never heard of him," Callie said.

"In Russia we had a leader in the early 1800s named Tsar Alexander. During the end of his reign, he became a devout Christian man. On a trip to the south of Russia he caught typhoid and was said to have died."

"Said to . . . ," Nate said.

"There were rumors that the Tsar secretly abdicated and became a devout monk and took the name of Feodor Kuzmich. He ministered in Siberia in the 1830s. And these rumors became even more persistent when the Soviet government opened Alexander's royal coffin in the 1920s and found it completely empty. No body at all.

"Anyway," Danya continued, "his great-grandson, Dmitry, a mystical character, came to our parish. He was attracted to my sister and claimed she had the gift of prophecy. After he laid his hands on her and prayed for her, she became a prophetess."

"So," Maria added, "I'm *not* a fortune-teller. Rather, I share what the Lord tells me to tell you about what he's doing in the lives of each of you. But Mrs. Randolph, not if you feel it improper."

Callie looked at Nate, who nodded his approval. Then she said, "I think that would be fine."

"Me first," Corrie insisted.

Maria gazed into her eyes for several moments while placing her hands on the girl's head. "You are going to have a long life. You will meet a handsome bachelor who will take you away from Hazel Creek to seek your fortune and happiness. I think he will be very rich."

Corrie squealed with joy and said, "You hear that, Abbie?"

"I heard it," Abbie said, smiling.

Maria laughed as she looked over at Nate. "I do not need a word from the Lord to see that you are a good man—a good husband and father." She hesitated and then looked deeper into Nate's eyes. "But be very careful, for danger lies ahead."

Nate laughed. "Well, I reckon that would be true of about anybody in Hazel Creek. We've all had some rough times—ain't easy livin' in the wilderness."

Maria went around to each of the girls and teased them, predicting they would all become famous one day—Whit as a singer, Corrie as an adventurer and writer, Anna as an artist—and finally she got to Abbie. "Without studying you, this I know, young Abbie. You are very special." Suddenly Maria reached out and put her hands on Abbie's head and stared into her eyes. "You are a little mother taking care of your sisters, and God will reward you for it. You and your future husband will care for many. You two will be healers and comforters."

Abbie smiled. "How 'bout Mama?"

Maria looked at Callie. "You have had many children, and you are a wonderful wife and mother."

"How many children is Mama gonna have?" Anna asked.

Maria continued to gaze at Callie. "Eight. The last one will be a little girl."

"Four more?" Nate exclaimed.

"No," Maria said, continuing to look at Callie. "I'm counting your lost children."

"Three boys," Callie answered softly. "What about this one?" she asked, rubbing her protuberant tummy with her free hand.

"She will be healthy."

"She!" Corrie exclaimed. "That's the same thing Maddie said."

"I, for one, hope they're both wrong. I need me another man on this farm," Nate mumbled.

"Well, you've got Danya," Maria said as she suddenly stood up. "We'll go now. Thank you for the food and for your good hospitality."

"I want to thank you also," Danya said. "We best be on our way. We need to find a place to set camp."

"I reckon it would be all right for you two to camp the night here," Nate said as the girls erupted in cheers. Nate and the girls walked them to the fence and then watched as the gypsies walked down to their wagon.

"Can they stay on our property for the winter?" Corrie asked.

Nate laughed. "You should ask Miss Maria. After all, she's the prophet."

"Pa!" Corrie moaned.

Nate put his arm around her shoulder and pulled her close. "Let's just start out with a few nights. If'n that works out, then maybe they might be able to help some on the farm. We'll just have to see."

Then Callie called from the porch, "All right, girls. Everyone to bed."

25

Ladybug

The morning air was crisp and cool, and the fog that covered the valley was as thick as the butternut squash soup Callie was cooking. She loved autumn in Hazel Creek—especially the fall soups. She sat near the cookstove, looking out the window, enjoying the warmth that still radiated off the black iron.

Enjoying the back-and-forth motion in her oak rocking chair, Callie closed her eyes and put her hands on her stomach. She could feel her child stirring, and as always, the miracle of a baby waiting to be born brought a sense of awe that touched her still—even with this, her eighth pregnancy.

But a fear also welled up, a sense of doom that had been growing in her heart the previous weeks. Bearing her other children had not been easy, but she'd always had a strong belief that all would be well. Now, however, there was pain that came every time the unborn child moved, and she grimaced as it struck her once again. She had not had a pain like this with any of her other pregnancies. She waited until it faded away, hoping the pain was just related to her age, but sensing there was something more ominous.

She laid her head back on the rocker and softly hummed one of her favorite hymns, "Day by Day," as she put her hand on top of the Bible in her lap. The Bible gave her great solace and comfort—and had since she had been a child. She loved reading and memorizing Scripture.

The verse she was memorizing this week was Psalm 71:18, and it represented her prayer for herself as she slowly whispered it: "Now also when I am old and gray headed, O God, forsake me not; until I have shewed thy strength unto this generation, and thy power to every one that is to come."

She started to open the Bible, but just then Jack, their gray tabby cat, jumped up into her lap and meowed.

"If you ain't a caution, Jackson Lee Randolph!" Putting her Bible on the side table, Callie waited until he turned around twice and then settled down on her lap. "You're always a-cravin' attention. You're more love-starved than any Randolph I've ever seen!" She stroked his head and back.

The sound of her family came from the open window. She could hear Nate singing "On Top of Old Smoky," energetically joined by the girls. She loved her husband's voice. And the girls' voices were true and sweet. Whit, even at her tender age, could sing on key better than anyone Callie had ever heard. She smiled as they all laughed together when they finished the last verse.

From just outside, Anna Kate's voice wafted through the window. The six-year-old was not singing but talking to herself as she played in the dirt. Callie could not make out the words as she stroked Jack's silky fur. She smiled as she heard the girls begin to sing "When You Wore a Tulip," another old favorite of hers.

Callie gently pushed Jack off her lap, ignoring his protests, and walked to the door. She was proud of her girls being schooled on the weekdays, but loved even more their being home with her.

She watched as Nate squatted down to Anna's level. The child was sitting flat in the dirt, and even from where she stood, Callie could see that her face was smeared.

"What in the blue-eyed world have you got on your face? Whatcha been eatin', child?" Nate said.

"Dirt," Anna said solemnly.

Nate laughed, then shook his head. "Why you been eatin' dirt?"

"I've made me a mud pie, Pa, and I ate it . . . or tried to, but it wasn't no good."

"Well, I swan, child! Why would you want to eat dirt, as good as your ma and Abbie cook?"

"I don't know, Pa."

Nate suddenly said, "Look. There's a ladybug on your arm. You see it?"

Anna lifted her chubby hand and stared at it. "A ladybug?"

"Yep. Look, you sing the 'Ladybug Song' when a ladybug lights on you. It goes like this:

Ladybug! Ladybug! Fly away home.
Your house is on fire. And your children all gone.
All except one, and that's little Ann,
For she crept under the fryin' pan.

"If you sing that song, that there ladybug will fly right off."

"Truly, Pa?" Anna demanded.

"Try it and see."

Callie smiled as Anna said the formula with a little help from Nate. She remembered how her pa had taught her the same rhyme when she was Anna's age. She watched Nate lean over and blow on the ladybug as it obediently rose in the air.

"Why, it did fly off, Pa!" Anna said with wonder. "Is her house really on fire?"

"I don't reckon so. It's just a little game you play."

"Pa, how come you're so smart? You know everythin' there is to know."

Nate laughed and reached out, picked up Anna, and stood up with her. "It's your ma that's smart, Anna. She's the smart one. I'm the pretty one."

Anna laughed and patted his cheek. "You ain't pretty, Pa. Why, I bet the Haint is prettier than you."

This amused Nate. He laughed, kissed her cheek, and set her down. "Reckon you're right, honey. You go on with your playin' now while I go check on your ma."

Callie quickly turned and returned to the rocker. She knew Nate would be irritated with her if he saw her up.

26

Gold

Nate came into the house, walked around the back of the rocker, bent down, and draped his arms around Callie. "How is my beautiful lady feelin'?" he whispered softly into her ear.

"All right. I can't complain." She didn't want him to worry any more than he already did.

"You never do." He smiled as he walked over to and pulled up a kitchen chair and sat down across from her. They talked for a while about how it might be nice to have Maria and Danya stay around and work on the farm. Maria could help Abbie and Emily in the house, while Danya had the potential to become an invaluable help around the farm. Nate told her how the harvest and haying were progressing.

Suddenly Callie grimaced and grabbed her abdomen.

"Another of your cramps?"

Callie breathed deeply for a few moments before smiling and sitting up.

"Has it passed?"

She nodded.

With some hesitation, Nate said, "Callie . . . are you worried about havin' this young'un?"

Callie looked down at her enlarged stomach and laid her hands on it. "God's given me a promise through Maria, Nathan. If she's truly a prophet, then this child will be strong and healthy. And I believe the Lord's promises are as good as gold."

Nate shook his head. "I wish God would talk to me like he does you."

"I think he does, but you've got to learn to hear him." Callie leaned forward, and when her husband reached for her hand and squeezed it, she said, "Maybe you just need to listen more carefully, Nate. He wants to talk to every one of us. After all, he says, 'My sheep hear my voice.'"

"I reckon that's so if the Good Book says it, Cal; but when it comes to hearin' the Lord's voice," Nate paused and tapped himself on the chest, "this here sheep is plum hard of hearin'."

"Sometimes he whispers real low-like." Callie smiled at him. "But more times than not, Nate, to me, he just speaks through the Bible. I find when I read it he *does* speak to me in my heart."

"Guess I do need to listen a bit more carefully," Nathan said as he leaned toward her and kissed her forehead.

Suddenly Nate turned toward the door. "Somebody's a-comin'," he said. He looked up. "It's Maddie. Maybe she can give you some tonic to ease you a mite."

Nate walked outside to the porch and watched as a small, stooped-over woman hopped off a mule that looked older than Methuselah.

Madeleine Satterfield was a thin old woman with sun-darkened skin. Her hair was gray and stuck out from under the straw hat she wore instead of her usual bonnet; her worn dress covered the top of her men's brogans. As she came to speak to Anna, she pulled her corncob pipe out of her mouth. "Mornin', child. How are ya?"

"I'm fine, Miss Maddie. I made a mud pie and ate it."

"Is that so?"

"Yep. But it didn't taste good, so I ain't gonna eat no more."

Maddie reached over and placed her hand on the child's head and then came up the porch. She greeted Nate, saying, "That child's eatin' mud pies, Nathan. Don't you feed her?"

"She just wanted to try one, Maddie. How are ya?"

"Well, I'm so tired I could scrape it off with a stick."

"Come on in and set a spell. I'm right glad you've come, Maddie. I want you to look Cal over."

"Why, it's the reason I stopped."

Maddie stepped inside the cabin, her sharp, dark eyes going at once to Callie; she was a combination herb woman, midwife, and all-around healer for the people of Hazel Creek, who for the most part couldn't afford a doctor. Even if they could, it was doubtful that they would go all the way to Bryson City to see one. And many of the mountain folks didn't trust the lumber company doctor in Proctor, Dr. Andrew Keller. Unless they were in the midst of a life-and-death emergency, most folks wouldn't visit him, although they increasingly allowed him to make private visits to their homes—especially since he didn't charge. But most of the mountain folks depended on Maddie.

Maddie smiled at Callie, saying, "That girl there you're a-carryin' is gettin' mighty anxious, I reckon."

"How do you know it's a girl?" Nate said. "Maybe it's a boy."

"Nope. You got you another girl child comin', Nate Randolph. Make up your mind to it. I can tell in a minute by the way she carries," Maddie said confidently.

Nate leaned against the cabin wall and watched as Maddie pulled up a stool in front of Callie. She took Callie's hands in hers and softly palpated as she questioned her intently. The old woman looked in Callie's mouth, carefully inspected her eyes, and then examined her swollen legs. She gently pushed her pointer finger into the swollen tissues of her ankles. After removing it, she watched to see if the indention would disappear. It did not. Nate noted that she frowned. Then she put her hand on Callie's swollen abdomen and waited for what seemed like a long time.

"Reckon I'll make you up a tonic when I come back from town, Callie. Will you be all right till then?"

"Oh, no need to fuss. I'm just fine."

"I'm sure you will, but the tonic will make you sleep better and it'll help with the swellin'." She looked at Nate and said, "I'm headin' into town now. I need to get some things at the store. Abbie can go with me if you'uns don't mind."

"She'd go in a flat minute," Nate said.

Abbie looked up from across the front fence, where Nate had seen her listening intently through the open door to the adult conversation. "Oh, yes, Pa! I'd *love* to go."

"Well, I reckon we can use a few things," Nate nodded. "You keep your eye on Abbie, Maddie, be sure she don't take up with none of them town boys—at least now that she and Bobby Lee are courtin'."

"Oh, Pa, don't say such things!" Abbie said.

"I heard the news," Maddie said. "Folks up and down the valley are just waitin' for weddin' invitations."

"Won't be any anytime soon," Abbie said as she started to climb the ladder to the loft. "I'll get ready now, Miss Maddie!"

Abbie looked down at her mama, who smiled and nodded her assent. The girl shot up the ladder like a squirrel dashing from a hunting dog.

Nate laughed. "Haven't seen her move that fast in some time."

He turned to the old woman. "Glad you asked her to go, Maddie. Abbie has a ton of responsibility on her little shoulders. But I don't know no help for it."

27
_____

Creation

A s Nate and Maddie walked out to the mule, Abbie scurried down the ladder and over to her mother, bending to kiss her good-bye.

"Here, Abbie. You take this," Callie whispered, holding out her hand.

"What is it, Mama?"

"I got some money that I been a-savin' up for Christmas. I know how much Maddie and you enjoy the movin' picture show. So, I want you to treat yourself and her to the dime picture show—if'n it's a proper show, ya hear?"

Abbie nodded as her mama dropped a small bag of coins into her hand. "And I want ya to get somethin' pleasin' for you and your sisters."

Abbie was shocked. Money was scarce in her family! She had never been given cash to spend. "You mean we're gonna play like it's Christmas already?"

"Somethin' like that. Especially since some of this came from the money Sanders had to pay for *your* walnut tree. So, just get some store-bought candy and a little present for each one of the girls, and look for somethin' nice for yourself."

"And for you and Pa?"

"No. This is *all* for you and your sisters."

"How about a small gift for Emily Rau?"

"I think that'd be mighty fine, Abbie."

Abbie took the money, which was tied up in a small piece of cloth. She recognized it as the cloth bag in which she had hidden her "tobacco." It felt heavy in her hand—likely gold coins.

"All right, Mama." Abbie peered into her mother's face and noticed that she looked tired. Little lines had appeared at the corners of her mouth. Her eyelids seemed puffier than usual—and that made her mama look older than she really was.

Abbie started to speak, but Callie shook her head. "You get along, now. We won't tell anybody 'bout this till after supper tonight."

As they headed away from the farm and toward Hazel Creek, Abbie's legs hung down the side of Maddie's bony, gray mule, and her arms were draped around Maddie's waist. She smiled as she glanced around at the steep hills. She had known no other sight all of her life except the Smoky Mountains surrounding Hazel Creek, and their lush beauty was never wasted on her.

A dainty, slowly drifting haze, which looked like smoke, rested on them now. Pa told her that was why they were called the *Smoky Mountains*—and that the smoky mist was the footpath of angels.

"Reckon we'll stop at the Faulkner place. Dove is doin' poorly. Lafe sent word for me to come."

"How'd you learn to heal people, Miss Maddie?"

"Learned from tryin' different herbs. When it didn't kill folks, I figured it was good for 'em."

"Oh, you're a-teasin' me!"

"I reckon I am a mite. My ma was an herb woman, and so was her ma. It just comes down to takin' what you learn and tryin' to add to it. Course, that old Cherokee medicine man, Jonathan Walkingstick, and his ma taught me some of the Cherokee medicine, so I use the best of both treatments to help my people."

Finally they came to a small cabin, where Old Scratch walked up to the hitching post and stopped without Maddie moving a finger. Abbie slipped off the mule and Maddie dismounted, unstrapped her carpetbag full of potions, and turned to meet the man who came out the front door.

Lafe winked at Maddie and smiled. "Who's that ugly gal with you?"

Abbie took no offense. She knew that of all the girls in her family, she was Lafe's favorite.

"I found her under a farkleberry bush," Maddie replied, laughing. "How's your Dove?"

"She's right puny, Maddie. Y'all come on in."

Abbie followed the adults in and found Dove Faulkner, a tall woman of sixty-nine, sitting at the kitchen table. Her hair was jet black, and she had dark eyes, signs of her Cherokee bloodline.

"Welcome," Dove said.

Maddie walked over to Dove, setting her bag on the table. "You do look poorly, lady."

"Think it's just my rheumatism actin'," Dove said, slowly taking off her shoe.

Abbie felt her eyes widen. Dove's great toe was bright red and swollen to twice-normal size.

"Haven't you seen the rheumatism, Abbie?" Dove said.

Abbie blushed for revealing her surprise, something mountain people were not to do, but said nothing as Maddie softly talked to and then carefully examined her patient. Finishing her study of her patient, Maddie sat down. "Don't think it's the rheumatism, Dove. Looks like the gout. Whatcha been doin' for it?"

"Lafe's been totin' me some cool branch water to soak it. And I've been takin' some willow bark."

"The soaks can be good, although I recommend alternatin' a hot soak with a cold one. Five minutes each, startin' and stoppin' with the cold. But I wouldn't recommend any more willow bark. It can help pain, arthritis, and even rheumatism, but it almost always makes the gout worse. Have you had the gout before?"

Dove shook her head. "But I've heard of it. Hewett Braun's wife says he suffers terrible from it—'specially when he gets to drinkin' Quill Rose's 'shine."

Maddie laughed. "If'n he drank mine, why, it wouldn't poison his system like that, I'll tell you that."

Dove smiled. "Reckon Lafe and I have lived as long as we have just because we don't drink the dew."

"And," Maddie countered, "reckon I'll live even longer than you'uns 'cause I do!"

Both women laughed. Then Dove reached out and took Maddie's hands in her own. "Why don'tcha come down to church with us sometime? It would do ya a heap of good."

Maddie scowled and looked down for a moment. Looking up, she said, "Looky here, Dove. I know church is good. That's why I go at Christmas and Easter. And," she said, looking over to Lafe, "I know church means the world to the both of you'uns. But my church service is in nature each week. And she's who I want to visit on most worship days."

Dove smiled and nodded. "When I was a young woman, Maddie, I was 'xactly the same. Loved the cathedral of the forest. And I guess I still do. But I found that her beauty was designed to point me to her Creator. It was the forest that actually led me to God."

Maddie cocked her head. "What in the tarnation are ya talkin' about, Dove Faulkner?"

Dove looked away as she thought for a moment. "How do I explain it, Maddie?" Then she looked back. "The Good Book explains it this way. It says that the invisible things of God, from the creation of the world, are clearly seen in nature. It says we can begin to understand him by just lookin' at the beauty of the things he has made."

Dove smiled and gave Maddie's hands a squeeze. "His eternal power can be felt when we're in nature, Maddie . . . when we hear his thunder, are washed by his rain, enjoy his rainbows, and his creation, and his creatures."

Maddie nodded. "It makes sense, Dove Faulkner, what you're sayin'. I do feel different when I enjoy the beauty of nature—"

"His creation," Dove corrected.

"His creation," Maddie repeated, smiling. "Now, lemme do some of my own creatin'. I need to mix up a tonic to try to quell the storm that's brewin' in your foot."

Dove laughed and hugged her old friend. "You're comin' around, Maddie. I know it. I think the Mountain Cur of heaven is sure enough on your trail."

"Well then, I might just try to outrun him."

Dove laughed. "He's mighty quick and never tires on his course, Maddie Satterfield. And I think when he finally catches up with you, he's gonna lick that old face of yours till there's nary a wrinkle left."

"Well, before he does, lemme tell you some things to do for your old toe. First off, be sure to move it up and down when you're soakin' it. Though it will hurt like fire at first, it'll help the swellin' and pain go down. As far as the soak, I want you to mix some Epsom salts in warm water and soak that toe several times a day. That'll get the blood movin' better. Now, I best mix up a tonic."

"Anything else?"

"Yep," Maddie said, looking at Lafe. "You need to mix a concoction of equal parts apple cider, honey, cherry juice, and crushed berries." She looked back at Dove. "You drink one-half cup of that four times a day, followed by a cup of pure branch water. Ya hear?"

Dove nodded and smiled at her friend. "Thanks, Maddie. I knew I could depend on you."

"You goin' into town, Maddie?" Lafe said.

"I reckon as how I am. I need a few things from the store and dispensary."

"I've got to go in myself. Lemme turn that ugly ol' mule of yours into the pasture. How 'bout we go in my wagon."

"That'd be right handy, Lafe."

28

Uptown

Ten minutes later Abbie was riding between Maddie and Lafe on the hard seat of his wagon. They had gone no more than a mile on the main road when Lafe began to straighten up. Abbie noticed he narrowed his green eyes as he stared down the road. Abbie followed his line of vision to see a man sitting on a large boulder by the side of the road, a rifle lying on his lap.

Lafe whispered in a hard voice, "Either of you know that man?"

"Ne'er seen him," Maddie replied.

"Maddie, got your pistol with ya?" Lafe said.

"Yep, it's in my bag on my lap. It's one of them new automatic .45-caliber pistols."

Lafe nodded. "My old Colt six-shooter's on my hip. Be of sharp mind, ya hear?"

Abbie could see Lafe move his right hand over the butt of his revolver. She knew he could still outdraw most men in the valley and could shoot a blackberry off a bush at fifty paces.

The trail narrowed, with barely enough room for the wagon to pass between the boulder and a sharp embankment that fell steeply to the roaring waters of Hazel Creek far below.

Abbie saw Lafe's lips draw tight. Suddenly it dawned on her the reason for the old man's concern. *This would be a perfect place for an ambush or a robbery*, she thought. Then she felt her eyes widen and her heart speed up as she recognized the Stetson hat and the dark, full-length duster the man was wearing.

As they neared the boulder, Lafe did not slow the horses, but shouted out, "Good mornin' to ya!"

The stranger nodded his head as he reached up and tipped his hat, pulling it down to more completely cover his face. He said nothing in reply.

As they quickly passed, Abbie turned back in time to see the man spit a stream of black tobacco juice across the trail behind them and wipe his lips with the sleeve of his duster. He then turned to look at her.

Abbie gasped as she saw an evil smile radiate through the bright red goatee below the tip of his Stetson. He slowly drew his pointer finger across his neck and then pointed at her. His threat could not have been more clear and she felt herself shiver as she quickly turned to face forward.

"I don't like him, either, Abbie," Maddie said. "There's somethin' downright wicked about the atmosphere around that man. We best find out who he is and what he's up to, don'tcha think?"

Abbie could only nod as she felt another chill go down her spine.

As they finally approached the outskirts of town, Abbie felt her concerns melt. "Miss Maddie, I enjoy comin' to Proctor once in a while."

"Why, darlin'? I kinda like stayin' away from it as much as possible."

"It's such a modern city, it seems."

Maddie laughed. "Honey, you've never been out of this valley to see a real city. But I can tell you this much: Proctor wasn't much before the Calhoun Lumber Company came out here in 1907."

"That's a fact," Lafe said. "Best I can recollect, there were only

four or five log houses, a small store, and the post office run
by . . . ?"

"It were Jimmy Bradshaw," Maddie said.

"Yep, that's right. I was right fond of Jimmy. Anyway, back then
there was nothin' but rough sled and wagon roads. There were no
bridges, only fords, and an occasional foot log across the creek.
Now, just over twenty years later, it's a full-fledged town with over
a thousand citizens."

"Calhoun's brought lots of finery to these parts, Abbie,"
Maddie said, "includin' convincin' the Southern Railway Company to run their train tracks here from Bryson City. Once
they did that, Calhoun was able to build the narrow gauge log-
gin' railroad that runs sixteen miles up Hazel Creek. Calhoun
owns it and it was his wife, Louise, who named the line the
Smoky Mountains Railway. He also owns the cinema house,
the stores you like, the school, most of the houses and buildin's,
as well as the town's electric power and phone company. And
it was his political pressure that led to the buildin' of the road
out here from Bryson City. But with the company came some
pretty surly characters—includin' some evil men, the bars they
drink in, and the women they cavort with."

"Pa doesn't like me comin' down here. I think he hates the town
and the company. But Maddie, I rightly enjoy visitin'—at least
once in a while. The town seems so full of life."

"It's sure bustlin' compared to two decades back—and it's sure
growing up," Lafe commented. "Just on Main Street in the last
few years there's the new blacksmith shop, the company commis-
sary, the hardware store, two cafés, the dispensary, the community
buildin' with the barber shop, and the renovated movin' picture
house—not to mention the brand-spankin'-new train depot down
by the river."

Abbie gazed up the hill at the boardinghouses, the Clubhouse,
and a slew of company offices and storage buildings.

"Course," Lafe complained, "most of the land in town is taken up by the sawmill and the mountains of lumber stacked high around it."

The wagon entered the edge of the small village, and the road widened. Small, quaint homes with charming front porches and picturesque picket fences bordered each side of the street. "Calico Street," Maddie explained, "is for the more common folks. Uptown, where the houses are a bit bigger, and so is the folks' pridefulness, we call the road there *Struttin' Street*."

"Pa tells me there are lumber towns up and down the river, Maddie. I'd like to go see one or two of them one day."

"That's a fact, Abbie. From where the Tuckasegee River meets the Little Tennessee River up near Bryson City, all the way down into Tennessee herself, there's nearly a dozen lumber or minin' towns. Way down valley, in Tennessee, there are the cotton mill towns. But most of them are pitiful little towns with cheap buildin's. And most don't have electricity and runnin' water indoors like here in Proctor. One thing about ol' Mr. William Rosecrans Calhoun: he builds one fine town. And he comes here to Proctor at least two or three times a year to check up on his businesses."

Lafe pulled the wagon up in front of a large, wooden building with a sign that read BARNES GENERAL STORE and said grudgingly, "Seein' that stranger at the bend in the road poisoned my whole day, but I'll hope to get over it."

Maddie laughed. "A gossip session at the café will set you straight, you old codger."

"Who you callin' old?" he said brusquely as Maddie slowly climbed down from the wagon. "I'll be back to pick you'uns up in a bit."

Abbie followed Maddie inside, where Millard Barnes warmly greeted them and then turned to Abbie. "How are you this fine day, Miss Randolph?"

Abbie felt grown up when Mr. Barnes addressed her as a lady. "I'm well, Mr. Barnes, thank you kindly. I came to buy some things."

"Perhaps a weddin' dress? We have a catalog full of fine ones. You're gonna make a mighty fine bride."

"Mr. Barnes, I think you're countin' my chickens before they hatch. I've only just started courtin' Bobby Lee."

"Well, I think you two are peas from the same pod. So, how 'bout buying your sixteenth-birthday dress?"

Abbie laughed. "Mr. Barnes, that's Pa's job. You know that."

"I do," Millard laughed. "So for now, you just look around and find what you like. If we ain't got it, we'll send for it, or else I'll tell you how to get along without it." Barnes laughed at his line, a phrase he used many times each day.

"Welcome, Abbie!" a voice called out from the back room.

"Hello, Mrs. Barnes. Are you well?"

"Not today, sweetie."

Etta Mae was considered an old maid when she married Millard at thirty-five years of age. He had been a clerk in this same store, which was her daddy's for a number of years, before finally asking for the hand in marriage of the owner's only daughter, one Etta Mae Jenkins.

Most local folks were shocked to learn that she allowed him to change the name of the store from *Jenkins Store*. But Millard insisted on this as a condition of marriage. And the local gossips contended Etta wanted a husband more than she did her daddy's name on a store.

In fact, she was so glad to get him that once they were married, she practically chained him up! She was known to be very jealous and could not stand for Millard to talk to any woman alone. She ruled like a tyrant over her mild-mannered bridegroom—making him the most henpecked man in town.

Another local rumor was that Mrs. Barnes was a sickly woman— for she was always complaining about this or that illness. In fact, on many days, like today, she could be found swooned on a day couch in the back room at their store as she succumbed to most every imaginable illness that might ever make its way to Hazel Creek.

But when Abbie once mentioned this to Maddie, she merely shook her head and grinned. "She enjoys ill health better than any human I ever saw," Maddie said. "She's healthy as a horse, really, but she craves attention, and that's one way she gets it. She'd be a real good-lookin' woman if she would spruce up and take care of herself a little better."

Abbie began to roam the store, which was always fascinating to her. The two side and back walls contained floor-to-ceiling shelves brimming with wares. The U-shaped counter ran in front of the shelves, all around the store, where the employees waited to serve customers. The center of the store contained about everything Abbie could imagine folks in Hazel Creek would ever need. She was not interested in the plowshares, yard goods, or the hardware, but she was very interested in the glass cases that had such exotic items as rings, pocketknives, broaches, and an array of candles. Her eyes were most quickly drawn to the shelves containing scores of jars containing different types of candy.

Supper had been cleared off the table. Abbie and her mama had not breathed a word of their secret. Finally Callie winked at Abbie and then said to the rest of the girls, "I have an announcement." She paused for a moment.

"What is it?" exclaimed Whit and Corrie, almost in unison.

"Well, it ain't Christmas, but I wanted to do something nice for you girls. Abbie, go get what you brought from town."

Abbie flew at once to the hiding place, a chest in her mama and pa's summer bedroom—across the dogtrot—that held old pictures and the valuables of the family. She slowly lifted up her grandmother's dress—the dress her mama had worn only on very special occasions. Just under it was what she was looking for. She took out the large sack and ran back to the cabin saying, "Here they are, Mama. Why don't you give 'em out?"

Callie took the bag on her lap and said, "You're all such good girls, and your pa and I wanted to please you."

Callie began handing out the candy and whoops of joy filled the Randolph cabin. Nate stood beside his wife as she sat there handing out the candy and then the small, inexpensive gifts. He squeezed her shoulder, knelt down beside the chair, and pulled her close. "That's a fine thing you've done, Cal."

"These are good girls we've got, Nate."

"Sure are, Cal, but *you're* the best girl of all," he said as he leaned over, kissed her on the cheek, and then took her hand as he sat down by her.

Abbie watched her sisters joyously taste their candy—especially Corrie!—and then looked on with a deep pleasure as she observed her mama and pa, holding hands, contentment and gladness radiating from their faces.

An early Christmas, she thought. *Reckon I'll remember this night the rest of my life.* Then she chuckled to herself. *It'll probably take half the night for the girls to calm down and get to sleep after Ma tucks us all in bed and gives us our bedtime prayers. But I don't think our family has ever been happier.*

29

Premature

After Sunday lunch, Abbie, Whit, and Corrie picked greens in the family garden. Returning to the cabin, they found their mama sound asleep in her rocker with Anna napping in their parents' bed.

Abbie had her sisters begin washing the mustard greens while she went over to check on her mama. She laid a hand on Callie's knee and was pleased to see her stir and then slowly open her sleepy eyes.

"Got some nice greens from the garden," Abbie said.

Callie smiled. "I'd like to see 'em." She began to stand.

"Are you sure?"

"Course I'm sure, honey."

Abbie thought her mama looked pale and weak, but helped her stand and walk over to the washing sink.

Callie was very complimentary of their hard work and the beautiful greens. "Let 'em dry, then we'll cook a mess."

The girls beamed, as they loved cooking with their mama.

Suddenly Callie slumped and groaned.

"Mama?" cried Abbie.

Before she could answer, Callie doubled over in pain, and another moan escaped from within her. Abbie gasped, "Mama, lemme help you get to the rocker!"

Slowly she walked Callie to her rocking chair. "Abbie, I've got cramps deep in my womb. They're shootin' straight through to my back."

As Abbie helped her sit, Callie groaned again, and Abbie was shocked to see blood pouring off the edge of the chair. She gasped as her mother doubled over, moaning in pain.

"Abbie," Callie groaned, "I've never had this kind of pain before! And never this early." She looked down at the floor and then, white-faced, looked up at her daughter.

"Abbie, no need to worry. A woman can have some bleedin' when her water breaks—it's more water than blood—probably a normal thing." She again doubled over in pain.

Whit and Corrie rushed to their mother's side. "What is it, Mama? The baby?" Whit said.

During her mother's cramps, Abbie could see that she couldn't speak; she could only nod.

"Do you want me to go get help?" Abbie said.

Callie shook her head and then as the contraction eased, she instructed, "Abbie, I want you to stay and help me. Whit, you go get Maddie. Corrie, run down to Maria's camp and have her come. Now!" Callie threw her head back as she cried out in pain. Whit and Corrie sprinted out of the cabin.

Abbie and Anna helped their mama crawl into her bed.

"Abbie, I'm gonna be all right. The baby's just decidin' to come a bit early. Anna, could you get me a washcloth and a cup of cool water?"

Abbie felt her mother tremble.

"Yes, Mama," Anna said.

"Thanks, dear. After you get 'em, we'll have a word of prayer." Callie's back arched as she let out a deep-throated moan.

As he walked from the woods with a freshly killed turkey, Nate saw something moving toward his cabin. It was Maddie and Whit straddling the back of Old Scratch, who was trotting up the road toward the cabin as fast as his legs could move. As Nate ran up to them, Maddie reined the mule to a halt. Whit jumped off. "Mama's hurtin' bad, Pa, and she's bleedin'! She sent me for Maddie!"

As her pent-up tears began to flow, Nate dropped the turkey and pulled Whit into his arms and hugged her. "It's okay, honey. I'm here."

Maddie shouted, "Nate, you go on! Whit and I'll be there right direct. Run on, now!"

Nate nodded, picked up the turkey, and then turned to sprint up the valley toward the farm. In moments he left Maddie and Whit behind.

As Nate came up to the clearing of his home, he heard a sound that made him stop in his tracks and the hair stand up on the back of his neck. Callie screamed—a bloodcurdling cry! He had never heard a sound like this—certainly never from his wife.

He ran as fast as he could to the cabin. As he approached the cabin, he saw Danya sitting on the edge of the porch whittling on a fresh piece of cedar.

"Callie's in labor," Danya said. "Maria's with her." He looked down at Nate's turkey and put down his carving. "Here, I'll dress the bird. You better get in there."

Nate nodded, handed Danya the fowl, and ran up the steps and into the cabin, where he found Callie balled up in their bed, moaning. Maria sat at her side massaging her lower back. He was shocked to see a trail of blood from her rocking chair to the bed.

Abbie and Corrie were silent, their faces pale and full of fear. Nate didn't see Anna, but he ran to Callie's side and slowly rolled her over to face him. She was whiter than the sheets.

"Nate. You're here." Callie whispered. "I think the baby's a-comin'."

"But it's too early!"

Callie tried to smile. "Must be another Corrie, Nate. Has her

determination. I think she's comin' when she wants to." Callie grimaced as another contraction began.

"Maddie's comin' up the road, Callie. I'll go get the ax."

Nate ran out of the house, leaped off the porch, and hurdled
the yard fence as he raced toward the barn.

Once in the barn, Nate ran to his tool bench and grabbed his
special ax—the one he used with each of Cal's seven previous deliveries. This tool represented one of the few and most important
tasks that he, as a mountain man, could perform during his wife's
labor.

As he wiped it off, he found his mind flooded with memories
of each of Cal's deliveries. They were always a time of anxiety for
him, since he knew the dangers of labor for mountain women
and was aware of many men who had lost their wives or babies
during difficult births. That's why his job, at this moment, was so
important.

He raced back to the cabin, where he found Maria and Abbie
comforting Callie as Maddie examined her. Cal seemed calmer
with Maddie in the room.

Corrie was sitting quietly at the table, while Anna crawled up
the ladder to the loft, where she and Whit were lying on their
tummies, looking over the edge. Abbie placed a cool cloth on
Callie's forehead.

As he approached, ax in hand, Maria and Abbie moved away
from the bed. Meanwhile, Maddie jumped up and walked to his
side. "I'll help you move the bed."

Nate saw Callie smile as he approached. He knew this would
help her pain. He nodded at Maddie, and together they pulled the
bed away from the wall about three feet. He picked up the ax and
stood above her as he slowly raised the ax above his head.

Anna screamed, "No, Pa!"

Whit turned to comfort her. "It'll be all right, Anna. Pa's
helpin'! You'll see."

Cal turned her head away from him as Nate swung the ax at

full strength, driving it deep into the floorboard under the bed next to the seven deep notches already there. He saw Cal wince as the blow on the floor reverberated through the cabin—and then he stood. After he and Maddie pulled the bed back, Callie smiled and he bent over to give her a kiss on the cheek.

"What's Pa doin'?" said Anna.

"It's a tradition as old as the hills," Whit answered. "When a pa drives an ax into the floor under the bed of his birthin' wife it'll cut the pain in two. Wouldn't a woman in these parts go through labor without Maddie, her husband's ax, and her family's prayers!"

30

Commencement

Maddie sat next to Callie. "You want me to call the other women?"

Callie nodded. She knew that for labor and delivery in these parts, the traditional wisdom was the more women who attended the birth the better. Men were not allowed in the cabin during birth.

"Corrie Hannah!" called Maddie. "I want you to get Danya to take you o'er to the Raus' cabin and call the ladies to come help me, you hear?"

Corrie looked at her pa, and he nodded. "Yes, ma'am!" said Corrie as she bolted out the door.

"Darla Whitney!" Maddie commanded. "You know where to find fresh squawroot and squaw weed?"

"Yes, ma'am."

"Then scoot. Take Maria with you, and go get me a mess." Looking to Abbie, she said, "I want you and Anna to help me boil some water. I'll be simmerin' the squawroot and squaw weed to make water for cleansin' your ma durin' and after the birth. Y'all get!"

Then she glared at Nate. "You too! Don't want no man in here!"

He nodded and turned to leave as Callie moaned deeply.

🙢 🙠 🙢 🙠

Tom Rau and his son David sat on the porch with Nate and Danya. As the men filled, packed, and lit their pipes, Nate could see through the cabin door that Whit and Maria had already washed, peeled, and begun to boil the squawroot and squaw weed they had gathered in the woods.

Sandy and Emily Rau were working in the cooking area with Abbie.

Nate turned to Tom. "How your dogs a-doin'?" Tom was known as an expert hunter. His hunting hounds were treated better than many people's children.

"My hounds are just fine," Tom replied, drawing on his pipe. "You be goin' for a bear this fall, Nate?"

"Danya and me just talked about it this mornin'. We're hopin' to track down Old Gray Back. He's gettin' long in the tooth and I wouldn't want him down here tryin' to feed around my farm or girls. Ain't that right, Danya?"

"Yes. Should be easy to hunt, especially since the mast is so good and thick," Danya observed.

"A well-fed bear," Tom added, "is not only good eatin', but a lot easier for the dogs to chase down and tree."

David was sitting away from the men on the edge of the porch and whittling on a stick. Nate admired his carving skills. "Danya, I believe this boy's got talent with his knife."

"Maybe I'll forge him a fine knife this winter," Danya said.

"That'd be mighty fine, Danya," Tom commented. "But speakin' of talent, David here says Whit's grades were the best in Miss Lumpkin's class."

"Seems to be a real smart girl. Reckon she got that from Cal."

Tom was quiet for a moment and then commented, "Nate, what you done to that other teacher, Simmons, last spring—well, I just wish I'd 'a' been there to have seen you hang his hide on the fence! Musta been a sight, I tell ya!"

Nate smiled. "Well, I'm glad that's past history." He then took a deep draw on his pipe.

"You sure?" Tom said. "Zach says the man ain't been found. Rumor is he's comin' back to seek revenge."

"Don't believe it," Nate said. "Man's too much of a coward."

Abbie and Emily were steeping some willow bark tea when Maddie called out, "Not too strong on the tea, girls! It only needs to be stout enough to take the edge off'n the pain. And be sure to cut it with some honey."

The tea mixture was one Maddie used often to treat pain, after she learned about it from the Cherokee midwives. But if the willow bark tea was made too strong, it became too bitter to swallow and could cause vomiting—something Callie did not need right now.

Maddie was pleased to have Callie out of the bed and walking around. She learned through the years that the worst place for a woman to labor was in a bed. She explained to Abbie, who was helping her mama walk, "Always want the woman to be movin' in the labor. It's the way God designed it; it keeps the pain down, and it speeds the labor. You want a long, hard labor, you just keep a laborin' woman in bed and on her back!"

Between contractions, Callie could sit, rest, sip some willow bark tea, or chew on a hardtack biscuit. As soon as each contraction began, Sandy, Maria, and Maddie had her up walking or leaning forward against the bed or table and rocking her pelvis. "That rockin'," Sandy told the girls, "helps the baby get into the birth canal in just the right position."

Finally, after several hours of labor, Callie whispered, "Maddie, it's time," as she sat on the edge of the bed.

Maddie washed her hands in the squawroot water, and then she carefully examined Callie internally. "Honey," Maddie whispered, "the baby's headfirst and comin'. You ready to birth this young'un?"

Callie nodded. Maddie could feel the contraction beginning to build in her abdomen. Maddie had Sandy and Maria apply pressure to her lower back, knowing this would help cut the pain. The younger girls sat at the kitchen table.

"Maddie!" Callie called out. "I feel the pressure. I . . . I think he's a-comin'!"

"I'm right here, Callie." Maddie knew that keeping her voice low and reassuring would help everyone in the room stay calm. Maddie smiled as she saw the first signs of the baby's head starting to show. "Oh, Callie. She's a-comin'. She's a big'un." Maddie looked around, then called out, "Corrie Hannah, bring me my stool. Quick, now!"

Corrie jumped up and grabbed a milking stool that the girls had cleaned and brought in from the barn. Maddie positioned it next to the bed as Callie began to push.

"That's good, Callie, nice and gentle!" Maddie's expert hands helped guide the baby's head as it appeared.

Callie's moan was deep and throaty. Maddie saw it was time for the final push. "Take a deep breath, Cal, and then bear down for me—but keep breathin' while you push, ya hear?"

Callie nodded and pushed. Maddie expertly guided the baby's head.

"Cal, hold your push while I clean the mouth. Take shallow breaths," Maddie instructed as she took a tiny cloth and used it to clean the baby's mouth and then gently squeezed mucus from the nose as the little one grimaced.

"Maria, you and Sandy help Callie stay in a sittin' position as she bears down, okay?" Maddie shifted on the stool. "Cal, just one more gentle push."

Maddie expertly maneuvered the little one's shoulders as the baby slipped out of the birth canal with a lusty cry. The girls cheered as Callie lay back on the bed.

Maddie held the baby in her arms, smiling from ear to ear, and then placed the baby to Callie's chest. As she did so, Sandy covered the baby with a blanket.

"What is it, Mama? Is it a boy?" called Corrie.

"I don't know, Precious. Let's look. Come over here, everyone."

With the girls crowding around, Maddie lifted the blanket, and they all gasped at the sight. Callie was beaming. "Girls, this here is Sarah Elisabeth. She's your sister."

"Mama!" cried Corrie. "Can I tell Pa?"

"You go ahead, child."

Corrie was out the door like a shot, and Callie could hear the cheers and backslapping from outside the cabin.

Maddie examined the umbilical cord, which connected the baby to the afterbirth still inside Callie's womb. She quickly pulled two pieces of yarn from her birth bag and tied them around the cord, about one inch from the baby's abdomen. She then took a knife and cut the cord—watching to be sure the knots on either side of the cut held—which they did.

Maddie then turned her attention to the afterbirth. "Sandy," she said to her helper, "time to get this baby to the breast." She knew that putting the baby to the breast could cause the body to cast out the afterbirth.

Sandy helped Callie turn little Sarah Elisabeth over so that her tummy rested on Callie's abdomen and her tiny head rested between Callie's breasts.

Maddie watched as Sarah Elisabeth began to root and squirm toward her mother's left breast. She had no idea why babies would instinctively snuggle toward their ma's left breast and not the right one, but she had seen it more times than she could count.

Callie helped her until little Sarah latched on and began to suckle.

Maddie smiled at Abbie as she wiped the perspiration from her mama's brow.

31

Afterbirth

Once the afterbirth was delivered into a bowl, Maddie examined the placenta and umbilical cord and, to her consternation, found that a section of the placenta was missing.

This wasn't rare, but she knew she would have to examine Callie internally, locate the missing piece, and remove it. Failing to do so could mean that Callie would continue to bleed or become infected—and either could be fatal. Maddie had seen one too many young women die after childbirth. She hoped to never see another.

"Callie, there may be a small piece of the afterbirth left up in your womb. I'm gonna try to get it out. And it may not be comfortable."

Maddie took Sarah Elisabeth off Callie's breast and handed her to Abbie to swaddle in a clean baby blanket. She again washed her hands and arms in the squawroot water and then gently examined her patient, finding a section of afterbirth attached to the wall on the inside of the womb. Normally any retained placenta could be easily removed—but not this one. The more she tried, the more uncomfortable it became for Callie. Maddie sensed she only had one try left.

"Callie," she instructed, "grit your teeth. Now!" Maddie used all of the strength left in her fingers. Callie screamed. The small piece of afterbirth was stuck—it would *not* move. Maddie removed her hand.

"Did you get it?" Sandy almost pleaded.

Maddie shook her head.

Sandy's face paled.

"Maddie," said Callie, "what's this mean?"

Maddie tried to smile. "Callie, I got most of the afterbirth. The piece what's left is mightily tacked down to your womb. I wasn't able to get it." Maddie turned to wash her bloodied hands in the squawroot water.

"Abbie," Maddie called across the room, "bring Sarah Elisabeth over here for your ma. Let's get her back on the breast. I'll go talk to the men."

As Maddie walked out to the porch, the men stood. Maddie walked up to them. "Congratulations, Nate." Maddie smiled, although her heart was tortured. "Just like I predicted and Maria prophesied, you've got a mighty pretty little girl." Nate nodded and Maddie continued. "Callie's doin' all right. She's a-restin' and a-feedin' the little one, but . . ."

Nate sensed there was bad news coming. "Maddie," he said, "but what?"

She looked away as Nate sank back onto his rocker. "Maddie, what is it?" he asked more urgently.

"Nate, there's a fair-sized piece of the afterbirth a-stuck in her womb. I can't get it out."

"What's that mean?"

"Maybe nothin' . . . or it could cause Callie some heavy bleedin'." Maddie paused to let the news sink in. Nate nodded his understanding. She continued, "Another possibility is that it would cause the milk fever to set in."

The color drained from Nate's face. It was common knowledge the milk fever could kill even a strong woman. "What do we need to do?"

Maddie thought a moment before replying. "Of course, we can pray. Lord knows Sandy and Callie are good at that." She paused again, then continued, "And I'll be usin' some of my potions to try to help." Looking away, Maddie decided to let Nate absorb what she was saying.

"You think that'll work, Maddie?" Nate asked quietly.

Maddie turned back to look in his eyes. "Nate, it might. But to tell you the truth, it usually don't. We might wanna try somethin' else."

"What might that be?"

"The company doctor could try some surgery."

Nate's eyes narrowed. "The company doctor? You mean Dr. Keller?"

"Yep. I ain't seen him do it. But I heard tell of a woman over in the Snowbirds—a Cherokee woman—who had a stuck-in afterbirth. He was able to do some surgery right at her cabin. Nate, he saved her life."

Nate was deep in thought for a few moments. He turned to Maddie. "Maddie, we don't need no lumber company doctor tryin' nothin' on my Cal!"

"Nate, he might be able to save Callie."

"And then what, Maddie? Then I owe the company for my wife's life."

He paused. She could see him trembling in anger and knew it would be unwise to directly challenge his stubbornness.

"They'll want our farm in exchange. Sanders has been doin' everythin' he can to get our property. I can't do it, Maddie. This was my pa's farm. He, my ma, and my boys are buried here."

Maddie took out her corncob pipe and filled it with tobacco. She wanted to let Nate's anger subside a bit and let him come to his senses. She sighed and commented, almost to herself, "Maybe that's it, Nate. Maybe that's what your choice is—Callie's life or the farm."

Nate took a deep breath and then walked by Maddie. "I'm gonna go see my baby girl."

Maddie followed. She watched as Nate approached Callie's

bed, where the girls were admiring the newborn quietly suckling her mother's breast.

"Come on over here and spend some time with our young'un, Nate," Callie said. "I know you want her named Sarah Elisabeth, but the girls and I think we'll be a-callin' her Sarah Beth."

Maddie saw Nate blink back tears.

32

Sanctuary

Despite the coolness of the autumn evening, Abbie chose to stay in the barn after she and Whit finished the evening milking. She was still a bit irritated that Bobby Lee had not come up to see her and her new baby sister.

But it wasn't too long in the barn before she found herself awash in childhood memories. She wasn't sure what it was about the family barn, but it was strangely comfortable and comforting for her—especially given all the commotion surrounding the delivery of the baby.

She looked fondly at Jean and Star as they ate their hay. Jean had filled out and was growing into a fine milk cow. Memories flooded her mind of the July Fourth celebration—of her pa fighting so gallantly for her, and Bobby Lee holding her hand and holding her close for the first time on the Ferris wheel. Life in Hazel Creek was never easy, but it was full of powerful memories.

This was the one building on their farm where she could come and leave her troubles at the door. Mr. Knight's and Mr. Sanders's threats, the lumber company's destruction of the valley, combined with her pa's worries and her mama's retained section of placenta, were almost more than she could bear. But here, in her sanctuary, she could leave the world behind and bask in the warm reminiscences of her childhood—recollections and remembrances that often left her wanting to not grow up, but to remain a child forever.

"Pshaw," she said as tears filled her eyes. "If growin' up means havin' to deal with pain and sufferin' and cruelty, I don't want any part of it."

Star let out a deep moo. Abbie wiped away a tear and walked over to her stall. "Of course, you're right, Star," she said as she rubbed her nose. "Bobby Lee will be there for me. He'll protect me. He'll provide for me. So, it's decided! I *will* grow up."

Abbie smiled as she caressed Star's soft ear. She loved the rural and earthy fragrances of the barn, and, of course, considered the animals that were stalled here part of the family. She found it curious that flatlanders apparently had so little respect for animal life, which she and her family considered sacred. Her parents taught her that God himself considered animal life sacred. *After all*, she thought, *it's right there in Genesis chapter nine—where God spoke to Noah and to his sons and established his covenant with man and with every living creature.*

She furrowed her brow as she tried to recall the verses she had memorized so long ago. *Aha!* she thought as she began to recite, pacing in front of her assembled congregation, mimicking Pastor Semmes as she held an imaginary black Bible draped over her outstretched left hand and waved her right index finger to make points.

Abbie took a breath before continuing to preach to her small congregation. "Couldn't be clearer than that!" Star and Jean were staring at her as they chewed their cud, as were the two family horses, all looking somewhere between confounded and comforted.

"You four are not only part of *our* family, but God loves you'uns also." She continued her sermon: "In fact, next time there's a rainbow above the farm, we all are gonna just look up at it and thank the Lord together for his goodness. Amen. And consider yourselves blessed that I won't be takin' a collection tonight. So, until the next rainbow comes along, I best get inside to Mama."

Abbie turned the wick of the lantern until the flame

extinguished. She latched the stall and then walked toward the barn door. Her step had a spring to it, reflecting the optimism she felt about her future marriage to Bobby Lee and the hope of a prosperous New Year. Despite the mysterious and eerie environment of the darkening barn, Abbie still felt great comfort there, knowing literally every inch of it—her sanctuary. She could walk it with her eyes closed and never snag her blouse on a splinter, peg, or nail.

Suddenly someone stepped out of an empty stall doorway, surprising her by blocking her path out of the barn. At first, she felt herself smile. *It's Bobby Lee!* she thought. *He* has *come to see me!* Her first instinct was to run into his strong arms and be held close to him. But then her nose caught an unpleasant odor.

"Bobby Lee," she said, "is that you?" At that instant she noticed his height and the hat he was wearing and then a vicious slap across her face both stunned her and knocked her to one knee. A dread filled her soul as he grabbed her by the arm and slung her onto her back in a hay-covered empty stall.

The attack was so abrupt that the terror that swept over her from head to toe completely paralyzed her. Before she could move, he was on top of her, pinning her to the floor. She opened her mouth to scream, only to feel him stuff something into it— she suspected it was a bandana, and the awful taste nearly made her gag. She was certain she would have vomited had it not been for what she felt next—the cold, sharp edge of a large knife pressing into her throat.

For a few seconds, he didn't move as he held the knife to her throat. She didn't move a muscle, knowing that a flick of his wrist could end her life. She felt her heart trying to beat out of her chest and was unable to control her panting, almost panicking at the lack of air. She remembered old Jonathan Walkingstick's advice, "Little Abbie, slow your breathin' and it will slow your heart. Keep in control," and began to slow her breathing.

Slowly, he removed the cloth from her mouth, but kept the

knife pressed against her neck. As her eyes adjusted to the dark, she could see the shadow of the Stetson hat he wore and his well-trimmed goatee.

"I know you and your family love going to church once or twice a week. And you and your sisters try to wear the mantle of being goody-goodies—of being so devout and self-righteous. But I know you're not. I've seen you and that Taylor boy together."

He chuckled an evil-sounding laugh and then continued: "I know when you go to school. I know when you go to town and when you're at the movie show. I know when you bathe and when you eat and when you sleep. I know your every move and I know every move of your so-called guardian angel—the Haint. He *cannot* protect you. No one can, not your pa, not that pitiful excuse of a sheriff, not that gypsy man—at least *not* from me."

No words could have struck her more deeply. No stranger could have caused her such utter shock.

"You hear me?" he sneered.

Abbie nodded as she felt her body trembling in absolute terror.

Suddenly there was a sound behind him and before the man could turn, something crashed across his head and shoulder, knocking him off Abbie. He quickly rolled to his side and then leaped to his feet, angrily facing his attacker, who stepped forward out of the shadow of the stall.

"You leave her be!" the Haint yelled, as he held one of the girls' baseball bats in his hands. "I'll whack you again, ya hear?"

Mr. Knight slowly sheathed his large bowie knife, and then took off his Stetson as he pushed it back into shape. "Yes, sir, Mr. Welch. I will be most pleased to retreat, that is, if you will permit me."

"You best leave quickly," the Haint hissed, "before I commence to beatin' you like a rug—like you deserve."

"I appreciate the mercy," Knight said as he began to put on his Stetson.

Abbie had not moved and felt herself continue to tremble in fear.

In a flash Knight slung his hat at Welch, causing him to duck and step back as Knight lunged across the stall and landed a roundhouse punch against Jeremiah's chin. Welch fell backward against the stall. As his head crashed into a post, he collapsed to the floor like a limp rag doll.

Before Abbie could react, Knight was back on top of her. He lifted his arm and quickly slapped the back of his hand across her face. The sting caused her to wince.

"That is payment for slapping me at the carnival, young lady." He then drew his knife and put it in front of her eyes. "Do you see this bowie's serrated edge? It is as sharp as a razor." He placed it against her throat. "I am half-tempted to slice your neck open right here. It would pay back your father for embarrassing me in front of my men with his illegal punches."

Abbie felt anger surging through her chest, but terror kept her from speaking.

Knight relaxed his arm, bent his face close to hers, and whispered, "Listen carefully, for I'm only going to say this once. Are you listening?"

Abbie nodded. Her mouth now felt like it was full of cotton.

"I am going to tell you something that you need to do for me. Are you ready?" he said softly but menacingly.

Too scared to speak, she was having difficulty even breathing. Somehow she forced her head to nod again.

Then he continued: "Like the God of Bethel told Jacob in Genesis chapter thirty-one, 'Now arise, get thee out from this land, and return unto the land of thy kindred.'"

He took a deep breath. "That is directly from the Good Book. But this is from me—you and your family must leave Hazel Creek and return to Tennessee. That is where your ancestors are from— that is where you need to return. And if your pa does not sell to the company, then I am to see to it that there are serious consequences. For example, maybe I will dig up the bones of one of your brothers. Would you want to wake up next to one of them?"

She shook her head.

"Perhaps I should consider burying you alive next to your brothers? Would you like to be buried alive?"

She shook her head again, feeling her tears falling down each side of her face.

"Or if your father stiffens his neck about selling, then perhaps you or one of your sisters would find their pitiful lives snuffed out—but not quickly. Maybe I will strangle one of them slowly— watch the horror in their eyes as I squeeze the life from them. Or how about you? Right here? Right now? In this malodorous barn, Abbie? Do you desire to die? Now?" he growled.

Abbie couldn't breathe or respond.

"You need to convince him to sell this place. I do not care how you accomplish it, but you better do it quickly. And you are not allowed to tell anyone about tonight. Do you understand?"

She nodded.

"In fact, if you tell even one person what happened here to-night, I will kill your father, your mother, and then every one of your sisters. I will slice their throats from ear to ear. I will take my time and watch them bleed to death slowly like one of the sacrificial sheep or cattle in the Old Testament. I will make them my sacrifice to the lord of the land. Maybe I will tie you up and tape your eyelids open. Then I will force you to watch the whole bloody affair. Then, sweet Abbie, I will cause you to feel more pain than you can imagine—before you die. And you *will* die."

He pushed the blade of his bowie knife into the skin of her neck. "Do you desire that?"

She could barely shake her head.

He sat up and was quiet for a moment before taking his knife away from her neck. "So, young lady, if you have any power of persuasion, you had best use it on him. For I shall return to make him a generous offer on this farm after his wife has had time to recover from birth. You need to be sure he does not refuse me. Do you understand?"

Abbie sensed her head nod.

"Good girl. Now, you stay still for ten minutes. Do not move. If you do, someone will die. Do you understand me?"

Abbie couldn't move even if she wanted to.

He bent down. "Say, 'yes, sir,'" he snarled.

"Yes, sir," she whispered as the man stood, sheathed his huge knife, and slowly walked over to Jeremiah, who was still out like a light. Then Knight kicked the man in the face, causing a grunt of air to rush out of his mouth, before turning and leaving the barn. After a minute she could hear a horse galloping away.

Nevertheless, she slowly counted to six hundred before getting off the barn floor. Because of the evil man's warning, she could not, and would not be able to, tell *anyone* what had happened. She could only hope that her facial bruise and scratched throat would be explained by a story of running into a stall gate in the dark barn.

Abbie slowly got up, and then ran to dip a rag into a bucket of water. She wrung it out and came back into the stall to care for Jeremiah's bleeding face. She knew she'd have to convince him to keep this horrible event a secret. Her family's lives depended upon it.

Because of Callie's worsening condition, no one noticed Abbie when she came into the cabin—and no one observed or commented on the "scratch" on her neck or swollen bruise on her cheek. As they could, everyone grabbed a bowl of stew for dinner between doing chores and caring for the baby and Callie. The whole evening, Abbie felt she was walking around in a fog, and bedtime couldn't come soon enough for her.

Abbie asked Whit to lead bedtime prayers and then she tucked in Anna and Corrie and turned off the lantern before crawling into bed next to Whit. She flinched as she lay her bruised face on the pillow.

"Too tired to journal?" Whit asked.

Abbie nodded, but could not say anything.

"What's the matter, sweet sister?" Whit asked. "You've been actin' a mite strange this whole evening—and you've been so quiet. Just ain't like you."

"It's Mama" was all Abbie could say. She wanted to pour her heart out to Whit, to tell her about the whole terrible affair. She wanted someone to talk and pray with. But she knew that the only person she could walk this path with was the Lord. And now she needed his wisdom and guidance more than ever.

33

Milk Fever

That night Nate, Tom, and David slept in the summer room across the dogtrot, while all the girls and women spent the night in the main cabin. During the night, Maddie had returned and given Callie a special herbal mixture that seemed to help for a short while. Callie and Sarah Beth were resting comfortably in the bed most of the night, except when the baby awoke for feeding.

Nate rose before first light and brought an armload of firewood inside. As the wood began to crackle in the fireplace, Nate heard some movement behind him.

"Nate?" called Callie softly.

He stepped over to her and sat on the side of the bed. He stroked her cheeks and then ran his fingers through her hair. He bent over to give her a kiss, and his lips felt the heat of her forehead.

The fever! he thought. He tried to hide his alarm as he whispered in her ear, "Mornin', Cal." He felt her reach up to embrace him and kiss his neck.

"I'm pleased she was born on the Lord's Day."

"Why's that?" Nate asked.

"It makes our name for her even more precious."

"How so?"

"Elisabeth means *God's promise* or *God is my oath*. And Sarah means *the princess*. So, this princess is God's promise to me born on the day we worship him."

Nate smiled. "And this promise is my princess."

"And God's oath to me."

"How so?" Nate said.

"In the Bible, Sarah was originally called *Sarai*. She shared an amazin' life with her husband, Abraham. She was exceptionally beautiful even into her older years. So, by namin' her Sarah, I'm claimin' the same for our daughter."

"Well, I don't know about her future life, but I sure know she's startin' out beautiful."

"Besides bein' your beautiful princess, your little Sarah Beth is a piglet," Callie sighed. "She was up 'bout every hour a-eatin'. Hope my milk comes in quick."

Nate was concerned about how weak Callie sounded.

"Cal, Maddie's worried about the little bit of afterbirth that's left in you. She's not sure her potions will work. She says Dr. Keller may have a surgery to help out. She wants to have him come up."

Callie looked at Nate. "How do you feel 'bout that?"

"My first thought, I'm embarrassed to admit, was that we couldn't pay—"

"Folks say that he doesn't take money from mountain folks what can't pay."

"I know that. What I meant was if'n we owe *him* anythin', then we owe Calhoun. And you know what they'll want . . . they'll want our farm or our trees or both."

Callie's eyes filled with tears.

Nate sighed as his eyes misted. "Been thinkin' about it all night, Cal—been tossin' and turnin' and prayin'. I reckon you mean more to me than any ol' farm. I'm a-willin' to take the risk of havin' him up, if'n it'll help you."

Callie reached up and brushed away a tear streaking down her husband's cheek. "Nate, I guess if I was honest, I'd have to admit to bein' a bit fearful myself. I mean, I trust the Lord, and I want to be with him in heaven; I'm not sure I want to leave you or our girls just yet."

"I want you to be here, too—to be with me and to raise our daughters."

Callie smiled. "Might not hurt to have the doctor's opinion—that is if you and Maddie feel it's right."

Nate sighed. "We do. You all right with that?"

Callie smiled and nodded as she reached out for his hand. Grasping it, she pulled it against her cheek and then softly kissed it.

Nate heard steps on the porch and turned to see Tom and David entering. He looked back to Callie. "Are you sure that's what you want?"

"I am."

"I'll send for the doctor." Nate leaned over to kiss her on the cheek as she fell back asleep. Turning to the loft, he called, "Girls! Time to get on up."

34

Doc

Just then there was a knock on the door and Maddie entered like a whirlwind, pushing the door shut behind her. After shedding her shawl and bonnet, and hanging them up, she walked over to Nate and Callie.

"It was a rough night, Maddie."

"I can see that in her face, Nate. Lemme take a look."

Nate stood as Maddie quickly examined Callie. When she turned, Nate could see the worry in her eyes. She nodded toward the door and they walked out to the porch.

"Callie's a mite weak, and the fever's gettin' higher. I'm fearful it's the milk fever."

Nate knew this was serious. "Cal's all right with Keller comin' to look her over. How you feel 'bout it?"

"I think it's right, Nate."

Nate nodded. "I'll have Danya go down by the tracks and wait for him."

"Nope, I need him for somethin' else. I'll go down to the tracks to flag him down. And in the meantime, before I ride down there, there's some things I want to try." They walked back into the cabin. Maddie turned to Sandy. "I'm gonna mix up a medicated douche for Callie. It'll have some witch hazel and arnica in it. You comfortable givin' it to her, Sandy?"

Sandy nodded.

"I'll also mix her another oral potion for the fever and the pain. I'll have to add slippery elm and aconite to the willow bark. It won't taste good."

Sandy nodded again. "Be happy to do it."

Maddie turned to Maria and said, "Sips of strong beef tea will help her energy."

Then Maddie was quiet for a moment, looking at Callie's rapid breathing. She turned and walked over to Emily, who was sitting next to Callie. "You and your pa best go down valley to tell the preacher. We're gonna need some powerful prayin'."

Emily's tears spilled down her cheeks as she nodded. She and her pa quickly departed.

Maddie called up to the loft. "Girls, I need you to gather up the nanny goats and get them in the barn. Then, if you could start milkin' 'em that will give us the milk we need for Sarah Beth."

"Yes, ma'am," the girls called out.

Maddie turned, noticing that Callie was still fast asleep—though restless and moaning.

She signaled to Nate to follow her to the porch, where she sat in a rocking chair and pulled out her corncob pipe, packing it with burley tobacco. She lit the small white pipe and began to puff. Finally, Maddie exhaled a plume of smoke and spoke. "Glad you decided to call the doc. It's time. It's not a minute too soon. Any more waitin'—well, it may be too late."

Nate thought for a moment and then nodded.

Maddie stood to leave and began down the steps. "I'll be back soon."

As Maddie left, Nate heard Sarah Beth begin to cry and Callie moan, and he hurried back into the cabin.

After Lafe picked up the girls for school, Sandy and Maria administered the potions. The douche and oral remedies seemed to help Callie rest. As she slept, Maria and Sandy sat by her bed and

Nate went to the porch to whittle while he prayed for his wife. Not only was it all he could do, but he knew there was nothing more important for him to do for her.

After a bit, he looked up to see a small man, below medium height, walking quickly up the road to the cabin. He was sinewy and intrinsically formidable—traits Nate liked. He was toting a knapsack and puffing on his pipe as he approached. *Looks like a train steamin' up the trail.* The man had a thick mustache and looked much younger than his sixty-two years.

The one physical feature that distinguished him from all other humans on Hazel Creek was that one of his eyes was a bright blue while the other was a deep brown. On his head sat his well-worn bowler with its hard felt body and rounded crown. Contrary to popular belief, bowlers and not cowboy hats like the Stetson or sombrero were the most favored hats on the frontier. Both lumbermen and railroad workers preferred the bowler because it wouldn't blow off in a stiff wind or from the window of a speeding train. A popular hat, it was worn by both lawmen and outlaws up and down the mountains.

As he approached, the man tipped his hat. "Howdy, Nate."

"Horace Kephart," Nate replied, "as I live and breathe." He gestured for the man to sit by him.

Kephart took off his hat, untied the bandana he usually had around his neck, and wiped the perspiration from his face. He leaned back in the creaky rocking chair. "Heard Callie's under the weather."

Nate nodded as he continued to whittle.

"She gonna make it?"

"Ain't sure. But sure am prayin' the Lord will turn things that'a way."

"Girls okay?"

"They're holdin' up. Sent 'em on down to school. Lafe took 'em. Course, they're worried about their ma."

Kephart took a puff.

"Heard you were up in Washin'ton, Kep. Still tryin' to get 'em to make a national park out here?"

"Yep," Kephart said. "Don't reckon the government could do a worse job of land management than Calhoun."

"I reckon settlers like me can do a better job than the government *or* Calhoun."

Kep nodded. "Were there only more like you, Nate. Too many sold out for too little. Not sure this valley will ever recover."

He pulled a cloth bag of Havana clippings from his shirt pocket and filled his tobacco burner. "When I came out here in '04, my taste was for the wild and romantic. I yearned for a strange land and a people that had the charm of originality. Found it here on Hazel Creek. But it ain't the same now."

"Guess you're right about that, Kep. So what brings you out? Headin' up to your cabin on the Little Fork?"

"I've gotta come out here, Nate. You know I spend most of my time in Bryson City, writing, but I'm rather fonder of the free life in the open air out here. I still love the thrill of exploring new ground, the joys of the chase, and the game of matching my woodcraft against the forces of nature, and with no help from servants or hired guides, I'll tell you that."

Nate smiled. "As long as you head away from the lumbered areas, that's what you'll still find."

"Don't look now, Nate, but here comes Doc Keller."

The doctor was still a way off down the road, but walking briskly toward the cabin.

"Maddie musta flagged him down at the railroad as he was comin' down the valley. But I tell you, I'm not sure how I feel about him comin' up here," Nate said.

"Nate, I know how you feel about Sanders and Calhoun. I know you don't like them a lick. But there are some good folks with that batch."

"Like who?"

"Like Gabe and Reba, and Rick and Linda, just to name a few."

Nate was quiet. Kep had a good point. He admired the black folks who helped him on his farm from time to time. He appreciated how Reba gave his girls singing lessons whenever Gabe worked on the farm. Reba often said she thought Whit had one of the best voices in the valley. "That Whit could be a professional singer," Reba once told Callie. "She's that good."

He kept his head down and kept whittling as the doctor drew closer.

"I heard tell that Keller left a rich medical practice in Philadelphia to become the company doctor for Calhoun—"

"To care for the mercenaries Calhoun calls employees."

"True enough, Nate. He does care for the company employees—that's his job. But he spends a lot of his time looking out for the mountain folks."

Nate kept whittling.

"Every day Doc takes the company's train all the way up the valley. Then he unloads his *skeeter*, that two-man cart he built, to travel down the tracks. It's funny to watch him in the flat areas, for he has to hand-pump the vehicle like wild. But most of the time he only needs to apply the hand brake to slow his coming down. He's told me it has the best brakes of any rail vehicle in the eastern United States."

"An industrious man, I guess," Nate said.

"You know that, Nate. And he's a good man. Like you."

Nate stopped whittling. "Don't go comparin' me with no flatlander. Ain't polite."

Kephart ignored Nate's comment. "They say that when he's comin' down the valley, he stops whenever and wherever he's waved down. He makes home visits, and he don't charge a cent for his time or his medicines. He even gives medicines to old Maddie."

As the tall, lanky man approached, Nate stood. Keller's flannel shirt and canvas brogans gave him the look of a logger. He had thick, wavy brown hair and brown eyes and was puffing on his pipe as he walked, carrying his black bag at his side. He walked up to the fence surrounding the cabin and stopped.

"Morning, Mr. Randolph. Morning, Kep."

"Mornin', Doc," Nate replied. "You can call me Nate."

"Mind if I come up?"

Nate shook his head. "Nope. Come on."

Doc Keller walked up to the porch. "I saw Maddie Satterfield out by the tracks. She came to get some medicine from me. I'm pleased she sees fit to teach me."

"Teach *you?*" said Nate incredulously.

"Yep. That woman knows more medicine and healing than most of the medical-school professors I had in Philadelphia. I tell you, were a patent medicine company to come to these parts and bottle just one-tenth of her treatments, they'd 'bout heal most of the country. She's one good healing woman."

Nate and Kep shared a surprised glance.

"I'm right honored she lets me work with her." He took a puff on his pipe and continued: "Maddie told me about Mrs. Randolph and the baby. She told me what she's done. She told me how she encouraged you, Nate, to send for me. She said you weren't inclined that way." The doctor paused.

Nate stopped whittling. He felt the color building in his cheeks and burning them. *What's he tryin' to say? Is he ridiculin' me?* In his rising anger, Nate whittled even harder.

Keller took a couple of puffs on his pipe and went on: "She said she persuaded you to let me come take a look. I told her I'd be obliged, but that I would *not* come up here as the company doctor, Nate. I'm here on my own accord . . . just to serve. No one will know I'm here unless you tell 'em. No fee. No obligation to me or any company. Just want to help if I can."

Nate continued to whittle for a few moments, too distracted about Callie to be aware of time.

Finally, Kephart leaned toward him. "Nate?"

Nate pursed his lips and then said, "I'd be pleased if you could save her, Doc. She's a mite important to me and my girls."

The doctor knocked the tobacco out of his pipe by rapping the bowl against the bottom of his boot, then put it in his shirt pocket as he stood. "I'll do an exam and report to you in a few moments, if you don't mind staying here. I assume there are ladies inside?"

Nate nodded.

"I won't do a thing without your permission. Okay?"

Nate nodded again as the doctor entered the cabin and closed the door behind him.

35

Atonement

The physician was inside for what seemed an eternity. When Callie cried out in pain, it took every bit of Nate's self-control to keep from running into the cabin—but he knew it wasn't his place.

Keller finally came out alone, closing the door behind him. He took out his pipe, packed and lit it, and then took a couple of deep puffs. "She's resting comfortable, Nate. It was a painful exam for her, even with the sniff of anesthetic I gave her."

Nate continued to whittle but didn't reply, just hoping the doctor could do the surgery to cure Cal—to bring her back to her smiling, good-natured self; to get her up and singing, gardening, and cooking again. It had been a hard pregnancy.

Finally, Keller said, "I'm sorry, Nate. There's nothing I can do."

Nate felt confused and said, "Maddie said you done surgery to save a woman with this trouble."

Keller looked across the mountains as he took another puff on his pipe. "Nate, if a woman has a piece of the afterbirth that stays in the womb, a good midwife like Maddie can get it out nearly one hundred percent of the time. If she can't, then I usually can. I have to do a simple procedure. I put the woman to sleep with a bit of chloroform and ether, then reach up into the womb with a curette that will pretty quickly and easily remove the tissue that's left."

"Cain't you do that for her?"

"It won't help Callie."

"Why not?"

"Well, she has a rare problem. It occurs when a part of the afterbirth grows deep into the muscle of the womb and just scars down in place. It doesn't affect the pregnancy, other than making the womb more uncomfortable, especially toward the end. Then it can cause labor to come early."

Nate realized this was what happened to Cal.

The physician continued: "When that happens, then only the part of the placenta that's not scarred to the womb can come out after the birth. The scarred part stays in, and nobody can get it out."

"Surgery doesn't help?"

"Nope. We don't have anything that works. Some women with this problem will bleed to death quickly, some slowly. Some die of the infection. In any case, there's nothing we can do but make the woman more comfortable until she passes."

"Nothin'?" Nate said tearfully as he stared at Keller, who shook his head.

"I'm so sorry to have to tell you this." He took a puff on his pipe and then turned toward Nate. "I can assure you it will be a peaceful death. The infection takes over the system. She'll get real still and sleepy. There will be minimal pain—little distress. Likely a slumber will come over her, and then she'll cross over to Glory. It's usually real quiet."

Nate noticed the silence. Even the birds were as quiet as night—as if they knew the gravity of the moment.

"What if I had sent for ya sooner?" Nate said.

"Wouldn't have made any difference, Nate. This die was cast many months ago, back when little Sarah was just being knitted together in the womb."

Nate slowly nodded.

"I best be on my way. Others to see. Maddie should be back soon." He was quiet for a moment. "I'm sorry, Nate. Powerful sorry. I can't even begin to imagine how hard this will be for you and your girls. But if there's anything I can do—anything a'tall, y'all let me know, hear?"

Nate nodded. "I appreciate you tryin', Doc. I do."

With that, Keller put on his hat, said good-bye, picked up his black bag, and left as quickly as he had come.

By noon Maddie returned with a large bag of herbs and potions. Callie had been in and out of consciousness all morning, but Nate had not left her side. When she awakened, Sandy and Maria gave her sips of water and tea.

Tom and Emily came back from updating Pastor Semmes. He told them he would quickly spread the word about Callie's illness and would call a prayer service for the church that very evening.

When Callie's fever climbed, the women sponged her shaking body with tepid water until the fever was gone and she was back asleep.

After the girls came home from school, Nate informed them of the doctor's opinion and their mama's prognosis. As he expected, it was a very emotional time. After he gave them some time alone, everyone gathered for the evening meal. But Nate couldn't eat. He sat on Callie's bed and whenever she woke, he'd be there to softly talk to her and kiss her. From time to time he would get on his knees and bury his head in the bed as he prayed.

As the light began to fade, Maddie came to sit on the bed with Nate. "Callie's not respondin' to any of the potions anymore."

Nate nodded.

Maddie reached over and took his hand. "Nate, there's one last treatment I can try. I've only used it twice before . . . and one time it worked like a charm. The other time—"

"What is it?" Nate interrupted, his eyes looking at Maddie expectantly.

"It's a mighty powerful potion and requires three injections into the cavity of the womb with warm flaxseed tea mixed with a bit of carbolic acid I got sent over from Bennett's pharmacy in Bryson. A doctor over there used it to save his own wife from a fatal termination with the milk fever."

"Reckon it'll work?" Nate whispered.

"Likely it won't harm none. And it's the last treatment I've got."

It took several hours for Maria and Sandy to complete the three treatments of Callie's womb, each separated by an hour or so. After finishing the last treatment and cleaning Callie, Maddie went to sit on the porch. Nate could hear her rocking.

He was grateful that the treatments did not seem to cause Callie any pain as he sat by her bed, gently stroking her hand and saying a prolonged prayer that had no words, just a moan from the depth of his heart, as the clicks from Callie's mantel clock seemed to echo across the cabin.

After a bit, he placed her hand on the quilt that had been their wedding gift from Cal's grandmother. The night was quiet and he didn't feel sleepy, so he put on a coat, stepped outside, and sat in a rocker by Maddie. They were quiet for the longest time until Nate finally broke the silence.

"I can't imagine life without Cal."

"You met in church, didn't you?" she asked.

He smiled. "Yep. I was seven and she was five. I was the oldest child in my family, and she the youngest of eight. Course, like most families out here, we both lost brothers and sisters when we were young. Cal's the only one left in her family. My youngest sister, the only other one left on my side—she moved to Raleigh some time back."

Nate and Maddie quietly puffed their pipes as the forest noises surrounded the cabin. Whenever the loss of children was mentioned in a mountain conversation, a brief silence would be observed in honor of the departed.

Maddie broke the silence. "Rumor is you'uns were childhood sweethearts."

"Don't know 'bout that. But we went to school together until I was thirteen."

"That's when your pa died?"

Nate nodded. "Cal finished school, but I had to work on the farm. We attended church together. I loved to watch her play the piano and listen to her sing alto in the choir."

He could see Maddie smiling in the dim light coming from the cabin window. "I heard you would nearly swoon every time you saw her," she said. "No one was surprised when you began to court and then got married."

"I hardly have a memory in life that doesn't include Cal."

"Best take her grandma's quilt off the bed and replace it with another you won't mind burning."

Nate nodded as he shook the spent tobacco from his pipe and began to repack it. Taking a kitchen match out of his pocket, he struck it on the bottom of his boot. As he raised it up to his pipe, he was so shocked to see a face at the edge of the porch that he gasped and dropped the match.

A deeply wrinkled, ancient face appeared in the light.

"I swan!" Nate said. "Jeremiah Welch, you old Haint. You 'bout scared the blood out of me."

"Didn't mean no harm," the man said as Maddie chortled.

"I know you didn't," Nate said.

Nate thought he saw something unusual and held the match close to Jeremiah's face. "Lordy, son. What happened to you?"

Jeremiah rubbed his swollen lip and bruised face. "Don't rightly know. I was in you'uns barn, in the hayloft, watchin' over Abbie and Whit while they was milkin'. Whit went inside and Abbie was a-preachin' to the cows and horses. Next thing I knew I was wakin' up. Abbie said I done falled out of the loft and hit my face on the side of a water trough. Have no memory of it a'tall."

"Come have a seat."

The slight old man nodded. "Believe I will."

"You are more of a bass than Gabe Johnson, Jeremiah. I always find it odd to hear such a deep voice comin' from such a small man. I think you should come to church with us sometime. You'd make our small choir sound even better," Nate said.

The old man smiled as he stepped onto the porch without a sound and sat next to Nate, who continued to rock slowly. "Don't reckon I'd be welcome in no church, Nate."

"Well, I think that one day you will be," Nate said.

Nate lit his and Jeremiah's pipes and the three were quiet for a bit.

Finally, the old man broke the silence. "Right sorry 'bout Mrs. Randolph. Anything I can do before the clock stops?"

"Thanks, Jeremiah. But I think other than prayin' and waitin', all that can be done has been."

"Don't think I've ever been sadder about anythin' than this," Jeremiah said.

"We've all had hardship in our lives," Maddie said. "Seems to come with livin' in the wilderness."

"That's true, Miss Maddie. And I've sure had my share of bad times."

"Haven't we all?" she said. "But what's been hardest for you, Jeremiah?"

"Probably when my pa, who was a Northern sympathizer . . . well, he were falsely accused of bein' a Southern deserter."

Maddie nodded. "That doesn't really matter anymore, Jeremiah."

The old man continued: "It does. You see, my pa come here to the wilderness of Hazel Creek to escape folks what were huntin' him—and perhaps his guilt. He met my mother and they fell in love. She were a full-blooded Cherokee. To some folks, that just added to his bad reputation."

Taking a puff on his pipe, Nate could only listen. He had heard tales of how Jeremiah's father was lynched for his "treasons" right in front of his four-year-old son's eyes.

"Lost him when I was tiny." Jeremiah Welch took a deep breath and then slowly let it out. "Then Mother left me for Glory when I was six. Guess I've been mad at the Lord ever since then. It's another reason my shadow ain't been seen in no church buildin'."

Nate had heard the tales that Jeremiah's mother had been raped and murdered by an outlaw gang. Jeremiah escaped the marauders by leaping out a back window of their cabin, but not before he witnessed the horrible scene. He chose to live in the forest ever since. He was rarely seen by anyone, although everyone thought they knew something about him.

"Got my schoolin' by sittin' outside the Cherokee schoolhouse and listenin' to the teachers. Would read books whenever I could get 'em. And when Mr. Horace Kephart moved up to the top of the Little Fork of the Sugar Fork Branch in '04, all the way from the St. Louis library, he taught me. Let me read books he brought with him from St. Louis. I read Dante, Shakespeare, Poe, Stevenson."

Nate was surprised. Like most, he assumed the Haint to be illiterate. Nate knew him to be well spoken—he just never knew Jeremiah was well read.

"Other than Kep and Maddie, you and Mrs. Callie are the only folks who have treated me with any respect, Nate. So, now that she's so sick, my heart is breakin'." Taking another puff, Jeremiah looked into the night. "Gonna miss her sorely. Valley'll be dark without her."

Nate stopped rocking and put his pipe down. "You see the future, Jeremiah?"

The old man shook his head. "I'm no fortune-teller, Nate." He placed his right fist over his heart. "But I have a feelin' deep in my gut. Not usually wrong."

"I hope you *are* wrong, old man."

"Me, too," he whispered. "But if not, I brought a gift." He reached into his black overcoat and pulled out a small flask and a tiny wooden bowl with a chunk of bread in it.

"I'm willin' to take her sin—to eat it. Not for money . . . but as a gift to her and you . . . a thank-you."

Nathan took a puff on his pipe, not certain for a moment on how to reply. He stopped rocking and faced his friend.

"Jeremiah, I know you to be a good man. But as Christians, me and Cal believe that the good Lord came and bore our sins on the cross. Cal's already been forgiven. So whenever he calls her home to Glory, I believe her chariot has already been reserved and paid for. Her admission ticket's already been punched."

Welch's head dropped. "No offense meant—"

"Lordy be!" Nate interrupted. "None taken. I'm rightly honored at the offer. I know it comes from the bottom of that big heart of yours."

The old man looked up. "I know Mrs. Callie has the faith. I just wanted to help out."

Nate leaned over and patted the old man's arm. "Just keep an eye on my girls, Jeremiah. You be their guardian angel. That's gift enough."

The old man smiled his toothless grin and nodded. "I'll just have to be careful where I watch from."

36

Glory Land

When Hezekiah crowed the next morning, Maddie lifted her head from the kitchen table and stretched out the kinks in her aging muscles. The Rau and Randolph girls were sound asleep in the loft, Sandy was in Nate's sitting chair, and Tom and David Rau were sleeping in the private bedroom. Maria and Danya had gone to their camp for the night. Maddie spied Nate lying on a quilt on the floor by Callie's bed.

Maddie knew Nate was exhausted from his vigil at Callie's side, for she had never known him not to be up before sunrise. She rose and stoked the morning fire and then tried to wake Callie but couldn't rouse her. She knew she had a difficult decision to make.

As the first cracks of dawn began to enter the cabin, Abbie came down the ladder. Nate sat up, rubbed his eyes clear, and looked at Maddie. He turned and studied Cal's porcelain face as he gently brushed her cheeks with the back of his hand.

Tears began to fill Nate's eyes as he looked out the window at the gathering morning light.

Maddie checked Callie one last time, finding her cheeks to be cold and clammy, her breathing slow and very shallow. Her brow and pillow were drenched with perspiration, but she was no longer moaning. Maddie suspected she was feeling very little pain. Maddie then leaned over to Nate. "Callie's fever ain't comin' down. She can't hold anythin' down and is dryin' up on us . . . which makes the fever worse." Maddie paused as Nate got up and sat on the bed. Maddie whispered, "Nate, she'll be a-leavin' us today, I 'spect."

Nate nodded and she knew he could see the tears in her eyes.

Abbie walked up to him, and he put his arm around her shoulders.

Maddie took Abbie's hand in her own. "I'm gonna have to leave you'uns. I plum hate to. But I have to."

"You gotta stay with us, Miss Maddie," Abbie pleaded.

"She can't, Punkin," Nate said.

"Why not?"

"It's tradition," he explained. "A mountain midwife can't attend a woman's death. If she does, she may carry the death with her."

"It's an old superstition in these hills, Abbie," Maddie said, "but one my mother taught me to never violate. I just wish I could've done more."

"Maddie, you delivered all my kids. You've cared for them when they've come down sick. What I got left's 'cause of you. Ya've done all ya could. Abbie and I know it, and Cal knows it. And we thank ya from the bottom of our hearts. But as far as I'm concerned, it's now up to the good Lord. If he can't give us the miracle to keep her clock a-tickin', then there's no one who can."

As he spoke, tears filled her eyes, and when they could hold no more, they streamed down her wrinkled cheeks. She nodded and left.

With the help of the Petrovs and the Raus, by midmorning the chores were finished. Abbie and Emily decided to stay inside with Sandy and Maria, but all of the younger children were outside playing. Danya was supervising some men from town who were helping with the harvest.

Abbie heard the whinny of a horse approaching the house and

the sounds of someone dismounting. As she opened the door, she saw Pastor Willie Semmes walking up to the porch. "Mornin', Abbie."

She nodded as her pa stepped around her to greet the pastor. They shook hands.

"How's she doin'?"

For a moment Nate looked away as he quietly said, "She'll be gone soon."

"Mind if I see her?"

"That would be fine."

As they entered the cabin, Willie removed his hat and placed it on the table. "Greetings, ladies."

He pulled a chair up to Callie, whose eyes were closed, and said, "Callie, we've folks a-prayin' up and down this valley. I suspect there's folks a-prayin' even over in Tennessee." He was quiet for a moment, and then to Abbie's surprise, her mama slowly turned her head toward him and opened her eyes.

"Pastor Semmes," she hoarsely whispered. "Sorry for the trouble." She took a deep breath.

"Save your strength, Callie." He gently stroked her hand and looked into her sunken eyes. "Callie, I've known you for many a year. I've known your walk with the Lord, and I know you're precious in his sight. Do you need to confess anything to God or man? I'd be pleased to hear it."

She nodded weakly, and Semmes bent over to put his ear next to her mouth. Callie whispered for a moment or two, but only Semmes could hear her words.

Then he began to speak softly next to her ear. Abbie could not hear what he said.

As he sat up, Callie closed her eyes, smiled, and breathed deeply. Semmes stood, keeping his head bowed, as if praying silently. After a moment, he turned and faced Nate and Abbie. "Let's go outside," he said as he walked past them and out the door.

They followed the pastor out to the fence, where he kept his back turned to them. After filling his pipe with tobacco, he lit it. A few puffs later, he turned to face them. It was then that Abbie saw his tear-stained cheeks.

"Nate, Abbie, I know Callie knows the Lord, and she knows she's a-goin' to heaven. She's at peace with him and with all men." He paused a moment. "I best be goin'. There's arrangements to be made."

Nate nodded, shook his hand, and thanked him. As the pastor mounted his horse and galloped away, they turned to go back in the cabin. Nate called to the young children to come, too.

Sandy and Maria were working in the kitchen. As the young children came in, Nate directed them to the kitchen table. While her pa walked to the kitchen and began to talk softly to the children, Abbie walked over to her mama's bed and slowly sat down. She felt the skin on her mama's forehead. *So cold. She's so pale,* Abbie thought. *But she looks to be at peace.*

Hot tears fell down Abbie's face. *She's so beautiful,* she thought, as she stroked her porcelain cheeks. *I could only hope to be half as lovely when I'm growed up.*

Callie's breathing was shallow as Abbie reached down and took her hand. Abbie held the cold hand, thinking it might warm in hers. "Oh, Mama," she whispered.

Callie opened her eyes, turned her head toward Abbie, and smiled.

"You know I'll be leaving, don't you, Abbie?"

Abbie nodded as tears streaked down her face. "I need you. I need your wisdom."

"I'm glad to know you'll be helping Pa care for my girls. I reckon I've taught you as well as I can. I think I'm ready."

"Not me, Mama," Abbie said. "There's a lumberman wants me to talk Pa into selling. Said he'll kill me if I tell anyone. I've been keepin' it a secret, Mama, but it's about to kill me not to."

Callie nodded. "I ain't gonna be able to help ya down this road,

Abbie. But Pa can. You gotta tell him. You ain't never kept no secrets from your pa. And now's not the time to begin. You tell him—and he and the Lord can help ya. Trust me about this. Will ya?"

Abbie nodded and heard her pa approaching as her mama looked past her. "Nate . . . ," she whispered. Abbie felt her pa's hands on her shoulder.

"Nate," Callie whispered, "I reckon the Glory Land's a-callin'."

"No, Cal. No! The girls and me, we need ya here," he pleaded softly. "Sarah Beth here—she's just a baby. She needs her ma. Don'tcha go a-leavin' us just yet!"

Callie's voice was faint. "Nate, you've always been so strong for me. I've always loved ya, and I always will."

Abbie felt her eyes again filling with tears as her mama, almost imperceptibly, squeezed her hand.

"Nate, you gotta be strong for our girls. Will ya promise me?"

Abbie now felt the tears pouring down her cheeks as she heard her pa sniffle.

"Nate, you have to promise me some other things. Get the girls to come here by my side, will ya?"

"Girls, come." The younger girls obediently came to stand at the foot of the bed.

Abbie knew how proud her mama was of her girls. Callie smiled at them and then turned back to Nate and Abbie. "First, you two gotta keep this family together no matter what. Ya hear?"

Abbie looked into her mama's eyes as her pa said, "I will."

Callie faintly smiled.

"Second, Nate, you gotta keep this farm for my girls no matter what. Ya hear?"

"You know I'll do my best."

"Third thing, Nate. You gotta keep right with the Lord yourself. All right?"

Abbie looked up at her pa to see him staring down at her mama, tears flowing.

"Nate, I know beyond a shadow of doubt that I'll be in Glory with Jesus. Nate, I'll be there. I'll be a-waitin' for ya. I want ya there with me! I want my girls with me at that great banquet table. Ya hear me?"

Abbie felt him squeeze her shoulders as Callie turned her head and deeply moaned. "Cal!" he said in a soft whisper. "Don't go! Don't leave me. Don't leave us!"

Abbie whispered, "Mama," as the younger girls began to weep.

"Lemme sit there, Abbie," Nate said. They quickly changed places, and she stood behind him. After the pain subsided, Abbie saw that her mama's breathing was even more labored. Callie panted as she looked back up at Nate. "Nate, there's one last thing, if it ain't too much."

She took a deep breath. "Nate, you get my girls educated, and you keep them churched, no matter what. Ya hear?" Callie looked panicked. Her forehead was glistening with beads of sweat.

"I hear, Cal. I hear."

"You promise me?"

"I know you're right, Cal." Nate took a deep breath and slowly released it. "I've always been active in the church. I've read the Bible through a couple of times and memorized many verses."

"But Nate, those are just outside things."

He nodded. "Deep down, far inside, I guess I've just drifted away from my Creator. And I know it's time to return home."

Abbie saw her mama smile a smile that seemed to fill the cabin and heard her pa take a deep breath. "Cal, I promise."

Callie's lips drew taut as she closed her eyes. Another cramp must have come on her, for she turned her head and moaned long and hard again. Abbie so wanted to hug her, but knew she could not.

Then Callie stopped breathing. Abbie clasped her mouth as she realized her mama was gone.

But suddenly her mama sat straight up, shocking everyone. Callie was smiling, and her eyes were bright and fully open, staring at the ceiling as if she could see something . . . or some-one . . . as she slowly reached toward the sky. An angelic smile spread across her face.

What does she see? Abbie wondered.

"Nate . . . girls . . . he's beautiful," she whispered. And then in an instant Callie slumped against Nate's chest and into his arms. She slowly exhaled and then was gone.

As the girls began to wail, Sandy turned and walked over to Callie's mantel clock, opened the front glass, reached in, and stopped the pendulum. The ticking of the clock stopped, preserving the time of Callie's entry into eternity.

Abbie felt a long moan rush from her throat as sobs erupted from her deepest soul.

37

Tolling Bells

Pastor Semmes tied up his horse just outside the church. He paused to look up at the white steeple that was topped by a fine chestnut cross, which had been hand built by Nate and Callie, as he replayed seeing David Rau gallop up to the parsonage to tell him the dreaded news about Callie.

His eyes lowered to the whitewashed sideboards, many nailed in place by Nate, and then painted by Nate and Callie, along with the rest of their church community.

This church was built with the blood, sweat, and tears of Nate and Callie Randolph. But, he thought, *it was founded on Callie's prayers.*

He walked to the church door, fumbling with his keys, ashamed his hands were so visibly shaking. Finally he opened the church door, walked to the front, and knelt in front of the altar for prayer. Then he just sat in the cool quiet of the church, deep in thought, before finishing with several minutes of a good cry.

He knew a mountain pastor could never let his congregation see him cry, but he also knew the shedding of tears was good for people. He pulled a kerchief out of his pocket and after drying his eyes and blowing his nose, he stood to face the altar. "Father, I don't always understand your ways. 'Spect I never will. I especially don't understand why you sometimes call your most precious ones to come home so early. I trust you, Father . . . but frankly, in the flesh I fear for Nate and his girls."

Semmes slowly turned and walked to the back of the church and the base of the steeple, where he located the bell rope. He rang the bell three times to announce to the community up and down Hazel Creek that there had been a death. He knew that everyone who heard the death bell's three tolls would stop whatever they were doing and stand hats off, heads bowed.

They all knew, as he did, that Callie was sick. They would be hoping against hope that maybe the bell was tolling for someone else—a stranger rather than one of their own.

Then Semmes rang the bell twice. Once would have communicated a male had died—twice for a female. After a second break of ten seconds, he slowly rang the bell thirty-two times—once for each of Callie's years on earth. Now everyone up and down the valley would know that a thirty-two-year-old female had died—that Callie Randolph was gone.

When the ringing stopped, Millard Barnes was standing in his store with his eyes closed as he prayed for his friend Nathan and the girls. Then he took a deep breath and headed toward his storage shed. He knew that one or two of the townsfolk would join him in a few minutes.

He would begin preparing a coffin, as was his habit with the toll of every death bell. Sometimes a small walnut coffin would be made for a newborn or small child. At other times the coffin would be extra big and crafted of pine if for a lumberman. For the mountain people there was never a charge; for the lumber company people and outsiders, there was *always* one.

He and the men would hurry to complete the box in only a few hours, and then they would hand deliver it, as it was important to place the body in the coffin before the rigor—the body stiffness—set in.

Millard thought, *This one must be very special! For her, cherry is the only appropriate choice, as she is one of God's most special ladies.*

He knew all of them would pour their hearts into her final ark and they would polish it with their private tears.

After the last bell, Sandy stood up. "Girls," she said quietly, "pack up about three days' belongings. Be sure to include some church clothes for the funeral. And Nathan, same goes for you. Tom will be here with the wagon to fetch y'all. I 'spect other women will be here shortly."

The children nodded. Abbie stood and handed the baby to Sandy. Their eyes met, and then Abbie turned and followed the other girls to the loft.

Sandy walked over to Nathan and put her hand on his shoulder. "I'm gonna put Callie in her mama's church dress. She loved that dress."

Nathan nodded. He felt numb.

"You want her weddin' ring to go with her into the ground, or do you want it for one of the girls?"

Nathan took a deep breath. He had not considered this question—he and Cal never discussed it. *I've never even imagined not havin' Cal with me*, he thought.

Nate was quiet for a moment, and then he replied, "I believe it might be best for me to give it to Abbie."

Sandy smiled. "It's what most folks in these parts do. I reckon Abbie would be mighty proud to wear her ma's ring. One last thing, Nate."

He looked at her sad eyes.

"I'd like to ask you if Abbie could stay with me to prepare the body. It's somethin' we women all have to learn at some time or the other. Won't be easy, but I won't let her out of my sight."

Nathan sighed deeply as he thought about the request. He wondered if Abbie might not be too young for such a thing or if it might not be too much of an emotional burden for her. And he needed her to help with the younger girls and the baby. But he

230 *V* WALT LARIMORE

also knew Sandy was right about Abbie needing to observe and learn the burying customs. *And*, he thought, *there's likely no better time than now.*

He nodded and turned to leave the room just as he heard the sound of a wagon.

He walked out to the porch to see Tom coming to take them to his home. He knew they would not be back in their home until after the funeral, after Callie was in the ground, and after the house had been scrubbed clean.

38

Dressing Up

A bbie watched from the porch as Mr. Rau pulled away with her family. Once they were out of sight, she turned back to the house.

"While I boil up some water, Abbie," Sandy Rau said, "I'll need you to go to the summer room, look in your ma's trunk, and find her ma's church dress. We'll need to iron it."

Abbie found herself staring at her mama's body, unable to move.

"What do you need me to do, Ma?" she heard Emily say.

"While we're waitin' for the others, can you go help Maria collect some more milk from the nanny goats? It'll need to be stored in clean jars down in the springhouse." Emily nodded and she and Maria left the cabin.

Sandy walked over to Abbie and took her hand. They sat on the side of the bed as Sandy softly stroked Callie's hair. "I'm gonna miss you, dear friend. Save a place on your bench in Glory. We're gonna have a lot to catch up on. We only part to one day meet again."

"I'm gonna miss you, too, Mama," Abbie said.

Sandy turned and pulled Abbie into her arms. When the girl's sobs subsided, Sandy sat back and wiped a tear from her own cheek. "My papa used to quote an old poem. It went like this: *'Days of absence, sad and dreary, clothed in sorrow's dark array—days of absence, I am weary; she I love is far away.'* But sweetheart, we *will* see her again."

Abbie felt more peaceful as she touched her mama's hand. "I guess you're right, Mrs. Rau. A good-bye isn't as painful when you know you're gonna say hello again."

They hugged.

"Take as much time as you need to be with your ma," Sandy said. "When you're ready, I'll be needin' your help in preparin' the body. In the meantime, I'll stoke the stove to heat up the iron while we wait for the others."

Abbie stood and looked out the window. "Sounds like they're comin' now."

"You feel like goin' out to welcome them, dear?"

Abbie nodded and walked to the cabin door. Stepping out on the porch she saw four women riding in a carriage. She was not surprised to see the passenger seat occupied by Maybelle Semmes. Driving the carriage, and whipping their poor old horse up the steep trail, was Etta Mae Barnes, looking much older than her thirty-eight years.

Riding in the backseat was Nancy Cunningham, one of Hazel Creek's spinsters. She was short and almost as thin as Maybelle, but what was most unusual was her hair. It hung almost to the floor. It had never been cut. Nancy owned and ran the Clubhouse, was a hospitable woman, and a nationally renowned chef. Abbie was glad to see her.

But the fourth figure was a surprise. There in the backseat, next to Nancy, was Dove Faulkner. She rarely left home after the deaths of three of her children, and from her visit with Maddie a few days prior, Abbie knew Dove had been ill. As the carriage stopped, Abbie stepped off the porch to greet them.

"You'uns go on in," suggested Etta. "I'll get this old nag into the barn and be up to the house in a lickity."

Maybelle hopped out of the carriage and ran to Abbie, embracing her closely. "How'd she pass?"

"Mrs. Semmes, you'd have to have been here to believe it," Abbie answered. "I think she saw the Lord, or maybe the archangel Michael, just before she crossed over. Pa said it was the most amazin' of any passage he'd ever heard of."

"She loved the Lord so very much." Maybelle straightened her arms to gaze into Abbie's eyes. "Your family gone?"

Abbie nodded. "They're all at the Raus'. Pa asked me to stay. Said I needed to learn the traditions."

"You all right? You could go to the Raus' and let us get started here."

"I'll be fine. Thanks."

Maybelle nodded and went inside.

Nancy was next out of the carriage. She reached into the back to pull out two burlap bags. "I brought a couple of bags of food. I'll begin the cooking, if that will be all right."

Abbie nodded as Nancy passed. "Just check with Mrs. Sandy. She's supervisin' everythin'."

As Dove limped up, she seemed even taller than Abbie had remembered. "Your toe better?"

Dove smiled. "It is, thanks to you and Maddie droppin' by. Not well yet, but better."

"Thanks for comin', Mrs. Faulkner." They quickly embraced.

"Has to be done" was Dove's reply. "We best get busy."

The cabin was abuzz with activity. Maybelle and Dove took off Callie's bedclothes and stripped the bed—leaving the body covered with a small sheet.

Sandy was giving orders. "Emily, you and Abbie take these out to the trash fire and burn them to ash. When you'uns are done, come back and get the bedsheets. All right?"

"Ma," said Emily, "why are we burnin' Mrs. Callie's night-clothes and sheets? Won't Abbie want them when she's growed up?"

234 *&* WALT LARIMORE

"It's the tradition. Don't want any death stayin' in the house. Gotta be burned. That all right, Abbie?"

Abbie felt herself nod, not sure whether she would want the sheets on which her mama had died. "Maybe we can keep one pillowcase, Mrs. Sandy? One she didn't rest her head on? That be okay?"

"I think so," Sandy said. "Y'all get on with the other linens, ya hear!"

"Yes, Ma," replied Emily.

"The rest of you, let's begin the work of preparin' the body and preparin' the food. There's gonna be many, many folks a-showin' up for the wake."

Abbie knew invitations were never extended—people would just begin coming. They all knew who was invited to any particular home and for any individual's funeral.

"When will they be here?" Abbie asked.

"Folks know that several hours are needed for the preparation of the body and the home. So they'll wait a bit. And from this moment on, the ritual must be done in silence."

Abbie knew that only women prepared a woman's body, and men prepared a man's.

"Any questions?" Sandy asked. "Okay, let's join hands and pray before we begin."

When Abbie opened the door, Millard Barnes greeted her, and she stepped out to the porch, being careful to close the door behind her. He took off his hat. "Abbie," he said, "sure is a powerful sad day in Hazel Creek."

"Yes, sir, it is."

"The boys are unloading the coffin. We'll put it on the porch."

"That'd be just fine. You'll be comin' for the wake?"

Millard nodded.

"My pa and sisters will be here when you come back. Pa will want you to see Mama in your coffin then."

Millard smiled and put his hat on. As he turned to help with the coffin, Abbie went back in. "Coffin's here."

Sandy called all the women to help.

After the body and cabin were prepared, Danya and Maria took Abbie to the Raus' home, where she quickly changed. As Tom Rau was bringing her and her sisters, with the exception of Corrie, back to her cabin, Abbie could see several carriages and wagons parked outside their barn.

She hoped in her heart of hearts that the cabin would be empty of anyone but her mama. She had even prayed that there might have been a miracle and that her mama would be sitting on the porch, rocking, and she would stand and wave at them as they drove up. She looked down at Sarah Beth, who was fast asleep in her arms. Abbie was thankful that she took to the warm goat's milk so quickly.

Whit and Anna sat in the bed of the wagon, on a bale of hay. Anna was giggling. Abbie smiled. She was glad in a way that her little sister was not aware of the many potential troubles that lay ahead. *Will Pa be able to keep us? Will he keep his promises to Mama? Will Whit, Corrie, and I be sent away to school—or worse yet, to Pa's cousins over in Cades Cove—on the other side of the Smokies? Or even more tragical than that, will we be sent to Pa's rich but stuffy relatives in Raleigh—the ones he dislikes so terribly?*

Pa and Corrie stayed at the Raus' with David. They would come over later. *Pa never was one to be around other folks or their funerals. Wonder if he'll come to the wake a'tall.*

As the wagon pulled up to the cabin, a bevy of women streamed out. Before Abbie knew it, the baby was lifted from her arms and a half-dozen sets of hands were helping her out of the wagon. It was all a blur.

Walking up to the cabin, she saw some women looking forlorn and others weeping. Some hugged her, some patted her back, and Etta Mae even patted her on the head. This irritated her. *I'm not a little girl anymore, Mrs. Barnes!* she thought to herself. *I'm fifteen years old for heaven's sake!*

Before she knew it she was at the cabin door. She wasn't sure if her mind blocked out the sounds or if everyone just got quiet. She stepped across the threshold, and then she saw it: her mama's coffin and her mama's body lying in it—and on their dining table no less!

Abbie slowly walked up to the coffin and just stared.

She looks so normal, thought Abbie. *Of course she does! I've been to funerals before. I've seen what a little bloodroot powder will do to the cheeks. Makes them look downright alive!*

Her mama's hair was done nice and she looked so lovely in her mama's dress. *When was the last time she wore that dress? Musta been the Spring Arbor celebration last year.*

Abbie found herself wondering, *What's her skin feel like now?* For a moment, she was taken aback by her own morbid curiosity. But then she reached out, palm up, and brushed her mama's cheek. *She's so cold and so hard!*

She jerked her hand away. *Mama's gone to Glory. I know she's happy. I know she's with Jesus,* she thought. *But what about us girls? What's this mean for me and Bobby Lee? What about Sarah Beth? What about Pa?*

Abbie was embarrassed about her selfish thoughts, but she just couldn't stop them. They swept over her like a summer thunderstorm. *What about me, Mama? What about our talks and our walks? How'm I supposed to care for the other girls? You ain't done teachin' me, Mama! You say I'm supposed to be responsible for the young'uns—well, how am I supposed to know what to do with ya gone?*

She felt the hot tears streaking down her cheeks and then a horrible thought crossed her mind: *God, why did you take Mama?*

You could have healed her. You shoulda healed her! I need her here. We all need her here! Abbie gasped and clapped her hand over her mouth as she bowed her head and sobbed.

After crying her eyes out, she blew her nose and wiped her tears. She looked up and whispered, "I'm sorry, Father. I do trust you. No matter what road you lay out before me, I'm willin' to walk it." And she meant it from the bottom of her heart.

39

Graven Image

Nate was sitting on the porch at the Rau home, silent while whittling a stick. He needed some time to think and to be alone. Losing Cal was painful enough, but facing all those folks at the wake would be pure torture for him. He suspected it would be just as difficult for Corrie.

She lit out into the woods once they got to the Raus' place. He knew she'd be able to find her peace there. He also knew that Jeremiah Welch was watching over her—albeit from a distance.

Nate already decided she would not have to go to the wake. Getting her to the funeral would likely be work enough. *It's gonna be hard for them all*, he thought. He was so deep in his thoughts and in his whittling that he didn't hear the horse approach until it was nearly at the porch.

He looked up to see Reginald Knight pulling the reins on his palomino and then pushing back his Stetson. Nate stopped whittling and stared in disbelief. He worried Knight might show up, but never believed he would actually be foolish enough to do so—and he was relieved he had the foresight to buckle on his holster and sidearm. *What's this snake want?* he thought as he sat back, put down his knife, and pulled his coat back. He wanted to be able to quickly draw his pistol if needed.

"I come in peace, Randolph," Knight said, dropping the reins and holding both hands up, palms facing Nate. "I'm not here for any violence."

Nate nodded and pulled his coat closed.

"Heard about your loss and wanted to come to extend my sympathies. I know I would be extremely upset if I lost my Elizabeth." He looked over to the Raus' barn and then back. "I'm up here to make you an offer."

Nate remained silent, figuring he had nothing to say to this scoundrel.

"Lord knows it is difficult enough to keep a farm and raise a family with two parents. I suspect it is right near impossible for a single parent. So to provide you some comfort and some luxuries, as well as the means to move to and live well in any city you desire, the company is prepared to make a very large offer for your property. We can have the cash to you tomorrow, or in your bank account in Bryson City this afternoon."

Nate felt an inexpressible anger welling up as his lips tightened.

"Of course, we know you and your girls need some time. We could allow you to stay on your farm while the girls finish this term of school. It would give you time to finish business. We'd not touch the property until spring anyway. There is no need to decide today. I would recommend you have a heart-to-heart talk with your oldest—what is her name? Ah, yes! Abbie, correct? Well, I would wager that she will see the sense in my offer. I suspect that she might even have more common sense than her father. I would recommend you discuss this with her."

"What makes you think I need to talk to my girl about this?" Nate asked, his eyes narrowing. He saw a brief look of confusion cross Knight's face. *Why'd he bring Abbie into this?* Nate thought. He slowly stood and tipped his hat back as he looked across the beautiful woods surrounding the Rau home. Taking a deep breath, while trying to control the rage he was feeling, he looked at Knight.

"You heartless pig," he heard himself snarl. "My precious wife's body ain't even cold—why she ain't even in the ground—and you come traipsin' up here, disrespectin' me, dishonorin' my wife's memory, and tryin' to drag my girl into your dirty business. Are you an idiot by birth or is your ignorance from gettin' your brains beat out one too many times?"

Nate saw Knight's facial muscles grow taut as he pulled his coat back, showing the handle of his bowie knife and his pistol.

"I reckon you know how quick my hands are, Knight," Nate said. "Are you stupid enough to try to outdraw me—or are you just suicidal?"

"Howdy, Nate," called a voice from the side of the cabin. Nate didn't take his eyes off Knight as a figure walked his horse toward them. "Afternoon, Mr. Knight," the voice continued. "You're quite a ways from your usual haunts. Suspect you're here to express your sympathy."

"I was. And I'm just leaving, Pastor," Knight said, pulling his coat together. He turned and picked up his reins as he turned back to Nate. "But when your grieving is over, Randolph, I'll be back. You can be sure. But before then, I'd suggest you have a talk with Abbie." Knight spun his horse around and spurred him out of the yard and down the road.

After Knight disappeared, Nate turned to see Pastor Semmes dismounting. "Howdy" was all Nate could muster as he sat down, picked up his knife, and turned his gaze back down to his carving.

The pastor tied his horse to the fence and walked up to the porch. He stood a moment, looking out over the valley, and then sat in the rocker next to Nate. He was quiet as Nate whittled.

Willie spoke first. "My guess is that man was not up here for any good purpose."

"Your guess would be right, Willie. I think he has it out for me. Glad you came along when you did."

"Me, too," the pastor said. "I was just at your house. The ladies have completed the preparation."

"Yep." Nate kept working the knife around the soft wood.

"I saw the casket," Semmes said. "Millard and the boys made it out of cherry. It's about the most beautiful casket I've ever seen. Danya carved some grapes and a grapevine on the side. As you know, our church don't allow anything fancy when it comes to a coffin. Feel it's breakin' the Second Commandment about graven images."

Nate stopped carving a moment.

Willie continued: "And I reckon I'm gonna make an exception here. Millard and Danya just wanted folks to know that Callie's life was about as fruitful as they come. So I'm gonna allow it. It's been stained and waxed. It's plum beautiful, Nate. Fit for a queen—suitable for the beautiful woman she was."

She was, Nate thought. He turned back to his carving as the pastor gave his comments time to seep in and then said, "Nate, I need to plan the funeral. Did Callie have any particular wishes?"

Nate stopped whittling and looked across the hills. Talking about Cal's funeral was the part he had been dreading. "Willie, I don't rightly know. We ne'er talked 'bout it. Don't reckon neither of us saw this a-comin'."

The pastor nodded. "She was a mighty important part of the church, Nate. I figure most folks would feel a church-building funeral would be right by her. I can pick out her favorite hymns. I'll keep the sermon short."

Nate kept looking down. Part of him was wishing he was out in the forest with Corrie—a place where he would feel more comfortable. He looked up across the virgin timber of the Rau property. *Maybe I'll sell my farm to the lumber company. Use the proceeds to send the girls to the fancy girls' school up in Asheville. It'll help each of the girls find a fine young man. Then I'll take my horse, my gun, and my dogs, and just go live deep in the woods like Horace Kephart used to do—or like Jeremiah does. Wouldn't be no worries. Wouldn't be no troubles.* He felt his cheeks blush as little Sarah Beth and Anna Kate came to mind. *Them little girls need me,* he thought. *And I promised Cal I'd raise 'em all up on this here farm.*

Willie interrupted him in mid-thought. "Talked to Abbie a bit. She told me about the promises you made to Callie."

Nate almost dropped his knife. *That's private! You got no right knowin' that!* he thought.

Semmes must have sensed Nate's anger. "Reckon one of the burdens a pastor has to carry is being aware of confessions, secrets, promises—the family laundry, if you would." He took in a deep breath. "Don't be angered at her, Nate. She needed to tell me— something about iron sharpening iron, and all that—and it'll stay with me."

Nate nodded and continued to whittle. He liked Willie Semmes. He thought Semmes's wife was a bit of a mismatch for these parts, but the pastor was a good man. "Pastor, you plan the funeral the way you think Cal would like it. The girls and me will be there. That all right?"

"That's my job, Nate." The men were quiet while Nate kept whittling and Semmes just rocked and looked over the hills.

"Nate, here comes Doc Keller."

The physician was puffing on his pipe and carrying his old black bag as he walked up to the porch.

He tipped his hat. "Pastor. Nate."

"Afternoon, Doc," replied Willie.

"Howdy, Dr. Keller," Nate said.

"Mind if I sit?"

"Not at all," Semmes said.

Doc Keller sat on the lower step between Nate and Willie with his back to them. He was quiet for a bit and appeared to be listening to the birds. "That solitary vireo has a beautiful song," the doctor commented. "But I haven't heard a single mockingbird all morning. I reckon they're as sad as everyone else in these parts." He took a deep puff on his pipe. "Nate, I'm plum sorry."

Nate whittled without replying.

The pastor took a deep breath. "She seemed at peace at the end, Doc."

"I'm glad. The infection is not a bad way to pass—if'n you have to."

They were quiet for a minute. Then the doctor spoke. "Tell you what, Pastor. When it's my time, that's just how I want to go."

Nate looked at Willie a bit incredulously. He smiled mischievously. Looking down at Keller, he said, "You mean you wanna die after havin' a baby, Doc?"

Keller began to laugh—first with just a chuckle, and then with peals of laughter. Semmes and then Nate joined him. All three men laughed with deep, rolling guffaws.

For the first time, Doc Keller turned to face Nate. "Well, I tell you, that would be one for the medical books."

He took a deep breath and looked back across the mountains. "Nate, you remember when we first met? You came down to the livery to work on some of the company engines, cars, and trucks. You are a natural with mechanical things. There's never been anyone better."

"I enjoy those machines," Nate admitted. "And I enjoyed learnin' to drive a truck on the Bushnell Road and drivin' errands up to Bryson City—and the money wasn't half-bad. But when I began to see what the company was doin' to Hazel Creek, it angered me. I figured it would be wrong to help a company what was destroyin' my valley."

"That's the problem, Nate. This isn't *your* valley. The company either buys the land or buys the lumber rights."

"They don't pay what it's worth, and you know it!"

"You're probably right, Nate. But nothing I can do to change them." Keller turned back to look over the mountains. "Truth be told, the morals of logging aren't really that cut-and-dried; they aren't clearly black-and-white."

"Whatcha mean?" Willie said.

"I've been in log camps in several states since I left Philadelphia, Pastor. I've taken a real fondness for the backlands of our great nation. And everywhere I've been, there are many folks, like you, Nate, and Mr. Kephart, who are appalled to see the desecration of the mighty forest. But there are just as many, maybe more, who are only too glad to get the jobs and the money they bring."

"Them folks aren't local," Nate said.

"I'm afraid some of them are, Nate," Keller said, taking a puff on his pipe. "I'm not saying one's right and the other wrong. I'm just saying there's folks on both sides of a very thorny issue."

"You tryin' to get me to sell, Keller?" Nate said.

"Heavens, no! I respect your right to preserve and protect your family's property, Nate. Truth be told, I think you're one of the finest men in this valley. I admire your grit and your integrity. But there are plenty of folks hoping you'll sell out one day—even just some of your timber rights—for if you do, then they'll get more work."

"They sound like they just want to make a dime on another man's back."

"Some do. Some just want to do right by their family. And lots of times I feel caught in the middle, I'll tell you that."

Nate thought, *He ain't bad a fellow. At least for a flatlander.*

Doc Keller took a moment to empty his pipe, fill it with fresh tobacco from a pouch, and light it. He took a puff and sat back, looking out over the hills. "Nate, the company is getting more aggressive. 'Specially that Sanders fellow and his hired gun, Knight. I don't rightly cotton to either of them."

"I'm with ya on that count," Nate said.

"You and Mr. Rau have the finest virgin timber left in this valley. I reckon they want to get their hands on as much of it as they can—by hook or crook." Doc Keller was quiet as he smoked his pipe. "Like I said, I like you, Nathan Randolph. I'm worried that there may be some folks in Proctor that don't."

Nate stopped whittling. "You think someone down there is a danger to me or my girls, Doc?"

Doc Keller slowly stood and turned to face Nate. "I do, Nate.

I do. You've got you one fine farm and an even finer family. I just want you to watch your back. Be careful!"

"Got to tell you the truth, though: I've suspected it for some time," Nathan said. "I appreciate your warnin'."

"Best I can do is to do the best I can do," Keller said.

"I don't got no grief with you, Doc. Fact is, I think you're a good man. I just got a powerful dislike for that company and what it's doin' to the valley out here. I know Hazel Creek ain't mine, but at times it feels like it should be. I've never known no place else. Never known no place without Callie, either."

The doctor looked down and kicked the dirt. He turned to Willie Semmes. "Pastor, if you need the train to carry the coffin to and from the church, you just let me know. I'd be mighty proud to arrange it for you."

"Won't be necessary," muttered Nate.

"Won't be no trouble and won't be no cost."

Nate looked up at the doctor. "Said it won't be needed."

"Okay, Nate."

Nate silently whittled, head down.

The physician nodded and turned to leave. When he could no longer hear the doctor's footsteps, Nate said, "Don't need nothin' from that company. 'Cept maybe for them to leave this valley before they strip away everythin' what's precious to us."

"Well," Semmes said, "I reckon I best go make preparations. You need anything, Nate?"

Nate whittled for a moment and then stopped. He looked across the hills and tears began to form in his eyes. He whispered, "I need my Cal, Willie."

The pastor nodded and turned to leave.

As Semmes rode away, Nate dropped his knife and whittling stick and lowered his head into his hands and began to weep.

40

Commitment

The American chestnut tree that shadowed the Randolph burial plot at the top of the ridge far above the family farm was a massive old giant that had overseen the coming and going of untold critters and countless generations of Native Americans that collected her mast each autumn.

She, like the others in her family, was a prolific bearer of mast, usually with three nuts enclosed in each spiny green burr and lined in tan velvet. Her fruit would develop through late summer, and then her burrs would open and fall to the ground near the first fall frost—some falling from her crown, which rose over 120 feet.

Her enormous forty-seven-foot circumference gave a strong hint of her age—and she spent her most recent century witnessing the colonization of her valley by white settlers. Moses Proctor, the first man to homestead on Hazel Creek, sat under her massive limbs in 1830 during his initial excursion into the valley. And now, for a quarter of a century, she served as the guardian for the Randolph family grave plot. She looked down to see Abbie being escorted by Bobby Lee and the two of them walking behind Pastor Willie Semmes.

As the burial party finished the steep climb up the trail and was nearing the top of the ridge, Abbie saw two black men, Gabe Johnson and Rick Pyeritz, standing off to the side, outside the small white picket fence that framed the graveyard. Beside the men were the pick and shovels they had used to carve a six-foot-deep hole in the hard rocky soil. She nodded as she recognized them, and they nodded back.

Abbie stood between Bobby Lee and the pastor as her pa and sisters entered the small family cemetery, followed by the men carrying her mama's coffin and a couple dozen of the sturdiest and healthiest folks of the many who had packed the church for the funeral service. Because the trail up the ridge was so terribly steep and difficult to climb, only the fittest would be able to attend the burial.

As the men set the coffin on the shelf of dirt by the grave, Abbie heard a staccato chatter-burst of sounds ring out from a nearby rhododendron patch. She immediately knew it was one of her mama's favorite birds—a white-eyed vireo, a shy little green bird that is almost impossible to see as it blends in so well with the bushes and leaves. She knew it to be a bird that not only had its own repertoire of songs, but could also mimic the notes of other birds. She wished she could run into the rhododendrons and hide with the birds.

Abbie looked down at the collection of graves, all facing due east, so that at the second coming of Jesus, the bodies would all resurrect to face the Lord himself—at least that's what she had been told. The graves were all marked with small fieldstones, as tombstones were just too expensive a luxury.

She felt Bobby Lee's strong hand gently envelop hers as she counted the six fieldstones. Under two of them were her grandparents, Nate's ma and pa, who had come over from Tennessee to stake their claim in the late 1800s. As she looked at three smaller stones, she felt tears form in her eyes. She had stood in this same spot as Pastor Semmes oversaw the burials of each of her three little brothers.

"That where your brothers rest?" Bobby Lee said.

Abbie pointed at the far one. "That's Nathan Hale Randolph

the Second. *Junior*, we called him; named after Pa. I barely remember him. Died of typhus when he was three. I was only a year
older than him."

She looked up to see her pa standing on the other side of the
pastor, at the head of the coffin. He was staring into the grave, his
face emotionless—but she knew his heart was broken. She took a
small handkerchief out of her sleeve and blew her nose.

"The middle one is where Samuel Johnson Randolph sleeps.
The Spanish flu took Sammy when he was six in 1918. The other
one is George Washington Randolph; Georgie. Killed by our
milkin' cow. Kicked in the head when he was just two years old—
when I was eight."

"Guess when the Lord calls, there isn't any stoppin' his call,"
Bobby Lee reflected. "That's how it was when he called my ma.
Saddest day of my life."

"I don't know if a person could ever be sadder than I am,"
Abbie said as she blew her nose again.

After Pastor Semmes began the burial service, most of it was
a fog to Abbie, and she could only remember a few scattered
events. She did remember her mama's coffin being lowered into
the ground. She found it painful to recall each person taking a
handful of dirt and casting it on Mama's coffin. She never forgot
the comforting feeling of Bobby Lee's arm around her shoulder as
Pastor Semmes recited the 121st Psalm.

Abbie, for some reason, found herself looking across the
crowd and into the rhododendron bushes and was surprised
to see someone standing deep in the shadows. As she glanced
around, she saw that no one else noticed him as the pastor continued the ceremony. The small, thin man's head full of thick,
uncombed gray hair streaming out in every direction made him
instantly recognizable to her. His black clothes hung like damp
rags from his gangly body, but what surprised her most was his
face, which was bright white, as if he were wearing the white
pancake makeup she had seen in the theater in town. Even

from the distance she could see that his face and lip were still swollen—and she could see the dark marks where his tears had streaked down his cheeks.

She knew he was there to show her mama his respect. She felt herself nod and as she did, his eyes widened and he disappeared as into thin air. But just seeing him brought back the horrible memory of her attack in the barn. She knew Jeremiah didn't remember it, but she did. She could only pray her pa would decide to sell the farm. If he didn't, she knew they might be returning to this cemetery more quickly than she could imagine. Would it be to bury one of her sisters, or her pa, or even herself? She trembled at the thought.

Then Pastor Semmes delivered the final prayer: "Most merciful Father, who hast been pleased to take unto thyself the soul of this thy servant, Callie Jean Randolph; grant to us who are still on our pilgrimage, and who walk by faith, that having served thee with constancy on earth, we may be joined hereafter with thy blessed saints in glory everlasting; through Jesus Christ our Lord. Amen."

Later, rather than sooner! she thought during the moment of silence.

Then the pastor's resonant voice began the benediction, and Abbie whispered it along with him, having listened to it at countless funerals since she was a little girl. She began to feel sobs racking her body and then felt Bobby Lee's strong arm come around her and pull her close as the pastor said, "Now the God of hope fill you with all joy and peace in believing, that ye may abound in hope, through the power of the Holy Ghost. Amen."

41

Potlikker

Abbie could not remember a time when she had not known how to make potlikker and the corn pone that always went with it. Even her dimmest memories were associated with the black iron pot hanging on a hook over the fire in the huge fireplace, bubbling with potlikker.

She must have been no more than five when her mama would let her stir the mixture and taste it from time to time. The dish had been as much a part of her existence as air or sunlight, for potlikker was considered essential for the family or for company.

After church, Whit, Corrie, and Anna went with the Raus up to their place to spend the afternoon. Although there were plenty of chores to do at home, Abbie knew the value of letting the children play—a luxury that she could no longer afford. Even though it was the Lord's Day, her pa decided to go hunting in the forest above their cabin. She knew it would do him good to spend some time in the woods.

As Sarah Beth slept, Abbie put a large ham shoulder in the pot of water in the fireplace and let it start its three-hour simmer. She was of the firm conviction that no one in their right mind would make potlikker without a ham shoulder, although she heard rumors that some flatlanders had tried it.

Then she cored a cabbage, cut it into four pieces, put them into the pot, and tossed in a pinch of salt, a bit of black pepper, and

two small pieces of red pepper. Next she washed and cut up collard greens, carrots, and onions, and threw them into the pot. She
covered the pot and let it simmer, adding water from time to time
to replace what boiled away.

It was midafternoon by the time she beat up a batter for a big
pone of cornbread, poured it into a greased iron skillet, put a lid
on it, and set it in the ashes. She had also heard rumors of people
that ate potlikker without corn pone, but that seemed a violation
of some sort of natural law to her.

In the late afternoon, Mr. Rau brought the girls back, and they
were all out playing in the sunshine except for Sarah Beth, who
was napping on Pa's bed, lying next to Lilly, who had grown into
a dog of enormous proportions and was not finished yet. She had
huge feet, and Maddie said, "If she ever grows into them feet,
she'll be as big as an elephant."

As Abbie walked over and stood beside the window, looking
out and taking pleasure in the girls' game of hopscotch, she heard
the cur jump off the bed. Suddenly she felt an enormous weight
on her feet and looked down to see that Lilly had come and sat
on them.

"Get off my feet, you monster! Why do you like to sit on
people's feet anyway?"

Lilly looked up and gave a muted howl. She was growing into
her big voice, a booming, baying sound that could be heard for
miles, but inside the cabin it was more a crooning sound. Her tail
beat the floor, and she leaned over against Abbie, almost knocking
her back a step.

"Get away, Lilly," Abbie said crossly. "You're too big to sit on
feet." She pushed the big dog away and shook her head.

Not only did Lilly love to sit on feet when she found someone
standing up, but if the person was in a chair and was not careful,
Lilly would leap up. She had more than once knocked one of the
girls over backward trying to sit in her lap. She was an established
and loyal member of the family now. Even Jack and Julius seemed

to tolerate her—as did Pretty Boy during his increasingly less frequent visits.

Abbie said, "Sarah Beth, do you want to taste the potlikker?" The baby continued to nap as Abbie walked back to the fire, took an old towel, and lifted the top off the black pot. She reached in with a big spoon and spooned up a sampling. She blew on it until it was cool and tasted it cautiously. *This is real good*, she thought.

She replaced the lid, put the spoon up, and then walked to the door. Anna and Whit were handling the ends of the rope as Corrie skipped.

As Corrie sang, the girls kept the speed, until finally Corrie missed.

"It's my turn!" Anna said, but at that moment she turned, for Abbie called, "Come in the house. It's time for dinner."

Abbie did not have to wait long, for, as always, the girls were hungry. The girls set the table while Whit ran to get a crock of buttermilk from the springhouse and poured everyone a large glassful. Abbie dished out the potlikker while Corrie took up the pone and cut it into parts. Corrie insisted on saying the blessing, and it turned out to be too long for Anna, who finally interrupted her, saying, "That's enough blessin'! Amen."

Corrie stared at Anna, her eyes flashing. "You're gonna go straight to the pit interruptin' a prayer like that."

"I am not! You might go for sayin' too long a prayer."

"All right," Abbie said, her voice loudly overriding the girls' argument. "Eat your dinner, or you can do without."

As always, the girls crumbled the pone into their bowls containing the potlikker, and they all ate as if they were starved. Abbie held Sarah Beth in her lap and fed her warmed goat's milk.

After feeding Sarah Beth, Abbie lay the baby in the crib. Then she joined her sisters in setting aside a plate for their pa, cleaning up after dinner, hauling in fresh firewood for the morning and nanny-goat milk for Sarah, and sharing their evening read of the Bible and memorization of one or two verses.

"When's Pa comin' home?" Anna said.

"Sometimes he'll stay out all night so he can be deep in the woods at dawn," Abbie said.

"I think Danya went with him," Corrie added.

"Can we sleep in his bed, Abbie?" Anna inquired.

Abbie laughed. "Well, I don't see why not."

"And can we read one more Bible story before we go to sleep?"

Abbie's first instinct was to say no. After all, they had to be up early to get to school in the morning—and it would be their first day back in school since their mama's death. Abbie knew they had a lot of catching up to do. But at least they wanted to read the Bible. She smiled. "I think that'd be mighty fine."

The younger girls cheered as Abbie looked out the window. The memory of Knight's attack in the barn rose like a rotten corpse to the surface of her mind. As much as she tried not to be haunted by the attack, she couldn't repress the nightmare.

Should I tell Pa? she wondered. *Of course you should!* a voice in her answered.

Immediately this voice was countered by an evil memory saying, *If you tell even one person what happened here tonight, I will kill every one of your sisters. I'll slice their throats from ear to ear. I'll force you to watch the whole bloody affair. Then, sweet Abbie, I'll come for you.*

Then she heard her Mama's voice: *"You ain't never kept no secrets from Pa. Now's not the time to begin."*

She felt a shudder go down her spine as her hand felt the healing cut caused when he pushed the blade of his bowie knife into the skin of her neck. *You want that?* the evil voice threatened. She shivered again and hoped against hope that her pa was safe.

42

Final Prayer

As Abbie finished reading her sisters the Bible story, she heard a noise on the porch. Just then the door flew open and in walked their pa.

"'Bout time for bed, girls," said Nate as he entered. As he put his rifle in the gun cabinet and hung his hat on a wall peg, they all jumped out of the bed and ran over to hug him.

"You get anythin', Pa?" Whit said as Abbie sighed the biggest sigh of relief that she could remember.

"Just saw Old Gray Back's tracks. That bear's wanderin' closer and closer to the cabin. Reckon me and Danya are gonna have to hunt him down sometime sooner rather than later."

After the girls were in bed, Nate came up to the loft, where he sat on the edge of Abbie's bed and cleared his throat. "I want to tell you girls somethin'."

The girls all sat up as he softly spoke. "I love you girls. The last few days ain't been very easy—'spect the times ahead won't be easy, either, but reckon we'll get through it all together."

Whit spoke first. "Pa, will you pray a bedtime prayer for us?"

Abbie saw his surprise. He never prayed out loud except at mealtimes. He had *never* prayed with his girls. Their mama did that, not him. She sensed he had no idea what to say or what to do. She reached for his hand.

"Pa," she said softly, "Mama taught me bedtime prayers. Maybe I could pray."

He looked relieved and nodded. "Girls, let's bow our heads."

Whit and Anna shuffled out of bed and knelt beside it. Corrie rolled her eyes and lay back on the bed.

Abbie sat by her pa, took his hand in hers, and bowed her head. "Dear Lord, we all miss Mama so much. Lord, I don't understand why you called her to Glory when we need her so. I don't know how we'll get on without her. But Lord, I'm so grateful she was our mama."

Abbie felt her voice cracking, and tears began streaking down her cheeks. She felt her pa grip her hand tightly and she continued. "Lord, thank you for a beautiful funeral and burial—and we're grateful for such wonderful friends. Thank you for their help and their love. Thank you for Pastor Semmes and our church. And now, Lord, we ask you for a peaceful night's sleep. And Lord, we ask you to guide Pa and guide us day by day. In Jesus' name. Amen."

Nate quickly stood and said, "Good night, girls. It's good to be back in our own home, ain't it?"

"Pa," Anna said, her lips trembling, "could we sleep with you tonight?"

Nate smiled as he pulled her into his arms. "Reckon y'all best stay up here tonight. I gotta leave room in my bed for Lilly, Jack, and Julius. Otherwise there won't be enough room for your pa."

"They miss Mama, too, don't they?" Anna asked.

"They do, little one. We all do."

The girls scurried under their quilts. Nate tucked in each girl, kissed her cheek, and then turned off the lantern and went down the ladder.

Abbie could see him walk over to the fireplace and sit down. She could hear him taking off his boots. Corrie turned her back and pulled the quilt over her head. Abbie thought she might be crying, but knew she needed to be alone.

Then Abbie found herself staring at the ceiling as light from the waning moon streamed through the window. After a few moments, she heard an unusual sound. *Is Sarah Beth stirrin'?* she wondered. Then she realized it was the sound of her pa softly crying.

Abbie snuggled into the feather mattress as she pulled the quilt tightly around her neck. As her body heat began to warm the bed and blanket, she prayed, *Lord, I'm so scared. Mama told me I had to be more responsible. Did she know you were callin' her to Glory? Had you told her you were takin' her home? Why couldn't she tell me?*

She thought about the soft sound of her father crying. *Lord, Pa is so scared. He's dependin' on me.* She took a deep breath and continued. *Lord, I don't know whether to tell Pa what happened in the barn or not. If I tell him and Knight finds out, he or one of my sisters could die. But if I stay silent, I'm goin' against everythin' Mama and Pa have taught me!* She wiped a tear from her cheek. *Lord, give me strength to make it through another day without Mama. Show me the way. Give me a lamp before my feet. Guide my path. Give me wisdom. But most of all, Lord, please keep our family safe and don't let nothin' happen to any of us. Amen.*

As her eyelids began to feel the weight of slumber, she found herself thinking back to the previous spring, when she watched two robins building a nest in the family peach tree. Day after day, she observed the ma and pa robin working together, slaving to build that little nest, to make it strong and secure and safe. They finally laid their eggs one day, and Abbie climbed up a ladder to see them.

The eggs were such a pretty blue. She wanted to touch or hold an egg, but Pa warned her not to. "The robins may reject the egg if it smells of a human," he told her.

Abbie felt herself smiling as she remembered the day the four little babies hatched. When they were hungry, they would squawk up a storm, and the parents faithfully cared for them and constantly fed them in a labor of love.

But one day their ma didn't come back. And for some un-known reason, neither did their pa. The babies squawked and squawked, but throughout the day and night, their squawks got weaker and weaker.

Her pa showed her how to mix squished worms and warm milk to feed the babies. Then he helped her set up a ladder so she could climb up every hour or so to give the little birds drops of food. When she was at school, her pa would feed the babies. And the babies took the food! And they grew.

Abbie shuddered as she remembered how afraid she had been when she went to the tree one afternoon and saw a large black snake climbing the trunk toward the nest containing her babies. She raced to the barn, grabbed a hatchet, and ran back to the tree, swinging the hatchet with all her might. The snake fell to the ground in two pieces. The head hissed as the two pieces twisted before going limp.

Then one day the four baby birds had grown and were gone. Abbie was pleased to think that they had flown away to start their own families, that they would have their own nests up and down the Hazel Creek valley, or maybe even over the ridge in the Eagle Creek valley. Maybe one would make it as far as a big city like Bryson City.

Suddenly a thought struck her like a thunderbolt and she sat straight up.

Oh Lord, what are you tryin' to tell me? Is it that I've got four ba-bies of my own? That Mama is gone, and Pa and me have to feed and raise them? Lord, show me what to feed them. Show me how to care for them. Lord, show me how to raise them.

She shuddered as she thought of the big black snake. *Most of all, Lord, show me how to keep the evil one away from them, how to resist him, especially Mr. Knight! Show me how to protect my sisters.*

Abbie shivered in the cold moonlit air and pulled the quilt around her. She reached for her journal and, in the moonlight that was streaming in the window, began to write furiously about her vision. She didn't want to forget a single detail. She knew now she had to tell her pa. There was no other choice. *The right thing almost always is the hardest thing*, she wrote, understanding the truth of her new conviction.

When done, she closed the journal, and looked down to see her pa standing at a front window that looked out over Hazel Creek valley. For some reason she felt compelled to get out of the bed, go down the ladder, and walk over to him. As she approached, he smiled and extended his arm. She stood next to him, enjoying his warm embrace.

"How come you're not asleep?"

"Been journalin'."

"Looky there. Ain't she beautiful?"

Abbie looked out and saw the moon shining overhead and nodded.

"Remember, the moon was full the night your mama died. Now she's wanin'—headin' into a new phase."

"Kinda like our family," Abbie said. "Gettin' ready to enter a different phase."

"Yep."

Suddenly something moved outside the cabin.

"You see what I see?" her pa said.

There, just outside of their front fence, stood a small, thin figure. He was almost impossible to see, as he was clothed in dark garments. However, his face and hands were a bright white as they reflected the moonlight. He took his right hand and slowly made the sign of the cross, and then, in an instant, turned and disappeared as a dark cloud covered the moon.

"Jeremiah. Our guardian angel and our secret, eh, Punkin?" Abbie felt her pa hug her close. "Reckon he and the Lord'll both be here to watch over and protect you girls."

"And you, Pa," Abbie said as she hugged him. "I need to tell ya somethin', Pa. I've never been so a-feared to say anythin' in my whole life." Abbie felt a chill go down her spine as the cloud passed and her gaze went back to the white ball, which seemed suspended in the sky like a beacon lantern trying to light the way into a now uncertain future. She watched as a large dark cloud covered the moonlight, and the valley and farm darkened. She wasn't sure that the Haint or anyone else would be able to protect her or her sisters from the evil that lurked in Hazel Creek. She never felt so lonely or so afraid, even under her father's arm.

"Go ahead, Punkin. Don't never be afraid to tell me nothin'." He sat down on the edge of his bed and gestured for her to sit by him. He was quiet as she poured out the entire terrible story of her attack in the barn and Knight's insistence that she convince her pa to sell the farm. She thought he'd explode in anger at any moment, but he just held her close and listened quietly as the story erupted from her.

After she finished, he hugged her close for a moment and then whispered, "So that explains the bruise on your face and the cut on your throat that night?"

She nodded.

"From the way he talked to me after your mama died, I suspected somethin' was up. Didn't know what. But now I do."

He pulled away from her. The moonlight illuminated his face. He seemed uncannily relaxed and calm—the opposite of what she expected. "It's mighty brave of you to tell me. And I'm glad ya did. We ain't never had no secrets between us, have we?"

Abbie felt her eyes fill with tears of relief.

"I'm mighty happy to have a daughter that can tell me anythin', and a daughter that I can tell anythin'. Not just every pa has that, eh?"

He pulled her back into his arms. "Rather than go saddle my horse and ride into town and slaughter and skin that old snake, how 'bout you and me just pray about what to do? That be okay?"

Abbie nodded as her pa began to pray.

FRIDAY, NOVEMBER 14, 1924

through

FRIDAY, MARCH 6, 1925

43

Scolding

"Lauren Abigail, I'd like to see you for a minute."

Abbie quickly gathered up her books and was about to leave school with the others. Bobby Lee was taking her and her sisters home today since Lafe was not available to pick them up.

She stopped abruptly and looked up with trepidation, as Miss Lumpkin would only call her *Lauren Abigail* when she was in some sort of trouble. She walked up to the desk and saw that the teacher was waiting until everyone was out of the room. A one-room schoolhouse had its advantages, but privacy was not one of them.

Abbie loved Miss Grace Lumpkin from the first day she put the skids to Rafe Semmes, and now she looked at her carefully.

Grace Lumpkin, at the age of thirty-three, was a study in classic beauty. She was of medium height with a wealth of brown hair done up in a bun and bright blue-green eyes. She had a clear complexion, very fair, so that when she grew embarrassed or angry, her cheeks showed redness.

"Abigail Randolph, I'm sorry to have to say this, but I am *very* disappointed in you."

Instantly Abbie felt her throat grow tight. After Josiah Simmons, this woman seemed like a breath from heaven. She knew that her schoolwork was not good, but by the time she got home and threw herself into the work of keeping a household running, serving as mother and oldest sister, she simply had no time to do the homework.

"I . . . I'm right sorry, Miss Lumpkin."

"I think it's important that each one of us does our very best, Abigail, but your work over the last month has become sloppy, and you apparently do no studying at all outside the classroom. I know it's been a very hard month for you due to the terrible loss of your mother. But I'm going to have to give you some very low grades if you don't improve—you may even be held back."

"I'll try to do better, Miss Lumpkin. I promise."

"That's all I wanted to say. I'll be looking for good things from you from now on—and expecting much better."

"Yes, ma'am."

"And Abbie . . ."

"Yes, ma'am?"

"If I can help in any way, I want you to let me know."

Abbie nodded and then blindly turned. Her throat was dry, and tears rose to her eyes. She wanted with all her heart to continue to do well in school! *Pa will be so disappointed, and Miss Lumpkin, she don't like me anymore.*

She moved outside and was only vaguely aware of the shouts of her fellow students, all of whom were delighted to be released from the classroom.

December was right around the corner, and the lush emerald green leaves of the summer forest had finished their transformation into the fiery colors of a Smoky Mountains autumn, and then fallen—as had Abbie's spirits since her mama's death.

Deep in the woods the fall wildflowers that carpeted the ground were now faded. All of the summer warblers, whose comic antics never ceased to amuse her, left to migrate to parts unknown. However, Abbie had not looked forward, as she usually did, to any of this. Her future seemed even more bleak and frigid than she could imagine—and the almanac predicted that the coming wilderness winter would be fierce. And on top of all this, she couldn't quit thinking about Knight's threat. Every time she tried to talk to her pa about selling the farm, he wouldn't even discuss it. He had promised her mama he would keep the farm and that was that.

She walked alone, wondering what her mama would say if she knew the threat hanging over the farm. *Lord*, she silently prayed, *who do I talk to? What do I do?* She was startled when Bobby Lee spoke.

"What's the matter? What did Miss Grace want to see you about, Abbie?"

Whit, Corrie, and Anna walked up to her. Abbie looked away, embarrassed. Then she decided they didn't need any more secrets between them. "She . . . she said I wasn't doing very good in my schoolwork, and she was disappointed in me."

Bobby Lee placed himself right in front of Abbie and put his hand on her arm. "She said *that* . . . to *you?*"

"Yes, and she's right. I ain't doin' good."

"Well, I'm gonna tell her a thing or two!"

Abbie was shocked when he darted toward the school door. "Bobby Lee, you can't!"

Corrie ran after Bobby Lee. Her bright red hair had golden glints as the sun bounced off it, and her green eyes were flashing. She wasn't sure about Bobby Lee, but Abbie knew Corrie was impossible to stop—for she could be like a mule once she set her mind on something.

The girls rushed to follow, and by the time they entered the room to stand by Corrie, Bobby Lee was already standing in front of Miss Lumpkin, who was cleaning the blackboard. Abbie and Whit, with Anna trailing behind them, followed Corrie into the room.

Bobby Lee's voice was firm as he said, "Miss Lumpkin, you ought not talk to Abbie like you just did. You've got her all wrong."

"Bobby Lee, come away from there!" Abbie commanded. "Don't you go botherin' Miss Lumpkin!"

Corrie spun around and looked daringly at her older sister. "I guess he's got a right to bother her if she ain't right."

"Corrie," Miss Lumpkin said, "I pride myself in knowing my students. And in you I see a potentially good one. I think your verbal skills and quick wit are far advanced for a girl your age. I find you outspoken, but with an eagerness to learn. Would I be accurate?"

Corrie seemed surprised, but nodded.

She looked at Bobby Lee. "And young man, I know you have a strong sense of justice and righteousness. Am I correct?"

"I hope so, ma'am."

"So," the teacher said, "how did I get Abbie wrong?" Looking from Bobby Lee to Corrie, she said, "How did I misjudge your sister? All I did was tell her she needs to do better."

"Well, I guess you don't know what all Abbie does, Miss Grace," Corrie said. "It's Abbie who takes care of *all* of us girls."

"That's right," Bobby Lee said. "Abbie has to work from the time she gets up, which is way before sunup, until the time she and her sisters leave for this school."

"I'm aware of the Randolphs' loss, Bobby Lee. But every farming family in this valley starts their days early. And their children get their schoolwork done."

"But after we get home," Corrie tried to explain, "she has precious little time to study. She's busy cookin' and ironin' and washin', and keepin' the rest of us in line. Miss Grace, Abbie would be right pleased to do all the work you give her, but Pa gives her more. And she doesn't stop until she has put all us to bed, and only then does she get to her Bible study and journalin'."

"I don't know how she even has time to sleep," Bobby Lee said. "And I know for sure she don't have time for courtin'."

He looked back to Abbie and his eyes softened. "Miss Grace, if you knew how hard she worked, you'd be proud of her, and you wouldn't be gettin' on her like you just did."

As Corrie and Bobby Lee were talking, Miss Lumpkin walked

slowly to the chair behind her desk and sat down. Her eyes went to Abbie, who worried Miss Grace might see her weariness and disappointment.

Abbie looked at Whit, who, although her eyes were as wide as saucers at Corrie's effrontery, was nodding, while little Anna tried to hide behind her.

Finally, Grace held up her hand and said, "All right, Corrie and Bobby Lee, that's enough. You've made your case. You can go outside now. And take Whit and Anna with you. I need to talk to Abbie . . . alone."

Miss Grace waited until Bobby Lee and the younger girls left the room, and then she stood up, came around the desk, and put her hands on Abbie's shoulders. "Abbie, will you forgive me?"

Abbie felt like a great weight lifted from her shoulders as she looked up and blinked back the tears. She managed a smile and said, "Why, it wasn't nothin', Miss Grace. And don't pay no never mind to Corrie."

"I'm afraid I'll have to pay some mind to her, Abbie. I can't begin to imagine how hard it must be for you trying to help your father care for the farm and raise your three younger sisters."

"No, ma'am, I've got four with little Sarah Beth."

"That's right. What do you do with her while you are at school?"

"Emily Rau, a neighbor friend of ours, and Maria Petrova, who lives on our farm with her brother, take care of her until I can get home."

"Well, it's good to know the gypsies are still there to help you and your father. I think that's admirable. I'll tell you what. You just do the best you can. I'll understand and I will help you all I can." She paused to look deeply into Abbie's eyes. "You're not angry with me, are you?"

"Oh, no, ma'am, I ain't . . . I mean, I am not. But I guess I've been a bit quick-tempered since . . . well, you can't imagine how empty my heart has felt since I lost Mama—that and folks threatenin' Pa to sell the farm . . . or else." Abbie paused as she felt emotion rising and her lower lip trembling. "Miss Lumpkin, I feel lost."

"I understand . . . completely," she said. Abbie saw Miss Grace's eyes soften and her shoulders slump a bit.

"You do?"

Grace's eyes misted as she turned her head to look out at the forest. "I lost my own dear mother this summer. No path in my entire life has been so hard . . . or so lonely."

"I . . . I didn't know, Miss Lumpkin."

Wiping a tear, Grace turned back to her.

Abbie felt her own eyes filling with tears.

"Don't, Abbie," Grace said, reaching in her desk drawer and handing Abbie a hankie.

"Other people's tears always make mine flow," Abbie said, smiling as she dabbed her eyes.

Grace smiled. "A dash of tears mixed into a cup of laughter—my recipe for emotional healing."

"I try to smile when I feel like cryin'," Abbie said, "and I act like I'm all right, even when I'm really fallin' apart inside."

"I know. When my dear mother passed, at first I felt like my own life was coming to an end. But I'm coming to believe that an ending is actually an opportunity to make a new beginning. What many think would be an end is where I am to start over from."

"What do you mean?"

Grace looked out the window again for a moment and then turned back. "Abbie, I love to write. In fact, I published stories in college and then in magazines since 1908. But now, with my mother's passing, I've decided to seriously pursue a career as a writer."

"Are you leavin' us?"

"Oh, heavens, no. No!" Grace laughed. "At least not this year. But I believe the desires that are in my heart were placed there by the Lord—they are his gift to me. What is his gift to you? What is your passion?"

Abbie thought a moment. "I guess my heart sings the most when I'm writin' or sketchin' in my journal, Miss Grace. I've thought about becomin' a writer or an artist, but don't see any way to make a livin' of it."

"Oh, Abbie. I know of people who make a fine living writing. In fact, I recently met Olive Tilford Dargan, who lives right here in Swain County. Have you heard of her?"

Abbie shook her head.

"Oh, then I'll have to take you to meet her sometime. She's written a number of novels, dramas, and books of poetry. About ten years ago she received a national prize for writing the best book by a Southern writer, and earlier this year she received an honorary degree in literature from the University of North Carolina at Chapel Hill. How about that?"

"She sounds more famous than even Mr. Kephart."

"I don't know about that. But she's just published a book about mountain folk."

"She has?"

"Yes. It's called *From My Highest Hill*. So she makes money writing. Mr. Kephart makes money writing. I think we could also."

Abbie smiled. "You think?"

"Abbie, I see great potential in your writing. Maybe you and I can learn how to be writers together."

"Oh, I'd like that! I would!" Abbie said, stars in her eyes. "Thank you, Miss Grace."

"You're welcome. So, tell you what—how about I give you and your sisters a ride home in my carriage?"

"Thank you, ma'am, but Mr. Taylor will be takin' us home."

Grace smiled. "The sheriff?" she kidded.

"No, ma'am. His son."

"Ah, your future husband?"

Abbie laughed. "I'm hopin' so, I'll tell you that!"

44

Posse

Abbie stood at the window looking out across the farm. She blew the steam off the mug of apple cider Whit handed her as she looked up at the gathering clouds. "Looks like Pa's right, girls. There's a blizzard blowin' in for sure."

Even with the first major storm of the season brewing, she still thought that Thanksgiving was her favorite part of the year. Although she knew they were a poor family, she was also old enough to realize how rich they were in love and friendships—and how blessed they were to have their farm, with its succulent virgin woodland, rich-soiled pastures, and wonderful cabin.

Harvest had gone extremely well, with Danya serving as farm manager, supervising Gabe and the boys from town in getting the crops and hay in on time. Their barn, smokehouse, corncrib, wood house, and springhouse were full to overflowing with the rewards of her pa's and Danya's hard work.

And the news that Bobby Lee shared at school that day—that one Reginald Knight had been transferred to another lumber camp—had taken a massive load off her shoulders. For the first time in weeks she and her pa felt almost carefree.

She turned back to look across the cabin as her sisters scurried around the cooking area, which, with their laughter, made the cabin an even happier place to work. The hearth fire was crackling, while above the mantel, the wall was full of hanging garlands of dried apples, garlic heads, onions, and a variety of variegated squash and gourds.

Abbie threw back her head to breathe in deeply the aromatic and savory fragrances that floated through the cabin like the clouds of mist that engulfed it each morning. As she took a sip of her cider, she inspected the kettles hung near the fire, each steaming in a way that indicated they were simmering just right.

Although she still missed her mama terribly, she knew she had to carry on—a chore made immensely easier with Knight's threat having been removed. Tomorrow would be the first Thanksgiving meal she would be in charge of preparing and she was determined to mark a new chapter in the story of her family. Her sisters agreed to pitch in to make the meal the best ever. And with friends joining them from up and down the valley, she felt an overwhelming pleasure to have the opportunity to do well—to please them and her pa.

She walked over to the old crib in which she and each of her siblings had been rocked through the years. Little round-faced Sarah was sleeping like an angel. Abbie smiled as she gently rubbed her curly blond locks. *Sarah girl, you're the curliest-haired baby this family has ever had!*

Laughter drew her attention to Anna and Corrie, who were sitting at the family table shelling corn for popping, while Whit was chopping meat for the stew.

Abbie walked over to the fireplace and gave a stir to the steaming kettle of cider.

"The cider's mighty fine, Whit," she said.

"It came out pretty good, didn't it?" Whit said as she gestured to the pies sitting on the mantel. "But I think your and Corrie's pies are the best ever."

"When they're cooled down," Corrie said, "me and Whit will get them into the pie safe. Don't want no varmints in here to poke their noses through the crust."

"What varmints?" Anna said.

"You," Corrie answered, softly poking Anna in the chest as she laughed.

"I ain't no varmint."

"I'm just joshin', Anna. Wouldn't want Lilly or Pretty Boy or one of them cats to get 'em."

"I can't wait until tomorrow. I think this meal's gonna be mighty fine, Abbie," Whit said.

"I'm sure hopin' so," Abbie said as she put her mug down, picked out two large choice pecans from a bowl, and cracked them against each other in her hand. Enjoying their sweet meat, she observed, "I guess it's 'bout time to punch the dough."

Abbie took the cheesecloth off the large wooden bowl that contained the fermenting dough. The heady scent was one of her favorites. She plunged her fists into the soft dough and began to knead it.

"Corrie, when you and Anna finish the corn, I need you to grind the spices I've put on the butcher block, but be very careful—"

"I know, Abbie," Corrie said impatiently as she and Whit said in unison, "spices are costly and not a single grain can be wasted!"

"If Mama said that once," Whit observed, laughing, "she said it a thousand times."

"Who all's comin' for dinner tomorrow?" Anna said.

"The Raus, Maria, and Danya," Abbie said.

Whit added, "Miss Grace, Pastor Semmes and his family, Sheriff Taylor, and, of course, Bobby Lee."

"Abbie wouldn't miss a holiday with Bobby Lee, would she?" Corrie said.

"Noooo," crooned Whit and Anna together as they laughed.

"You girls quit your squawkin' about Bobby Lee," Abbie scolded. "We can get tonight's dinner on the table as soon as I get the bread into the Dutch oven. Pa will be in from the barn before you know it."

"Someone's comin' up the road," Corrie said as she ran to the window and her sisters gathered behind her. "It's a bunch of horsemen."

"Pa musta heard 'em. He's comin' from the barn," Whit said.

Abbie sensed there was a problem since the six men were galloping fairly quickly toward the cabin. She could see the sheriff leading the pack. As Zach reined his horse to a halt, he quickly dismounted, threw the rein over the hitching post, and ran to meet Pa.

"What's goin' on, Abbie?" Anna asked.

"Hush!" Abbie said. "I'm tryin' to listen."

As the two men finished their conversation, Pa ran toward the cabin as Zach ran toward the barn. Abbie opened the cabin door as Pa ran in.

"What is it, Pa?"

Nate closed the door and took off his hat. "Zach's hitchin' up my mount, Abbie."

"Why, Pa?"

"Needs me on his posse. Word's come of a man bein' shot and killed just over the ridge in Eagle Creek."

"Who, Pa? Anyone we know?"

"'Fraid it is, Punkin. It's Joseph Post. Sheriff Taylor thinks it may have been someone from the lumber company what shot him. They've been wantin' his land mighty bad. Three posses are convergin' on the area to see if we can catch the murderer. One's ridin' up Eagle Creek from Fontana; another one's ridin' up from Cades Cove and then down Eagle Creek from where Quill Rose used to have his still. We're gonna go up Sugar Fork and see if he's tryin' to escape this way."

"Pa, you can't go!" Anna cried as she ran into his arms.

"Can't be helped, darlin'. Zach and the men need me. 'Sides, you know I can't cook. I need you'uns to stay here and get tomorrow's meal ready." He looked up at Abbie. "You all can do it, right?"

The girls nodded.

"Now, I'll ride down to let Maria and Danya know I'll be gone the night."

"Whatcha gonna eat?" Abbie asked. "Want me to get you a bag to take?"

"Zach has vittles Bobby Lee packed up for us," he said as he stood, pulling an extra shawl and his heavy overcoat off the wall. Reaching for a box of bullets, he put it in his coat pocket. "Punkin, I need you to see to the evenin' milkin' now. Jean and Star's udders are full. And I want you back in the cabin before the storm hits. Then get your sisters fed and to bed." Nate turned up his collar, put on the overcoat, and then pulled on his heaviest mittens.

"Whit, put an extra comforter on each bed. I reckon the wind's gonna be fierce and the temperature below zero, if'n I'm readin' the signs right. There's plenty of wood on the porch, so keep the fire goin' all night, you hear?"

"Yes, Pa."

"Corrie, you and Anna get the pies in the safe. I want a bite of each one tomorrow and don't want Lilly's nose print on a single one."

Whit smiled. "We'll do it, Pa."

"I'm dependin' on you girls to get ready for tomorrow's company. I'm right sorry I won't be here to help."

"Yes, sir," they all said as he gave them each a hug and then quickly turned and left.

The girls all ran to the window and watched as Zach brought Nate's horse from the barn. The men mounted and spurred their horses down the property to Maria and Danya's camp. After only a moment, they were racing down the road toward the Sugar Fork as the snowflakes Pa had predicted began to swirl and a strong gust of wind shook the window.

⚜ ⚜ ⚜ ⚜

The snowflakes became so thick the girls could not even see to the gypsies' camp. As dusk began, the gusts of wind increased in frequency and ferocity, but inside, the younger girls were busy and warm, hardly noticing the strengthening gale churning down Hazel Creek. Abbie felt she was the only one worried about Pa and the posse.

Looking out the window, Abbie said, "I best go milk Star and Jean, and get 'em some hay down."

"I'll help you, sister," Whit said.

Abbie was delighted to have her offer. Since the attack, she had been afraid to venture out alone.

The girls sat on the bench by the door and pulled on their boots, winter overcoats, and thick mittens. Pulling a woolen cap over her head and ears, Abbie gave Corrie and Anna their marching orders before she and Whit quickly opened the door, stepped out onto the porch, and slammed the door behind them.

They ran through the frigid air to the barn, which by comparison was warm, and then hurried through their chores. As the dusk deepened, they put some of the milk into the springhouse and then ran back to the cabin with enough milk to last the baby through the night. Once under the porch roof, they shook the snow from their caps and coats, stomped it off their trousers and boots, and reentered the cozy, fragrant atmosphere of their cabin.

"We got dinner ready, Abbie," said Anna.

Abbie took off her outer clothes, latched the door firmly, and turned to see her sisters sitting at the table, with dinner completely ready. She looked down at the crib to see Sarah sound asleep.

"I fed her while you were out. She was a little piggy tonight," Corrie said.

"Well, I'll be tarred and feathered!" Abbie said. "You girls are somethin' else."

"We are!" Corrie commented.

"We are, indeed!" Anna added as all the girls laughed.

Abbie and Whit took their places at the table, and the girls held hands as Abbie thanked the Lord for the food and prayed a blessing of safety on her pa and the other men.

When dinner was over and the dishes and pots cleaned and stored, Abbie and Whit began spinning—Abbie on the larger wheel and Whit on the smaller. During winter evenings, most homes in Hazel Creek had a basket or two of wool ready to be twisted into yarn for knitting.

Corrie kept up the fire as she and Anna popped the corn. They ate the popcorn and sang songs as Lilly and their cats lay on the hooked rug in front of the fire, luxuriously soaking in the warmth. Between songs the girls chattered like vireos about the plans for the next day and the goings on up and down the valley.

"Reckon people will be able to get here through the snow?" Anna said.

"They'll get here," Abbie reassured her. "Mama's turkey and stuffin' recipe would bring them through the blizzard of the century."

"I reckon Bobby Lee would get here to be with Abbie even if'n he had to claw his way over an ice field."

The younger girls laughed as Abbie scowled. "You'uns are makin' too much outta him. He's just a boy."

"He's just a boy whose knees turn to mush when he sees you, Abbie," Corrie said.

"And your cheeks turn the color of bloodroot when you see him," Whit added.

"Don't pay them no never mind, Anna," Abbie said. "They don't know nothin'. In fact, I'll sing you a song that they don't even know. It's called 'Come All Who Roam.' I like the first line: 'A woman never knows when her day's work's done.'"

Her sisters applauded as Abbie began to sing the ballad while she and Whit continued to step up and down to spin their wheels.

After she finished the ballad, the younger girls broke out in applause once again.

"That was really good, Abbie," Whit commented as she spun. "Who taught it to you?"

"Believe it or not, Dove Faulkner."

Just then, the mantel clock struck nine. "Time for bed, girls."

"Aw, one more story, Abbie," said Anna.

"Maybe after our bedtime prayers," Abbie promised as she stood. "We've got to rise early in the mornin' to begin the preparations."

45

Preparation

Abbie woke the girls well before dawn. Although sunrise would be about six-thirty, with the blizzard's thick clouds she predicted the first light would be delayed. It was still snowing heavily and very dark outside, but the girls all roused without complaint. After all, it was Thanksgiving Day, and there was much to do.

After Abbie refreshed and stoked the fire, she fed Sarah and watched as her sisters broke the thin ice covering the wash barrel in the corner of the room and gave themselves an invigorating scrub before scrambling into their clothes.

Corrie and Anna were soon dressed and off to the barn to milk the cows and goats, gather fresh eggs, and haul more firewood to the porch for the day's cooking.

Before long, Whit and Abbie had a copper kettle of buttery grits steaming and at the table, along with a small pile of applewood smoked bacon, sourdough toast, and jam. The table was set and ready and Sarah swaddled comfortably in her crib by the time of sunrise—even though the sun's warm rays were nowhere to be seen.

"Looks like the storm clouds are low and thick," Whit commented, looking out the window.

Abbie joined her. "Yep. And looks like it might last the day, don'tcha think?"

Whit nodded as they noticed the two young Randolphs stomping through the snow toward the cabin, each carrying a load of firewood.

After putting the wood on the porch pile, they shook off the snow and came through the door Abbie opened for them.

"Come in. Quick, girls! Don't want to let all the heat out of the cabin."

"Musta had three to four feet of snow last night—hard to tell with all the drifts," Corrie said as she took off her thick winter gear. "One of 'em is completely up to the eave of the barn—and it's still comin' down like crazy."

"You gals certainly finished your chores awful quick," Abbie commented.

"You're not accusin' us of takin' shortcuts, are ya?" Corrie asked.

"Should I?"

"Yep. Turns out Mr. Danya had already been up here workin'. He stomped a path to the barn. We gathered the eggs while he fed the livestock. He milked the cows *and* the nanny goats—all we had to do was take some of the milk to the springhouse and bring some here to the cabin. Then we all carried wood together."

"'Cept he carried more than me," Anna said matter-of-factly as Corrie helped her out of her coat and boots. "The snow was over my head! But thanks to Mr. Danya, we have paths to the barn, the woodshed, *and* the springhouse."

"Does he want to come in for some breakfast?"

"Naw," Corrie said. "He went back to make coffee and cook breakfast for Miss Maria. Then he said he's gonna take his Percherons and the flat sled and clear a path on the road for the folks who are comin' up today. Said he and Miss Maria would be over here early to help us prepare."

"Well, isn't that thoughtful? Bless his heart," Abbie said.

"What about us?" Corrie said.

"Good job to you girls also! And we've got breakfast for ya."

"Smells yum-yum good," Anna said.

As the girls sat at the table, Whit commented, "This is my favorite winter breakfast."

"Mine, too!" Corrie agreed. "I love grits—'specially on a snowy day."

The girls bowed their heads and held hands as Abbie asked a blessing on their food and their pa. "Bring him home safe, dear Lord," she prayed.

"Today," Anna added.

"Amen," they said in unison before they set into their breakfast.

For a few moments, the girls hungrily devoured the hot breakfast. Finally, after licking a final dab of blackberry jam from her upper lip, Abbie wiped her face with a napkin, pushed back from the table, and said, "Now, about dinner preparations."

The silverware was put down all around.

"This is our first Thanksgivin' without Mama. Since she's not here to cook it, we're just gonna have to do our best. Of course, the pies and breads are ready. And Whit and I know how to roast a tom turkey, and Whit makes a puddin' about as well as anybody on Hazel Creek."

"Hey, I can cook," Corrie complained.

"And I can stir," Anna added.

Abbie smiled. "Of course you'uns can. Heckfire, if'n ya can't get some vegetables cleaned, prepared, and boiled, Mama would be sorely disappointed."

"Have ya ever roasted a turkey by yourself?" Corrie asked.

"Should we wait for Mrs. Rau?" Anna asked.

"You girls will just have to wait and see what Whit and I can do—ain't that right, Whit?"

"If you say so, Abbie," Whit answered cautiously. "But it *will* be our first one by ourselves."

"Tell ya what. Whit, let's you and me get the table cleaned and get started. Corrie, how about you and Anna go to the springhouse and bring in the tom and a ham?"

"From the springhouse?" Anna said.

"Yep," Whit answered. "Took them from the smokehouse to the springhouse a few days ago. Didn't want 'em to freeze in this weather."

As soon as the breakfast dishes were cleaned, dried, and put in their proper place, the girls rolled up their sleeves, put on their favorite aprons, and got out all the utensils they would need.

"Mama always had everythin' handy," Whit said.

"Whit, I'm thinkin' we'll have everythin' ready by two o'clock or so," Abbie said as they began their work.

"Weren't we plannin' on havin' dinner at five?" Whit said.

"We were. But I suspect folks will be a-comin' up early. And with the storm still blowin', I would think most folks will want to be a-headin' home long before sunset—which ought to be about five o'clock. I think dark will be set by five-thirty."

"Good idea," Whit said.

"I'm just prayin' Pa will be home by then," Abbie said, looking out the window at the swirling snow.

Just then the two younger girls stomped their way back to the cabin. Abbie laughed as she saw the girls laboring under their loads. She quickly placed two trays on the butcher block and helped Corrie lift the enormous turkey onto its platter.

"I shouldn't have fed him so much this summer, Abbie," Corrie said. "But he sure would gobble with glee every time I went to throw him some corn."

"Just more of *him* to gobble up!" Whit commented, laughing as she stirred the pudding mixture.

"How's the plum puddin' comin'?" Corrie said.

"I'm feelin' pretty confident about it," Whit said. "I've watched Mama do it so many times that I feel I could do it blindfolded. I've already mixed in the spices, sugar, suet, and a bit of Pa's brandy."

"Corrie, before you take off your coat and mittens, how about you get the vegetables for me?" Abbie said.

"You mean I gotta go out again? It's cold enough to freeze the nose off a bear."

"Should be the last trip. And the root cellar's not that far. Just take a bushel basket to haul everythin'."

"Anna, can you start settin' the table for dinner?"

As Corrie quickly unlatched the door and left the cabin, securely latching the door behind her, the sisters continued their preparation until Lilly stood up from in front of the fireplace and began to growl. The hair between her shoulder blades and the base of her tail was standing straight up. Abbie wiped her knife and furrowed her brow.

Then at almost the same instant, Abbie heard Corrie scream. Lilly sprinted to the door barking insanely. The three girls flew to the window just as Corrie leaped onto the porch, flew in through the door, and slammed it behind her as she latched it and sucked in air trying to catch her breath.

"What is it, Corrie?" Abbie implored, running over to her sister, who was panting and white-faced.

"A bear, Abbie! A monster bear! I think it's Old Gray Back. Get the gun!"

"It can't be a bear. They're hibernatin'."

"It *is* a bear, Abbie! A big'un. And he's comin' toward the cabin now!" Whit shouted as she and Anna gaped out the window. "He's comin' toward the steps!"

Anna screamed.

46

Beast

Abbie dropped the knife and ran to her pa's gun cabinet. She had no idea why Old Gray Back would be out of his den, especially during an early winter blizzard.

She knew that it was not at all unusual for black bears in the Smokies to waken during the wintertime—they were known to leave their dens during warmer winter days. But what worried her the most was that the bear might be rabid. A hungry bear could be irritable, a mother bear downright mean and nasty, but a rabid bear could be insane and totally unpredictable. And a wild bear thrashing inside a cabin—she didn't even want to think about it.

As Abbie raced to the gun cabinet, unlatched the door, and began to look through the contents, she remembered October a year ago when the Forets in Graham County barely survived an encounter with a rabid bear. The bear emerged from the thick woods surrounding the Foret property near Robbinsville and broke through a stout fence to attack the family goats. The family all started yelling from their porch to scare the bear away. But it didn't work.

"The bear immediately left the goats and bounded toward the house, coverin' the thirty-five yards in an instant," John Foret told Pa. "We all ran in and I barely got the door bolted shut before he tried to crash through. When I seen the bear wasn't gonna give up, my sons took over holdin' the door against the creature's lunges, while I ran to get my shotgun. That ended his terror."

Anna's cries and Lilly's baying melded into a cacophony of terror as Abbie quickly pulled out Pa's trusty 12-gauge double-barreled shotgun. She knew a big bear would have a bulky hide covering a thick layer of fat over dense muscles and large bones. And she remembered Mr. Foret saying it took two shots to kill the rabid creature attacking his family and cabin.

Suddenly the bear was at the door, growling and clawing the door wildly, as both Whit and Anna screamed. The door shook violently on its hinges from the powerful blows of the brute, but the latch held. Abbie quickly placed a shell in each chamber and put several more in her pocket and ran toward the door.

The bear's attack on the door was becoming more ferocious as he threw himself against it again and again.

"Whit, Corrie!" Abbie screamed. "Push the bench against the door and lean on it with all your power, girls!"

Then the attack suddenly stopped. The girls were panting as they listened to the bear's growls outside the door.

"Whatcha see, Anna?" Abbie said.

Anna peered out the window, looking to and fro. "Don't see him," she said, as she unlatched the window and began to open it.

"No!" Abbie shrieked as she hurdled herself toward the window, but before she could slam it shut, the bear's head was through the window, snarling as its massive teeth snapped wildly in the air. Abbie threw Anna back and spun around toward the window. She knew the bear must be standing on his hind legs.

The bear stopped growling and began to make more of a grunting sound. She could hear his back claws scratching the logs as he attempted to climb up the wall and through the window. Without thinking, Abbie pumped the gun and pointed it at the bear's head as she began to walk toward the window. She could barely control her terror or her shaking. The closer she came to the bear, the wilder the bear became, now snarling in rage and fury.

"Shoot him, Abbie!" Corrie screamed.

As Abbie moved closer and aimed the shotgun, one of the bear's paws suddenly shot in through the window and grabbed at the end of the barrel. Abbie fired instinctively. The shotgun blast struck the bear in its face, blowing it backward out of the window. For a moment there was silence, except for Lilly's incessant barking.

Abbie ran to the window and carefully looked out. The wounded bear was collapsed in the yard, about ten feet off the porch.

"Pull the bench away!" Abbie commanded as she helped the girls push it back. "I gotta get out there and finish him off!"

"Just shoot him from the window!" Whit ordered.

"Cain't get a good shot on him from there, Whit," Abbie answered as she began to pull the bench away from the door.

"Don't go out there!" Whit yelled. "Mr. Danya will have heard the blast. He'll be here in a second."

Abbie unlatched the door, pumped the shotgun, and then pulled the door open only a crack—ready to slam it shut if needed. She pointed the shotgun ahead of her as she slowly and very cautiously stepped out on the porch.

The bear was lying in the snow, not moving, but she could see that he was still breathing heavily. Then she heard a deep guttural sound. She could not tell if he was softly growling or moaning.

"Leave him be," Corrie said. "Let's barricade ourselves inside until Mr. Danya gets here."

Abbie looked into the blowing snow, not able to see the gypsies' camp. "They may not have heard the gun given the storm," she said. "I gotta finish him off." She turned to look at Whit, "Hold Lilly. Don't let her loose. You hear?"

Whit nodded as she reached down to grab the dog's collar.

Abbie turned to step out.

"No!" cried Anna.

"Got to, little one," Abbie said. As she turned toward the bear, she realized they had all seen bears in the woods, but none of them had ever been so close to such a large bear. As she slowly moved forward she couldn't remember ever seeing such a formidable specimen on Hazel Creek. She was putting one foot in front of the other, approaching the edge of the porch. Suddenly the porch creaked, and the cracking sound must have set off both the bear's panic and instinct in one last explosive surge of energy.

He shot up off the snow, standing on his rear legs, growling wildly and pawing at his bleeding and mangled face. Abbie knew it was time to put him out of his misery and quell her sisters' terror as she dropped to one knee and calmly, but quickly, placed the butt of the gun against her shoulder.

"Shoot him, Abbie! Don't miss!" Whit yelled as Lilly bayed wildly.

The bear let out a series of horrible growls and began to claw at the air as he stepped toward her. He wasn't ten feet from her, and Abbie suspected he had been blinded by the buckshot blast. She aimed at his head and neck, knowing a bear's chest bone was too thick to be penetrated by a shotgun. She knew the shot would have to find its mark, for if she missed, she'd have no time to reload before his final attack. She wished now she had reloaded after her first shot.

The bear bellowed an awful growl and continued to slowly walk toward her. Abbie took in a deep breath and held it as her finger began to pull the trigger. To her horror, the gun only clicked, and her eyes widened as she realized it had misfired. The click drew the bear's attention, and in terror she saw his cold black eyes focus on her.

"No!" Whit screeched.

As Abbie quickly ejected the shell and fumbled for another, Lilly broke free and ran by Abbie, launching herself off the porch and at the bear's throat. Before she could lock her jaws on the bear's massive neck, the huge animal grabbed her and threw her to the side. Lilly crashed against the side of the cabin and fell limply to the floorboards.

Abbie grabbed a shell and thrust it in the chamber, but before she could snap it shut, she saw the bear fall to its haunches and then in a final fit of fury, launch itself into the air at her.

Suddenly everything turned to slow motion. As the bear vaulted through the air, its massive jaws wide open in a rasping, throaty death bellow, she knew that her young life was coming to a horrible end. There was no time left to react or move. She was frozen in place, awaiting the final blow. She hoped it would be quick and painless—and felt sad that her sisters would have to see her die like this. Her last thought was that she wished to be buried next to her mama.

Abruptly, completely unexpectedly, and in the twinkling of an eye, the enormous bear's hurling flight stopped in midair, as if he hit some invisible wall, and the massive body crumpled to the ground at her feet. At the same instant, she both felt and heard an explosion that left her ears ringing.

Instinctively she whipped around to see smoke curling up from the end of her pa's .30-06 rifle. Holding the rifle against her shoulder, in a classic shooting pose, and more beautiful, poised, and confident than even Annie Oakley herself, was one Corrie Hannah Randolph.

Abbie could only hear a high-pitched ringing in her ears as she turned back to the bear. It was not moving or breathing. She stood and slowly backed up, snapping the shotgun shut and ready to use it should the mammoth animal have any life left. She felt her sisters crowding behind her as they looked down at the massive carcass.

Abbie felt the gun slip from her hand and fall to the boards as she turned around and pulled her sisters into her embrace. As Whit and Anna began to sob together, Abbie looked down at Corrie and felt herself begin to tremble again.

"Pretty good shot, there, Corrie Hannah," Abbie said as the tears began to pour down her cheeks.

"We was just lucky," Corrie said.

"I'd rather call us blessed," Abbie replied, her lip quivering.

"Blessed it is," Corrie replied, burying her head in Abbie's chest as she also began to sob.

47

Thanksgiving

Stomping on the outside porch announced the arrival of Maria just after noon.

Anna raced to the door to unlatch it. "Welcome, Miss Maria! Here, lemme take your coat."

"You're too small to reach the pegs," Maria said, laughing.

"Am not!" Anna complained. "I can stand on the bench and reach 'em just fine."

As the coat was hung, Maria took off her winter boots and called out, "How's the preparation going?"

"It's all ready but the stuffin'," Whit said. "The turkey's roastin' fine."

"I can smell him."

"Where's Danya?" Abbie said. She was in front of the fireplace stirring a large pot.

"I told him he had to clean up good and proper," Maria said. "After butchering the bear and tacking up the hide in the barn, he was smelling rank. So I told him to heat up some water and put the lye soap to his hide if he wanted to come into the Randolph cabin to eat."

"Bet he'll smell pretty," Anna said as she jumped down from the bench and took Maria's hand. "Come see Lilly, Miss Maria."

Anna and Maria walked over to a blanket near the fire where Lilly was lying. Maria stooped down, gently examined her, and then stroked her fur. "I think she's gonna be fine, Anna. Just a couple of broken ribs, which should heal in time. Just keep giving her your love."

"I will," Anna said.

"That dog may have saved Abbie's life," Corrie said. "Distracted that bear just long enough for me to get off a shot. I swan, I don't think I've ever been so a-feared."

"Me, too," Abbie added. "Thought I had taken my last breath."

"Well, all that's over," Whit said. "Come on, Miss Maria. Let's all set up for dinner. We've just about got it done all by ourselves, and company will be along soon."

"And," Corrie added, "so will Pa . . . or at least I hope he will."

"Everything smells so good," Maria said, standing and putting on an apron.

"That old bear messed up our timin', Miss Maria," Abbie said, turning to look into the Dutch oven. "'Bout caused me to burn the tom on one side, while the kettle almost boiled over."

"We *were* a bit distracted," Whit said.

"Well, I declare. You've got a point!" Abbie said. "We couldn't help it, could we? I mean, after all, we were almost Thanksgivin' dinner ourselves."

Maria's hearty laugh bounced off the rafters and the girls all joined in. As good humor filled the cabin, the fear and trauma of the attack was ushered out.

Suddenly the door flew open and a gust of chilling wind swirled in as Danya entered.

"The snow has let up a bit and here comes your pa!" he exclaimed as the girls cheered and ran to the door, ignoring the frigid air.

"There's folks with him," said Whit, clapping.

"Lots of 'em! There's one sleigh with the Raus," Corrie said, pointing.

"And another one followin' with the Semmeses," Abbie said. "And is that Miss Grace sittin' next to Rafe?" The girls laughed. "I bet he's 'bout undone by that. Ain't it a sight?"

"Looky there, Abbie," Whit added. "I see the sheriff and his handsome son followin' on their regal steeds. Why, it's a regular Thanksgivin' parade!"

"Oh my goodness, girls! I'm so happy we got dinner ready early," Abbie said.

Maria pulled Abbie under her arm and gave her a hug. "Let's just pray it tastes half as good as it smells."

Anna cheered with delight.

"Hooray for Corrie," Abbie added, putting her arm around her little sister, "who saved my life!"

The sleighs were unloaded, and the women scurried inside while the men took the horses into the barn. After hugs all around, Abbie watched her pa's eyes widen in delighted surprise to see the food preparation in full swing.

As he hugged each one, he asked, "Well, did you girls have any adventures while I was gone?"

When they glanced at each other and laughed, he looked confused.

"You begin, Abbie," Whit said, and so Abbie recounted the hair-raising tale while everyone listened with rapt attention. "Then," Abbie concluded, "Danya came and butchered the bear."

"Land sakes!" was all Nate could say.

"The meat's in the smokehouse and the hide is tacked up in the back of the barn," Danya said.

"Can you eat rabid bear?" the pastor asked.

"Yep. The rabies only affects the brain," Danya answered. "If Maria and I had known what was happening, we'd have come running quicker. The gunshots gave me a terrible scare as it was."

"Never saw him move so fast," Maria added.

"It musta been frightful," Nate said.

"It was, Pa." Abbie looked up as the wind shook the windows. "But bein' here with all of you is plum comfortin'. So let's stop the somber talk and begin us a jolly time. Whatcha say, Pa? How about we frolic?"

Nate laughed and put his arm around Abbie. "You're right, Punkin. It's exactly what your mama would say. And it looks like a feast fit for a king. But, I swan, girls, you'uns never cease to amaze your pa!"

He gave them each another hug, and everyone immediately went to work to finish the preparations, with Maria, Maybelle, Grace, and Sandy taking over the cooking area.

Zach and Pa regaled the men with their story. They had not found the criminal who shot Mr. Post but had spent the night at the Post cabin and attempted to comfort the widow and her children.

"Hopefully, one of the other posses found him," Zach said. "I'll find out when I get down to the telegraph office in town."

"If they find him, will he hang?" asked the pastor.

"Hope so, Willie," said Zach. "Sure deserves it—takin' that good man away from his family."

"What's the widow gonna do?"

"Paula said she rightly don't know. But I'm hopin' and prayin' she and the kids can survive the winter." Zach looked out the window at the gale just outside. "Sure startin' out to be a mean one."

"What in the world put it into your head that we would actually come up here on such a dreadful day?" Semmes said, rising to walk to the table.

"We knew you could smell our cookin' all the way down at the parsonage," Corrie explained.

"Well, it's sure a plentiful table."

"Everyone, let's sit," Nate called, as he pointed out each place— sitting Abbie and Bobby Lee next to each other.

After the pastor led a lengthy Thanksgiving blessing, and indeed, there was much to be thankful for that day, the girls began to tell more details of the stories in which the blizzard, the bear, and the preparation of the feast were oddly mixed. Everyone expressed satisfaction with the stories, the fellowship, and the delicious dinner.

"Everythin' is perfect!" Nate observed, to Abbie's infinite delight.

"From one tom to another," Tom Rau commented, "this is 'bout as tasty a smoked and roasted turkey as there ever was, Abbie."

"I've never tasted better vegetables," Maria said.

Grace added, "And girls, the dressing is delicious. I may just give up my hopes for a writing career and stay right here in Hazel Creek."

As the children applauded, Zach observed, "If the snow continues to thicken and drift, we may have to stay up here on the Sugar Fork until the spring."

"The bread is wonderful, and so are the preserves," Maybelle declared, with her mouth full of the food she was praising.

"Nowhere in Russia are they eating a feast like this today," Danya said, beaming.

Maria slapped his arm. "Danya . . . of course."

"Of course what?" he said.

"Of course they're not. There's no Thanksgiving in Russia."

"Well, there should be," he said.

"Abbie," Pastor Semmes announced, "your ma would be proud."

If it was possible, Abbie felt herself blush and beam at the same moment as she nodded. "I think she'd be proud of all us girls."

"Well," the pastor continued, "I suspect we all know who was the chief cook, and as pastor, I declare you ready to be a wife."

Everyone clapped, except Abbie and Bobby Lee, who looked at each other and smiled.

"Well," Bobby Lee began, "since we have the pastor and we have the witnesses, want to go ahead and tie the knot today?"

Abbie turned to face him. "Bobby Lee, are you askin' me to marry you?"

"Um . . . er . . . uh . . . no," Bobby Lee stammered, blushing. "I was just joshin'. I mean, I don't have no proper ring and we've not really had a proper courtship just yet."

Corrie piped up, "Last spring John Bradshaw and Patricia Tuttle got hitched up. And they didn't have no ring or no courtship."

"Well, I'm plannin' to court your sister the proper way." Bobby Lee turned to face her, taking her hand into his. "Lord knows this beautiful lady deserves it."

As Abbie hugged him, cheers broke out around the table.

48

Joy

After the dinner dishes were cleared away and the plum pudding served and enjoyed by all, the women chatted in front of the fire, while the girls were shooed off to play the games of four square, hopscotch, and sleeping lions. The boys and men put on their coats and went out to admire Danya's work on the bear's hide. It was such a joyous afternoon that not a single person seemed to notice the continuing storm.

When the men came in, Nate and Tom tuned the fiddles and commenced to play as everyone sang "The Jam on Gerry's Rocks" and then "I'll Take You Home Again, Kathleen," followed by a rousing rendition of "Grandfather's Clock." All were songs popular up and down the valley.

When the instruments struck up the first chords of "Monkey Musk," there were cheers all around as everyone leaped to their feet and took their places for a dance. All up and down the cabin they stood—even Danya and Maria—and then away they went, allemanding and promenading, clapping and laughing, until the last chord, by which time everyone was breathless—even the musicians.

The final course, apples, slices of pie, and cider, was accompanied by more conversation and singing, until Zach finally finished the afternoon with a declaration that the town folk all needed to get home before dark and that "I and my valiant son will safely lead the entourage to their destinations."

After the horses were either saddled or placed in their harnesses, and foot warmers were filled with hot coals, hugs and kisses were given all around.

Bobby Lee walked up to Abbie and gave her a hug. "Abbie, you did an amazin' job," he whispered in her ear, making gooseflesh rise on her arms.

"It *was* a good meal, wasn't it? I'm just glad Mama taught me how."

"Not just the meal, Abbie . . . although that was wonderful." He pulled back to arm's length. "I mean, protectin' your sisters . . . facin' that bear. He was a monster. My pa says he's the biggest he's ever seen. Why, there must not be a braver girl in the whole valley."

She felt her cheeks blush as she looked down. "Actually, Corrie was the hero, not me."

With his finger, he gently lifted her chin. "I appreciate your humility, Abbie. But the award for leadership and courage goes to you today. You're gonna make one amazin' wife, Lauren Abigail."

Then he gave her a tender, soft kiss on each cheek. Although it must have lasted only a second, to Abbie it seemed like minutes, and she wished it would never end.

"You kids cut that out!" Zach called out from his horse. "Bobby Lee, there's a pause in the storm that's come just in time to get these good folks home."

Bobby Lee smiled at Abbie and affectionately touched her nose with the tip of his finger. "I think I love you, Abbie Randolph."

"Think?" she said, chuckling.

"Know," he said, smiling.

Before her eyes could widen in surprise, he turned, leaped from the porch, and dashed to his horse, bounding into the saddle. And then, in an instant, everyone was leaving. Abbie felt herself tingle as she watched the entourage departing. When the jingle of the last sleigh bells muffled in the distance, Pa finally spoke. "Children, let's go in."

He closed the door behind them as they all took off their mittens and coats, and then the family worked together to finish getting the cabin back in order. Whit fed and changed Sarah Beth before swaddling her and placing her back in the crib.

After dusk, Nate spent some time comforting Lilly, then called out, "Girls, come sit by the hearth."

After they were gathered in front of him, he began. "I couldn't be more proud of you girls. *All* of you."

The girls beamed.

"I think we have special cause to be thankful. I expected this Thanksgivin' to be full of sorrow—with your mama not bein' here. But you girls and our friends have changed what could have been a grievous mournin' into an amazin' joy."

He reached up to the mantel and pulled down his pa's Bible. "I promised your mama I'd try to do better teachin' you girls in the Scripture. So, I've prepared a little sermon."

"Oh, no," Corrie winced. "*Not* a sermon!"

Nate laughed. "Bad choice of words, Precious. I just thought that before we go to bed, I might give thanks where thanks are due." He sat in his rocker. Anna crawled into his lap as he opened the Bible, while the older girls pulled up their chairs and sat quietly in the firelight.

"I just wanted to read you your ma's favorite passages about Thanksgivin'. She has them listed in the front of this here Bible." He opened the Bible, looked in the front, and then flipped pages.

"This here one's from the Epistle to the Colossians, chapter four and verse two. 'Continue in prayer, and watch in the same with thanksgiving.' This verse tells me that we're to be thankful not just today, but every day."

As Pa turned the page, Abbie looked around and saw her sisters smiling as they listened with happy hearts. Even Corrie seemed to be listening as he flipped a few pages. "This one is from the Epistle to the Philippians, chapter four and verse four. 'Rejoice in the Lord always: and again I say, rejoice.'"

"I like *that* one," Anna said, clapping, as her sisters smiled.

"And here's verses six and seven. 'Be careful for nothing; but in every thing by prayer and supplication with thanksgiving let your requests be made known unto God. And the peace of God, which passeth all understanding, shall keep your hearts and minds through Christ Jesus.'"

"I like that one, too!" Anna exclaimed.

"I like 'em, too, Anna. And I thank God for *each* of you. Each of you is a gift of joy to me."

"We love you, too, Pa," Anna said, giving him a hug.

"Here's the last verse I'll read."

"You promise?" Corrie said.

Nate smiled. "Promise. But I want you'uns to listen carefully to this one. I believe this is what your ma would say to you, if'n she was here."

The girls all sat up and leaned forward, even Corrie.

Nate turned the pages of the old book. "It's from the second chapter of Colossians and starts with the fifth verse." He cleared his throat. " 'For though I be absent in the flesh, yet am I with you in the spirit, joying and beholding your order, and the stedfastness of your faith in Christ. As ye have therefore received Christ Jesus the Lord, so walk ye in him: Rooted and built up in him, and stablished in the faith, as ye have been taught, abounding therein with thanksgiving.'"

He closed the Bible and smiled. "I believe that while your mama is not with us in the flesh, she's watchin' us . . . that she's with us in spirit. I see her in each of you. And I think she's joyful to see what you'uns done today and shares my pride and joy in you with me."

Everyone was quiet for a moment. "All right," he said. "Time for a family hug and then everyone up to bed."

When the good nights were over and the bedtime prayers said, Abbie sat on Corrie's bed and whispered tenderly, "I'm thankful for you, dear sister."

"For what?"

"For all your help today. And for savin' my life."

"Don't be silly, Abbie. You would've had that gun loaded again and that bear dead before he'd landed a paw on you. I'm sure of it."

"Well, I ain't as sure as you. I'm just joyful you were there."

Corrie smiled. "Me, too. After all, if we ain't got each other, just what else is there?"

Abbie laughed and tousled her sister's hair.

"Girls," came their pa's voice from downstairs. "You'uns go on to sleep. Don't want you wakin' your baby sister."

"Yes, Pa," they said in unison, as they hugged.

Pretty Boy

In the wilderness, there are very few things devised, no matter how ingenious, that the average raccoon can't break into given time. Pretty Boy, the coon that visited the Randolph cabin a couple of days a week, was the most mischievous and clever of all the coons the girls had ever known.

Dawn was just peeping over the mountains, and the mist that surrounded the Great Smokies formed a veil that dimmed the rounded outlines of the eternal hills. Pretty Boy came as usual to try the door—which he did more often during the winter when vittles were harder to come by. As a rule it was a fruitless attempt.

This morning, however, Nate left early to go to Tom Rau's place to help him slaughter hogs, and he must have forgotten to drop the latch when he went out because the door pushed open easily.

Pretty Boy scurried inside using that peculiar gait of coons—with his back end high and little claws scratching on the wooden floor.

The fire Nate started was crackling, giving off plenty of noise to cover any clatter he might make. His nose twitched as the good smells came to him. He found a chair pushed up to the cabinet, leaped up on it, sat up, and gazed around at the possibilities.

Another leap brought him to the top shelf and he walked over to where several jars containing flour, meal, and sugar rested. It took him less than thirty seconds to discover that the tops lifted off. He first sampled the flour, but was not able to taste much as most of it lay in the bottom—so he pulled it over to spill it out. Again finding it lacking in taste, he chose to pursue greener territories that called to him. He pulled over the meal, also spilling it out, but wrinkled his nose once again at the disagreeable flavor.

Next came the sugar, which he quite enjoyed for a bit—at least until his eyes settled on an unusual shaped jug. His curiosity overcame him, and he walked across the shelf toward it. Sniffing the cork, he worked at it with his paws, and finally grasping the top of the jug, seized the cork in his teeth, pulled it out, and let it fall.

He tried to stick his tongue down and since that did not work too well, he pulled the jug over on its side. The dark molasses came glugging out, and Pretty Boy began lapping it up as fast as possible. It mixed itself with the flour, the cornmeal, and the sugar, and Pretty Boy's hands were sticky, and his belly and his hind feet were soon covered with the sticky mess.

Suddenly paradise found became paradise lost. A very loud voice came to Pretty Boy.

"You ornery critter!" Abbie shouted as she scurried down the ladder from the loft. She grabbed the broom and ran toward Pretty Boy, but he was too fast.

At once he dove off the shelf, hit the ground, scurried out the door, and dashed across the snow-covered yard to their massive magnolia tree and climbed to a limb twenty feet off the ground. There he sat down on a branch and watched curiously and calmly as he began to lick his handlike paws and then his stomach.

"What's the matter, Abbie?" Anna had come down the ladder, followed by Corrie, both dressed in nightshirts. The girls stood rubbing their eyes and yawning as they watched Abbie, who stood in the doorway with the broom in her hands.

"It's that dratted coon of yours, Anna! Look at the mess he's made!" Abbie leaned the broom against the cabin wall and moved back to the cabinet, standing with her hands on her hips. She glared at the mess and said furiously, "I'm gonna shoot that pesky coon! He won't give us as much stew meat as that bear did, but he'll make a mighty fine stew just the same."

"No! I'll clean it up," Anna said with alarm as Corrie sat down.

"You sure will. He's your problem, not mine."

"What's the matter?" Whit asked from the loft, after waking from a deep slumber.

Anna walked across the cabin and stared at the scene with her big blue eyes. She did not seem to be alarmed as she tracked through the mess on the floor.

"Now look what you've done!" Abbie shrieked. She skirted the trail that Pretty Boy left, picked Anna up, and put her on a chair as she said over her shoulder, "Whit, come down and help Corrie get this mess cleaned up. And I mean I want it to sparkle. I'll clean off Anna's feet."

As Whit came down the ladder, Abbie continued, "I wish you'd look at what Pretty Boy has done. He's ruined all of our sugar, our cornmeal, and our flour. And most of the molasses is gone."

"Don't let 'er shoot him, Whit," Anna pleaded, her eyes bright with alarm. "He didn't know any better."

"Well, somebody shoulda known better than to leave the door open. The last time he got in here," Abbie said with disgust, "he found the potatoes and ruined every one of them."

"I don't see why I have to clean this up," Corrie said petulantly. "He's not my old coon. He's hers."

"I don't care whose coon he is," Abbie said as she dried Anna's feet. "I've got to fix breakfast. Now let's all get started before Pa gets back. Anna, help the other girls."

With molasses-free feet, Anna at once began working to clean up the mess. She worked hard, and with Corrie and Whit's help, she got the worst of it up.

Glancing at Abbie, who was over at the fireplace frying eggs and making biscuits, she reached stealthily into the pie safe, picked up two old biscuits, put on her coat, and moved out the door. She looked around and saw that Pretty Boy was nosing around the smokehouse. Walking over to him through the snow, she squatted down and held up a biscuit. "Here, Pretty Boy. It's a biscuit for you."

She watched with delight as Pretty Boy held the biscuit as well as she herself could and began nibbling on it. There was a pan sitting beside the smokehouse that had some melted water in it. From time to time Pretty Boy would stoop over and dip the biscuit in the water and then swallow the treat.

After feeding him both biscuits, she reached out and stroked his head. "Don't you get in the house and be naughty no more or Abbie will shoot you. You hear me?"

She got up and went into the barn, where she filled a can with chicken feed and began to scatter the feed as the chickens came clucking around her, scratching and pecking at the seeds as they fell. She threw the rest of the seed out and put the can back.

As soon as she got inside the cabin, she heard Abbie saying, "Whit, you go out and milk the cows, okay?"

"I don't want to. I don't feel good."

"You feel all right. Now you do what I tell you. Go milk the cows."

Whit put on her coat, and Anna followed her outside. When they got to the barn, Star and Jean greeted them with welcoming moos. Anna watched as Whit grabbed her three-legged stool, plopped it down, and then shoved the bucket under Star's udder and began milking. She watched with fascination, listening as the milk drummed with a rhythm into the bottom of the pail. "When can I start milkin'?"

"When you get older."

"Well, I'm six and a half already—will be seven in March."

"You're not strong enough. Now, go away and leave me alone."

Anna leaned to one side and saw that tears were running down Whit's face. "You still cryin' for Mama?"

"Yes, now go away."

"It's been two months. You can't cry all the rest of your life. I'm sad, too, but I ain't cryin'."

"Get away and leave me alone!" Whit screamed.

"All right!" Offended, Anna marched back into the cabin, put her coat on its peg, and walked over to where Abbie was taking biscuits out of the Dutch oven. They were golden brown and smelled good. "Can I have one?"

"No. Wait until breakfast. It won't be but a few minutes. Put the plates on the table."

As Anna began to set the table, she looked over at Abbie and said, "Whit's cryin' again. She cried last night, too."

"I know. I heard her."

"Why, she can't cry forever, can she? I cried, too, but you can't *always* cry."

"She'll have to get over it just like the rest of us. Now go bring in some stove wood."

"Why can't Corrie do it?"

"Both of you go fill that wood box."

Corrie was cutting slices of ham and said, "I'm cuttin' ham."

"You do what I tell ya, Corrie."

"You're gettin' downright bossy!" Corrie said as she wiped the grease off her hands onto a dishrag. As she walked toward the door, she said, "Come on, Anna. Let's leave this witch in the cookin' area."

The two girls made several trips, Corrie throwing the wood into the box as hard as she could to make more racket. As she brought the last load in, Julius, their rather elegant orange cat, came to rub himself against Abbie's leg. He was Abbie's favorite. Julius slept with her every night and usually awoke her in the morning by tapping her lips gently with a soft paw. "Get away, Julius!" Abbie cried and shoved him with her foot.

"You don't have to be mean to Julius!" Corrie complained. "He ain't done nothin'."

Instantly Abbie was convicted about her behavior and walked over to Corrie. "I'm sorry, sister."

"Ain't nothin'," Corrie said, throwing more wood in the box.

"Can you finish breakfast? I need a minute."

Corrie nodded, and Abbie walked out on the porch. Her eyes were drawn up to the ridge high above their cabin. There she saw the towering head and shoulders of the large chestnut beneath which her mama was buried, and a lump came to her throat.

Lord, forgive me for not bein' a better ma to my sisters. It's just so much. I don't know how I'm gonna bear it all.

She felt Julius rubbing against her leg. She bent over and picked him up, hugged him, and said, "I'm sorry, Julius." As Sarah Beth began to cry, Abbie put the cat down and went back inside and picked her up. "Are you hungry, sweet one?"

Sarah Beth just cried all the more.

"All right. I have some warm milk ready for you. Let's sit down here and eat this breakfast. If you eat enough, you'll grow up to be pretty as our mama."

Once Whit came in, the girls sat down to eat. Abbie sat in their mama's place. She had taken this place the very day after the funeral, and now the girls seemed to take it for granted. She asked the blessing and the girls began to eat.

"Girls," Abbie began, as her lip began to tremble, "can you forgive me for bein' spiteful? I've not been the big sister I should be. I'm sorry. I'll try to do better."

Whit reached out and took her hand. "I ain't been the most helpful sister to you. Please forgive me."

"Me, too," Corrie and Anna said in unison as they offered their hands.

Abbie squeezed her sisters' hands. "Then, like they say, all for one and one for all."

Anna laughed as she winked at her sisters with both of her eyes, a trick she had recently picked up. She winked at everyone now, finding that the trick delighted everyone else. All the girls laughed together.

They ate and talked, speaking mostly of the business of the farm. Whit said less than any of them, and Abbie cast a glance at her from time to time. *What in the world am I gonna do about Whit? She's got to come out of it.* Then her conscience got the best of her. *What am I gonna do with myself? I've got to be less aggravatin' to the girls; I mean, I'm plum annoyin' to myself!*

As she took a sip of milk, she prayed, *Father, I've been both touchy and cantankerous with my sisters. I admit that to you and ask you to forgive me. Help me be a better sister and a better mama.*

50

Traditions

It had been a tradition in the Smoky Mountains for generations: during the year before a child's sixteenth birthday, the youngster received an extra special gift. For a boy, it might be his own hunting rifle or a horse. For a girl, it was usually a hand-sewn dress made by a local seamstress, or if funds were adequate, the extraordinary gift of a store- or catalog-bought dress.

Abbie hoped her pa wouldn't keep her waiting until her sixteenth birthday, which would not occur until next May, and that he might give her her gift early—perhaps sometime during their Christmas break from school, as this was what many parents on Hazel Creek did.

For a number of years, she and her friends swooned over the newest dress fashions in the Sears, Roebuck and Montgomery Ward catalogs—or even the occasional *McCall's* magazine that would make its way into their hands. She hoped her pa would enlist the assistance of Sandy Rau in choosing an appropriate pattern from the *McCall's* book for Reba Johnson to sew from—not to mention to choose just the right material with the help of Etta Mae Barnes, as she knew her materials and certainly understood dress design. Or if not that, maybe her pa had saved enough to allow Sandy and Etta Mae to choose the perfect catalog dress and have it sent to the general store for Maybelle to alter, clean, and iron before its presentation to her this very Christmas.

Abbie hummed to herself and spun around as she imagined her new dress swirling around her and saw Bobby Lee and the boys with their mouths hanging open in amazement. *Good thing I'm courtin'*, she thought, *otherwise, I'd just be too much of a temptation for all those boys!* She laughed at the thought of it all and how she was looking forward to her present.

After an early lunch, Abbie figured her pa would cancel their afternoon chores, a family Christmas custom, to begin the preparation for their Christmas Day lunch—the centerpieces of which would be a smoked tom turkey and a molasses-soaked ham.

After working on the fixings for that night's dinner and the next day's feast, the family would pull up chairs in front of the fireplace where Pa would read the Christmas story from the Gospel of Luke in their family Bible. After hot chocolate and hanging stockings on the fireplace mantel, the younger girls would put out a large cookie they baked that afternoon, along with a small cup of sweet milk—both for Santa—and a carrot or two from their root cellar for the reindeer.

However, the midafternoon began with a different kind of surprise. Nathan came into the cabin but he didn't remove his hat, coat, or boots. It was cold enough that ice had formed on his mustache and beard.

"Girls," he called out, "you'uns keep up with the kitchen chores. I've got the turkey and ham defrosted in the springhouse. Ya hear?"

The girls said, "Yes, sir!"

"Abbie, I need you to bundle up good and come with me."

Abbie smiled. Not only was she delighted with how well her pa's spirit had improved since Thanksgiving, but she noticed that all the girls, herself included, seemed to be getting back to a new normal. Sure, they all missed their mama, but they also understood that life needed to move on without her.

Now, she thought, *he wants to take me to see my store-bought dress! He's hidin' it at Miss Maria's. Or maybe the Raus'!*

"Whoopee!" she said, as she skipped to the coatrack and threw on her hat, scarf, winter coat, and gloves.

"It's a bitter cold out there, Abbie. Bundle up tight. And don't forget your heavy boots."

Once outside, Abbie saw Danya's workhorses hitched to her pa's sled. Whatever he had in mind, she was sure it was not looking for a hidden gift. She felt a cloud of disappointment cover her. *Drats! Pa's just plannin' for me to help him with more chores.*

Her pa hopped up into the seat and pulled the reins into his hand while Abbie reluctantly climbed up beside him. The frigid north wind bit through her coat, intensifying her unhappiness.

"Where are we goin' to that we can't get to in your truck, Pa?"

"Where the snow's too deep and the trail too steep. You'll see, Punkin."

Nathan slapped the reins and galloped the workhorses down toward the branch, pulling up at the gypsy wagon. Over the months, Danya had erected a cooking and eating tent, a small work shed to hold tools, and a small barn for his horses. Just down the rise, he had constructed an outhouse.

As Nate whistled, Danya bounded from the shed, waving at Nate and Abbie as he jogged over to the sled. He was carrying two leather straps strung with bells. He hung the silver sleigh bells from the harness around the necks of the horses and then hopped into the back of the sled. Once he was holding on to the back of the seat, Nathan galloped the horses back toward the cabin and around the rear of the barn.

"Danya, let's put on the high sideboards," he said. "Here, help me out."

The high sideboards! Abbie thought. *This means Pa's plannin' a bigger job than I had hoped.* She felt even more dejected.

"I'll do it, Mr. Nate!" Danya protested.

Nate nodded. As Danya lifted the first sideboard, Nathan indicated it was time for Abbie to get down. "We need to help Danya fill the sled with wood," he said.

Danya gave Abbie a mysterious smile as the three of them turned toward the woodshed. They each carried armloads of chopped wood to the sled.

Abbie turned toward the sled. "What are we doin', Pa?"

"Tell ya what. Instead of carryin' wood, Abbie, you load Danya's arms," Nate commanded dismissively. "As much as he can carry. We'll fill the sled in no time at all."

Danya carried armload after armload to the sled, dropping it in the wagon for Nate to arrange, until the sled was loaded to a point that Abbie wondered if the horses would even be able to pull it. Finally, her pa declared the job done.

"Danya, go to the dry barn and grab a sack of flour and a sack of corn. Abbie, you come help me."

Abbie followed her pa over to the smokehouse. Once inside, the delicious fragrances made her mouth water. Her pa chose a big ham, put it in a burlap bag, and handed it to her to carry while he shouldered a side of bacon and then picked up their tom turkey in his arm. After putting the sumptuous delicacies in the back of the sled, he got onto the seat as Danya loaded the two seventy-five-pound meal sacks onto the back of the sled. Then Danya jumped up and sat on the pile of logs and bags in the back.

Once they were settled, Nate slapped the reins as the large Percheron workhorses strained against the heavy load. When they reached the Sugar Fork Branch, instead of turning downstream toward Hazel Creek, Nate pulled the reins to head upstream.

"Pa," Abbie said, no longer able to contain her curiosity, "where in the world are we goin'?"

51

Gift

As the Percherons leaned against their large harnesses, the silver bells ringing, pulling the heavy sled uphill, Nate responded. "Punkin, last week Danya and I crossed over into the Eagle Creek valley to hunt—"

"Pa, after what happened over there to Mr. Post, I don't rightly hanker to you goin' over there anymore. Seems too risky."

Her pa smiled. "That's why I take Danya with me. Right, Danya?"

"Yep," Danya said.

"Anyway, when we were over there, we stopped by the Post cabin."

Abbie nodded. Her mama would take the girls over to the Post homestead once a year or so to visit. Joseph and Paula had three young children. After receiving the terrible news that Joseph had been shot and killed, Zach and Doc Keller investigated and concluded that someone had shot him in the back of the head with a .22 pistol, but they could find no evidence to arrest anyone—so the case went cold. But the rumor up and down the creek was that someone in one of the lumber companies that was working the watershed had killed him in cold blood—and the gossips insisted the killer was one L. G. Sanders or one of his henchmen. It would not have been the first time such a thing had happened in the region.

"Turns out Mrs. Post ain't doin' so well. Their woodpile is about gone, and accordin' to the almanac, this winter's only just begun— and it's gonna be a fierce one. Her oldest boy, Jimmy, is only six and can't be much help. She's sold a few of her choicer trees, but the company over there didn't pay her much. She's in a hurtin' way. I . . . well . . . I just thought we might help her out a bit."

Abbie blew out an exasperated breath, propelling some of her wayward hair from her eyes.

"What's the matter, Punkin?"

She crossed her arms and turned her head.

"You angry about somethin'? About me givin' away some of our wood . . . or our tom turkey?"

Abbie only shook her head. *I so wanted that dress this Christmas*, she thought. *It ain't right!* The lost dream of getting a Christmas dress piled on top of the incessant grief she felt from losing her mama made her feel like her soul was drifting without an anchor. She knew what it was like to lose a parent. *I know how hard it is to get by. But it ain't right for Pa to take them gifts and not give me mine!*

As their pace picked up, Abbie felt something hit her foot. She looked down and noticed three sacks bouncing under the seat. For some reason, she had not noticed them before.

"What's in the sacks, Pa?" Abbie asked. She was sure she knew the answer and was sure her irritation carried into her voice.

"In one sack we have boots. When Danya and I were up there at the Post place, we saw them kids didn't have proper shoes. What they wore had more holes than a colander. It's a wonder they haven't gotten frostbit. And their coats were in tatters. Ready for the quilt bin if you ask me. So, I took some of our savin's and paid Maria, Reba Johnson, and Linda Pyeritz to make a pair of lamb shearlin' boots and a coat for each child . . . and a nice pair of boots for Mrs. Post. And the other two sacks . . . well, they contain nuts, fruit, and candy from Calhoun. Danya's gonna play Santa, aren't you, Danya?"

HAZEL CREEK   *313*

"Yes!" Danya said, laughing.

Abbie didn't see the humor. "Are those our gifts, Pa? The sacks Calhoun gave the girls?"

"Calhoun?" Danya said.

Abbie turned to him. "Yes. Each year Calhoun decorates a large Christmas tree down in front of the town church."

"It's somethin' to see," Nate commented. "Covered with fancy glass balls and tinsel."

"And under that huge tree, Danya, Calhoun places a gift for every child in Hazel Creek what's under fourteen."

"What's he give?" Danya said.

Abbie answered, "A bag chock full of apples, oranges, nuts, and candy. And if a family won't come to town to pick up the gift, Calhoun has his men load 'em on the train and take 'em up the valley to any child that didn't get one. So, Dr. Keller brought up four bags, one for Whit, Corrie, Anna, and Sarah." Abbie turned to her pa as anger began to bubble up again. "And now you're givin' away *their* gifts? How can ya, Pa?"

Nate was quiet a moment. "Well . . . I figured we could spare a couple of the bags. I mean, we were given *four* of 'em."

"But Pa!" Abbie said, "They belong to the girls. Not you!"

Nate just stared forward.

She felt her face warming with emotion. "And besides, don't the Posts have neighbors that live closer to them than us? Why don't *they* help them? Why give *our* gifts?"

Abbie saw her pa's jaw flinch. He was getting angry himself.

Finally, in almost a whisper, he turned to her and said, "You know, Abbie, if Sanders or Knight had their way, you wouldn't have a pa, either. If that's ever the case, I would hope and pray that our neighbors would be sure that you girls were cared for and that you would have a nice Christmas. The Post kids don't have a pa, and I just thought it wouldn't be Christmas for them without a few gifts and a bit of candy."

A chilly silence ensued as they each were enmeshed in their

own thoughts. After a few miles of going uphill, the horses snorted as the wagon crested Welch Ridge and headed downhill. Finally, Abbie sighed and turned to her pa. "I apologize for my anger, Pa. It wasn't right of me."

She felt his arm encircle her shoulder and pull her close. "Punkin, you're forgiven." He gave her a hug. "What's one thing you can do to make me love you more?"

Abbie felt herself smile. She knew the answer to this question as he often asked it of her. "Nothin'," she answered.

"That's right. And what's one thing you can do to make me love you less."

"Not get so angry at you?"

Nate laughed. "Well, that would be nice, but, nope. The correct answer is nothin'. Nothin' you can do to make your pa love you less."

She lay her head on his chest.

"You kinda remind me of old Joseph in the 'Cherry Tree Carol,'" her pa said. "You remember it?"

Of course she did. It was one of her favorite Christmas carols. But she had no idea what it had to do with her anger. Her pa began to sing it:

As Joseph and Mary were a-walkin' the green
There were apples and cherries there to be seen.
And then Mary said to Joseph so meek and so mild:
Gather me some cherries, Joseph, for I am with child.

He stopped for a moment. "You gonna join me?" Not waiting for her answer, he continued:

Then Joseph said to Mary so rough and unkind:
Let the daddy of the baby get the cherries for thine.

He laughed. "Sounds like Joseph was angry, eh? Like you?"

Abbie remained silent, but admired how her pa hit the nail on the head. *He can read me like a book.*

Then the baby spoke out of its mother's womb:
Bow down you lofty cherry trees, let my mammy have some.
Then the cherry tree bent and it bowed like a bow,
So that Mary picked cherries from the uppermost bough.
Then Joseph took Mary all on his left knee,
Sayin': Lord have mercy on me and what I have done.

"Come on, Abbie. Join me!" Nate encouraged.
Abbie reluctantly joined in as she watched the trees pass by.

Then Joseph took Mary all on his right knee,
Sayin': O my little Savior, when your birthday shall be,
The hills and high mountains shall bow unto thee.
Then the baby spoke out of its mother's womb:
On old Christmas morning my birthday shall be,
When the hills and high mountains shall bow unto me.

Her pa leaned over and gave her a hug. "You know what that carol's about?"

Abbie shook her head, wondering what he was getting at.

"Joseph became angry because he didn't know the whole picture yet. But later he found out and when he did, I bet he was plum ashamed for his anger. And as a testament to the lesson he learned, the cherry trees still bow their branches for us to pick their fruit."

Abbie pondered his words, as their meaning began to sink into her heart.

He was quiet for a few moments and then said, "Abbie, I kept this trip a secret from ya. I wanted it to surprise ya and I wanted ya to be part of the surprise for the Posts. I *did* talk to Whit and Corrie about it. Both of them volunteered their gift bags—freely and happily. I coulda gone to town and purchased a couple of those bags—Barnes has them at his store. But your sisters wanted to be part of the surprise. They wanted to be part of the givin'."

Now Abbie felt perfectly ashamed of herself. Her pa's words struck deep and a wave of conviction pierced her heart. She turned to look at the passing trees as hot tears streamed down her cheeks. She could imagine nothing worse for a child than having a parent murdered—except maybe being an orphan. *How could I be so selfish?* she wondered.

"Forgive me?" she asked.

"Already have," he responded. "You're forgiven and it's forgotten."

52

Deliverance

No one spoke as they rode the final two miles down the trail toward the Post homestead.

Abbie continued to feel bad. Finally her pa put his arm around her and pulled her next to him. She felt a surge of gratitude to the Lord for him. She leaned against him, feeling a wave of warm comfort come over her. The only sounds were the occasional gusts blowing through the trees and the rhythmic beat of the silver bells as they trotted down the trail.

Abbie noticed that either Danya or her pa had placed sprigs of holly berries as decoration on the top of the horses' bridles between their ears, and it made her smile. Suddenly she felt better, her heart lighter, as she knew her pa was correct—their mission was the exact right thing to do. *Besides*, she thought, *there's plenty of fruit and candy in the remainin' two gift bags to share with all of my sisters!*

At last they reached the wagon trail leading up to the Posts' cabin, and the horses leaned into the yoke until they reached the homestead clearing. The sun was just beginning to drop in the western sky as Nate reined the horses up toward the cabin. The horses' snorts and the silver bells announced their approach, and Jimmy opened the door as the sled pulled up to the front of the cabin. He had a rifle in his hands.

"Who's there?" the boy cried out.

"It's Nathan Randolph, Jimmy. Me and my daughter Abbie and our friend, Danya. Mind if we come in?" Nate shouted as he pulled the sled to a halt.

The door cracked open a bit more and a woman looked out. Recognizing them, she smiled and patted her son's shoulder. "Jimmy, it's the Randolphs from over on Hazel Creek." She looked back at the visitors. "Come in! Come out of the cold. Welcome!"

As Abbie entered the cabin, she noticed how cold it was inside—unlike the warmth she was used to in their cabin. Mrs. Post had a thick blanket around her shoulders and the two younger children were sitting on a bearskin, covered by a quilt, in front of a fireplace that contained only a few small coals—not nearly large enough to heat the cabin. Jimmy placed the rifle on a rack by the door as Nathan entered the cabin and closed the door.

Mrs. Post lit a lamp with trembling hands and then fumbled to adjust the flame. "Sorry it's so dark and cold in here," she apologized. "We're a bit low on wood and kerosene this year."

She turned to face them, and Abbie could see the embarrassment in her eyes. "Won't you take off your coats?" Looking at Nate she said, "Where's your friend? What's his name?"

"Daniel," Nathan said. "But we all call him *Danya*. And before we take off our coats, Paula, I'd like to bring a few things in."

Before she could reply, Nate turned and left.

"Please, Abbie. Have a seat."

Abbie sat on a bench by the fireplace. There was virtually no warmth coming from it.

Then the door burst open. "Children, I have a surprise!"

The children spun around to face Nate. Seeing that he was carrying a ham and an enormous tom turkey, they leaped off their chairs, cheering, and raced toward him, causing him to laugh.

"What a wonderful surprise!" Paula exclaimed.

"The surprise is not the meat, Paula. Here, this is the surprise. Santa is here!"

The children turned to face the door as they heard a sonorous tenor crying out, "Ho, ho, ho!" Stooping to enter the cabin, in strode Danya, wearing a red cap, and a red blanket rimmed with a border of white lamb's wool draping his shoulders.

Abbie smiled as she saw his beard had been streaked with white kaolin. In his massive arms, he carried two of the gift sacks and the side of bacon on top of a large pile of wood. Danya's smile radiated. "Ho, ho, ho!" he cried again.

A smile spread across the widow's face as tears streaked down her cheeks.

Nate laid the meat on the kitchen table. "Children, get the wood from Santa and stoke the fire. Abbie, get the gift sacks from Santa and let the children open 'em."

The children ran over to Danya, who squatted down as they took the goodies from his arms. Danya beamed as he continued to say, "Ho, ho, ho!"

"Come on, Santa, let's go get the rest!" Nathan instructed.

Abbie helped the children put wood on the fire and then open the bags of candy, nuts, and fruit. At the same time she watched as Mrs. Post walked over to the meat, stretched out her trembling fingers and touched it, then brought her hand to her nose. As she slowly breathed in the delicious scent of the smoked meat, she closed her eyes and smiled.

As the wood began to catch fire, warmth began to spread across the cabin, which almost immediately began to grow lighter and brighter—as if daybreak was beginning to shatter a frozen forlorn winter night—as if the cowardly darkness was racing to hide from the comforting warmness of light.

When Santa and Nathan reentered the cabin, carrying the sacks of flour and corn, the children again cheered as their mother's mouth fell open. She gasped and brought her hand up to her mouth.

The men placed the bags on the floor against the side of the cabin.

"Corn and flour for the children," Danya said. "From Santa!"

He smiled as the children ran over to hug him. "That's not all," he added. He handed Mrs. Post the sacks containing the boots and coats. "Mrs. Claus and our elves made these for your family."

She reached out and took the bag from his hand. As she hesitantly opened the drawstring, she once again gasped, slowly sat down on a bench beside the kitchen table, and removed the boots and coats one at a time.

Abbie watched as Mrs. Post bit her lower lip to try to control its quivering. As she gazed at the items, tears filled her eyes and once again began to tumble down her cheeks. She looked up from Nathan to Danya to Abbie as if she wanted to say something, but no words would come.

"Tell her what else we brought, Abbie," Nathan instructed, pointing with his thumb over his shoulder, toward the door.

Abbie smiled. "Pa and Dan . . . er . . . Santa has brought a sled full of wood."

"Abbie, while Santa and I unload the wood for Mrs. Post, why don't you help the children with their boots and coats. And then you children can try them out by bringin' in enough wood to fill the wood box."

Abbie insisted that each child try on his or her boots and coat before going outside into the cold and snow. She was amazed that each one fit perfectly. She wondered how the ladies had known what sizes to make—how they had guessed so correctly about the boot sizes just from her pa and Danya's description.

Abbie again felt a deep conviction about her own selfishness. *How could I not want to be here . . . doin' this?* And then she felt a smile spreading across her face as a warmth filled the cabin and her soul—as she both remembered and experienced the reality of the words of Jesus, which she mouthed. *It* is *more blessed to give than to receive.*

53

Homeward

The rest of their time in the cabin was a blur of memories that Abbie knew would last a lifetime. Several times her eyes filled with tears and a lump developed in her throat. She laughed watching the children open the bags of nuts, fruit, and candy—the gifts from her sisters. She felt her heart swell with a joy she had never known before.

She remembered watching the children run around the cabin in the perfect-fitting comfortable boots, and observing their ma standing there in her new boots, radiating gratitude, and still unable to speak.

Abbie always enjoyed giving gifts, but could never remember any gifts that had so much effect or made so much difference. She sensed in her soul that these gifts might literally save the lives of this destitute family as they struggled not only against one of the bitterest winters in memory, but also against poverty caused by a heartless lumber company.

As the fire blazed, so did each child's spirit. They giggled as Santa told stories about his elves, who he claimed were actually the "Little People" reputed to live in remote hollows in the Smokies. The children inquired about Mrs. Santa, and Abbie laughed as he described his sister making their boots, while Mrs. Post looked on with an ear-to-ear smile.

Mrs. Post finally gathered the children around her, took

their family Bible down from the mantel, and gave it to Nate to read the Christmas story from the Gospel of Luke. After the story, Nate and Danya led several Christmas carols. As they finished with the "Cherry Tree Carol," Abbie couldn't keep her tears back anymore. They tumbled down her cheeks as the group formed a circle, holding hands. To her delight, her pa led in prayer.

As they were putting on their coats to leave, Mrs. Post said, "God bless you, each of you. You are an answer to our prayers. I know the Lord sent you. Nathan Randolph, you are an angel." She hugged him and then turned to Danya. "You, sir . . . well, you are an archangel, or at least the biggest angel I've ever seen. So, bend over and lemme hug you." Her smile radiated as she laughed and hugged his neck.

Danya took each of the kids in his big arms and gave them a hug, saying, "Ho, ho, ho." They clung to him—even Jimmy—as if they didn't want him to ever leave.

Paula turned to hug Abbie and whispered in her ear, "Thank you, Abbie. I guess I don't have to say, 'May the Lord bless you,' for you and I know that pure religion is carin' for the widow and the orphan. You've done that today, sweet sister. Therefore, I know for certain that he *will* bless you."

On the sled ride home, Abbie didn't even notice the biting cold wind. Rather, she basked in the bright light of myriad stars sparkling in the dark night sky of a new moon and savored the warmth of a thousand happy memories welling up from her soul.

As they crossed the ridge and the horses trotted into the Hazel Creek valley, her pa turned to her. "Punkin, you need to know somethin'."

He took a deep breath, and the steam formed in the air as he let it out. "I had been savin' a bit of money away to buy you somethin' special this year. But after Danya and I saw the Posts . . . well . . . I just knew I needed to give that money to the ladies for the boots and coats. I know it was the right thing to do, Punkin. I spent the money I was savin' for you for the Posts. I hope that you'll find it in your heart to forgive me."

Abbie could not have been happier. She scooted closer to him and he put his arm around her.

"Of course, Pa." She remembered a memorized verse from her childhood: "If thou wilt be perfect, go and sell that thou hast, and give to the poor, and thou shalt have treasure in heaven"—words she understood now in a fresh new way.

"Besides," he said, chuckling under his breath, "we can always trade us one of our cherry trees for a new dress. Yes?"

"We could buy a fancy house in town for what Sanders would have to pay us for one of our cherry trees, Pa."

She felt him hug her.

"But I think I'd rather have those trees as they are than any old dress that's simply gonna fray and wear out over time."

"If your mama's lookin' down right now, I 'spect she's mighty proud of her oldest."

For the rest of Abbie's life, whenever she saw a lamb-shearling boot or coat, or a molasses-soaked ham, or a smoked tom turkey, or a sled full of chopped wood, she would feel inner warmth . . . remembering the joy she felt riding home beside her pa that night.

After the girls were tucked into bed, Abbie changed, fed, and swaddled Sarah Beth as she and her pa talked about their remarkable day.

As she hugged him good night, he said, "One more thing, Punkin. Take a look under your ma's pillow. I do have an early Christmas present for you."

Abbie was not surprised that he kept her mama's pillow on his bed. He had been very pleased when he learned she had not burned it with the rest of their bed linens from her mama's deathbed. She suspected he was clinging to the memory of where they had last slept—where her head had last rested.

Abbie reached over and lifted up the pillow, seeing under it a small velvet-covered box. "What is it, Pa?"

"You'll have to open it to find out."

She held it gingerly in both hands, pausing a moment, wondering what it might be. Then she slowly opened the top of the box, and sitting in it was a silver band. She immediately recognized the Edwardian wedding ring trimmed in milgrain and highlighted with an intricate fine-carved pattern that had been her mama's.

She gently lifted the ring and looked inside; she could read the engraved inscription with her mother's and father's initials and their wedding date: *NHR to CJR 08/01/08.*

Abbie looked at her pa, tears filling her eyes. "Mama's?"

Nate nodded.

"I thought it was buried with her!"

Nate's lower lip trembled. "I want it to live on with us, just like her memory."

Abbie looked back down at the ring she had admired on her mama's finger for her entire life. Slowly, she handed it to her pa.

"Will you do the honors?"

He smiled, took the ring, and slipped it on her left ring finger.

"It fits perfectly!" Abbie said.

"You can keep it on until some young man presents you with another."

Abbie slowly shook her head. "No, Pa. I'll *never* take this one off." As she hugged him, she began to weep. "Never, ever."

54

First Footer

"Why black-eyed peas?" Maria asked as Whit stirred the slowly simmering pot over the fire in the Randolphs' cabin.

"It's an old Southern tradition," Abbie said.

Whit continued, "We have them on New Year's Eve, but many say they should be the first food eaten on New Year's Day—that is, if you want luck and prosperity throughout the year ahead."

"My ma taught us that the practice of eatin' them for luck dates back to the Civil War," Maddie said as she chopped vegetables.

"Before the Great War, black-eyed peas were planted primarily as food for livestock," Grace explained. "Later, they became a food staple for slaves in the South. As a result, General Sherman and his troops ignored the fields of black-eyed peas. They destroyed or stole other crops, thereby giving the humble, but nourishing, black-eyed pea an important role as a major food source for the surviving Confederates. At least that's what Grandpa Lumpkin taught us down in Georgia where I grew up."

"Where in Georgia?" Abbie said.

"Why, Lumpkin County, of course," Grace replied, laughing.

Corrie said, "We serve 'em with greens—"

"Yep," Whit interrupted. "Sometimes collards and other times mustard or turnip greens."

"Remember," Abbie said. "Mama told us the peas represent coins, and the greens represent paper money. In the lumber camp they use cabbage in place of the greens. But we believe that's bad luck."

"Don't forget the corn bread," Whit said. "It represents gold."

"And," Corrie added, "for the best chance of luck every day in the year ahead, a girl's gotta eat at least three hundred and sixty-five black-eyed peas."

"This is all almost too much for me to remember," Maria said, laughing.

Maddie looked at her. "What were some New Year's Day traditions in Russia?"

"Russian New Year traditions include a New Year's Tree, which we called *Novogodnaya Yolka*. The tree is decorated with sweets and has a bright star on top. Another tradition is the arrival of Father Frost along with his granddaughter Snegurochka, the snow girl. Children wait for them as they bring New Year presents and keep them under the New Year's Tree. To make Father Frost happy, children sing songs."

"Okay," Abbie continued. "Here's the penny." She handed it to Maria.

"For what? Is this my pay?" Maria said, laughing.

"No, silly," Abbie said. "Mama would always add a shiny penny to the pot just before servin'. It's another Randolph tradition. Then when served, the one whose bowl contains the penny receives the best luck for the New Year."

"Unless, of course," Corrie said, "the person swallows the coin, which would be a terrible way to start off the year."

Everyone laughed.

"In Russia," Maria said, "men and women kiss at midnight. By kissing the person dearest to you right at midnight, you are guaranteed that the relationship will continue throughout the next year. In fact, if you don't kiss someone at the stroke of twelve, you'll gain only a year of coldness and misfortune."

"Then Abbie, we must kiss tonight," Bobby Lee said as he entered the room with an armful of wood for the firebox.

"Why wait?" Corrie said.

"Corrie!" Abbie cried.

"Girls, girls," Grace cautioned.

"The last several years," Maria said, "I've only had Danya's cheek to kiss. But I'm hoping to have another man to kiss by the next New Year."

"Who?" Whit asked. "Sheriff Taylor?"

Maria only smiled.

"I've been noticin' he's been comin' up here a bit more to see you," Abbie said.

"I think he's sweet on you, Miss Maria," Bobby Lee added.

"Time to change the subject," Maria ordered, smiling.

"Here's another one from Georgia," Grace said. "We call it *first footing*. It means that the first person to enter your home after the stroke of midnight will influence the entire year that's coming up. So, in my mind, he should be dark-haired, tall, and handsome."

"Like Bobby Lee," Corrie kidded.

"It's even better, Corrie," Grace instructed, "if he comes bearing certain small gifts such as a silver coin, a bit of bread, a sprig of evergreen, and some salt. Blond and redhead first footers bring bad luck, and female first footers should be shooed away before they bring disaster down on the household. My father would aim a gun at them if he had to, but he would never let a woman near his door in the New Year before a man first crossed his threshold."

"I've never heard such a thing," Maria said.

"Ah, the first footer is also called the *Lucky Bird* and should knock and be let in rather than unceremoniously use a key. Also, after greeting those in the house and dropping off whatever small tokens of luck he has brought with him, he should make his way through the house and leave by a different door than the one through which he entered. No one should leave the premises before the first footer arrives, for the first traffic across the threshold must be headed in rather than striking out."

"Bobby Lee," Maria said, "since you're tall and handsome and have that dark hair, I suggest we station you just outside the door near midnight to ensure you are the first footer as soon as the mantel-clock chimes sound."

"I'll volunteer," Bobby Lee said, "as long as Mr. Randolph will lemme stay."

The girls all clapped.

"In Russia, we also let the Old Year out at midnight. No matter how cold, all the doors of the house must be opened right at midnight to let the Old Year escape. We believe the Old Year must leave before the New Year can come in. In some homes, not only are the doors flung open, but also all the windows. It helps him in finding his way out."

"And don't forget," Grace added, "we're to make as much noise as possible at midnight. We're not just celebrating; we're scaring away all the evil spirits, so we must do a good job of it!"

"That's right," Maddie added. "Evil spirits and even the devil himself are said to hate loud noise. By makin' as much of a din as possible, we make sure Old Scratch and his minions don't stick around."

"That's the same reason church bells are rung on a couple's weddin' day," Whit said, nodding her head.

"And," said Nate as he entered the cabin, "don't forget the weather."

"That's right!" Maddie said. "If just after midnight the wind is blowin' from the south, there will be fine weather and prosperous times in the year ahead."

"But," Nate added, "if it comes from the north, it will be a year of bad weather and bad luck."

"What about if it's from the east?" Corrie wondered out loud.

"The wind blowin' from the east brings famine and calamities," Maddie explained. "But the strangest of all is this, if the wind blows from the west, the year will see plentiful supplies of milk and fish but will also see the death of a very important person."

"And," Nate added, "if there's no wind at all, a joyful and prosperous year may be expected by all. So, here's to a windless midnight. Although," he said, pushing the door shut against the blustery wind, "it don't look very likely."

"Well," Abbie said, her hands on her hips, "I don't take to all the superstitions. Like the Good Book says, 'Choose you this day whom ye will serve . . . but as for me and my house, we will serve the Lord.'"

"That's perfectly fine," Maddie said, chuckling, "but let's just be sure Bobby Lee crosses the threshold at midnight, as the windows and doors fly open, carryin' good-luck gifts, a bowl of black-eyed peas with greens and corn bread—"

"And," Maria added, "no wind at his back." The group applauded and laughed as they continued the dinner preparation.

55

Eleventh Day

The Twelfth Day of Christmas was always a special day for the Randolphs. Of course, on the church calendar it was the last day of Christmastide, the days between Christmas and Epiphany, which was on January 6—tomorrow.

The day dawned without a cloud in the sky. The air was crisp, clear, and a cold thirty degrees. But all of the signs promised a high in the forties, and it was a glorious break between the blizzards that Nate expected would continue into March. And for the girls, there was still a week before school would start again.

Yesterday, Maria and Whit had been put in charge of baking the Three Kings' Cake, which everyone would enjoy after dinner on Epiphany—celebrating the end of the twelve-day journey of the Magi to Bethlehem to visit the baby Jesus. The cake, in the shape of a Christmas wreath, would contain a tiny metal baby or coin—symbolizing the baby Jesus. The person receiving the piece of cake with the baby would be called *king* or *queen of the feast* and would for the rest of the evening wear a paper crown the girls made.

After breakfast and the chores were complete, Nate was working with Danya, Abbie, and Corrie to load the sled with firewood. Nate wanted to get another load over to the Posts' cabin before any more bad weather set in. He figured that this load, added to their Christmas Eve delivery, would give them enough wood to last well past the winter blizzards. And he had worked with Pastor Semmes to collect gifts from other families in the community that they would bring with them today. In addition, the pastor had contacted a sister congregation in Eagle Creek that agreed to check on and care for the family the rest of the winter.

As they loaded the sled, the girls were trying to teach Danya the lyrics to "The Twelve Days of Christmas" song, which they enjoyed singing each evening during Christmastide.

"Which of the twelve gifts would you want, Danya?" Abbie said.

Danya thought a moment and then smiled. "Danya would like a maid a-milking or a dancing lady. Either would be nice—or maybe both!"

"One wife in a cabin is quite enough," Nate said, laughing. "Two would be entirely too many."

"How about you, Abbie?" Danya said as he dropped a massive load of wood into the sled.

"The golden rings would be my choice," she said.

"You'd be happy with just one," Corrie kidded, "if'n it came from Bobby Lee. Right?"

Abbie laughed.

"For myself, I'd like a lord a-leapin'," Corrie said. "As long as he was a true lord and truly rich."

"Corrie, we're already rich in so many ways," Nate commented.

Corrie smiled. "A little more never hurts, Pa."

"I swan, child," Nate said, "the Good Book says our conduct should be without covetousness; that we are to be content with such things as we have. Like my pa used to always say, 'If ya ain't content with what ya have, you'll ne'r be content with what ya want.' So, I hope you're not developin' a love of money."

"Why not, Pa?"

"It's like the Good Book says, Precious: 'For the love of money is the root of all evil.'"

"Where's it say that?" Corrie said.

"It's in first Timothy, chapter six, and verse ten," Abbie responded. "I think that would be a good one for you to remember, sister."

"I prefer first Corinthians, chapter twelve, and verse thirty-one," Corrie said.

"What's that one say, Corrie?" Danya inquired.

"It says, 'but covet earnestly the best gifts.' So, followin' the Bible mandate, I'm gonna marry a man that can give me the best gifts—like coffee and candy—and who can take me to all the big cities where his baseball team is a-playin'. While he's a-playin', I tell ya, I'll be a-shoppin'. You can be sure!"

"You're a mess!" Nate exclaimed as they all laughed.

After they loaded the sled, Nate and Danya sat on the front seat, while Abbie arranged a quilt on the pile of wood to serve as her seat and a warm, protective coat for the trip up valley. Nate slapped the reins and giddied the horses toward the long driveway down to the Sugar Fork. Just before they turned onto the main road from their land, heading up toward Welch Ridge and Eagle Creek, they saw Zach and Bobby Lee riding up the trail toward them.

"Welcome!" Nate shouted as he pulled the horses to a halt to wait for the Taylors to ride up.

"Howdy, Nate," Zach said. "Happy Epiphany eve to you and yours."

Bobby Lee smiled and waved to Abbie, who could not have been more delighted if Father Christmas himself had arrived.

"And yours!" Nate responded.

"Pastor spread the word you all were headed over to the Post cabin to make a delivery."

Nate nodded.

"Actually, we're headed the same way. I heard a tale about some men camped up on the ridge that may be up to no good. So, Bobby Lee and me are off to investigate. Mind if we ride up with you?"

Abbie could see that they each had a rifle in a scabbard strapped to their saddles, and Zach had a pistol on each hip.

"Would enjoy havin' you'uns ride along," Nate said. "And I'm sure Abbie wouldn't mind. That right, Punkin?"

Abbie felt herself blush as her pa laughed.

Bobby Lee dismounted, grabbed his rifle, and tied the reins to the back of the wagon. "Abbie, if'n you don't mind, I'll just sit by ya and hold ya tight so ya don't fall off the sled and get left behind. Wouldn't want your pa to lose my girl!" He smiled at Abbie as he hopped onto the pile of wood and sat by her.

"Well, now that we're all settled, we're off!" Nate said as he reined the Percherons up the trail.

Bobby Lee pulled Abbie close as he laughed.

As they approached the top of the ridge, both Percherons snorted and balked. Nate tried to rein them in, but then saw their concern, as a tree appeared to have fallen across the trail.

"There's an ax under the seat there, Danya," Nate said. "Guess we'll need to chop a path for the sled."

Zach rode up, dismounted, and tied his horse up to the back of the sled. Abbie was surprised to see him pulling his rifle out as she and Bobby Lee climbed down, prepared to help Danya and her pa.

As the group approached the tree, Danya said, "I'll make short order of this. Guess the snow was too much for her."

"Nope," Nate said, walking toward the stump. "Looks like she's been chopped down." He looked into the woods and Abbie saw him pull his coat back, exposing the handle of his pistol. "I wonder why?" he said to no one in particular as he squatted down to inspect the stump. "Looks fairly recent, too." Small puffs of smoke rose from his pipe as he ran his hand over the stump.

Before anyone heard the crack of the rifle, Nate's pipe shattered into pieces, and a gravelly voice commanded, "Drop the ax, gypsy.

The rest of you put your hands up! Anyone who doesn't put his hands up will be shot through the heart!"

Nate looked around for the source of the command as another shot came. Just then Nate's hat flew off, and all hands flew into the air. Four rifles were pointing at them from behind the trunk of several massive trees.

"Sheriff Taylor, drop your rifle, or I'll drop you."

Abbie watched her pa glaring at their ambushers' guns.

"Now!"

Zach squatted down, placed his rifle on the ground, and then stood up.

"Randolph, Sheriff, drop the pistols!"

Nate put his pistol on the top of the hard-packed snow and watched Zach pull back the left edge of his coat, revealing his pistol.

"Slowly!" a voice commanded.

Zach pulled it out and slowly laid it down.

"Didn't know you were left-handed, Sheriff," the voice said. "I've always found that the cack-handed are a bit more feeble and simpleminded. So, I guess I shouldn't be surprised you're a southpaw."

As Zach and Nate stood, the four men walked out from the brush hiding the base of the tree. Abbie gasped as she recognized the Stetson shadowing a bright red goatee. But the shock of seeing Knight again paled to her astonishment when she recognized one of the other men carrying a rifle.

"Is that who I think it is?" Bobby Lee whispered.

"Oh my goodness!" Abbie gasped.

56

Retribution

"Josiah Simmons," Zach growled. "Surprised to see a snake like you outside of its den on a cold winter day. Isn't it a bit inclement for a city boy like you to be out here in a man's wilderness?"

Simmons aimed the rifle at the sheriff, but Mr. Knight pushed his rifle barrel down toward the ground. "Not yet, Simmons. Leave this to me."

The ambushers walked toward the locals, but stopped at a safe distance of ten paces or so.

"What's your business?" Zach said.

"Just come to deal out a bit of reprisal, to deliver a bit of delayed justice," Simmons said.

"I believe that's my job," Zach said sternly.

"If you had done your job, Randolph here would be in jail, and I'd still have my job and my reputation. So, I suppose you're disqualified for this type of work now. That's why I've hired some men who can help me finish what needs done."

Knight kept his eyes fixed on Zach and Nate. Abbie knew he was a cold, heartless man and suspected he could shoot a man through the heart without a second thought.

"We heard you all were coming this way, Randolph," Knight said. "I am deeply thankful to your gossiping pastor for clueing us in to your trip of mercy. But imagine my surprise when I saw you all *and* Taylor riding up the trail toward us together. It was too good to be true."

"Guess it's your lucky day," Nate said, glaring back.

"But not yours, Randolph. I was planning to meet you in your barn and take care of business there, just like I did with your daughter. The difference is that you would not be walking out as she did."

Nate shot a look at Abbie, who couldn't look him in the eyes but kept staring at the men. Nate turned back to Knight. "You sound mighty sure of yourself."

"I am," he said, and before anyone could react, Knight aimed his rifle and pulled the trigger, causing an explosion of snow and ice just in front of Nate's right boot. He jerked back a step as the shot echoed across the ridge.

"That leaves me enough bullets in the magazine to put one in each of you."

"Why don't we just take Taylor and Randolph and send the others away?" Simmons asked. "I don't have business with the kids or the gypsy."

"Not on your life, Simmons. I have business with the gypsy. And the kids could be witnesses against us. We're just going to have to lay all of them down. We'll make it look like a small-time robbery. They happen all the time around here. In this cold, your bodies won't decompose any. And folks cross the ridge enough that they'll be found soon."

"We can't kill 'em, Knight!" Simmons cried out. "I hired you and your two men to help me get revenge on the two. Nothing more. Just want them beat up real good."

"I'm afraid you'll be getting more than you bargained for, old man," Knight snarled.

"You can't kill 'em, Reginald."

"Why not?"

"Because I said so! And I'm paying the freight on this job,"

Simmons said as he walked up to Knight and tried to speak so as not to be heard by anyone else, but his voice carried. "I hired you to scare these men. Beat them up a bit—in fact, as much as you want. Get me a bit of retribution, but keep them alive. You hear me?"

Simmons backed away as he commanded Knight. "Now you do what I say!"

"Or what?" Knight said.

Simmons lifted up his rifle. But before he could reply, Knight whipped out his pistol and aimed it at Simmons. The bullet blew through his brain and flung him back in a crumpled heap on the snow. Abbie screamed and Bobby Lee wrapped his arms around her. Nate, Zach, and Danya all stepped forward as the three remaining men with rifles turned and aimed at them.

"You all stand down!" Knight instructed. "Simmons always was a coward—that's why he could only beat on children. I knew he did not have the fortitude to carry out what needs to be done. But do not be mistaken—me and my men do."

"Let Danya and the children go, Knight," Nate requested. "I'll have them give a vow of silence—to you, to me, and to the Lord. Their word will be good."

"Can't take that chance, Randolph."

"A few months ago, I showed you and Sanders mercy when you'uns were rustlin' my tree. I could've put a hole through your heart and no one would have thought nothin' 'bout it. I reckon I'm askin' you to show the same to me and let the children and Danya go."

"Randolph, you didn't show me any mercy when you cold-cocked me in the boxing ring. A right illegal blow if you ask me."

"It was a fair fight and you know it."

"I do not see it exactly the same way, Randolph. And lumbermen are still snickering about it. A man does not embarrass me and live to talk about it. And you, gypsy, you didn't show me any mercy when you about strangled me on my company's property—land on which you were trespassing. Both of you men have made what I consider fatal mistakes."

"Okay, Zach and I will deal with you'uns—man-to-man. But let Danya and the children go."

"You know the Old Testament story of Jehoram?" Knight said.

"What's a king of Judah got to do with this?" said Nate.

"When he became king, he killed all his brothers and some of the princes of Israel to keep them from dethroning him. There is no need to leave folks behind to seek revenge, is there?"

"I'm *not* leaving this place," Nate heard Danya bark. "Let the children go!" the large man commanded.

"I do not think I will be able to accommodate your request, gypsy, but thanks for the offer." Knight stepped onto the trail, out of the deeper snow. He slipped a bit on the ice of the trail, but quickly recovered. "All right, here is my offer. You each keep your hands up. I want you to turn around and walk to the edge of the trail. Then I want you to sit down with your hands clasped behind your heads."

For a moment, no one moved, until Knight aimed his rifle and let a shot go that just missed Danya.

Bobby Lee pulled one hand down. "Here, Abbie. Take my hand. If I'm gonna die, it's gonna be holdin' the hand of the one I love."

Abbie nodded and reached out and took his hand. They turned and sat down together as Knight and his sidekicks began to walk toward the men.

"You men turn around, or I'll be just as happy to shoot you standing where you are."

"Is there no other way, Knight?" Zach asked.

"It's a beautiful day to die, Sheriff," Knight growled. "Go ahead and turn around. My finger's beginning to itch."

At first it was almost imperceptible—a movement in the brush behind the riflemen. For a moment Nate thought it might be a small bear, but as he slowly stood, Nate recognized the wild hair of a small man who wasn't more than ten paces behind Knight. The Haint held a finger in front of his lips, as if to tell his friends, "Be quiet."

"Last chance to turn, gentlemen," Knight said. "I'd be happy to shoot you right where you are."

Jeremiah raised his hands to his mouth and then bowed down once. When he stood he let out a frightening cry that sounded like a cross between a wolf and a coyote.

The three riflemen turned toward him in utter surprise, at least one firing at the Haint, who instantly ducked, as there was an immediate reaction by the mountain men.

In an instant Danya unsheathed his knife as he dropped to one knee and hurled the massive blade with expert precision.

Knight, seeing the movement, immediately pointed his rifle at Danya and released three rounds. Danya spun backward, blood flying from his chest.

Abbie screamed as Bobby Lee threw her to the snow and covered her body with his while he covered her head with his chest and arms. He held her close as the shots rang around them.

Zach drew the pistol that had remained hidden under his coat on his right hip and released a series of shots that exploded into the man on the right's chest, hurling him back into the snow.

Before the first shot, Nate had dropped to the snow, grabbed Zach's rifle, and rolled under the trunk. Coming up on the other side of the tree, he aimed first at Knight, but when he saw his body flying backward through the air, Nate aimed at the remaining man, who was walking forward with his rifle at his hip, shooting off round after round at him.

"Drop it!" Nate screamed. "Or I'll drop you."

To Nate's surprise, the man stopped in his tracks.

"Go ahead and drop the gun, and you won't get hurt!"

The man smiled an evil smile and then, in the twinkling of an eye, he pulled the rifle to his shoulder and began to fire. The first bullet ricocheted off the tree, showering Nate with wood splinters.

But before he could get the second shot off, Nate aimed and shot in the same instant. A red circle exploded in the middle of the stranger's forehead, and he reeled backward, his body spasming like a beached fish.

He was dead before his limp body thudded onto the icy road.

57

Kep's Back

The party was in full swing when Abbie noticed a man striding rapidly up the road toward their cabin. Even from a distance, she recognized Horace Kephart by his knapsack, puffing pipe, and well-worn bowler. It was his spring arrival on Hazel Creek, as he wintered in nearby Bryson City.

As he approached, he tipped his hat. "Howdy, Abbie."

She ran out to him and gave him a long hug.

"What's all the doings?"

"It's Anna Kate's seventh birthday and we're throwin' her a big party. Everyone's here. The Walkingsticks came over from Cherokee; Miss Maddie and the Faulkners are here, along with the entire Rau and Semmes clans, of course; Miss Lumpkin, the Barneses, Dr. Keller, Mr. Danya are inside—while Mr. Taylor and Miss Maria seem to be makin' a date of it. He dropped by her camp with a carriage and brought her up to the cabin."

"Are they an item?"

"That appears to be the case. I think Mr. Taylor is more than a mite interested in her."

"Any others here?"

"Heavens yes, friends from up and down Hazel Creek."

"Well, I'm glad to hear it. Will be good to catch up with them all. And I've brought some books for you girls that I think you'll enjoy."

"Are you in from Bryson?"

"Nope. I've been in Washington trying to talk some sense to those dadburn politicians. I don't have any liking for politics, Abbie, but I'm convinced it can't be left to the politicians. Fortunately, more and more plain old citizens are testifying up there to what Calhoun and his ilk are doing to our Smokies."

"I just hope they'll leave before they cut the whole valley clean."

"Well, I'm working on it, honey. Now, how's that new milk cow of yours doing?"

"Jean? She's not new. Why, she's been with us since last summer."

"At my age, Abbie, that's new. Show her to me."

He offered her his arm as they walked to the barn. After admiring the health of Jean and Star, he emptied, repacked, and lit his pipe.

"I heard about the killing of Joseph Post and then the shooting up on Welch Ridge. You were there?"

Abbie nodded. "It was terrible, Mr. Kephart—"

"Kep is fine."

"Me and Pa and Mr. Danya were takin' some wood and supplies over to Mrs. Post. Sheriff Taylor and Bobby Lee were headin' up that way, so they rode with us—"

"And I've heard you're engaged to one Mr. Bobby Lee Taylor?"

"No!" Abbie said, laughing. "We're just courtin'. But I hope that's the way it's headin'."

"I think I'll need to interview him, if you don't mind. After all, I'm practically an uncle to you girls."

Abbie laughed again. "Just take it easy on him, all right?"

Kep nodded as he took a puff. "Go on." He listened and his eyes narrowed as Abbie recounted the ambush and the horrible events that followed.

"After the shootin' finished, I couldn't help it, but I screamed. I knew for sure I had lost Pa. I couldn't imagine life without parents. I think I panicked out of the sheer terror of it all."

"What happened next?"

"Pa called out for me. When I heard his voice, Kep, I felt *so* relieved. Immediately I yelled to him I was fine. Bobby Lee helped me up. Pa and Sheriff Taylor checked the men that ambushed us and found them all dead. Bobby Lee and I rushed to Danya, who was lyin' on the road. He was bleedin' and not movin'. I just *knew* he was dead. But when we rolled him over, he moaned. He had been shot three times, but fortunately two wounds were graze wounds—one gashed his arm, one glanced off of his skull—that's the one that knocked him silly—and another ripped the side of his chest. He was bleedin' bad. Bobby Lee and me stopped the bleedin' with pressure. I tell you, Kep, had those shots been any closer to his brain or heart, he'd be in the earth."

"Was Jeremiah shot?"

"Yep. But the bullet just nicked him on the arm. He's healing up fine."

"Simmons was killed up there?"

"He was. He had hired the other three men."

"How'd he die?"

"Mr. Knight killed Mr. Simmons. Mr. Simmons didn't want to kill us, but Knight did. So he shot him. It was then I knew we were all goners—nothin' but a miracle could save us. And that's when Jeremiah showed up. He was behind the killers and let out a shriek that froze the blood of those men. Shocked 'em for a second. But it was all the time Pa and the sheriff needed to get their guns. Pa grabbed a rifle off the ground and Sheriff Taylor still had one on his hip. So when the gunfight broke out, Pa shot one of the bad guys, and Sheriff Taylor the other—but only in self-defense, after the guys tried to kill 'em."

"And Knight?"

"He was the one shootin' at Danya. And even though he was hit, Danya unsheathed his huntin' knife, threw it at Knight while he was still shootin' at him, and the knife buried itself deep in his chest—all the way to the handle—and from at least twenty paces. Cut his heart plum in two. He was a goner before he hit the snow."

"Then?"

"Pa helped me bind up Danya, while Mr. Welch and the sheriff stacked the men's bodies off the road. Then Bobby Lee chopped the tree off the road and we made our delivery to the Posts."

Kep laughed. "So, y'all just left the bodies on the ridge and went on a social call?"

Abbie furrowed her brow. "Well, why not? They wasn't goin' anywhere. They just straightened 'em out so they'd get stiff in an easy-to-bury posture and covered 'em with some snow."

"Well, if that don't beat all. Then?"

"At the Posts', Mrs. Post cleaned Danya and Jeremiah's wounds, coated them with sulfur paste, and bandaged them. After she brewed 'em some willow bark tea, they was 'bout back to normal—'cept Danya when he tried to move too fast. But they're both doin' better now and Danya is already back at the farm doin' light work."

"What happened after that?"

"After our visit with the Posts, we just went back up the ridge, picked up the bodies, put 'em in the back of the wagon, and went back down to our farm. Simple as that. We left Danya and Jeremiah in Miss Maria's care, and Pa dropped Bobby Lee and me at the cabin to care for the girls. Then he and the sheriff took the bodies to town."

"Any charges filed?"

"Mr. Sanders wanted them filed, you can be sure about that. But the sheriff from Bryson came over the next day and investigated. He talked to all of us, visited the scene, scribbled a lot in his notebook, and then declared the whole thing self-defense. They say Sanders about exploded when he found out; he became so mad he threw a chair out of a second-floor window of the company office—and there was a man sittin' in it! He told folks no one could do that to one of his family members and to one of his employees and get away with it. So Pa, Sheriff Taylor, and Danya are all havin' to be more careful than usual. They think Sanders may come after them sometime."

"I can certainly understand why. But were any charges filed against Sanders?"

"Why? For threatenin' my pa?"

"No. Everyone knows he was behind the shooting of Post— even though it can't be proven. Everyone knows how angry he was about your pa getting Simmons fired and then whipping Knight in front of the whole town. Lord knows he's threatened your pa more than once. And the professional killers he hired would sure seem to link him to the ambush. He had the motive and means. I admit it's circumstantial evidence, but seems like that would be enough to bring him up on something."

"Apparently the sheriff doesn't think so. And rumor has it the district attorney over in Sylva agrees. But ever since the shootin', it seems Sanders has been lyin' low. We think Calhoun may have put the reins on him. No one knows for sure."

"Sounds like it was terrible."

"It was, Kep. But now that's in the past, like so many other bad memories of this year. And now it's time for a frolic."

"Mr. Jeremiah Welch going to make a showing?"

"Haven't seen him, but don't expect to. He's not much for parties or social occasions. But if he did he'd sure shock Corrie or Anna. They don't believe he's real. But, me, I love him like an uncle."

"Like your uncle Kep?"

Abbie laughed and hugged him. "Yep."

"So how about you take me to this shindig?"

"Let's go," Abbie said as she took his arm.

58

Never Alone

"Abbie!" called a voice from outside the barn.

"In here!" Abbie shouted.

"Welcome, Mr. Kephart," said Bobby Lee as he walked in. "I didn't know you were in the valley."

"Just arrived, son," Kep said as they shook hands. "Understand you two are courtin'. That true?"

Bobby Lee beamed. "I'm mighty proud to reply in the affirmative."

"You know I'll need to interview you—seein' I'm Abbie's honorary uncle."

"I'd be honored, Mr. Kephart. She's a special girl and I'd be happy to be interviewed by the president of the United States if that's what it takes."

Kephart laughed. "Be careful what you wish for, son. I was with President Coolidge at the White House just last week and could definitely make that happen."

"Well I'll be hog-tied!" Bobby Lee exclaimed.

Kephart took Abbie's arm and placed it in Bobby Lee's. "Also, I understand you're responsible for saving this fair lady's life."

"Not really."

"Not really? They say in town that when the bullets started flying, you lay her on the ground and protected her with your body. Son, that's courage if I've ever heard it. Why, it's as self-sacrificing and gallant as one can get. Heckfire, I'd even call it chivalrous."

"Like a Knight of the Round Table, I'd say!" Abbie added.

"If I could, I'd give you a medal. But in the meantime, I'll extend my gratitude."

"Thanks, Mr. Kephart," Bobby Lee said shyly. "Well, they're ready for the cake and ice cream inside. I was sent to fetch Abbie."

"Kep," Abbie said, "why don't you go on in. Tell Pa we'll be along in a moment."

Kephart looked askance at the couple and smiled. "In a moment?"

"In a moment," Abbie laughed.

Kep turned and left. After he left the barn, Abbie turned and faced Bobby Lee.

"They're waitin' for us," Bobby Lee said.

"Kep'll keep 'em occupied for a few minutes, Mr. Taylor." Abbie put her arms around his waist and looked into his dark eyes.

"Um . . . is this okay? I mean, we're only courtin'."

Abbie smiled. "I think it's acceptable, but only if the boy and girl are in love with each other. And only if it goes no further."

He nodded.

"I guess I haven't rightly thanked you for savin' my life, Bobby Lee."

His eyes softened. "It was just instinct, Abbie. I didn't even think about it."

"Good instincts come from good character," Abbie said. "Mama used to tell us, 'The reputation of a lifetime can be made in a moment.'"

"I'm just thankful to the Lord that he protected us all."

Abbie felt her eyes fill with tears.

"What's the matter?"

Abbie wiped her eyes. "We both could have become orphans. We both could be alone without any parents. It's too horrible to think about."

"No," Bobby Lee responded, "not alone. Never."

"What do you mean?"

"I mean this: God has placed us together on this journey—we're on the same path. With or without our parents, I will be with you—forever. Also, our guardian angels will be with us. And the Lord has promised us that he will never leave us, and he will never forsake us, and no one can snatch us from his hand."

She hugged him, grateful to receive his reassurance.

"So Abbie, you will *not* be alone. Never, ever!"

As he returned her hug, and she settled into his warm, comfortable embrace, she thought, *This is good. This is very, very good.*

She released him and they smiled at each other.

"Come on," he said. "Let's get back to the party."

They turned to walk out of the barn and toward the house. Behind them the hayloft door silently opened. A thin old man with unkempt gray hair streaming out in every direction looked out at the couple and smiled an ear-to-ear, toothless grin.

Yarn

The Fryemont Inn, which was situated on a mountain shelf over-looking the quiet village of Bryson City, offered secluded comfort, excellent dining, and scenic vistas. The regal poplar-bark-covered building was built in 1923, and the inn was listed in the National Register of Historic Places—and rightfully so. The history of the place was so thick you could cut it with a knife.

I offered my arm to Mrs. Abbie as we slowly walked up the stone steps to the front door. Each step seemed an effort for her frail legs. However, when we entered the lobby, she seemed to come alive and looked around in wide-eyed wonder.

"I feel like I have been transported back in time." She walked over to and felt the chestnut-paneled walls and then looked across the lobby full of comfortable furniture. "I can't remember the last time I was here, but it looks exactly like it did before."

She turned to look at an eight-foot by eight-foot tongue-and-groove oak table in the middle of the lobby, in front of the fireplace. "I remember that table from when I was a little girl. Whit and I called it a *game table*, but Mrs. Lillian Frye said it was called a *parlor table*." She laughed as the memories coursed through her mind. "We played checkers on it. My, did we ever have fun!"

I escorted her through the porch doors, which opened to the fresh mountain air and a rocking-chair porch overlooking Bryson City and the Great Smoky Mountains National Park. As she gazed upon the mountains, she took a deep breath. "Brings back a lot of memories," she said.

"Want to sit a spell?"

"No time to sit and rock," she said, laughing. "You promised me lunch. One doesn't turn down an invitation from one's physician, now, does one?"

"So, am I your physician now?"

"I have so decided."

I smiled and offered my arm once again. We turned, and I slowly escorted her down the hallway to the dining room, stopping to admire the photos hanging on both sides—many black-and-white, others sepia—all from the early days of both the Fryemont Inn and Bryson City. She was beaming as she explained to me—a newcomer to the area—places and people. Her eyes widened at one photo showing a group of musicians. They were gathered on a rocking-chair porch with fiddles in hand.

"Gracious me!" she said as her hand covered her mouth. "This is the group that Mr. Barnes hired to play for my fifteenth birthday party! They are the same band that provided music for the silent films at the movie theater in Proctor every Wednesday and Saturday."

She giggled and she leaned toward the photo to look more closely. "At the theater, their skills were especially needed when the film broke, which it did quite frequently." She pointed at a tall, handsome man with a gleaming smile and a small, beautiful woman standing next to him. "Gabe and Reba Johnson. Oh, how I loved them."

As we entered the dining room hallway, there was a large glassed-in montage of memorabilia. "Looky there," she said, pointing. "There's Amos and Lillian Frye with Eugenia Rowe."

"I've heard of Amos and Lillian. He was a timber baron who

built this establishment in 1923. Lillian was his wife and the first female attorney in western North Carolina. But who is Eugenia?"

"Eugenia Rowe was Lillian's sister, and she was out of her head."

"Good evening, Doctor," the hostess said, walking up to us.

"Good to see you, Sue," I replied. Sue Brown and her husband, George, had owned the inn for nearly thirty years. "Sue, this is my friend, Mrs. Abbie. She's residing up in Mountain View Manor, but grew up on Hazel Creek. She visited here as a child and knew the Fryes."

"And Eugenia," Mrs. Abbie added.

"Welcome back, Mrs. Abbie," Sue said. She pointed to another picture. "Here's another one of Eugenia. I tell you, stories of her abound. I'm told she was a spinster schoolteacher and fancied herself an artist. She was a follower of the "I Am" religious movement of the time, and she used to sequester herself in the attic, or . . ." Sue laughed. "Perhaps they shut her up there. Anyway, she'd draw primitive scenes of the mountains with crayon and scribble her beliefs and her challenges to the Almighty. In fact, years ago we found an old mattress at one end of the attic, under the eaves, surrounded by her writings on the backs of old rate cards, box tops, and anything she could get her hands on."

She turned. "Let me show you to your table."

As we walked, Sue continued, "Folks at the old Belk Department Store told us that Eugenia would come in, sit down, open every box of stockings, take them out, look at them, and drop them on the floor. Mrs. Abbie, do you remember when Hanes stockings came in boxes?"

Abbie laughed. "I do!"

"They used to cringe when they saw her coming in the store. She didn't buy anything; it was just kind of a ritual."

Sue handed us our menus. "Take your time to look it over," she said. "And take particular note of today's specials."

The dining room evoked another era. The gleaming hardwood

floors reflected the glow of the fire in the huge stone fireplace. Overhead, brass and wood paddle fans hung from the raftered, vaulted ceiling, as music from the early 1900s enveloped us in the ambience that had begun in the lobby.

Every week for the past month, when making rounds at the nursing home, I would sit for a while with Mrs. Abbie and listen to her stories about growing up on Hazel Creek. My wife had suggested I bring her to lunch here as a special treat, and Mrs. Abbie had jumped at the suggestion.

After we were seated, we were offered fresh-baked bread, soft creamy butter, and homemade jams. Abbie leaned toward me and whispered, "I bet they're still usin' Bobby Lee's recipe. I'll have to tell you the story one day. But"—she paused as a song caught her attention—"this is one of my favorites. It's Frank Sinatra's version of 'Sentimental Journey.'" She softly sang along for a verse.

"My husband had a voice that sounded just like Old Blue Eyes," she said. "I loved when he sang this to me—although no one in Hazel Creek had a voice as pretty as my sister Whit."

"Have you ever thought of going back?" I said.

"To Hazel Creek?"

"Why not? The North Shore Cemetery Association works with the National Park Service to barge folks across Fontana Lake each summer for—"

"Decoration Day," she interrupted as she furrowed her brow. "I've thought about it from time to time—just never done it. Think I'd rather just enjoy the many, many warm memories I have from so long ago." She accompanied Sinatra on the next verse, lip-syncing his words about taking a sentimental journey home.

"Many more memories are rushin' back now," she said, looking out the window and at the massive hemlock trees just outside. "Sometimes they are so real, they sweep over me like a warm evening breeze. Other times they are cold and heavy, like a wet quilt. Sometimes they overwhelm me with joy, and other times they hold me a prisoner of time itself."

She turned back to face me. "I have so much more to tell you that I think you'll find interestin'. Stories of another man who was killed for his property, moonshinin' durin' the Prohibition, a tale of an old doctor's sage advice, and a Cherokee chief's wisdom—and a story I think you will find very intriguin' . . ."

"How so?"

"It's a yarn about a young doctor who came to Hazel Creek— as wet behind the ears as you—and even more handsome."

She smiled as I felt myself blush. "Well, I'll tell you this, Mrs. Abbie, I'm learning that you can spin yarn with the best of them."

She laughed—laughter still as clear and refreshing as a mountain stream, as it must have been eighty-five years before. I looked forward to hearing more of her stories.

To Be Continued

Most of the geographical locations and landmarks mentioned in this book exist or existed, but the use of their names and functions for the purposes of this book is purely fictional.

However, a number of historical characters appear in the book, including Tsar Alexander, Senator Kelly Bennett, Jimmy Bradshaw, George and Sue Brown, Fanny Brice, Louise Calhoun, William Rosecrans Calhoun, Olive Tilford Dargan, Zina Farley, Harve Fouts, Horace Kephart, Fedor Kuzmich, Grace Lumpkin, Moses Proctor, Aquilla "Quill" Rose, Eugenia Rowe, Louise Thomas, Frances Christine Fisher Tiernan, and President Calvin Coolidge, albeit used fictitiously.

All other persons mentioned are the product of my imagination and any resemblance to persons, living or dead, is entirely coincidental.

ACKNOWLEDGMENTS

The nidus for this book was planted thirty years ago, when I had the privilege of practicing family medicine in Bryson City, North Carolina, from 1981 through 1985. During those years I was introduced to Hazel Creek and made many trips into the Great Smoky Mountains National Park and, any number of trips hiking and fly-fishing up and down Hazel Creek and her many tributaries—even doing volunteer work on the creek with the park rangers. We were called *Volunteers in the Park*, or VIPs. In those years in Swain County I learned a great deal about real-life medicine, the Smoky Mountains, the wonderful mountain people there, and life.

The seed of this book was fertilized twelve years ago when I began writing the first of three autobiographical books, *Bryson City Tales*, for then I met a new friend, a man who would become my first fiction-writing mentor—Gilbert Morris. Gil and I were introduced through my daughter Kate, who was initially a faithful fan of his, only to later become dear friends and pen pals.

After we met, Gilbert gave me the gift of writing the foreword to *Bryson City Tales*. Not too long after that, he approached me about the possibility of the two of us writing a book together. Thus the idea for this book came initially from Gil and he reviewed my first drafts of it.

After I began the process of intensively researching and writing this book under Gil's tutelage, we decided not to author it together. He encouraged me to develop and write the story alone. But the idea for this book and much of its early formation owes much to this wonderful man.

I'm thankful to Duane Oliver for his research on Hazel Creek and for spending hours talking to me about the area, its lore, its people, and its history. Duane, who retired from his professorship at Western Carolina University, is descended from the first settlers of Hazel Creek, grew up on Hazel Creek, and is the author of a number of books about the area that were invaluable to me, including *Hazel Creek from Then till Now, Along the River: People and Places,* and *Cooking and Living Along the River.*

Thanks also to Tom Horton, John Mattox, Tom Robbins, and Mort and Laney White, all of whom helped me with early research. The writings of a number of authors, listed in the bibliography, have also informed my vision of, passion for, and writing about the southern Appalachians in general, and the Great Smoky Mountains in particular.

Thanks also to National Park Rangers John Garrison, Joe Ashe, Mike Sharp, and John Mattox for trips into the park and teaching me about the park and her history in the early 1980s. I'm especially appreciative for the time and teaching of Arthur Stupka, the first Park Naturalist of Great Smoky Mountains National Park.

Like Charles Frazier, when he wrote *Cold Mountain,* I was dependent upon Horace Kephart's record of life on Hazel Creek from 1904 to 1907, *Our Southern Highlanders.* No doubt those familiar with his work and writing will see his reflections embedded in these pages. I'm also in the debt of Libby Kephart Hargrave for sharing memories and writings of her great-grandfather.

I'm grateful to George Ellison, a writer, historian, and naturalist, who resides in Bryson City and whom I first met in 1981, for reviewing the manuscript. George is an expert on Horace Kephart, the Smoky Mountains, and the Cherokees.

I also owe a special debt to John and Ella Jo Shell, the former proprietors of the Hemlock Inn when we lived in Bryson City, for the information and hospitality they provided as this book's vision became a reality. Thanks also to Mort and Lainey White (Lainey is John and Ella Joe's daughter) and the staff of the Hemlock Inn, who treated Gilbert Morris and me like royalty during a research week in Bryson City in 2001.

Thanks to the coffee shops and restaurants that allowed me to utilize their space (and Internet access) as I wrote: Serranos in Monument, Colorado; CC's in Baton Rouge, Louisiana; and Panera Bread in Tulsa, Oklahoma, and Colorado Springs, Colorado. I'm appreciative to the St. Inklings (aka "the Stinklings"), the writer's group with which I meet. Thanks to Paul McCusker, Al Janssen, Larry Weeden, and Jerry Jenkins for the encouragement—and to Barnes & Noble for allowing us to inhabit their café every other week. A special thanks to Paul for suggesting the "red goatee."

I'm grateful to my friend Steve Dail for advice about early-twentieth-century camping, woodcraft, hunting, horses, wagons, and guns. Thanks to Bill Judge, my mentor and a former inductee into Florida Dairy Hall of Fame, for helping me write accurately about livestock.

And I deeply value the many hours that Barb and Kate Larimore spent poring over copy after copy of drafts of the manuscript. Thanks also to John Blase, Vicki Clark, Zanese Duncan, Annette Finger, Lee Hough, Harry Kraus, and Donabeth Urick for detailed and valuable manuscript review. My appreciation goes out to dear friends who served as readers of the manuscript: Beth, Bonnie, Cheri, Diane, Paula, Elizabeth, Judy, Kathy, Kim, Margie, Ralinda, and Shugie. It's a better book because of each of your suggestions.

Thanks to Lee Hough and Donna Lewis at Alive Communications, who not only represent me but also have become good friends. Appreciation, affection, and admiration are due to my longtime legal and business counselor, and dear friend, Ned McLeod.

I'm indebted to my friend, writer and editor Dave Lambert, who expertly guided, edited, and critiqued early drafts of this book—and encouraged me to pursue and continue writing it. Dave's expertise, suggestions, comments, observations, and considerable skill resulted in a much, much better book than the manuscript I first submitted to him.

I'm thankful to Becky Nesbitt, the editor in chief, and her team at Howard Books and Simon & Schuster, including Holly Halverson, for the trust they've extended to me in agreeing to publish my first solo novel—and for applying their considerable skills in shaping and improving this book. Thanks to Jessica Wong for much assistance and Tom Pitoniak and Stephanie Evans for their amazing editing skills that remarkably improved this book. I also owe much appreciation to Kirk DouPonce of Dog Eared Design for the beautiful cover artwork and Jaime Putorti for the beautiful design.

To the real-life Lauren Abigail, Darla Whitney, Corrie Hannah, Anna Katherine, and Sarah Elisabeth—thanks for lending me your names. I love each of you dearly. And to the real-life Rau and Pyeritz families—this is what happens if you complain to a novelist that your name has never appeared in a novel. Jack, Julius, and Lilly, you'll always have a special place in our family.

Finally, I'm indebted to Bryson City and her people, who welcomed me into their community. I thank them for all they've taught me.

Walt Larimore
Monument, Colorado
September 2011
www.DrWalt.com
www.DrWalt.com/blog

At Home in the Smokies: A History Handbook for Great Smoky Mountains National Park. Washington, DC: National Park Service, 1978.

Brown, Margaret Lynn. *The Wild East: A Biography of the Great Smoky Mountains.* Gainesville: University Press of Florida, 2000.

Brunk, Robert S., ed. *May We All Remember Well. Volume 1: A Journal of the History & Cultures of Western North Carolina.* Asheville, NC: Robert S. Brunk Auction Services, 1997.

Bush, Florence Cope. *Dorie: Woman of the Mountains.* Knoxville: University of Tennessee Press, 1992.

Chase, Richard. *Grandfather Tails.* Boston: Houghton Mifflin, 1948.

———. *The Jack Tails.* Boston: Houghton Mifflin, 1943.

Coggins, Allen R. *Place Names of the Smokies.* Gatlinburg, TN: Great Smoky Mountains Natural History Association, 1999.

Dabney, Joseph. *Smokehouse Ham, Spoon Bread, Scuppernong Wine: The Folklore and Art of Southern Appalachian Cooking.* Nashville, TN: Cumberland House, 1998.

Duracher, Frank. *Smoky Mountain High: The Consuming Passion of Cecil Brown.* Alexandria, VA: Crest Books, 2007.

Ellison, George. Introduction to Horace Kephart, *Our Southern Highlanders.* Knoxville: University of Tennessee Press, 1984, ix–xlviii.

————. Introduction to Horace Kephart, *Smoky Mountain Magic: A Novel.* Gatlinburg, TN: Great Smoky Mountains Association, 2009, xix–xl.

————. Introduction to James Mooney, *History, Myths, and Sacred Formulas of the Cherokees.* Fairview, NC: Bright Mountain Books, 1992.

Erbson, Wayne. *Log Cabin Pioneers: Stories, Songs, & Sayings.* Asheville, NC: Native Ground Music, 2001.

Holland, Lance. *Fontana: A Pocket History of Appalachia.* Robbinsville, NC: Lance Holland, 2001.

Hyde, Herbert L. *My Home Is in the Smoky Mountains: Tales from Former North Carolina State Senator Herbert L. Hyde.* Alexander, NC: WorldComm, 1998.

Kephart, Horace. *Camping and Woodcraft: A Handbook for Vacation Campers and for Travelers in the Wilderness.* Knoxville: University of Tennessee Press, 1917.

————. *Smoky Mountain Magic: A Novel.* Gatlinburg, TN: Great Smoky Mountains Association, 2009.

————. *Our Southern Highlanders.* 1913; rept. Knoxville: University of Tennessee Press, 1984.

Kephart Hargrave, Libby. Foreword to Horace Kephart, *Smoky Mountain Magic: A Novel.* Gatlinburg, TN: Great Smoky Mountains Association, 2009, vii–xiv.

Larimore, Walt. *Bryson City Seasons: More Tales of a Doctor's Practice in the Smoky Mountains.* Grand Rapids, MI: Zondervan, 2004.

————. *Bryson City Secrets: Even More Tales of a Small-Town Doctor in the Smoky Mountains.* Grand Rapids, MI: Zondervan, 2006.

————. *Bryson City Tales: Stories of a Doctor's First Year of Practice in the Smoky Mountains.* Grand Rapids, MI: Zondervan, 2002.

Lumpkin, Grace. *To Make My Bread.* Urbana: University of Illinois Press, 1995.

Mooney, James. *History, Myths, and Sacred Formulas of the*

Cherokees. 1900; rept. 1 Fairview, NC: Bright Mountain Books, 1992.

Oliver, Duane. *Along the River: People and Places; A Collection of Photographs of People & Places Once Found Along the Little Tennessee River, an Area Now Part of the Fontana Lake Basin & Southern Edge of the Great Smokies Park.* Hazelwood, NC: Duane Oliver, 1998.

———. *Cooking and Living Along the River.* Hazelwood, NC: Duane Oliver, 2002.

———. *Hazel Creek: From Then till Now.* Hazelwood, NC: Duane Oliver, 1989.

———. *Mountain Gables: A History of Haywood County Architecture.* Waynesville, NC: Oliver Scriptorium, 2001.

Porter, Eliot. *Appalachian Wilderness: The Great Smoky Mountains.* New York: Ballantine Books, 1950.

Rivers, Francine. *The Last Sin Eater.* Wheaton, IL: Tyndale House, 1998.

Shields, Randolph. *The Cades Cove Story.* Gatlinburg, TN: Great Smoky Mountains Natural History Association, 1981.

Venable, Sam. *Mountain Hands: A Portrait of Southern Appalachia.* Knoxville: University of Tennessee Press, 2000.

Weller, Jack E. *Yesterday's People: Life in Contemporary Appalachia.* Lexington: University of Kentucky Press, 1966.

1. What surprised you about life on Hazel Creek?

2. Did you have any misperceptions about mountain people? If so, what were they and how did this book change them or support them?

3. With which character do you most closely identify and why? What do you see as his or her strengths and weaknesses?

4. Which of the Randolph sisters did you like the most and why? Do you have any predictions about what may become of them in the next book?

5. The lumber company believed in the right of subduing the earth and ruling over it. Was their view correct? Can you think of any verses to support that belief? What obligations do we have to wisely care for the earth and natural resources? Can you think of any Bible verses that support your view?

6. Many of the characters in the book depended upon scripture memory as they faced various obstacles. Do you see this as a strength or a weakness, a comfort or a crutch? Do you believe you need to memorize more scripture or not? Why or why not?

7. Could you identify with Abbie's reluctance to be forced to give gifts to the poor family on Eagle Creek? Have you ever been reluctant to give to others in need? Does the Bible give any direction on this issue? If so, what examples can you think of?

8. Nate decided to allow Maria and Danya (strangers to him) to stay on his farm. Do you think this was wise or foolish? Would you do the same today? Why or why not?

9. How did Nate's faith change as he was challenged by Callie's death and witnessed firsthand how faith works in the lives of others?

10. Have you encountered someone whose faith seemed so real that they inspired or challenged you? Who was that person? What attributes did he or she exemplify to you? Do you demonstrate your faith in a way that speaks to others? If so, how?

The Visitor

The tall, slim young man seemed almost awkward in his movements as he boarded the morning train in Bryson City.

His height, at six feet three inches, made the passenger seats quite uncomfortable for him. He shook back a thick shock of auburn hair as he glanced at the Bryson City train depot. *I wonder*, he thought, *will this be the last time I see civilization?* Then he laughed. *If you call* this *civilization!*

As the train pulled out of the station heading toward Bushnell and then on to the Hazel Creek Depot, he settled into his seat, praying no one would come by to sit with him. His long arms and legs would make sharing the small bench seat even more miserable. As the locomotive strained to pick up speed, Wade had time to think back on his childhood in the Republic of Liberia in West Africa. He had been educated in missionary schools there. When he arrived in America to attend college he could speak French fluently and Latin passably. *As if that will have any merit in this wilderness!* he thought.

While in college he'd become a fair piano player and he excelled at imitating several famous singers. The prior two evenings he enjoyed playing and singing popular songs with the other guests after the astonishingly excellent dinners he enjoyed at the

Fryemont Inn. *These skills will have even* less *merit in the back-woods!* he thought.

His mother had died of cholera when he was a child and his father remarried a nurse at the mission within a year. Wade had taken a steamer the previous summer to visit them at their mission deep in the jungles of Liberia and spend a summer of study with the missionary physicians. He deeply loved his father and genuinely admired the doctors with whom he had worked. As a result, he thought he was sensing a call to be a missionary—but would it be in the same wilderness in which his father served or another one? *Maybe working in Hazel Creek will help me decide*, he thought.

He also found himself worrying almost incessantly about what his future patients might think of him. Would they have any idea just how well trained he was? Would they appreciate his skills? Would they think that his coming to their wilderness meant he was some sort of medical-school failure instead? How would he let them know he had graduated at the top of his class—summa cum laude, not Lordy how come?

I know what I'll tell them! he thought. *I'll tell them I was offered an exclusive apprenticeship with a well-known established Philadelphia physician but chose to come to the wilderness for a year to serve my fellow man. Of course, that was true—but did it sound too sanctimonious?* He smiled. *Probably!*

Maybe, he finally concluded, *I should just be me.* After all, "actions always speak louder than words," his father had often taught him.

When the train pulled past the small depot at Bushnell, a tiny bird on a post caught his eyes. *That's a hooded warbler!* He furrowed his brow for a moment as he tried to remember, and then his eyes brightened. *Ah, yes! Wilsonia citrina!*

As an amateur ornithologist, he had studied birds on three continents and even knew most of their scientific names. He had seen pictures of the hooded warbler but had never actually seen one in real life before. He smiled. *Well, I do love birds and botany. And I love to read—particularly westerns. Maybe it won't be as bad out here as I'm imagining. Maybe this will be the adventure of my life.*

Then he felt a frown spread across his face. *This is going to be terrible. I'm going to miss my friends. I'm going to miss Philadelphia. And, most of all, I'm going to miss the young ladies. How many will get married while I'm out in this godforsaken wilderness. Why did I ever agree to this?*

As the train chugged on, he pulled a well-worn book out of his day pack and opened up *The Travels of William Bartram*. It took his mind off his worries and the concerns of the world. And Bartram was one of his favorite writers. He had been a naturalist who extensively traveled in the southeast colonies of what would become the United States in the late eighteenth century and wrote extensively about the Great Smoky Mountains. Wade opened the book to a favorite passage:

This world, as a glorious apartment of the boundless palace of the sovereign Creator, is furnished with an infinite variety of animated scenes, inexpressibly beautiful and pleasing, equally free to the inspection and enjoyment of all his creatures. Perhaps there is not any part of creation, within the reach of our observations, which exhibits a more glorious display of the Almighty hand than the plants, which excite love, gratitude, and adoration to the great Creator, who was pleased to endow them with such eminent qualities, and reveal them to us for our sustenance, amusement, and delight.

I wish I could write like this! he thought as he watched the hills rush by, fully clad in vibrant multihued spring flowers. He felt himself smile. *It is beautiful out here. Okay, Father,* he silently prayed, *forgive me for calling your creation "godforsaken."*

❧ ☙ ❧ ☙

"Hazel Creek!" the conductor called out as he walked toward the back of the train. "Last stop before Eagle Creek and the end of the line!"

Wade could already feel the train slowing down. For over twenty miles they skirted the edge of the Tuckasegee and then the Little Tennessee rivers. Wade closed his book, gathered his belongings, and then made his way out of the car. As he ducked his head to step off the train, he heard his name and turned to see an older man in a plain brown coat approach.

"Dr. Chandler?"

Wade saw a tall and lanky man with wavy brown hair and eyes waving at him. He took his pipe from his mouth as he walked forward. "I'm Andrew Keller. Welcome to Hazel Creek!"

Wade smiled and firmly shook his new mentor's hand. "Good to meet you, sir."

"If you'll just come with me, I'll have some of the men bring your bags to the Clubhouse, where you'll be staying until we can get you a proper house. Let me walk you up there."

Keller turned to walk down the platform and Chandler almost had to run to keep up with the older man. He was happy that he was in fair shape and enjoyed Keller's recitation of the history of the area as they walked up Hazel Creek toward Proctor. Reaching the edge of town, Keller stopped.

"Down there to the left is the mill. Trees are floated down Hazel Creek, or brought down the valley by train. Here they are cut and kiln-dried, then shipped to all over the United States and even to Europe. The Calhoun Lumber Company is known to produce the finest hardwood lumber in the world. We'll take a tour down here a bit later, but let me walk you through town and up to the Clubhouse. Nancy Cunningham is waiting to welcome you up there."

Wade's attention was distracted by laughter. He turned to see three beautiful women spilling out of a general store, giggling. They didn't see him until the tallest of the girls almost ran into him.

"Oh my goodness!" she exclaimed. "Please excuse me."

He was struck dumb by her beauty. Her radiant smile was framed by shimmering auburn hair and capped with luscious dark brown eyes.

She continued to look up at him as she demurely cocked her head. "I don't believe I've metcha before. I'm Abbie Randolph."

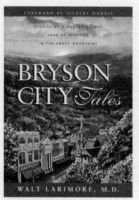
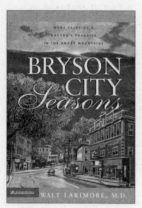

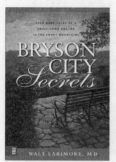

Bryson City Secrets
Walt Larimore, M.D.

More enchanting tales of the people and events that shaped a young doctor's life and faith during his early practice in the Smoky Mountains ...

There are places in Bryson City where the smell of home cooking is a little too tempting for an empty stomach. Don't, for instance, pass the Fryemont Inn when the windows are open—not unless you plan to come inside and enjoy fresh-baked rolls, gourmet cooking, and an owner who is as warm and inviting as the food. She's just one of the friendly faces you'll meet in *Bryson City Secrets*.

Told with winsome humor and deep affection, *Bryson City Secrets* is a story-lover's delight, continuing Dr. Walt Larimore's reminiscences of his early years of country medical practice. Pull up a chair and feast on this rich fare of Smoky Mountain personalities, highland wisdom, and all the tears, laughter, tenderness, faith, courage, and misadventures of small-town life.

Softcover: 978-0-310-26634-1
Ebook, ePub: 978-0-310-86123-2

Best of Bryson City Tales
Walt Larimore, M.D.

"We walked out onto a side porch, with woven-seat rocking chairs strewn across it, to look out at the hills that were literally ablaze with color--reds and yellows were painted across the promontories, with amber and orange hues specked the bluffs. The spectacular view all the way to the peak of the distant Frye Mountain reminded us of why so many chose to visit this wilderness area during the fall color season."

But the little mountain hamlet of Bryson City, North Carolina, offers more than dazzling vistas. For Walt Larimore, a young "flatlander" physician setting up his first practice, the town presents its peculiar challenges as well. Schooled in the latest medical technology, the eager doctor--his wife, Barb, and two-year-old daughter, Kate, in tow--is about to discover that there are some things in rural practice for which medical school just hadn't prepared him. But he's about to learn. His patients will often be his best teachers, and his classroom will range from hospital corridors and smelly barns to homey kitchens and mountain streams.

With the winsomeness of a James Herriott book, *Bryson City Tales* sweeps you into a world of colorful characters, the texture of Smoky Mountain life, and the warmth, humor, quirks, and struggles of a small country town. It's a world where the family doctor is also the emergency physician, the coroner, and the obstetrician, and where wilderness medicine is part of the job, search-and-rescue calls in the national forest are a way of life, and the next patient just may be somebody's livestock or pet. And it is the place where the practice of medicine will forever shape Dr. Larimore's practice of life and faith.

Sharing the joys, heartaches, frustrations, and rewards of rural mountain medical practice, *Bryson City Tales* is a tender and insightful chronicle of a young man's rite of passage from medical student to family physician. Laughter and adventure await you in these pages, and lessons learned from the strengths, foibles, and simple faith of Bryson City's unforgettable residents.

Softcover: 978-0-31026634-1   Audio download: 978-0-310-261470-7   Ebook, ePub: 978-0-301-861249

Available in stores and online!

LIVE LIFE INSPIRED.

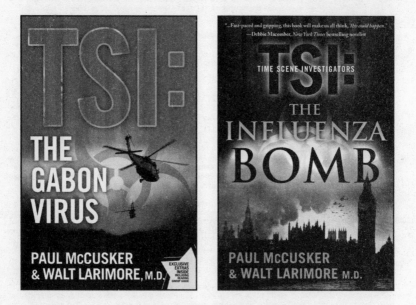